DEAR CHILD

ROMY HAUSMANN

Translated from the German by
Jamie Bulloch

Quercus

DEAR CHILD

Romy Hausmann was born in East Germany in 1981. At the age of twenty-four she became chief editor at a film production company in Munich. Since the birth of her son she has been working as a freelancer in television. *Dear Child* is her thriller debut. Romy Hausmann lives with her family in a remote house in the woods near Stuttgart.

DEAR
CHILD

ROMY HAUSMANN

Translated from the German by
Jamie Bulloch

Quercus

First published in the German language as *Liebes Kind* by
dtv Verlagsgesellschaft mbH & Co. KG, München, in 2019
First published in Great Britain in 2020 by

Quercus Editions Ltd
Carmelite House
50 Victoria Embankment
London EC4Y 0DZ

An Hachette UK company

Liebes Kind by Romy Hausmann
© 2019 dtv Verlagsgesellschaft mbH & Co. KG, München
English translation copyright © 2019 by Jamie Bulloch

A CIP catalogue record for this book is available
from the British Library

HB ISBN 978 1 52940 144 8
TPB ISBN 978 1 52940 142 4
EBOOK ISBN 978 1 52940 145 5

10 9 8 7 6 5 4 3 2 1

Typeset by CC Book Production
Printed and bound in Great Britain by Clays Ltd, Elcograf S.p.A.

MIX
Paper from
responsible sources
FSC® C104740

Papers used by Quercus are from well-managed forests and other responsible sources.

For Caterina, of course.

'Nothing is sadder than the death of an illusion.'

Arthur Koestler

Student, 23, missing in Munich

Munich (LR) – The Munich police are searching for clues relating to the whereabouts of Lena Beck, 23, from Munich-Haidhausen. According to eyewitnesses, the student was at a party on Tuesday night in the Maxvorstadt district until around 5 a.m. On the way home she telephoned a friend. Her mobile phone has been switched off ever since. A police search of Munich on Friday produced no leads. Lena Beck is 1.65 metres tall, petite, and has blonde, shoulder-length hair. She was last seen wearing a silver top, black jeans, black boots and a dark blue coat.

On the first day I lose my sense of time, my dignity and a molar. But I do have two children now and a cat. I've forgotten their names apart from the cat's – Fräulein Tinky. I've got a husband too. He's tall, with short, dark hair and grey eyes. I look at him from the corner of my eye as I sit huddled next to him on the threadbare sofa. In his embrace, the injuries running right down my back are throbbing, as if each of them had their own heartbeat. A cut on my forehead is stinging. From time to time everything goes blank or I see white flashes. Then I just focus on trying to breathe.

It's hard to tell whether it is actually evening, or whether he's decided that's what it is. Insulation panels are screwed over the windows. He creates day and night. Like God. I try to persuade myself I'm already over the worst, but I can't stop anticipating that we'll be going to bed together soon. The children already have their pyjamas on. The boy's are too small, whereas the girl's sleeves go way over her wrists. The children kneel on the floor a couple metres from the sofa and hold their hands up to feel the residual warmth of the wood-burning stove. The fire has burned down to a black heap, with only the odd ember still glowing red. The high-pitched voices with their jolly chitter-chatter blend into the sheer abnormality of this situation. I can't understand exactly what they're saying. It's as if I'm hearing them talk through cotton wool, while I contemplate how I'm going to kill their father.

THE NIGHT OF THE ACCIDENT

HANNAH

It's easy to begin with. I straighten my back and take a deep breath. I climb into the ambulance and travel with it. I tell the men in the orange coats Mama's name and that her blood group is AB negative. AB negative is the rarest blood group and it doesn't have any antibodies against groups A and B. That means Mama can have blood from all the other groups. I know this because we talked about blood groups in class. And because it's in the thick book. I think I've done everything right. It's only when I unintentionally think about my brother that my right knee starts trembling. Jonathan will be frightened without me.

Concentrate, Hannah. You're a big girl now.

No, today I'm a little girl and I'm stupid. It's cold, it's too bright and it's beeping. I ask where the beeping's coming from, and one of the men in the orange coats says, 'That's your mum's heart.'

My mum's heart never beeped before.

Concentrate, Hannah.

It's a bumpy ride and I close my eyes. Mama's heart is beeping. She screamed and there was a bang. If my mum's heart

3

stops beeping now, those will have been the last sounds I heard her make: a scream and a bang. And she didn't even wish me goodnight.

The ambulance does a little jump then comes to a stop.

'We're here,' the man says. He means at the hospital.

A hospital is a building where illnesses or injuries are treated with medical assistance.

'Come on, little girl,' the man says.

My legs move automatically and so quickly that I can't count the steps. I follow the men pushing the rattling stretcher on wheels through a large glass door beneath the glaring sign that says 'Accident and Emergency', and then down a long corridor. As if by command, helpers swarm from both sides and lots of voices all talk nervily at the same time.

'You can't come in here,' a fat man in a green apron says, nudging me to the side when we arrive at another large door at the end of the long corridor. 'We'll send someone to look after you.' He points at a row of seats along the wall. 'Go and sit down there for the moment.'

I want to say something, but the words won't come out, and in any case the man has already turned around and disappeared through the door with the other helpers. I count the chairs along the wall – seven. He – the fat man in the green apron – didn't say which one I should sit on. I've started chewing my thumbnail without realising it. *Concentrate, Hannah. You're a big girl now.*

I sit with my knees up on the middle chair, picking pine needles and small brown bits of bark from my dress. I got quite dirty this evening. I think of Jonathan again. Poor little Jonathan who stayed at home and has to do the cleaning. I imagine him crying because he doesn't know how to get rid of the stains from the carpet in the sitting room. I'm sure we've got the right cleaning fluid in the store cupboard, but Papa's put two padlocks on the door. A precautionary measure. We need to have lots of these. You always have to be careful.

'Hello?' A woman's voice.

I leap to my feet.

'I'm Sister Ruth,' the woman says with a smile, and takes my hand to shake it. I tell her my name is Hannah and that it's a palindrome. A palindrome is a word that reads the same forwards as well as backwards. To prove it I spell my name, first from the beginning and then from the end. Sister Ruth is still smiling and says, 'I understand.'

She's older than Mama; she's already got grey hair and she's slightly round. Over her light yellow apron she wears a colourful cardigan which looks nice and warm and has a sticker with the face of a panda on it. It says, 'Be Happy.' That's English. The corners of my mouth twitch.

'You haven't got any shoes on, child,' Sister Ruth remarks, and I wiggle the big toe of my left foot through the hole in my tights. Mama stitched it up on one of her good days. I bet she'd be angry if she knew that I'd made the hole in my tights again.

Sister Ruth takes a tissue from the pocket of her apron because she thinks I'm crying. Because of the hole in my tights or because of Mama. I don't tell her it's actually because I'm blinded by the harsh light from the fluorescent tube on the ceiling. I just say, 'Thank you, that's very considerate.' You always have to be polite. You always have to say please and thank you. My brother and I always say thank you when Mama gives us a cereal bar, even

5

though we can't stand cereal bars. We don't like the taste. But they're important because of the vitamins. Calcium and potassium and magnesium and Vitamin B for the digestion and blood formation. We eat three of them every day unless we've run out. Then we have to hope Papa comes home soon and has been shopping on the way.

I take the tissue, dab my eyes, blow my nose, then give it back to Sister Ruth. You mustn't keep anything that doesn't belong to you. That's stealing. Sister Ruth laughs and puts the tissue back in her apron. Of course I ask her about Mama, but all Sister Ruth says is: 'She's in the best hands.' I know that's not a proper answer, I'm not stupid.

'When can I see her?' I ask, but don't get an answer to that either.

Instead Sister Ruth says that she's going to take me to the staffroom to see whether there's a pair of slippers I could wear. Jonathan and I have to wear slippers at home too because the floor is very cold, but mostly we forget and our tights get dirty. Then Mama gets cross because it's not washing day, and Papa gets cross because Mama hasn't cleaned the floor properly. Cleanliness is important.

The staffroom is big, at least fifty paces from the door to the wall opposite. In the middle are three tables, each of which has four chairs arranged around it. Three fours are twelve. One of the chairs isn't straight. Someone must have been sitting there and not tidied up when they left. I hope they got into trouble. Because tidiness is important too. The left-hand wall of the room is filled with a metal cupboard with lots of individual lockable compartments, but there are keys sticking out of almost all of them. There's also a loft bed, which is metal too. Straight ahead are two windows. I can see the night through them. The night is black and there aren't any stars. To the right is a kitchen unit. There's even a kettle out on the work surface. Hot water can be very dangerous. Skin burns at forty-five degrees. At sixty degrees the protein in the skin cells congeals and the cells die off. The water inside a kettle is heated to one hundred degrees. We've got a kettle at home too, but we keep it locked away.

'Why don't you sit down?' Sister Ruth says.

Three fours are twelve. Twelve chairs. I have to think, but I'm distracted by the black night without any stars beyond the windows.

Concentrate, Hannah.

Sister Ruth goes to the cupboard, opens one compartment after another, then closes it again. She says 'hmm' a few times, drawing it out, and the metal doors clatter. Looking over her shoulder, she says again, 'Come on, child, sit down.'

First I think I ought to go for the chair that's not straight. But that wouldn't be right. Everyone needs to tidy up after themselves. Take responsibility. *You're a big girl, Hannah.* I nod at nothing in particular and count to myself, eenie, meenie, miney, mo. There's one chair left over, which would give me a good view of the door and which I'll put back neatly later when Sister Ruth tells me the time to sit down is over.

'How about these?' she says with a smile, turning to me with a pair of pink rubber shoes. 'They're a bit big, but better than nothing.' She puts them by my feet and waits for me to slip them on.

'Listen, Hannah,' she says as she takes off her cardigan. 'Your mum didn't have a handbag when the accident happened. That means we couldn't find an identity card or any papers belonging to her.'

Grabbing my arm, she holds it out straight and fiddles the sleeve of her cardigan over my hand.

'So now we don't have a name or an address. And no emergency contact number either, unfortunately.'

'Her name is Lena,' I say to be helpful, like I was in the ambulance. You always have to be helpful. My brother and I always help Mama when her fingers tremble. Or when she forgets things, like our names or when it's time to go to the toilet. We go with her to the bathroom so she doesn't slide off the toilet seat or do anything else silly.

Sister Ruth is now on to the other arm. The warmth that's still in the cardigan spreads cosily across my back.

'Yes,' she says. 'Lena, great. Lena without a surname. The paramedic already made a note of this.' When she sighs I can smell her breath. It smells of toothpaste. She tugs on my chair, which scrapes across the floor, until she can squat in front of me without knocking her head on the edge of the table. Table edges can be very dangerous. Mama often hits her head against the table when she has one of her fits.

Sister Ruth starts fastening the buttons of the cardigan. On my thigh my finger draws the zigzag pattern of her parting. Right, straight, left, straight, left, straight, left again, like a jagged lightning bolt. Sister Ruth suddenly looks up as if she'd sensed me staring at her head.

'Is there anyone we can call, Hannah? Your papa, perhaps? Do you know your telephone number by heart?'

I shake my head.

'But you do have a papa?'

I nod.

'Does he live with you? With you and your mama?'

I nod again.

'Shall we call him? Surely he should know your mama had an accident and that the two of you are in hospital. He'll be worried if you don't come home.'

Right, straight. Left, straight, left again, like a jagged lightning bolt.

'Tell me, Hannah, have you ever been to a hospital before? Or your mama? Maybe even this one? Then, you see, we could look in our really smart computer for your telephone number.'

I shake my head.

'In an emergency, open wounds can be sterilised with urine. It disinfects, coagulates the proteins and relieves the pain, full stop.'

Sister Ruth takes my hands. 'You know what, Hannah? I'll make us some tea and then we'll have a bit of a chat, you and I. How about that?'

'Chat about what?'

I see, she wants me to talk about Mama, but I can't think of anything to say to begin with. I just keep thinking of the big bang when the car hit Mama and the very next moment she was lying on the cold, hard ground in the beam of the car headlights, her arms and legs all twisted. Her skin was far too white and the blood flowing from all the little cuts in her face far too red. Crimson. The glass of the headlights shattered on impact and flew straight into Mama's face. I sat on the side of the road, closed my eyes, occasionally blinking in secret until the flashing blue lights appeared in the darkness: the ambulance.

But I don't have to tell Sister Ruth all of this. She already knows that Mama had an accident. Mama wouldn't be here otherwise. Sister Ruth stares at me. I shrug and blow ripples on my tea. Rosehip, Sister Ruth said, and she told me it was her daughter's favourite when she was small. 'Always with a big spoonful of honey in it. She had a real sweet tooth.' *Sweet tooth.* I don't believe there is such a thing, but I like the sound of it.

'I think we urgently need to speak to your papa,' Sister Ruth says. 'Have another think; maybe your home telephone number will come to you.'

'We don't have a telephone.'

'What about your address, then? The name of the street you live in? Then we could send someone by to pick up your papa.'

I shake my head very slowly. Sister Ruth can't understand.

'Nobody must find us,' I whisper.

LENA

The air just after it's rained. The first and last squares of a bar of chocolate, which always taste the best. The aroma of freesias. David Bowie's Low *album. A curry sausage after a long night out. A long night out. The hum of a fat bumblebee. Everything the sun does, whether it's rising, setting or just shining. A blue sky. A black sky. Any old sky. The way my mother rolls her eyes when she has a spontaneous visitor and the washing-up hasn't been done. The old Hollywood swing in my grandparents' garden, the way it squeaks and sounds as if it's singing a weird song when you swing back and forth on it. Those silly tablecloth weights that look like strawberries and lemons. The summer wind on the face and in the hair. The sea, the sound of it roaring. Fine white sand between the toes . . .*

'I love you,' he moans, rolling his sticky body off of mine.

'I love you too,' I say softly, doubling up like a dying deer.

'. . . Serial rib fracture on the left-hand side involving the second to fourth ribs. Subperiosteal haematoma . . .'

HANNAH

'Are you saying you're not going to tell me where you live?'

Sister Ruth is smiling, but it's not a proper smile, more like half of one with just the right side of her mouth.

'My daughter loved to play games like this when she was small.'

'Sweet tooth.'

'That's right.' She nods, pushing her cup to one side and leaning slightly further across the table. 'And of course those games are fun. But you know, Hannah, I'm afraid it's not always the right time for games. Like now, when it's really quite serious. When someone has an accident and is taken to hospital, we have to contact the relatives. That's our duty.'

I try not to blink when she looks at me in this very particular way. I want her to blink first, because that means she's lost.

'Sometimes, when someone's badly injured, like your mama, we have to make important decisions.'

The person who blinks first loses. That's how the game works.

'Decisions that the injured person can't take for themselves at the moment. Do you understand that, Hannah?'

Sister Ruth has lost.

'Oh well.' She sighs.

I put my hand up to my mouth and pinch at my bottom lip so she can't see me grinning. You should never laugh at anyone, not even if they've lost a blinking competition.

'I just thought we might have a little chat until the police arrive.'

The police are an executive organ of the state. Their task is to investigate punishable and illegal acts. And sometimes they come to take children away from their parents. Or parents from their children.

'The police are coming?'

'That's perfectly normal. I mean, they have to work out how the accident happened in which your mama was injured. Do you know what "hit and run" means, Hannah?'

'"Hit and run" describes the unlawful disappearance from the scene of an accident by a road-user after a road traffic accident which is their fault, full stop.'

Sister Ruth nods. 'It's a crime the police have to investigate.'

'Does the man involved get into trouble, then?'

Sister Ruth narrows her eyes. 'So it was a man driving the car, was it? Why do you ask, Hannah?'

'Because he was nice. He sorted everything out and called the emergency services. And he gave me a coat when I felt cold while we were waiting for the ambulance. He didn't actually leave until just before the ambulance arrived. I think he was just as frightened as Mama and me.'

I don't want to look at Sister Ruth anymore.

'And anyway, the accident wasn't his fault,' I say with my mouse's voice. Papa invented the mouse's voice for Mama's bad days, because he thought she would get upset if we talked too

12

loudly. 'Mama needs her peace and quiet,' he would always say. 'Mama's not feeling so well today.'

'What do you mean, Hannah?' Sister Ruth says. She seems to know the mouse's voice too, because she's speaking like this now as well. 'Whose fault was it then?'

I have to think carefully about what I say.

Concentrate, Hannah. You're a big girl.

'My mama sometimes does silly things by accident.'

Sister Ruth looks surprised. Surprise is when you hear something unexpected or when something unexpected happens. It can be a nice surprise, like a present someone gives you even though it's not your birthday. My cat Fräulein Tinky was that sort of surprise. When Papa came home and said he'd got something for me, I thought it might be a new book or a board game I could play with Jonathan. But then he showed me Fräulein Tinky. She's been mine ever since, just mine.

'Hannah?'

I don't want to. I want to think of Fräulein Tinky.

'Have you got problems at home, Hannah?'

Mama doesn't really like Fräulein Tinky. She even kicked her once.

'Do you have problems with your mama?'

And she's really clumsy, no matter what Papa says. Sometimes she can't even light the stove without his help.

'Hannah?'

Once it was cold for more than a week at home and we froze so much we were just tired all the time. But she is my mama all the same. And when I think of her, I know that I love her. Love, it's like happiness. A very warm feeling that makes you laugh for no real reason, even though nobody's told a joke. The way Sister Ruth laughs when she talks about her daughter. Sweet tooth.

'Please talk to me, child!'

'I don't want the police to come and take Mama away!' I protest. That was my lion's voice.

HANNAH

Sometimes we play a game, my brother and I. It's called 'What does it feel like?' We've been playing it for ages. I can't remember exactly, but I think we've been playing it since Mama first told us about 'happiness'.

'Happiness is a particularly positive feeling, a state of being pleased or content, full stop.' That's what I read out of the thick book that knows all the answers. Jonathan nodded at first, like he always does when I read out the relevant passage. But then he narrowed his eyes and asked what it actually meant. I told him he was an idiot and he wasn't listening properly. You always have to listen properly. Not listening is impolite. But I read it out again anyway. I mean, Jonathan is my brother, whether or not he's an idiot. 'Happiness is a particularly positive feeling, a state of being pleased or content.' Then I said 'full stop' very slowly and very clearly, so he knew that this was the end of the passage.

But Jonathan's eyes were still narrowed and he said, 'You're the idiot. Of course I understood. I meant what does it feel like, inside you, that sort of thing.'

'What does happiness feel like?' we asked Mama. She took us in her arms and said, 'Like this.'

'Warm,' Jonathan declared, estimating that Mama's body

temperature was slightly increased. I pressed my nose into the cool between her neck and her shoulder. She smelled of meadow. Happiness feels warm, almost like a slight fever; it has a smell and a heartbeat that goes like the second hand on the kitchen clock.

We also discussed what a fright feels like, Jonathan and I. 'A fright is like a slap in the face,' Jonathan suggested.

'Which comes as a surprise,' I added.

And we were right. That's exactly what a fright is like. And you can see it in someone's face too. The eyes are big from the surprise and the cheeks turn red in a flash, as if they've been hit by a large, hard hand.

That's exactly what Sister Ruth looks like right now. I screamed at her in my lion's voice, 'I don't want the police to come and take Mama away!'

'Hannah.' Sister Ruth's voice is now slightly squeaky. That must be down to the fright too. My first thought is that I have to tell Jonathan about this, we must remember it: fright = slap + surprise + squeaky voice. My second thought is that he's at home at the moment, struggling with the carpet, then my third thought is that Sister Ruth said the police are on their way. Now I become sad, with tears.

Sister Ruth has probably noticed that I'm feeling a bit weak at the moment and so she's forgotten the fright I gave her. Her chair scrapes across the floor when she gets up, then she walks around the table and presses my head into her fat, soft breasts.

'I know all of this is a bit much for a little girl like you. But you needn't be afraid, Hannah. Nobody wants to do anything bad to your mama or you. Sometimes families just need a bit of help, but they don't realise this themselves. Is it possible that your family needs help at home, Hannah?' She squats beside my chair and takes hold of my hands that are in my lap.

'No,' I say. 'We know how everything works. We have our own rules, you see. It's just that Mama forgets them sometimes. But luckily she's got us, we remind her of them.'

'But still she does silly things? That's what you said earlier, wasn't it? That she sometimes does silly things by accident?'

I lean forwards and make my hands into a secrets funnel. Jonathan and I invented the secrets funnel, but we're not allowed to use it when Papa's at home. Sister Ruth turns her head so that I can put the secrets funnel to her ear.

'She wanted to kill Papa by accident,' I whisper.

Sister Ruth's head spins around. Fright, I can see it quite clearly. I shake my head, grab her face and turn it back into the right position for the secrets funnel. 'You don't have to tell the police. Jonathan is taking care of the stains on the carpet.'

LENA

He wants three, he says, as he gets to work on the onion. He very calmly removes the outer layer, which sounds like a plaster being ripped from the skin. It's a painful sound to my ears. I'm standing right beside him in the kitchen, staring at the knife in his hand. A carving knife with a thin, serrated blade, sharp enough.

'Are you listening to me, Lena?'

'Of course,' answers the woman who I'm beginning to hate with every fibre in my body. He gets everything from her; he grasps his opportunities valiantly and he has already helped himself plentifully. To her body, her

pride, her dignity. Yet still she smiles at him. This woman makes me sick.
'*You want three.*'

'*I always did. What about you?*'

The woman always wanted three as well. I've never wanted any myself, but my opinion doesn't count. Some days I wish I could get used to it. On others I know that it must never happen. I gather the last of my reserves, small shards of a broken will, memories and reasons, and hide them in a safe place. Like a squirrel burying supplies for the winter. I can only hope that nobody, neither he nor the feeble woman, ever discover my hiding place. The secret place where there is a sky and kitschy tablecloth weights.

'*Fancy a glass of wine?*' *He places the knife he's just quartered the onion with beside the wooden board and turns to me. The knife, just lying there. Half an arm's length away, within reach. I have to force myself to take my eyes off it. To look him in the eye again with the inane grin on the lips of the feeble woman.*

'*Yes, lovely.*'

'*Wonderful.*' *He smiles back, then takes a step towards the dining table, where the two brown paper bags with the shopping still stand unpacked.* '*Red or white? I got both because I didn't know which you'd prefer with the spaghetti.*'

Him standing there, slightly hunched over the bags, his back half-turned to me, his right hand already in one of the bags. The knife lying beside the board, just half an arm's length away, within reach. Now! the inner voices cry.

'*Lena?*' *The paper bag rustles as he takes out the first bottle.*

'*If it's up to me, then red.*'

'*Yes, I'd rather red too.*' *Content and with bottle in hand, he turns around again. The feeble woman is holding on to the worktop for support.*

One finger twitches pitifully for the knife. Only a few centimetres separate the two, yet it's an impossibility. He cooks for me. We eat together and raise our glasses of red wine to my getting pregnant as soon as possible. He wants three children. We'll be a very happy family.

'Atrial fibrillation!'

HANNAH

Sister Ruth left the room so quickly that she almost tripped. Because she said I should sit there quietly and wait for her, I don't move. When Sister Ruth returns with a sketch pad and some sharp pencils, she says, 'I've had a great idea, Hannah.'

I'm to draw something, okay. But I'm not sure whether it really is a great idea. The pencils are certainly lovely colours: red, yellow, blue, black, purple, orange, pink, brown and green. But they're really sharp. I take the red pencil and carefully run my thumb over the tip – yes, really very sharp. We do drawing at home too, but with crayons. We write with crayons as well.

'Why should I draw something?'

Sister Ruth shrugs. 'Well, first, it'll give us something to do to fill the time until you can see your mama, but also we can say we're really busy when the police come and ask stupid questions. What do you think?'

'So what should I draw?'

Sister Ruth shrugs again. 'Hmm, perhaps you should just draw what happened today before you came here with your mama.'

Without realising it, I've started chewing the end of the pencil. Tiny little bits of wood have chipped off and are sticking to my tongue. I lick the back of my hand to get rid of them.

'No,' I say. 'I've thought of something better. I'm going to draw a picture for Mama, then I can give it to her afterwards.'

'Okay, that's a good idea. And have you got any idea what you might draw?'

'Yes, maybe,' I say, thinking about it. 'Something that I know will make her happy.'

Now Sister Ruth is excited. She tells me and I can see it in her face. Her eyes are quite round and she's pulled her eyebrows up so high that there are lines running across her forehead. I put the red pencil to one side and take the blue one. I put it on the paper really carefully. Sharp pencils can be very dangerous. I begin by drawing Mama's face. Sister Ruth asks why it's blue. I click my tongue and roll my eyes. Sometimes Sister Ruth is a bit of an idiot too, like my brother. 'Because I don't have a white pencil. And anyway, you wouldn't see the white pencil on the white paper,' I explain.

Then I draw Mama's body wearing a beautiful long dress. It's blue too, although it ought to be white, then her beautiful long hair in yellow, and after that the black trees with branches like fossilised monsters' fingers, which are trying to grab hold of Mama.

'That looks dangerous, Hannah,' Sister Ruth says. 'Tell me a bit about the picture.'

'Well, this is the story of my mama and my papa and how they fell in love. Late one night, Mama was out in the woods. Can you see how beautifully her hair is shining in the moonlight?'

'Yes, she really looks very pretty, Hannah. Was she out alone in the woods?'

'Yes, and she was terribly scared, and that's why she's not laughing, can you see?'

'What was she so scared about?'

'She'd got lost. But then . . .'

Now I draw my papa, stepping out from behind a tree.

'Along comes Papa and finds her. This is the best part of the whole story. He's standing there as if he's appeared from nowhere, and he saves her.' I redo Mama's mouth so she's smiling. Her smile is really fat now, like a fat, red banana. 'And they fall in love at first sight.'

Satisfied, I put down the red pencil I've just used to draw a few hearts. A red heart is a common symbol for love. I've drawn six red hearts for even more love.

'Wow!' Sister Ruth says. 'It almost sounds like a fairy tale.'

'No, it's not a fairy tale, it's a true story. Exactly as Mama always tells it.'

Sister Ruth leans a little further across the table.

'What's your papa got there in his hand?'

'That's a cloth he's going to tie over her eyes because he wants to surprise her. You see, she mustn't know where they're going to go now.'

'Where are they going to go, Hannah?'

'Home, of course,' I say. 'To the cabin.'

LENA

Be grateful.

God has blessed you.

You have a lovely home.

You have a family.

You've got everything you always wanted.

The voice in my head is merely scratching the surface. My stomach is burning. Emptiness. Emptiness can't burn. Oh, but how it can burn, this emptiness. My jaw tenses with the strain when my trembling fingers try to take off the lid of the hot chocolate tin. It's stuck. It's bloody well stuck. I can feel the sweat collecting beneath my hair and making my scar sting. On the work surface beside me, next to the milk, are two cups, a red one and a blue one, both with white dots, both melamine and unbreakable. The children need to have breakfast, now. Breakfast at seven-thirty. What's so difficult to understand about that? The children need an ordered daily routine. The children need a balanced breakfast.

What sort of a mother are you, Lena?

What sort of monster are you?

Behind my back, I can hear them running riot – please, children, not so loud! *The kitchen, the dining area and the sitting room all run into one another. As they chase each other through the house, their screeches fly from one corner to the next like a bouncy ball out of control –* be quiet, please! *Now and then, one of them leaps over the armrest of the sofa and flumps on to the cushions, making a sound like a loud, heavy sigh, again and again –* I want you to stop now! *The pressure inside my head is unbearable and it feels as if it's about to burst. The lid is stuck. The fucking lid is stuck.*

'Mama?'

I give a start. All of a sudden my daughter is standing beside me, pushing her chin inquisitively across the edge of the work surface. How small she is. A tiny, delicate girl with thin blonde locks and very white skin. Like a little angel. But not one of those neat, red-cheeked cherubim porcelain figures my mother collects on her dining-room dresser. More like an angel where something's not quite right. The prototype that almost worked but not completely.

'Hannah,' *I say. It sounds like a statement, totally lacking in affection.*

'Do you want me to help you, Mama?' Her round, pale blue eyes show that she hasn't taken offence at my cold tone, or merely that she doesn't want to take offence. I nod wearily and push the hot chocolate tin towards her. She opens it in seconds with a skilful twist, and beams at me: 'Da-da!'

Hannah is just about to go away and play when I grab her arm, probably too tightly, seeing how small and delicate she is. I let go again at once. 'I'm sorry. Did I hurt you?'

She frowns and grimaces as if I'd just said something very stupid.

'No, of course not. You'd never hurt me, Mama.'

For a brief moment, a feeling covers my inner emptiness like a heavy, warm blanket. I attempt a smile.

'Maybe you could help me some more?' As if by way of proof, I hold up my shaking hands, but Hannah has already nodded, stood up on tiptoes and grabbed the neon-green plastic spoon which is also on the work surface. She measures out the powder, two spoons for each cup, carefully pours milk on top and stirs, while slowly and monotonously counting the number of times the clanking spoon circles the cup.

'One, two, three . . .'

The counting, the clanking. The voice inside my head that continues scratching steadily at the surface. The voice that says: she is your daughter and you have to love her. Whether you want to or not.

'. . . seven, eight . . .'

It's getting more difficult to breathe. My knees feel like jelly. I make a grab for the edge of the work surface, for some support, but I grasp thin air.

'. . . thirteen, fourteen . . .'

In slow motion the ceiling tilts, the floor ripples, I sink into my weakness, sliding almost sedately into the redeeming blackness, thank you.

'Papa!' I hear Hannah as if under water. 'Mama's had another fit!'

'Stabilise circulation!'

HANNAH

Sister Ruth asks me what I mean by 'the cabin'. To begin with, I want to bash her over the head and make her work it out for herself, but then I think that I ought to help her.

'A cabin is a little house made of wood. In the forest.'

Sister Ruth nods as if she understands, but her eyebrows are pulled into a frown and her jaw is now hanging a little lower, as if it had somehow slipped from where it should be. If you're smart, you can see a lot in someone's face.

'Are you telling me you live in the forest? In a cabin?'

I nod slowly and say, 'Well done.' I get praised when Mama tests me and I get something right. She always says, 'Well done, Hannah,' which makes thinking about things much more fun. Maybe Sister Ruth feels the same.

'Have you ever lived anywhere else, Hannah? In a proper house?'

'A cabin is a proper house! My papa built it specially for us. We've got proper air too. The recirculation unit has only slightly malfunctioned two or three times. It needs to be humming gently the whole time, otherwise there's something wrong. Luckily I've got a really good sense of hearing. If something's wrong with the recirculation unit I notice at once, long before we start to get headaches. But Papa repaired it straightaway. He said it was just a little loose connection, nothing serious. He's a pretty good handyman.'

Sister Ruth is blinking a lot. 'What,' she says, but then stops. I don't say anything either, because I think she's finally understood that she needs to make an effort herself. Mama always waits a while if I can't immediately think of the right answers when we're doing work. 'It's not going to help if I always give you the solutions straightaway. You have to get used to using your own head. Think, Hannah. Concentrate. You can do it.'

'What,' Sister Ruth says again. 'A recir . . . ?'

'Recirculation. It's hard to say, isn't it? Do you know what I do when I come across a difficult word?'

Again Sister Ruth says nothing.

'I say the difficult word over and over again in my head until it's stored there. That's why my vocabulary is much better than Jonathan's. Sometimes I only have to say the word twice inside my head, but sometimes I have to do it ten times.'

Sister Ruth still isn't speaking. Maybe she's trying my trick and practising the difficult word in her head.

Finally something happens and her mouth starts moving again.

'Will you now tell me what a . . .' – she takes a deep breath for the difficult word – ' . . . recirculation unit is?'

'Well done,' I say, pleased at Sister Ruth's progress and at myself. I'm a good teacher. I get that from Mama. 'The recirculation unit makes our air,' I tell her, trying to speak as slowly as possible so Sister Ruth can follow me. 'A person can't live without oxygen. Every day we need to breathe in and out between ten and twenty thousand litres of oxygen. In terms of volume, that's roughly ten to twenty thousand times as much as in one pack of milk. The air we breathe in contains about twenty-one per cent oxygen and nought point nought three per cent carbon dioxide. The air we breathe out contains about seventeen per cent oxygen and four per cent carbon dioxide, full stop. The recirculation unit ensures that the good air comes into our cabin and the bad air is taken away. We'd suffocate otherwise.'

Sister Ruth puts a hand in front of her mouth. I can see she's trembling slightly. All of her, not just her hand.

'Why don't you just open a window if you need air, Hannah.' I think that's a question, but it doesn't sound like one. You're supposed to go up at the end of the sentence if you want to ask something. I start arranging the pencils on the table in a long, straight line, from light to dark, beginning with yellow and ending with black.

'Hannah?' Sister Ruth's voice goes up this time. I look up from my line of pencils and into her eyes.

'Will you at least tell me who Jonathan is?'

'He's my brother.'

'Does Jonathan live in the cabin too? With you and your parents?'

'Yes, of course. He hasn't done anything wrong. Why should we send him away?'

'Tell me about the stains on the carpet.' Now Sister Ruth is looking very strict and she's even winning the blinking competition. But that's just because my eyes have started weeping again. I blame the light and because I'm tired.

'Hannah? Earlier you said that Jonathan was taking care of the stains on the carpet. What stains, Hannah?'

I shake my head and say, 'I'm tired and I want to see my mama.'

Sister Ruth reaches for my hand across the table. 'I know but, believe me, the doctors really will let us know as soon as you can go and see her. Maybe you'd like to draw another picture in the meantime? Tell me, is your brother older or younger than you?'

I tear the picture of Mama and Papa in the forest from the pad and put it to one side. Then I pick up the blue pencil and start drawing Jonathan's face on a new piece of paper.

'Younger,' I say. 'By two years.'

'Okay, don't say anything, let me guess. That means he's . . .' Sister Ruth says, looking as if she's working it out. 'Hmm, it's hard. I reckon that makes him . . . six?'

I look up from the piece of paper. Poor, stupid Sister Ruth. She doesn't seem to be any good at maths.

'Thirteen minus two,' I say, trying to help, but she just gawps at me.

'He's eleven, of course!' I solve the sum for her. Sister Ruth really has a lot to learn in her life.

'Hannah?' Now she sounds as if she's about to cry. 'The cabin. And the circulation unit.'

'*Recirculation* unit!' I say in my lion's voice.

Sister Ruth flinches. Fright, again. Wide eyes and red cheeks. She just won't make an effort. 'I'm not going to put up with this!' my lion's voice continues and I slap the table. The pencils jump; the green one rolls over the edge and clatters on the floor. You mustn't be stupid deliberately. I bend under the table to get the green pencil and when I reappear, she apologises. That's something, at least. You always have to apologise if you do something wrong.

'I didn't mean to upset you, Hannah,' she says. 'It must be a very difficult situation for you. I understand that. But I'd like to understand the rest too. I'd really like to know what it's like at home. I don't know anyone else who lives in a cabin in the woods.'

I turn the paper around and keep drawing Jonathan's trousers.

They're his favourite trousers, the blue ones he's only allowed to wear on Sundays.

'Hannah?'

I look up.

'Do you understand me?'

I nod, then go straight back to my picture. I've also given Jonathan his favourite red T-shirt. It really glowed when it was still new. I think he'd be pleased if he knew he was wearing his favourite clothes in my picture. To finish, I draw his curly hair. It's almost black like Papa's. Then I start drawing my own face right next to Jonathan's. I'm going to put on my favourite dress too, the white one with the flowers. We're all going to look very beautiful in my picture.

'So you can't open the windows at home, Hannah? That's why you need the unit?'

'The recirculation unit,' I mutter.

'Doesn't the cabin have any windows?'

'Of course it does.' I need the yellow pencil for my curly hair.

'But you don't open the windows? Why not, Hannah?'

'It's too dangerous. That's why they're boarded up.' I wonder if it's a lie if I draw myself with a red hairband. I don't have a red hairband, only a dark blue one. But a red one would go much better with the flowers on my dress.

'Did your papa do that, Hannah? You said he's a good handyman.'

'Yes.' My hand moves very carefully to the red pencil and I look Sister Ruth in the eye. There's no way she can know I don't have a red hairband, but I'm slightly worried she'll see from my face that I'm trying to cheat. Worry isn't proper fear, but it's not a good feeling either. Worry is more like the feeling of sickness you get when you've got a tummy ache and you don't know if you're going to have to throw up or not.

Papa was very worried when Mama was away. He told us that he wasn't certain she'd be coming back to us and then he cried. Papa had never cried before. I put my hand up to his face and felt the sticky tears running down his cheek. He didn't say it, but I immediately knew that it was partly my fault that Mama went away. It was because of the Sara thing. Jonathan knew too. He just stared at me and wouldn't talk to me for several days, until I reminded him that he didn't particularly like Sara either.

'You know what, Hannah, I was just thinking. You've gone to so much trouble drawing your brother that it shows just how fond you are of him. Maybe we should send someone to your house to see how he's getting on with the carpet? Or to help him?'

I grab the red pencil without taking my eyes off Sister Ruth. But it doesn't seem to bother her that I'm going to cheat with the colours.

'Or,' she continues unfazed, 'we could bring him here, to be with you. Then you could wait for your mama together. Some things seem only half as bad if you've someone important to you close by.'

'I'm not sure Jonathan would like it here,' I say. My imaginary red hairband looks really lovely with the flowery dress. 'I think he'd start trembling if he had to be here.'

'But you're brave and you're not trembling.'

'Yes, that's true,' I say. 'But maybe I'm just more courageous than Jonathan. Because I'm older or a bit smarter or both. He was much more terrified than me by the blood too. And by the noise.'

'What noise?'

'Well, where do you think the bad stains on the carpet came from?'

Sister Ruth looks as if she's thinking, but I now know that she's not particularly good at this. 'Like if you drop a watermelon on the floor,' I say, to spare her more embarrassment. 'What it sounds like when you bash someone's head with something. Bam!' I say in my lion's voice. Speaking normally again, I add, 'And afterwards it's very quiet for a while.'

MATTHIAS

Four thousand nine hundred and ninety-three days.

I have counted and cursed each one of them. My hair has turned greyer, my heartbeat uneven. The first year I drove down her last route every day. I had flyers printed and stuck them on every single lamppost. On my own initiative, I questioned supposed friends and set a few people straight. Several times a day I would call my long-term friend Gerd, Gerd Brühling, who was looking for her in his role as chief inspector and head of the investigation team. I terminated my friendship with Herr Brühling when he failed to find her. When I reached the stage where I began to feel my efforts were pointless, I was determined at the very least that the lies should stop. I gave endless interviews, fifty or more.

Lena has been missing for 4,993 days. And nights. That's over thirteen years. Thirteen years during which every ring of the telephone might signal the one message, the only message that would change everything. Our daughter had been abducted and they were demanding a ransom. Our daughter had been fished out of the Isar, blue and swollen beyond all recognition. Our daughter had been found, raped, slaughtered and thrown away like rubbish, perhaps abroad, somewhere in eastern Europe.

'Matthias? Are you still there?' Gerd's voice is squawking with excitement.

I don't answer, I just try to breathe. The receiver is shaking in my sweaty right hand. With my left, I grope for some support on the chest of drawers. This space, the hallway in our house, is losing its solidity; the stairs, the carpet, the wardrobe seem to slosh towards me, as if driven on by waves. The floor beneath my feet is soft. Beside me is Karin who, still half-asleep, hauled herself downstairs when I didn't return to the bedroom. Nervously fiddling with the tie of her cream-coloured towelling dressing gown, she hisses, 'What's up, Matthias? What is it?'

With great difficulty, I swallow the lump in my throat, the news and its significance, the thirteen fucking years. Hundreds of times both Karin and I have imagined Lena dying in the most terrible way possible, torturing ourselves with thousands of possibilities. In our thoughts we'd started to disregard only one of these possibilities: what if the telephone rings and they tell us they've found her alive?

'Lena,' I gasp.

Karin closes her eyes and takes a few unsteady steps backwards until her back hits the wall and she sinks to the floor. She puts her hands to her face and starts to sob, not loud and histrionically, no, not like that. Too much time has passed, 4,993 days, leaving too little hope. No, the sounds she makes are like sad, feeble hiccoughs.

'No, no,' I say, finally managing to speak, and hold my hand out to her.

'Matthias?' Gerd says on the phone.

'What do you mean, no, no?' Karin says, slumped against the wall.

'They believe she was abducted. But they've got her. She's alive,' I say in a voice that's barely loud enough to reach my ears. I say it again: 'She's alive.'

'What?' Karin gets awkwardly to her feet. I grab her arm when it looks as if she might lose balance again on her wobbly legs.

'Yes,' the squawking Gerd says on the other end of the line. The information he's just given me is vague. I don't know if he can't, won't or isn't allowed to tell me any more. Only this: running a description through the database of missing people threw up a number of similarities. He said he's going first thing tomorrow morning to Cham on the Czech border to confirm Lena's identity. Cham, only two and a half hours from Munich, so close. Lena is so close, perhaps she's been so close the whole time. And I didn't find her.

'I'm coming with you,' I bluster. 'Let's go. Not tomorrow morning, let's go right now.'

'No, Matthias, you can't do that,' Gerd says, in the tone of a grown-up trying to placate a stubborn child. 'It's not the way things are done . . .'

'I don't care,' the child says doggedly. 'Actually, I don't give a fuck! I'm going to get dressed. You come and pick me up.'

I hear Gerd sigh.

'You owe me this,' I add before he can launch into an unnecessary, long-winded explanation about the usual procedure. 'Let's go.'

Gerd sighs again and I hang up. I decide to give him half an hour. If he doesn't appear, I'm going on my own and that's that. To Cham, to Lena. I put my arms around Karin. Her warm tears seep through my pyjamas.

'She's alive,' I murmur into her hair. How wonderful that sounds: she's alive.

Within the next fifteen minutes we're dressed, and Karin has even combed her hair. Side by side in the hallway, we're itching to leave, both of us focused on the front door. We will immediately see the beam of the headlights through the frosted glass if Gerd drives up. Karin says what I'm only thinking: 'Let's not wait.'

I nod eagerly and grab the car keys from the hook.

To Cham. To Lena. She's alive.

I've been in a bubble since Gerd's call earlier on, but when our old Volvo turns on to the motorway slip road, it suddenly bursts. Now I'm wondering whether we ought not to have waited for him after all. And whether it was right to bring Karin. Gerd's words on the telephone play back in my head. 'Listen, Matthias, we can't be sure yet. But I've had a call from a colleague in Cham, where a woman ran in front of a car in a wooded area near the Czech border. Apparently she's called Lena. They suspect that the accident is somehow connected to an abduction, which is why they trawled through the missing persons database. There are some points of resemblance, such as the scar on the forehead. But she suffered serious injuries as a result of the accident. She's in casualty and nobody can talk to her right now. Are you still there? Matthias?'

'Lena,' I gasped at Karin.

'Yes,' Gerd said. 'I'm going to set off for Cham first thing in the morning. Until we can unequivocally confirm the woman's identity . . .'

Me: 'I'm coming with you.'

'Karin, I think I have to warn you,' I say when I realise that Gerd's reservations don't just relate to disregard for police procedure. I ought to have told Karin earlier, as we were getting dressed, but I could barely utter anything other than a mere 'she's alive', over and over again, in wonder, in disbelief, in awe.

'Gerd says she's in casualty. She might be seriously injured. Could you bear to see her like that?'

'Are you crazy? She's our daughter!'

Karin is right. Lena needs us there with her, especially in her condition. I put my foot down and push our old Volvo to its limits. After more than thirteen years, only one hundred and eighty kilometres separate us from our child.

'Ciao, Paps! See you soon! And thanks again!' I hear her say as clear as a bell, and in my mind I see her skipping down the steps to the front garden. On the afternoon before she disappeared, she came to see us for a coffee. Her bicycle had been stolen from campus and I made sure I handed over the money behind Karin's back. Karin thought the girl ought to be more independent and, like lots of other students, get a part-time job. I thought that was a very bad idea. The girl ought to concentrate on her studies. Well, now the girl needed a new bike, so I'd given her the three hundred euros.

Ciao, Paps! See you soon!

Ciao, my angel, see you in 4,993 days . . .

'Matthias?' Karin is waving my mobile. Only now do I notice the ringing and the blue display light illuminating the dark interior of the car.

'Gerd,' I presume, and I imagine him standing outside our house at this moment, ringing the doorbell a few times and realising that we've left without him. I glance at the dashboard. He'd have been on time.

'Don't worry, answer it.'

Gerd moans so loudly into Karin's ear that even I can hear it. Karin apologises. 'We couldn't just wait, surely you can understand.'

Gerd tells her to tell me that I'm still an idiot – I hear this too and can't help grinning when a feeling briefly flickers, a slight wistfulness. Gerd and I used to be best friends, in the past, in another life.

'Yes, yes, don't worry,' Karin says to Gerd before she says goodbye, and at the touch of a button the car becomes dark again. 'He said to meet him at the hospital. We're to stay calm until he gets there, also on account of his colleagues at the hospital.'

I snort; the wistfulness is gone.

'Like I give two figs about Herr Brühling's colleagues. We want to know what's happened to our daughter and that's that.'

I can hear Karin rummaging around in her handbag; I suspect she's putting my mobile away. But then I hear the familiar sound of a packet of paper tissues being opened. From the corner of my eye, I see her wiping her face.

'Abduction,' she sobs. 'But if she was abducted, why didn't anyone contact us about a ransom?'

I shrug.

'It wouldn't be the first time some sick bastard abducts a young woman to keep her.' I immediately think of Mark Sutthoff. What if he did have something to do with Lena's disappearance after all? Good God, I could have had him . . .

'*Keep* is a dreadful word,' Karin says, her voice mingling with the images inside my head. My hands on Mark Sutthoff's collar, his back pressed up against a wall, his face as red as a lobster.

Where is she, you bastard?

'I know,' I say.

Karin snuffles. 'Do you think she'll recover? I don't mean from the injuries in the accident.'

'She's a strong girl, she always was,' I say with a smile of encouragement, and stroke Karin's knee.

We spend the rest of the journey in silence, apart from the occasional clearing of a dry throat, either Karin's or mine. I know what's going through Karin's mind. She's wondering whether the person we'll be getting back today can still in some way be our daughter, after all these years and everything she may have been through. In the past, Karin often said things like 'I hope it was quick, at least', or 'I'm praying she managed it'. What she meant by *managed it* was her wish that Lena's death had been quick, without any physical or mental torture, no suffering. Sometimes I found it difficult not to go for the jugular when she spoke like that, even though I secretly thought the same. I sense that we're miles apart, even though we're sitting in the same car with just the central armrest separating us. Karin is frightened, Karin has her doubts. Me, on the other hand, all I'm thinking is that there are doctors for everything, for both body and soul, that it's all going to be fine now. Why else would Lena have survived if she wasn't capable of living? If she didn't want to cling on to life? Maybe I'm too naïve and Karin is too pessimistic; maybe the truth is somewhere in-between, like the central armrest. Maybe it's handy and quite simple.

'She's strong,' I assert again and Karin clears her throat.

LENA

Someone screams, 'No!' and 'Oh God!'

My stiff body is wrenched away. Shaken. Warmth, a firm embrace.

'Lena! Oh God, Lena!'

I blink. Give a weak smile. He came back after all, at the last moment. The children, they're alive, their arms clasped around his neck. He has an arm around me. His face is pale with horror. I put out my cold hand, feel a tear.

'I'm so sorry,' he says, and I say, 'You saved us.'

'Patient stable.'

HANNAH

I think I've done something wrong. I'm sure I have, because I've already counted to 2,676 and Sister Ruth still isn't back yet. I mimicked the noise of the watermelon for her. *Bam!* Then she said she had to ask whether we could go and see Mama, and while she was away I should keep drawing the picture of my family. I've given Papa a red patch on the side of his head but now I don't know what else to do.

I'm tired. The night outside the windows has already turned a bit grey. I haven't been up this late very often, only when Sara was still with us and kept us awake with her howling. You always have to have enough sleep so the body can regenerate. I lay my head on the table and close my eyes. Mama always says you can choose what you dream if you think hard enough about something before going to sleep. I want to dream something really nice. About Mama and me finally going on another trip, just the two of us because I'm her favourite child.

So I think as hard as I can about the first time we went away together. I was a bit anxious to begin with, but Mama said, 'It's a wonderful place, Hannah. You'll love it there.' And she said we weren't to tell anyone we were going away.

'Shh,' she said, putting her finger to her lips. 'Our trips are a secret.'

'But you mustn't lie, Mama!'

'We're not lying, Hannah. We're just not telling anyone.'

'What about Jonathan? He'll get scared when he wakes up and finds nobody at home.'

'Don't you worry about him. He'll sleep for a long time. And we'll be back by the time he wakes up, I promise.'

We made ourselves look beautiful. Mama even let me put on my favourite dress, the white one with the flowers. Then we tiptoed out of the house to the car. I sat in the front, next to Mama. The road we drove on was as smooth as paper and reflected the sun. In places it shimmered in the heat like little, colourless fires. I pressed my nose against the cool glass of the window. The sky was a canvas, with snowy-white clouds against a blue background. I traced the outline of a cow cloud on the window.

Mama laughed. A song was playing on the radio that we knew, and Mama's laughter ruined the melody until she started singing along. We left the main road and turned into a residential area. Mama parked the car in the shade of a large tree. It was a maple. You can tell by its five-fingered leaves that look like a big green hand.

We'd been invited to a party, and it was taking place in a garden. Mama was right, it was a wonderful place. We were expected; people were laughing, waving and calling out, 'There you are!' Mama tried to introduce me, but I couldn't stand still with excitement. I slipped off my sandals and ran barefoot through the garden, sniffing the hydrangea flowers that were as large as cabbages, then I threw myself on the lawn on my tummy. The grass smelled of the washing powder we always use. I picked blades of grass and daisies and let a ladybird run over the back of my hand. A man with really light blue eyes and grey hair sat on the lawn beside me and said, 'It's so lovely you came, Hannah.'

I showed him the ladybird on my hand and he told me that ladybirds were really useful because they ate greenfly and spider mites. I was amazed, such a tiny creature.

'They're also said to bring good luck,' the man said. I liked that.

Someone called us to eat. At the back of the garden a long table had been set up. I put the heel of my right foot to the toes of my left, then kept going like this until I measured the length of the table: thirty steps. There was chocolate cake and straw-berry tart and custard with raspberries the size of my thumbnail and biscuits and pretzel sticks and barbecued sausages. I wanted to try everything, but Mama said we had to get back. Jonathan would wake up soon. The sleeping pills never work quite as long as we'd like.

'Can I at least have a piece of chocolate cake, Mama? Just a little bit, please? I eat really fast.'

Mama shook her head. She took a cereal bar from her handbag, tore off the wrapper and gave it to me. 'Too much sugar's unhealthy, Hannah. When we're back home we'll read what too much sugar can do to your body. Now get your sandals, we've really got to go.'

She hurried towards the garden gate without saying goodbye to the other guests. When I caught her up just before she got to the car, I turned around again. Standing by the garden fence and waving at me was the man who'd told me about ladybirds. I raised my hand, but only briefly so Mama didn't see. Then we were back home.

'The excessive consumption of sugar and sugary foods can lead to the following symptoms,' Mama began reading from the fat book, which is always right. She'd taken it from the shelves in the sitting room as soon as we got back. 'Tiredness, lack of motivation, anxiety, digestive problems, flatulence, diarrhoea or constipation, nervousness, sleep and concentration disorders, as well as tooth decay. You see?' She slammed the fat book shut, very loudly. 'Be glad you didn't have to eat the cake.'

I nodded. My mama looks after me. She only ever wants the best for me.

A moment later Jonathan was standing in the doorway. He must have just woken up.

'What are you two doing?' he asked, rubbing the sleep from his eyes.

'Nothing, Jonathan,' Mama said with a smile, and winked at me.

We had a secret, my mama and I. We belonged together for ever, my mama and I . . .

'Hannah?'

I blink.

'Hannah?'

I lift my head from the table.

Two strangers are standing in front of me. A man in a grey suit and a tall, thin woman with short brown hair. My body flinches with shock. Now I'm sitting up, my back very straight, like you have to do when sitting at the table for mealtimes. The woman offers me her hand. I hold out both of mine and turn them slowly so she can see my fingernails, then my palms. Before I can finish showing her she takes my right hand and shakes it. The woman and the man say, 'Hello, Hannah,' and tell me that Sister Ruth isn't coming back right away because she has to have her break first.

'She's looked after you so nicely all this time,' the woman says, smiling. Then she tells me her name is Dr Hamstedt, but she doesn't look like a doctor. She's not wearing a white coat. I want to tell her that, because she might just have forgotten her coat and could get into trouble, but I don't get the chance because now it's the man's turn. He doesn't want to see my hands either, even though he's a policeman. He even shows me his ID and laughs because he looks very different in the photo than in real life.

'I was young and handsome back then.'

I think this is supposed to be a joke, but the moment my mouth begins to twitch the man turns serious again.

'Hannah, I urgently need to check that everything's all right at your home,' he says, taking the chair Sister Ruth was sitting in earlier. Then he stretches his neck to look at the pictures I drew and taps his finger right where Papa has a red patch on his head.

'After what Sister Ruth told me I think something terrible happened there last night. I think you and your mother might have been so frightened that you ran away and then she had that accident in which she was injured.'

Now he takes my first picture, showing Mama and Papa in the woods, and points at the cloth that Papa's holding.

'You mustn't be afraid, Hannah. Tell me where the cabin is. I'll look after everything. And nothing bad is going to happen to you, I promise.'

'Listen to Inspector Giesner, Hannah. You can trust us.'

'Where's the cabin, Hannah? Can you tell me how to get there?' – the policeman again.

'Don't worry, you're safe here' – the woman.

I don't find these people unfriendly. The policeman, in particular, is much nicer than I thought he'd be. But I don't want to talk to them. I want Sister Ruth to come back, or at least I want to go to sleep. I think they understand this because they leave me in peace when I lay my head on the table again and close my eyes. I try to think of something nice to begin with, but it doesn't work, because I'm trying so hard to listen to the man and woman for a sign they're getting up and leaving the room. But they stay sitting there until I've counted to 148. Then I finally hear their chairs scrape across the floor and, shortly after that, the door.

MATTHIAS

We turn into the hospital car park. It's not quite four o'clock.

Karin reaches for my hand. Hers is cold and wet. She says something. I can't hear anything apart from my own pulse in my ears. We don't run, we don't storm the building, we take cautious, little steps. Everything runs on autopilot. We enter the foyer through a door and walk the short distance to reception, where a woman is sitting. My mouth is moving. I want to tell her that we're the parents of Lena Beck, who was admitted as the victim of a road accident. That we have to go to casualty. I don't know how I sound. Or if the sentences coming out of my mouth are the same as those I've composed in my head. Now the woman at reception moves her mouth too and picks up her telephone. Karen grabs my sleeve and drags me a few paces away from the glass box where the woman is sitting and making a phone call. Karin's face is white and her eyes are quivering in their sockets as she looks at me. When I notice her shifting nervously from one leg to the other, I put my arm around her shoulders. I want to tell her to calm down, and evidently I do say that because I see her nod in response. A doctor comes or an orderly, I don't know which, but at any rate he's wearing a doctor's coat. With him is a man in a grey suit. Names fly past my head, my hand is shaken. We follow the two of them to a lift. It moves, but I don't know whether we're going up or down. Time is pulling the strings. The lift stops, one of the men touches me on the shoulder, probably to signal I should get out. Karin has taken my hand again and is squeezing it. Our procession takes us halfway down a corridor then comes to a halt. Karin abruptly lets go of my hand. Only because this unsettles me, I suddenly become alert again.

'It would be better if only one of you came in with us,' the doctor says. 'Although she's had treatment, she's still unconscious. We want to let her come round in her own time, especially as we can't rule out the possibility that she's in shock.'

'Which means I can't talk to her,' I say rather stupidly.

The man in the grey suit, who I now identify as a police inspector, says, 'First we need your help to identify her beyond any doubt. Then we can discuss everything else.'

'I'll do it,' I say to Karin. She nods. It's what we'd already agreed years ago. I would do the job of identifying the dead body of our daughter shrouded by a thin sheet on a mortuary slab. I would hold her hand one final time and give her a last kiss on her cold forehead. Tell her that we love her.

Only we're not in some forensics basement, but in a hospital, and our daughter is alive. The doctor leads me by the arm towards a nearby door, which divides the corridor from a separate area. Behind me, Karin asks the inspector what's going to happen now. I don't hear his answer as the door closes behind the doctor and me. All of a sudden, I feel unsure; I begin to wonder what she looks like, our daughter, with the injuries sustained in the accident and whatever else has happened to her. When she disappeared, she was in the fourth semester of her teaching degree, a young girl just spreading her wings. Now she's thirty-seven years old, a proper woman, who might have been married and had her own children, if she hadn't been wrenched from her life on that one night.

'Please don't be horrified,' the doctor says as we're standing

43

outside her room. Although he's already holding the handle, he's hesitating. 'She has a few injuries to her face, cuts mainly. But it looks worse than it is.'

I make a grunting sound. I don't have enough air for anything else. My chest feels tight. The doctor pushes the handle. The gap in the door widens.

I close my eyes and am drowned by images. My Lenchen, the tiny bundle in Karin's arms. Fifty centimetres tall, 3,430 grams in weight, a minute hand clutching my thumb. 'Welcome to the world, my angel,' I say. 'Your papa will always look after you.' My Lenchen with the missing tooth and the huge bag of sweets for her first day at school. Lenchen insisting she must be called Lena from now on because all the other names are too childish. Lena, having dyed her beautiful blonde hair black, sitting on the sofa in our living room with her knees up and scratching holes in her jeans with a safety pin. Lena, now blonde again, and my pride and joy. Who looks ravishing in her dress at her school prom, has a great set of exam results and so many plans in her head. Lena the student, and Lena when I see her the last time before she disappears. Skipping down the steps into the front garden after visiting us, turning around again and giving me a jolly wave. *Ciao, Paps! See you soon! And thanks again!*

Then I go in.

Her bed is in the middle of the room. I hear machines beeping. Her eyes are closed. There are indeed injuries to her face; it's covered in cuts that look like tiny triangles. The left-hand side is blue and swollen. It looks as if she's been stitched above the eyebrows. The small scar to the right on her forehead is clearly visible nonetheless. And yet . . .

The first glance ought to have sufficed. But the significance needs to sink in; it takes time, it sinks heavily, it sinks without ever stopping. All of a sudden I slap my hand over my mouth and stagger away from the bed.

'That isn't Lena,' I gasp into the palm of my hand. 'That isn't my daughter.'

The doctor takes my elbow; he keeps me on my feet or pushes me out of the room, perhaps both at the same time.

'It's not her,' I say, over and over again.

'I'm sorry,' the doctor says. *I'm sorry*, as if that were sufficient.

HANNAH

If I had the choice I'd love to be beside the sea now. With my mama – just the two of us because I'm her favourite child – in the most beautiful place on earth. She actually owes me a trip to the seaside because the last one didn't go to plan. You always have to be in a good mood when you go on a trip. I caught every wave, throwing myself on my tummy with gusto, as if I'd already guessed that this might be the last time we'd be able to go away together. Mama had changed. She lay in the sand on her back and stared at the sky. I thought it was because of Papa. Every time he was away she was scared he might not come back. Although she didn't say this, I could tell. She was nervous and agitated, counting the cereal bars, and she kept asking me whether everything was okay with the recirculation device. I've got an excellent sense of hearing, the best of us all.

I really wanted to cheer her up so I struggled my way back through the waves to the beach. I turned around to look at the water again, in case we had to leave right away because of Jonathan – his sleeping pills never work quite as long as we'd like. I saw the sun glistening on the sea as if a huge load of diamonds had been tipped on to it. The sky and the water were one, everything was blue, nothing but blue from top to bottom, *remember this, Hannah, don't ever forget this beautiful, infinite blue.* I closed my eyes and breathed in the salty air which sat stickily on my lungs. *Don't forget this, Hannah, just don't ever forget it. Das Meer,* the sea, *la mer* covers almost three-quarters of the earth's surface. Marine flora produces around sixty per cent of the oxygen present in the earth's atmosphere. When I was sure I'd stored it all in my mind I trudged through the hot sand to where Mama was lying.

'Mama?'

She said nothing. I shook my hair over her like a dog would its wet coat, and I really wanted her to leap up and chase me across the beach. Like she usually did. But that day she just lay there, totally stiff, staring up at the sky as if she weren't really there.

'You wanted to go in the sea too,' I moaned, flopping down in the sand beside her.

'Oh, Hannah,' she said, rolling on to her side so she could look at me. 'I'm really sorry about everything.'

'What do you mean, Mama?'

'You all have such a difficult time, just because of me.'

She meant the black eye. 'That was just a silly accident,' I said. 'It's not that bad.'

'You're smart, Hannah. And you're getting bigger. One day you will think it's bad.' She felt for my hand and squeezed it too hard. 'If someone asks about me, you're going to tell them the truth, okay?'

'You know I don't lie. Papa always says that lying – '

'I know,' she interrupted me. You should never interrupt any-body. It's impolite. She made a laughing sound. 'Oh, just forget what I said, Hannah. I bet it's just my hormones.' Hormones are biochemical messengers that trigger certain biological processes. Like the fact that she was crying now and little high-pitched sounds were coming out of her mouth. I'd never heard her make any sound when crying before, even though the sound she was making was very soft. I've got excellent hearing.

Mama pulled my arms until I was sitting in the right position for a cuddle.

'I love you, Hannah.'

'For ever?'

'For ever and ever and ever . . .'

I hear the door open and look up. This time it's Sister Ruth. Finally she's back.

'Well, Hannah? How are you?' she asks with half a smile. It's the stupid smile she does when she's a bit embarrassed. Probably because she left me alone and sent those two strangers instead.

'I'm happy you're back,' I say.

'Me too,' Sister Ruth says with a real smile this time.

I dart around the table even though I didn't ask permission to get up, and give her a hug. Sister Ruth strokes my head. Her hand is over my ear again and I can hear the sea. *Das Meer*, the sea, *la mer*, the most beautiful place on earth.

'I've got some good news for you,' Sister Ruth says through

the roar of the sea. 'We can go and see your mama now, if you like. She's not awake yet, but the doctors are done with her for the moment.'

I nod into her soft belly. I want to go to my mama, but I also want Sister Ruth to cuddle me for a bit longer.

'Can you hear that?' Sister Ruth asks. Only now do I pull my head back. She means a sound. A strange fluttering, somewhere in the distance, but clearly audible. Sister Ruth points at the window. I can make out white and red flashing lights in the grey night. Whiteredwhitered, flashflashflashflash.

'What's that?'

'A helicopter. The police are now flying above the area where your mama had the accident.' Sister Ruth squats before me and takes my face in her warm hands. 'They're going to find the cabin, Hannah. They'll get your brother out of there.' Now Sister Ruth is smiling a proper smile, and because I can't think of anything better to do, I smile too.

'What do you think? Shall we go and see your mama now?'

I nod. Sister Ruth takes my hand and we leave the staffroom.

MATTHIAS

Sympathy. Words of solace. For over thirteen years now I know how little any of this means. That people say things simply out of politeness. Karin still makes the effort to nod through her tears, while the inspector wastes his hollow phrases on us. 'I'm really very sorry, Herr and Frau Beck.'

Gerd has arrived now too, and he's standing with us in this ill-fated semicircle on the casualty corridor. I stare at the shirt he's wearing beneath his well-worn, open leather jacket, which he hasn't buttoned up correctly in his rush tonight.

'This is why I wanted to come here on my own,' he has the nerve to say.

I swallow some ugly words.

'Your disappointment is now even greater, of course.'

I swallow again.

'So, who is this woman?' Karin asks, sobbing. She took one look at me as I came out of the casualty ward and knew immediately. 'It's not her, is it?' she asked. I tried to shake my head, but couldn't even manage that.

'Frau Beck,' Gerd's colleague says. 'This is an ongoing investigation. I hope you understand that we can't give you any information.'

'Because suddenly it's got nothing to do with us anymore, Karin,' I translate for her. 'It's not our daughter, so they can't tell us anything.'

'What my colleague Inspector Giesner means . . .' Gerd chimes in. He's trying his best to remain calm, but in my ears his voice hits all the wrong frequencies.

'You dragged us out of bed in the middle of the night, saying you've found our daughter!' I hiss.

'I said there were similarities that we had to check,' Gerd hisses back. The other inspector retreats a few steps, evidently uncomfortable with this situation.

'I said from the outset that there was no certainty the woman was Lena.' Gerd rubs his forehead and sighs, then he turns to Karin. 'I'm terribly sorry, Karin. I shouldn't have given you any false hopes. That was unprofessional of me. You know that for me this is a personal matter . . .'

'You've been behaving unprofessionally for over thirteen years,' I fire off, but I'm ignored.

'So what does this mean for us, now?' Karin howls.

Gerd sighs again. 'It means that . . .'

'That we can wait another thirteen years for her, Karin,' I interrupt gruffly. I no longer want to hear any of the clichés, the niceties, those dumb phrases to boost morale. 'She's not coming home.' I feel the anger starting to burn behind my face; my cheeks are glowing as if gripped by fever.

'Matthias . . .' Karin grabs for my arm, but I'm not going to calm down. I want Gerd to realise the harm he's caused.

'It means we no longer have a daughter, that's what it means! She's dead! She's probably been dead for over thirteen years! Only the brilliant Herr Brühling can't even bring her body home so we can give her a decent burial!'

'Matthias . . .' Karin's fingernails dig through the material of my jacket. All of a sudden her face is paler, while her eyes are wide open and fixed on something. 'There,' she whispers.

I don't understand.

'There she is.'

I follow Karin's gaze across the corridor. I stop breathing, my heart.

'Tha – that's Lena . . .'

Karin's right. That's her. She's coming towards us across the corridor, holding a nurse's hand. Our child, our little Lena, my Lenchen.

LENA

I vaguely recall the screeching sound of the brakes, my own voice screaming, then abruptly dying away, the impact and how surprised I was not to feel any pain, at least not initially. Then it arrived, the pain, and it swept through me with such violence that I passed out. I don't know how long for – ten minutes? An hour? – but then I suddenly came to again. As if I'd been sitting in a pitch-black room and someone had switched on the light. I was awake and totally clear-headed.

I knew instantly that I'd had an accident. I knew instantly that I was in an ambulance. I heard a beeping, which was translating my heartbeat for the outside world. I heard the sirens. I knew we were driving fast; I could feel the bumps in the road and the vehicle taking the corners. The pain I felt in my body was beyond words. I tried nonetheless to move, to check I had feeling in my limbs. Where there's feeling – even if it's pain – there's life that can be recovered, I thought. If I strained I was able to wiggle my toes and bend my fingers: a good sign. Only my head wouldn't move; my neck was stretched and fixed. They'd put me in a brace. I couldn't see what was going on beside me. There was no right, no left, only a rigid up, the yellowed ceiling of the ambulance. Directly above me a piece of silver-grey insulating tape was stuck to the roof, possibly covering a small crack or a hole or even a discouraging bloodstain that wouldn't wash off. I felt a slight pressure on my chest and behind my knees, but I expect that was just tight straps. I mustn't fall from the stretcher during the journey and do myself even more harm. So absurd.

'I think she's coming round,' a man's voice said.

Seconds later a paramedic leaned into my restricted field of vision and shone a light in my eyes. I was supposed to follow the light. I tried as best I could, but my vision went blurred and the light spot just became a bright, frayed surface. The pain was fluid, oozing its way out.

The paramedic put the light aside and said, 'Don't worry. We're taking you to hospital.' I felt his thumb, in a latex glove, wipe a tear from my cheek. The beeping translating my heartbeat became quicker and more irregular.

'Nice and calm, now.' The paramedic tried to maintain professional distance and said he was sorry.

I began writhing under the straps that suddenly felt too tight.

'Calm down. Listen, everything's all right. You were knocked down by a car, but we'll be at the hospital very soon. You've almost made it.' The paramedic held on tight to my legs. I wanted to scream, but I just kept wriggling beneath the straps. 'I'm going to give you something to calm you.'

The beeping of my heart immediately became slow and regular again, which I found completely wrong.

'Could you tell me your name?' the paramedic asked. 'Do you remember your name?'

My eyelids began to flutter.

'I don't think we're going to get anywhere,' I heard him say, now as if from far away. 'She must be in shock.'

'Lena,' a second voice said. One that wasn't real, which came from the sedative, from the shock.

'Her name's Lena,' the voice said again, as if to substantiate the truth of it.

I tried moving my head, but it was fixed, facing upwards

52

towards the yellowed roof. And it was tired, this stupid head. So tired. My eyelids snapped shut. Hannah, said the last thoughts in the fug of my mind before it went black. It was Hannah's voice I'd just heard. Hannah was with me, in the ambulance . . .

I stifle a gasp. I don't want them to notice that I've woken up. Time has passed. A segment of film that's missing from between my last thoughts in the ambulance and now. I'm in the hospital, lying in a bed. I'm feeling really light-headed now; I expect I've been pumped up to the eyeballs with drugs. The crook of my right arm is twitching. They've put me on a drip. I can smell disinfectant and hear the familiar beeping of an ECG machine. All around are voices and activity.

'Can you hear me? Can you give me a sign, move a finger?'

I do nothing. I focus on my breathing and keep my eyes closed like a stubborn child. I don't even blink when your crazy father stands by my bed and completely flips out.

'It's not her! That isn't my daughter!'

I think he needs to be supported as he leaves my room.

Whereas I just lie there like a hunk of dead meat, just as all those nights I lay there while your husband sexually abused me. My eyes are screwed up tightly. I know that all hell will be let loose the moment I open them. I'm scared, Lena, terribly scared.

MATTHIAS

Karin's expression. Her pale face and her wide, staring eyes.

Lena, coming down the corridor towards us, holding a nurse's hand.

53

Our child, our little Lena, my Lenchen, maybe six or seven years old. Far too small for that enormous cone of sweets, my addled brain elaborates when the images from the past wash up again and mingle with reality. Those blonde locks, that pointed chin, those eyes, my God, those eyes.

I thrust my hand out for some support and end up holding on to Gerd's arm.

'Lena . . .'

'Oh God,' I hear Karin say before Gerd snatches his arm away from me. My eyes follow this harsh gesture and I see that he's grabbed Karin under the arms because her knees have given way.

'What . . .' he exclaims, before he too turns his head to the left, towards the girl. 'How . . . is that possible?'

His colleague from Cham, who's kept his distance up till now, also hurries over to us.

'Lena!' Karin calls out.

The nurse holding Lena's hand stops in her tracks. Lenchen nervily steps behind her. She seems to be scared by the commotion.

'Shh! Be quiet! Quiet, for goodness' sake!' I cry, but Karin is totally beside herself.

'What on earth's going on?' she gasps, and then shrieks, 'Lena!'

The nurse nudges the girl back down the corridor.

'No, no, no! Wait!' I bellow, and start after her before I'm suddenly yanked back. Unfamiliar arms clasp me from behind.

'Lenchen!' I croak, then Giesner wrestles me to the floor like a raging animal. While I thrash around pitifully beneath him in the last throes of our struggle, Lenchen disappears again and the corridor is empty apart from us. Silence.

'Please come with me, Herr Beck,' Giesner says after a few seconds, helping me to my feet.

With an orderly leading the way, he and Gerd take us to the nearest empty room. Gerd helps Karin over to the bed, on to which she sinks as if she's just had the plug pulled out. The orderly asks whether we need a doctor to give her a sedative.

'No, thanks,' I decide without really considering the state she's in. 'She's fine.'

Once the orderly has left the room, Giesner says, 'You owe me an explanation.'

'Lena,' Karin and I say in unison. 'The girl back there in the corridor looks just like our daughter,' I tell him. 'When she was a child,' I add quickly when I realise how crazy we probably sound. Parents in severe psychological distress harassing a small child they've never met before – that's how we must come across to Giesner. Although, if the girl is a carbon copy of our daughter, she can't be a stranger. Can she?

'It's true,' Gerd says, unexpectedly coming to our help. 'Like a clone.'

Giesner now gives him a sceptical look too.

'I'm a friend of the family. I've known Lena since she was born.'

Friend of the family, I ruminate quietly, but then pull myself together. This isn't about Gerd and me, it's about Lena. No, it's about the girl.

'Wait a moment.' I remember, and feel for my wallet inside my coat. Behind transparent plastic, the colours slightly faded, is my Lenchen, smiling with a gap in her teeth and her enormous cone of sweets. I pluck out the photograph and offer it to Giesner.

'Here, take a look for yourself.'

55

Giesner takes the photograph and gives it a thorough examination.

'Hmm,' he says several times in succession. Just 'Hmm'.

'Who is the girl?' Karin asks with a brittle voice from the background.

Giesner looks up from the photo.

'According to her statement, the girl is the daughter of the accident victim.'

I shake my head.

'But that doesn't make any sense. The woman there,' I say, nodding vaguely behind me in the direction of the door, 'isn't Lena.'

'Matthias, are you sure?' Karin asks. 'Maybe after all these years you just didn't recognise her. Does she have the scar?' In small, brusque movements she runs her finger underneath her hairline to the right of her forehead. 'Should I go and have a look at the woman?'

'She has got a scar, yes. But it's not her. I would recognise my own daughter,' I say, sounding unintentionally abrupt. 'I'm sorry, darling. It really isn't her.'

'But what if I just took a look? Just to be sure?'

'It's not her, Karin!'

'Let's all calm down first,' Gerd chips in. 'Karin, you won't go into that room. I'll do it. I'd recognise Lena.'

'You're not seriously saying that I couldn't recognise my own daughter?' I can't believe it.

'Of course you could, Matthias.' Gerd sighs. 'But the fact is, there's something here that's eluding us. We've got to find out who this woman is and why a little girl, who looks just like Lena, is claiming to be her daughter.'

'Hmm,' Giesner says again, giving me back the photograph of Lenchen. He turns to Gerd. 'Do you know whether a DNA profile exists for Lena Beck?'

Gerd nods eagerly like a model pupil. 'We created one back at the time with a sample from her toothbrush.'

'Well, then,' Giesner says to Karin and me. 'That means we just need a sample from the girl. It wouldn't take long, a simple saliva test would do it. We can create a DNA profile for the girl and then check the two profiles for matches. Then at least we'd have an answer to the question of whether the girl's related to your daughter. What we still need to find out is the connection between the girl and the accident victim . . .'

'Let's ask the girl,' Gerd says with a determination I last heard in his voice over thirteen years ago. 'We're going to find your daughter, Matthias,' he said back then, his feet cockily on his desk and a cigarette in the corner of his mouth, like a cop from a bad American film. 'If it's the last thing I do, I'm going to bring our Lena home.'

Giesner sighs. 'I've already spoken to the girl, with the help of a specialist too. We didn't get far.'

'You've spoken to her?' I gasp. 'What do you mean, you didn't get far?'

'Dr Hamstedt, our specialist, can't come up with a sure diagnosis in such a short period of time. So far we've only got pieces of the puzzle, but hopefully we'll know more when we find the cabin Hannah's told us about. I've dispatched a chopper, which is flying over the tract of woodland and I've also got a team searching the area where the accident took place.'

'Hannah . . .' I repeat, but just to myself. So that's her name:

Hannah. I try to catch Karin's eye, but she's looking past me, at Giesner.

'What cabin?' she asks. 'Is that where Lena is, in that cabin?'

Giesner clears his throat.

'Inspector Brühling's right. You need to calm down first.' He motions to Gerd to follow him to the door. Gerd nods.

When they've left, Karin says, 'What the hell's going on here?'

LENA

Briefly I consider escaping from here, but how would I manage that? I can still barely move, I'm hooked up to devices that might give off an alarm if I fiddled with the electrodes and on top of this, there's always someone coming into my room. It's as if they're trying to keep me awake with their hustle and bustle. To begin with it's just people from the hospital, popping in to change the intravenous bags or check the ECG. That's bearable – I just keep my eyes closed and breathe.

But then the two policemen turn up and decide to take up permanent residence beside my bed. One of them, as I can make out from their whispered conversations, has come especially from Munich, whereas the other belongs to the Cham force. They keep saying, 'The girl'.

Hannah. So I didn't imagine her – she *was* there, she came with me in the ambulance. Here to the hospital. Hannah's here.

I overhear words such as 'abduction' and 'cabin'. The ECG I'm wired up to registers my sudden agitation with a nervy sequence of sounds. Right beside my head one of the policemen – 'Cham', I think – presses the emergency button. I hear them scurry on either side of my bed as they wait for one of the medical personnel.

A man arrives, who first checks the ECG clip on my middle finger and then presses a cold stethoscope bell to my chest.

'Everything's fine,' he tells 'Cham' and 'Munich'. 'Maybe she just had a bad dream.' One of the two policemen mutters a reply.

I hear the door click shut – the nurse has gone again – then a chair scraping its way across the floor to my bed, followed by a second one. They seem intent on sitting here for as long as it takes for me to regain consciousness so I can answer their questions.

It's precisely what I've spent many a night thinking about when his closeness, his hot breath on my neck and his sticky skin on mine has kept me awake. What would I say if I ever got out of this hole?

Then I sorted the details. From the outset some were piled together with the unsayable things, the indescribable perversions that made him a monster and, in particular, me his victim. I didn't want to spend the rest of my life as the poor woman from the cabin. I would be strong, sit up straight and tell them the bare minimum, with a clear focus. Silently I count three breaths, like one last little reprieve, then I wrench open my eyes. It's time, Lena.

A policeman, the one in the grey suit, rushes immediately into my field of vision. The other one gets up from his seat too. Both are now bent over me, their questions already present in their expressions. The ECG goes mad.

'Hello,' the one in the suit says. 'Please relax. Everything is absolutely fine. I'm Frank Giesner from Cham police, and this is my colleague, Gerd Brühling, from Munich. Do you understand? We're from the police.'

I try to nod, but fail.

'Can you hear me?'

'I think we should get the nurse back in here,' Munich says, pointing at the emergency button. Cham takes him up on his suggestion.

'You've been brought to hospital because you were hit by a car. Could you tell me your name?'

I roll my eyes and groan in pain.

'Listen, we know about the cabin. We're already looking for it. Nothing's going to happen to you. You're safe here.'

The door opens; it's the nurse coming back into the room. Cham and Munich step away from my bed in sync.

'She woke up,' Munich tells the nurse, who checks my pulse and says, 'I'll get Dr Schwindt to come and give her an injection. It might take a while, though, as it's the shift changeover, and that's always chaotic.'

I open my mouth to protest, but all that comes out is a noise, a strange noise, somewhere between an exhausted gasp and a hysterical giggle. By the time I'm over it the nurse has gone again. I need to stay clear-headed; that's all I can think about.

'Have you found him?' I say, my voice cracking.

Cham makes a vague movement with his head, while Munich can't stop staring at the scar on my brow.

'Like I said, we're still looking for the cabin. But please don't worry. You're absolutely safe here. Would you tell me your name?'

I convince myself that it's a simple and perfectly logical request. There's nothing sinister or threatening about it. On the contrary, if the police know who I am they can notify my relatives. Tell my mother that I'm still alive and that she should come and pick me up. Take me away from here; I just want to get away from here. And I'm ready to talk to them; I've taken a deep breath and opened my mouth. But again nothing comes out except for a few more hysterical sounds. I've swallowed my identity and I giggle once more.

This goes on for quite a while, and the policemen are very patient. On their faces I now see another expression apart from bafflement: pity. As far as they're concerned, I'm the poor woman from the cabin. When I realise this, the laughter subsides. Not immediately, but in fits and starts. For a moment I sound like a stuttering engine. Finally, there's silence. Followed by my answer.

'Lena. My name is Lena.'

HANNAH

I recognised him at once, from that party in the garden, the first trip I did with Mama. He told me about ladybirds and how they're lucky. I remembered his grey hair and his very bright blue eyes, which are the same colour as one of Mama's Sunday dresses. Although the dress has white stripes as well. But then I wasn't quite so sure, because the people he was standing with in the hospital corridor were all talking so loudly that they frightened Sister Ruth and she took me back to the staffroom. We walked so quickly that I had to push my toes upwards so I didn't lose the big pink rubber shoes.

She'd actually promised that we'd go and see Mama, but now she closes the staffroom door behind us and says, 'I think we're going to have to wait a little longer before we can see her, Hannah.'

I look at the floor and see a fuzzball. It's purple, probably from Sister Ruth's colourful cardigan which I'm still wearing.

'Don't be sad, little one,' she says, lifting my chin. 'We'll go and see her as soon as we can, I promise. But first I want to find out what was going on out there.' She takes her hand away and pushes me further into the room, back to our table. 'They've all gone a bit nutty.' I think she's saying that to herself rather than to me, because now she's babbling away weirdly and not looking at me anymore. You always have to look at people when you're talking to them. 'Making such a row and frightening people. As if you hadn't been through enough already. Who do they think they are?' She shakes her head a few times. 'Go on, Hannah, sit down. I'll make you some tea and then I'll find out what all that nonsense was about.'

I nod and sit down. Sister Ruth goes over to the kitchen unit. Behind me I can hear her turn on the tap and fill the kettle.

'I think I know,' I say.

'Hmm?' Sister Ruth didn't hear me because the tap was running.

'I think I know!' I shout, but the tap's now been turned off.

'What do you mean, Hannah?'

Clack: the lid of the kettle is shut. *Click*: the kettle is switched on.

'I think I know who they are,' I say.

Now it's silent behind me. Sister Ruth doesn't understand again.

'I think that was my grandfather who was shouting.'

'Your . . . ?'

'A grandfather is the father of either parent or, colloquially, an old man.'

I turn around to Sister Ruth so I can see from her face if she's understood. She hasn't, of course. She's just gawping again. I sigh.

'They also shouted *Lena*,' I tell poor, stupid Sister Ruth. 'That's what my Mama is called, don't you remember? And I recognised him too.'

I don't bother waiting for Sister Ruth to try and think this through herself. Instead I start telling her about our first trip. Mama and I drove down the shimmering road to the garden where the lawn smelled like our washing powder and there were hydrangeas with flowers as big as cabbages, and where there were only unhealthy things to eat. And I told her about my grandfather who sat on the grass with me and talked about ladybirds.

'Ladybirds are very useful creatures because they eat greenfly and spider mites,' I say, repeating what he told me. 'They're also said to bring good luck.'

Sister Ruth scuttles back from the kitchen and flops on to her chair. The water in the kettle has already boiled and I bet it'll be cold by the time she makes my tea.

'Are you telling me you've actually met that man before?' she asks when I've stopped talking.

I nod.

'We did many trips together, Mama and I. We went to the sea and to Paris. The Eiffel Tower was built to celebrate the one hundredth anniversary of the French Revolution and it's 324 metres high.' I lean over the table and whisper to her, 'But you mustn't tell anyone that.'

'I don't understand . . .' Sister Ruth babbles away again.

'You mustn't tell anyone that we went on trips. It's a secret. Otherwise we'll get into trouble, Mama and I.'

'With your Papa?'

'Yes.' I nod. 'Mama is so silly. She can't even turn on the cooker on her own. Papa would definitely say it's much too dangerous for her to drive a car, and with me in it, and so far away. And I bet Jonathan would be cross too.'

I didn't want to think about Jonathan again. I feel so sorry for him because he's got to scrub away at those silly stains on the carpet. To distract myself I smooth down my dress. There are pockets on either side. The bottom seam of the right-hand pocket is coming away, so I can only put things in the left-hand one.

'Why should he be cross with you? Didn't you take him with you on your trips?'

'He wouldn't have enjoyed them at all.'

Sister Ruth cocks her head.

At first I don't want to tell her, because I'm slightly ashamed. But then I think it's not my fault I'm Mama's favourite child and she prefers going away with me alone.

'It's more that . . . I think he'd be cross if he knew we slipped him sleeping pills,' I say, preferring to keep my eyes fixed on my dress rather than looking at Sister Ruth. Mama really will have to sew up my pocket when we're back home.

LENA

It was a Thursday in May when I vanished from the world. Alice was pushed down the rabbit hole, tumbled head over heels and was knocked out when she hit the bottom. I reckon he must have injected me with an anaesthetic before whisking me off to the cabin. The first thing I remember is the stench of sweat, urine and stale air. Then, as if from far away, the noise of a key turning in a lock and the click of a light switch. I didn't flinch until he jabbed at my leg several times with his foot.

'How are you, Lena?' asked the man standing there, smiling down at me.

My eyes darted across the room, taking in shelves that filled most of the wall opposite: provisions, preserving jars, sacks of potatoes, a dark object which from the shiny silver zips I identified as my overnight bag, then several canisters, a pile of wood in the corner. I looked up at the bulb hanging from the ceiling, and down to my ankles, then my blotchy jeans and my sweat-soaked top, down my arms to my wrists, which were bound to the waste pipe of an old sink with a sort of loop made out of cable ties. Finally, my eyes returned to the man, who was still smiling and repeated his question with a patient voice: 'How are you, Lena?'

Lena, that wasn't me, that wasn't my name.

The cogs in my brain started whirring. This was a misunderstanding; he must have got me mixed up with someone else. I whimpered into my gag like a beaten dog as I tried to understand the mix-up that had clearly happened here, all the while tugging so wildly at the cable ties that they cut into my wrists.

He shook his head sympathetically, turned around and went towards the door. *Click*: the light. Then the door, metal scraping in the lock, the key turned twice.

Me, alone, in total darkness. I started to scream and kept tugging at the cable ties – both pointless. With the gag in place my screaming sounded like a throttled grunting, and the cable ties were secure. I'd been abducted. Shackled to a waste pipe. A dreadful mix-up. And the darkness too, making the whole situation here even more terrifying. It seemed as if the room had dissolved. I was drifting in a formless black sphere, unable to anchor my thoughts. I conjured up the man's face. His grey eyes, his slightly crooked nose, his smile, his dark, wavy hair. I'd seen him only fleetingly and yet the image was quite clear, etched into my mind, just like his voice.

How are you, Lena?

Lena, Lena, Lena . . . I knew a Lena. A trainee in the advertising agency I'd worked for. A spoiled, cocky girl. Rich parents, very rich parents. Now it dawned on me. It was *her* he was after! The Lena with the rich parents. A ransom, that was the point of all this. What would happen next? Would he kill me if he realised his mistake? Let me go? Demand a ransom for me instead? I pictured my father stacking bundles of banknotes into a briefcase. A briefcase he no longer possessed, and money he'd never had anyway. I saw my mother in black clothes and a black hat, chewing her bottom lip as she wondered what else there was to say about me, apart from the fact that I'd been a disappointment to her for most of my life, and Kirsten, who for the first time ever was in agreement with her. I even thought of old Frau Bar-Lev from the second floor, joining the squad of those shaking their heads and complaining about how sloppily I'd cleaned the communal stairs in our building. The devil comes for wicked girls. My thoughts went round and round in circles, raging, spinning, unable to anchor in this black sphere with just the stench of sweat, urine, stale air; I drifted, drifted, I was away.

I woke up. I was back. Still here.

With tears in my eyes I blinked at the light bulb dangling from the ceiling on a cable which had been tied to make it shorter.

'How are you, Lena?'

He had returned and was standing over me, smiling, like before.

I calculated that I'd been his prisoner for just over half a day now, although my senses and my intellect were at odds over this. In the darkness time stood still. And yet I still felt just about okay, so couldn't have been here much longer. I was tired and had a headache, which I interpreted as an initial sign of dehydration, but my brain was still functioning. Even if all it could offer me was: *after two or three days without water, you'll be dead.*

'Have you calmed down?'

I resisted the impulse to scream and just gave him a silent nod.

'Very good,' he said, then turned around and went to the door.

I waited for the click of the light switch.

It didn't happen. The light stayed on. And he even left the door slightly ajar when he went out.

Forgetting to breathe, I stared at the door, open. I tugged fitfully at my shackles, without taking my eyes off the door, the open door, just five or six strides away from me, beyond reach.

I blinked away a few stupid tears. I wouldn't get very far in any case. He must be coming back soon; why else would he leave the light on and door open? All I could do was wait. With great difficulty and so far as the restrictions of my shackles would allow, I tried to change the position I was sitting in. My body had become uncomfortable. A rough wooden wall pressed into my back. My legs felt swollen, my neck stiff and my shoulders were burning from my arms having been stretched out to one side for hours. The sink I was bound to lay on my right. The position of my arms was similar to that of a baseball hitter waiting for the ball. And waiting. And waiting. My heart was racing. Where was he?

He was fetching the knife.

*

This was what they did, wasn't it? The madmen. The psychopaths. They went to fetch a knife, an axe, a chainsaw, with a smile on their lips. They had their own mad code, and his question 'How are you, Lena?' had in reality been a very different one.

In his reality he'd asked me whether I was ready to die, and I'd shown my acquiescence with that silent nod. I'd given him my permission. At this very moment he was probably admiring the long, broad blade of his favourite knife. Angling the handle so he could see his face reflected in the metal. Imagining how easily it would slice through my flesh, how effortlessly it would sever stubborn muscles, arteries and veins.

I hyperventilated into my gag. At any moment he would step through the door with a knife in his hand. I would be dead before the hunt to find me had even been launched. 'Typical,' my mother would think, when yet again I failed to turn up for coffee at the weekend as promised. Just 'typical', not 'something must be wrong'. What about Kirsten? Kirsten might even believe I was not coming on purpose. 'She's always been a drama queen . . .' I heard her voice say in my head.

At any moment.

Now. The door. He was back.

My eyelids began to flicker. My heart and my breathing were going so quickly that I felt dizzy. I drew my legs up and shuffled backwards against the wall. As if through a thick pane of frosted glass I saw him come closer, closer, until he was standing right in front of me, holding something – not a knife.

'Are you thirsty, Lena?'

It took a few seconds before I realised what he was saying

and saw that the object in his right hand was not a knife, but a bottle of water.

'Are you thirsty, Lena?' he said again.

When he held out the bottle I nodded in time to the intense thumping inside my chest, and growled like a greedy animal in the hope that he would remove the gag. But he just stood where he was, towering over me, waving the bottle in front of my eyes. And smiling.

I shook my head helplessly. He lowered his right hand, then held out his left, which was holding a packet of hair dye. The woman in the picture looked delighted with her new, bright blonde hair. The sight of her triggered a feeling, a bad feeling that started in the pit of my stomach and gradually engulfed my entire body.

He nodded thoughtfully.

'First we'll dye your hair and after that you can have a drink.'

I calculated my chances. *After two or three days without water, you'll be dead.*

'Take all the time you need to think about it.'

He shrugged and turned to go.

I squealed into the gag and thudded the floor with my bound feet.

He turned around slowly.

'That is the right decision. And because right decisions are always rewarded, you may have a sip now.'

He placed the packet of hair dye on the edge of the sink, squatted down, put the bottle of water beside me and untied the gag. Then he picked up the bottle and unscrewed the cap. With one hand he lifted it to my mouth, with the other he supported the back of my head. A sip was a sip, I had to realise. I thanked him all the same and sucked up a stray drop from my bottom lip.

'And now we're going to make you beautiful.'

His knees clicked as he stood, and he went over to the shelves behind him. When he turned around again he was holding a pair of scissors.

'I think this is one big misunderstanding,' I began with a croaky voice, as he cut the cable ties from my wrists. 'You must have mistaken me for someone else. I'm not Lena.'

He stopped in between cutting the third and fourth cable tie.

'My name is . . .'

'Be quiet!' he barked, so loudly that I gave a start. There was a snip and the last cable tie released my hands.

'How many times have I told you not to lie to me?'

'But I'm not lying –'

'I told you to be quiet!' His face had suddenly turned red and a blood vessel stood proud beneath the skin on his left temple, throbbing angrily. My gaze fell on the scissors that were still in his hand.

'I'm sorry,' I said softly.

He muttered something; I stared at the scissors.

'What do you want from me?' I asked cautiously.

He reached up to the sink and swapped the scissors for the packet of hair dye.

'I want to make you beautiful, Lena.'

His words exploded in my head, paralysing my thoughts, a mental blackout. A shrill scream, a firm shove against his chest. His head hit the ceramic of the sink. 'Fucking hell!' My body threw itself forwards and somehow I got to my feet. The door, only a few metres away. I staggered on a pair of legs that hadn't carried my weight for a while, my circulation, *pull yourself together*, movement behind me, the door handle so close. I reached for it, almost touching it, but then was torn away. His hand had grabbed my hair and jolted my head. I landed on my back and my scalp burned as if alight. I clung to his forearm, tried to get my footing, he was shouting and I was too. 'What an ungrateful bitch!'

'What do you want from me, you fucking madman?' He dragged me back to the sink and let me fall hard on the floor. I doubled up and sobbed so intensely that I started retching.

'The world is out of joint, Lena,' he began, panting, but otherwise perfectly calm. 'People have become ungrateful. Ungrateful and lacking in respect. Promises have become worthless, nothing is binding anymore. Who these days remembers the importance of rules, when all you hear is people saying there's no need to stick to them? I'm not criticising you, Lena. You're confused. Nonetheless, I have to make you aware of the consequences of your misdemeanours.'

He paused to allow what he'd said to sink in. I heard him take a deep breath and a hunch I had made me do the same. Then I closed my eyes. The first kick was to my stomach.

Do you know, Lena, at that time I still had no idea what he meant by 'rules', but I had understood one of them. I had to be you, or I would be dead. Call it instant conditioning if you like. Call me cowardly, or crazy, I don't care. But please don't say it's astonishing that when the policeman asked me my name there was only one answer I could come up with to begin with: 'Lena. My name is Lena.'

'Surname?'

The Cham policeman takes a small notebook and pen from his

inside jacket pocket. The undertone in his curt follow-up question doesn't escape me.

I shake my head. Lena doesn't have a surname.

'Well, you're not Lena Beck at any rate,' Munich states, shifting to the front of his chair. I grab my forehead, where the scar has started to burn. I couldn't say whether this is because of his penetrating stare or the sweat oozing from every pore of my body.

'Who are you?' Cham asks again, calmly, emphasising each word in turn.

Within seconds my answer seems to have turned me into an impostor; I can't ignore this. And maybe the suspicion in his voice is justified. Perhaps I am an impostor. Perhaps it's not just your husband's fault, but equally mine too. It's still easier to convince myself that all those dreadful things happened to Lena rather than Jasmin.

Somewhere in the world Jasmin is leading a happy life. Breathing in the air after it's rained. Squabbling over the first and last piece of a bar of chocolate. Taking in the bouquet of freesias. Dancing and bawling to David Bowie. After a long night's drinking, sharing a beer and a curry sausage with some feckless aberration she considers to be love. Jasmin, untroubled and with all the freedom in the world, doing those lovely, silly things that life is made of. The things I tried to recollect when your husband was lying on top of me and I just wanted to die.

I wipe the tears from my chin and sniff.

Munich clears his throat.

'Let me tell you something, *Lena* . . .'

MATTHIAS

On the horizon the dawn is chomping light grey strips in the sky. I can literally see the new day devouring the night. It's just before five o'clock. I'm standing at the window of the hospital room where we're waiting for Gerd and Giesner. Karin is still sitting on the bed. In the window I can see the reflection of her dangling legs. Her head is bowed and she's squeezing her hands in her lap. From time to time she lets out a gentle sigh. In my head I replay the last hour and try to understand. The woman we thought was our missing Lena is a stranger. My thoughts momentarily turn to Gerd again. Gerd, the failure, whom we have to thank for all this upset. He has swept the last pitiful remnants of our hope into a small heap and wilfully set fire to it. All that's left now is ashes.

I stare up at the heavens, in a touch of Christian faith. You've been up there for a while, haven't you, Lena?

I don't realise I've started sobbing until Karin's face appears in the window beside mine. I feel her hand on my back. She lays her head on my shoulder and closes her eyes. We both know. Lena didn't reappear this evening, so we finally have to resign ourselves to the notion that she's not coming back, ever. It's just that now, in the cold reality of the hospital, this idea suddenly feels so different from previous times when, at home on the sofa or in bed at night, we would go through what might have happened to our daughter. Up till now these have merely been theories with a certain room for manoeuvre. I understand that over the past thirteen years, this room for manoeuvre has been the one, tiny place we've been able to exist, had space to breathe. Now there's no space at all, now we're floating in a vacuum somewhere, up in the sky, like two sad astronauts who've had their air hoses severed. I reach for Karin's hand. I don't want to go adrift alone, out there in the empty darkness. Karin nods as if she's able to read my thoughts. I embrace her, holding her as tightly as I can. Her heart beats against mine. The new day is in the sky. So her name is Hannah. You called her after my mother. That's lovely, Lena. That's really lovely.

LENA

'Student from Munich, twenty-three years old, one of those young, carefree girls. In her fourth semester studying to become a teacher. Her father swears blind she wanted to be a teacher from a very young age. I was certain she'd do something creative, like become a writer, perhaps. She had a very fertile imagination and used to come up with the wildest stories. Or an actress, that would have suited her too. At any rate, she was one of those girls who turned heads. Who could enter a room and only had to smile to make everyone speechless. Long, blonde hair, blue eyes, great figure. She disappeared on her way home from a student party. Without trace – she simply vanished into thin air. No witnesses, nothing. The last people to see her were other guests at the party, and they said she'd had a few drinks and maybe taken some other things too, you know. There were plenty of theories. The route home must have taken her along the Isar, across Reichenbach Bridge. Maybe she fell into the river and drowned. We had divers go down several times, but they found nothing. We checked out her boyfriend, but he couldn't have had anything to do with her disappearance, even though for a long time Lena's father refused to accept this. She could have been kidnapped too, but there was never a demand for ransom money. She could have just as easily fallen into the hands of a people-trafficking gang. Abducted and sold abroad. Sexual slavery, I'm sure you've heard of this. Well, as you can see, there are all manner of possibilities. But the fact is, we simply don't know what happened to Lena Beck thirteen years ago. It remains a mystery to this day. Back at the time I promised her father that I'd find her. Do you know what they teach you during police training? No? Never make promises. Promises that aren't kept break people. And this father is a broken man, believe you me. He misses her so much, still, every day. I miss her too, we all do. That scar you've got – Lena had one because when she was four or five she fell against the edge of a bookshelf. And it happened in my sitting room, can you believe that? Her father was beside himself. How did you get yours?'

I think I take my first breath since Munich started talking about you. It seems to be the same for Cham: I hear him breathe deeply.

'He did it to me,' I reply, carefully touching the spot which will probably still mark me long after the cuts I sustained in the accident have healed.

'Could you tell me who *he* is?'

I nod.

'The man who abducted me.'

The man who called me Lena and beat me.

After the assault I lay curled up into a ball in my old place beside the sink. I held tightly in my fist the tooth I spat out as he was kicking me. I counted six kicks and three punches. Although he'd now left me alone, I could still see bright lights exploding before my eyes, no matter whether I closed them or not, fireworks ignited by pain. My body felt like one big bruise under constant pressure.

He stood over me, massaging his knuckles.

'Can we continue now, Lena?'

Without waiting for an answer, he bent down to me, grabbed my wrists and pulled me to my feet with a vice-like grip. I whimpered. I couldn't stay upright on my legs and collapsed again immediately.

'You've got to make a bit of an effort, Lena.'

This time he took me under my armpits and heaved me up. Then he dragged me to the sink, which had a mirror on the wall above it. It was an old, very tarnished mirror, that barely showed anything save for my blurred face. But I could still make out the brown trail of dried blood that ran from my nose down to my chin. Looking for some support I propped myself on the sink and stared at the plughole.

'Oh, Lena,' he said to the back of my neck. 'We really got off to a bad start, didn't we?' He put his arms around my waist and started unbuttoning my jeans.

'We'd better clean you up first. You'll feel like a brand-new person afterwards, just you see.'

This, by the way, is one of those parts of my story that ended up on the pile of unsayable things, if you're interested. An episode I'm dreadfully ashamed of because I simply failed to resist. I ought to have rammed my elbows into his side, pushed him away or at least screamed.

Jasmin would never have let that happen to her. She wouldn't have waited passively while he filled the sink with water from a canister. She wouldn't have stood there naked, her arms out to the side and her legs apart, allowing him to wash her. She wouldn't have let him scrub her body with a scratchy flannel until her skin was red and sore. She wouldn't have put up with being dyed blonde without protest, or cried silently over her molar, which now lay in a small brownish puddle of blood and water splashes on the rim of the sink. He'd already noticed while undressing me that I'd wet myself at some point that day.

'Tsk, tsk, you really must learn to get a grip on things,' he'd said, his eyebrows raised and nose wrinkled. 'You're a grown woman, Lena.'

Jasmin wouldn't have apologised quietly. She would have spat in his face and shouted, 'Fuck off!'

I, on the other hand, nodded politely when he wrung out the flannel for the last time and asked, 'That's much better, isn't it?'

I let him dry me, rinse out the bleach, and towel and comb my wet, freshly dyed hair. I even thanked him when he handed me the bottle of water. A reward, as he said.

Clothes were lying ready for me on the shelves. I don't know if he'd had them ready from the outset or brought them later. White underwear, sheer tights with a silky lustre, white blouse, knee-length dark skirt and shoes with straps, a size too small for me. I peered at my own things, which lay in an untidy pile beneath the sink, then back to the shelves, where my overnight bag sat right at the top, out of reach. It looked crumpled, like an empty wrapper. He must have taken everything out of it.

'They say you should never judge a book by its cover,' he began. I tried not to look when he bent down, holding the white panties, and directed my legs into them. I put my head back and stared at the ceiling.

'But the truth is, tasteless clothes make a tasteless woman.'

Between the wooden beams I spied a gratifying spider's web to distract me from his caresses as he put on my bra. *Incy Wincy spider climbed up the water spout*, I hummed inside my head. My mother used to sing me this song when I was small and she still a mother. She would sit on the edge of my bed, twisting her fingers funnily to imitate the spider's movements. *Down came the rain and washed poor Incy out* . . .

'You are going to stick to my rules, Lena. Tidiness, cleanliness, discipline, respect, honesty, fidelity, loyalty. Whenever I come into a room you will position yourself so I can see you and you will stick your hands out. Do you understand? I want to check that your fingernails are clean and that you've got nothing hidden in your hands that could hurt me – or you, for that matter. Your times for using the toilet are seven o'clock in the morning, twelve-thirty, five in the afternoon and eight in the evening. I will help you with your personal hygiene. Unfortunately we don't have running water here, only these canisters.' He nodded towards the canisters I'd already seen. 'But it's fine so long as we're not too wasteful. We have our own generator and are fairly well equipped otherwise. You'll like it here.'

With a rasping noise he pulled up the zip of my skirt and tugged from behind at the shoulder seams of my blouse before walking around me and running his splayed fingers through my hair.

'Don't think we can't talk to each other, Lena. We certainly can. I want you to be happy and I promise I'll do everything I can to ensure that you are. In return, however, I need to sense that you've understood the rules and, most of all, that you're going to abide by them. Otherwise our life together isn't going to work.' He eyed me up and down. 'Almost perfect.'

Life together – the words hammered inside my brain. *Life together*, as he reached for a lipstick that was also on the shelf, *life together*. He put lipstick on me in coarse strokes.

'Just one thing missing now.'

His left hand held the back of my neck as he put the lipstick back on the shelf and picked up the scissors he'd used to cut the cable ties from my wrists. I started breathing heavily. His grip around my neck became tighter. The scissors scratched all the way down my forehead. Blood roared in my ears. Blood ran into my right eye.

You've got a scar, Lena.

I'm going to have one too, soon.

'We'll see if that worked,' he said, dabbing with the flannel at the spot below my hairline. 'Otherwise we'll have to redo it. You'd best keep the flannel on it for a while or you'll ruin your blouse.' He moved my hand up to my brow. 'Hold it tight, Lena. It would be a pity if the blouse got stained.' I pressed the flannel to my head and let out a whimper.

'We ought to have done it before you got dressed. Why didn't I think of that? I mean, that's your favourite blouse.'

I couldn't see anything anymore; there was blood in my eyes, my lids were twitching, my circulation, the room overturned, up was down and I fell as if in slow motion, hit the ground, passed out.

The next thing I remember was opening my eyes and gasping for air, as if I'd been underwater for a long time. I was lying on my back, on something soft, my forehead throbbing from a burning pain. Above me I could see a blurry strip of brown, and a moment later I recognised it as the wooden beams of a ceiling. I tried to sit up, but it didn't work. From the scraps of information I could take in, I concluded that I was in a sitting room. A thick carpet, an old-fashioned, cast-iron stove with a fire burning inside, a wall of books. The surface below me sagged. I realised it was a sofa; I was lying on a sofa, wrapped in a woollen blanket and with a cushion beneath my calves, probably to stabilise my circulation. Someone had sat beside me. A hand touched mine. A little hand.

'Are you awake?' I heard a child's voice whisper, then the face of a boy appeared in my field of vision. He had very white skin, a narrow, handsome face with light blue eyes and thin, black locks. I looked at him as I might a work of art which I found both beautiful and repulsive.

'Jonathan!' another voice called out.

I squinted and felt another movement below me when the terrified boy leaped to his feet.

'I didn't mean to wake her, Papa! I just wanted to see if she was rested yet.'

Papa. It was his son. The monster had a son.

'You can set up the chessboard, Jonathan,' I heard, then, 'Lena . . .'

Once more the sofa cushion sagged under an additional weight.

'Open your eyes, Lena. I know you're awake.'

I blinked.

'You look beautiful,' he said, sweeping a strand of hair from my face. His eyes were fixed on a particular spot on my forehead. 'It's come out well, I think. I did go over it again with the knife, then I stitched it up straightaway.'

A dry sound emitted from my throat.

'Oh, come on, Lena. You were out cold anyway and didn't have a clue what was going on.' He smiled. 'It couldn't have gone any better for you, could it?'

I raised my trembling hand to touch my forehead. I felt the stitches and the sharp end of a thread that stabbed my fingertip.

He grabbed my hand and moved it down again.

'Don't touch it, Lena, or the wound really will get infected. We can take the stitches out in a few days.'

I began to sob.

'Please, you've got to let me go. I want to go home.'

He leaned so far forwards that the tips of our noses almost touched; his weight was painful on my torso that had suffered his kicks and punches.

'You are home, Lena,' he whispered back, brushing my forehead with his lips.

I turned my head away and buried my face in the cushion of the back rest. Its slightly musty smell reminded me of the furniture in my grandparents' house. He thrust his hand roughly between the cushion and my cheek, and turned my face back, forcing me to look him in the eye.

'Do yourself a favour and think about this carefully, Lena. Ask yourself if I'm joking. If I'm just trying to frighten you. Or whether I'd be capable of killing you.'

'Not joking,' I wheezed. I was finding it increasingly difficult to breathe under the weight of his body. But at least my brain seemed to be sort of functioning again. The thought that it now conveyed was a very definite one, a thought that had probably been there for a while, but had become entangled in the jumble of other thoughts: the clothes I was wearing.

'I'm only going to tell you once, Lena, so listen carefully.'

The underwear, the tights, the skirt, the blouse and especially the shoes – all of them too small for me. They'd clearly belonged to someone else.

'From now on you're going to be a good mother and a good wife. And you're going to stick to my rules. Do you understand?'

'Where is your son's mother?'

For a moment he actually looked surprised.

'Where is his mother?' I asked again, more insistently this time. My heart had flipped up from my chest and was now beating in my throat.

'*You're* his mother.'

He sat up. I inadvertently sighed with relief when I was finally able to breathe freely again without the weight of his body on me.

'And get up now. That's enough rest.'

There was another child, a girl. I first became aware of her when he helped me sit up. As stiff as a poker, in pyjamas that were far too big for her, and with a serious, pale face, she stood in the frame of an unhinged door. How long she'd been there, I didn't know. The girl seemed to be clutching something to her chest. I could make out a spotted red coat. And ears. A little animal.

'Hannah,' he said. 'Mama's woken up.'

The girl's expression didn't change. I guessed she was slightly younger than the boy. She was shorter and a little more delicate than him, with the same pointy chin and the same thin hair, but hers was blonde.

'Oh, come on, Hannah,' he said, waving impatiently at her to come in. 'Don't be afraid, come here and bring Fräulein Tinky with you. Mama's finally come back home.'

The girl narrowed her eyes. Of course she must realise that something wasn't right here. There was a strange woman hunched on the sofa in their sitting room. Surely she could see I wasn't her mother. My lips silently mouthed, 'Help me.'

The girl stared at me, her eyes still narrowed, without blinking. Then she turned around and disappeared into a hallway or a neighbouring room.

I slapped my hand over my mouth in disbelief and panted into it, while my body was suddenly seized by cold panic. There was a roaring in my ears. As if from a great distance I heard him say, 'The children have really missed you. You've all got a lot of catching up to do.'

'But that's . . . that's not possible,' I said, my voice sounding distorted and alien.

'They're your children. I'm your husband. We are a happy family.'

'Those aren't my children,' the distorted voice whimpered.

'We're a happy family. I'm your husband,' he kept saying. 'I'm your husband and they are your children. You don't have anybody anymore, apart from us. You'll feel better when you understand that.'

I wobbled my head clumsily, meaning to shake it, but out of the blue I seemed to have forgotten how. His hand shot forwards, grabbed my mouth and squashed my cheeks hard. His pupils darted about, he ground his teeth. A predator, a hunter, a monster and from now on my husband. My husband who didn't joke, something which right now he seemed to be intent on reminding me: 'Do you know what it sounds like when you bash someone's head in, Lena? It's like dropping a watermelon on to the floor. *Bam!*'

I recoiled in horror.

'That's what it sounds like: *bam!* An interesting sound.'

The policemen say nothing. They're just sitting in silence, their faces suddenly vacant; I can't read anything in them. I'm gripped by the absurd fear that I've said something wrong. And now there's something else, too, something cold, wrenching: guilt. I feel guilty because I'm wearing the scar that belongs to you.

'He abducted me to give his children another mother,' I say in conclusion, then sink back exhausted on my pillow, maybe to evade their looks too. I stare at the ceiling. 'What's the date today?' I ask.

HANNAH

Sister Ruth has made a fresh cup of tea and is now buttering some bread for me. With a knife from the cutlery drawer that someone must have forgotten to lock. I told her it isn't time to eat, but she probably got a fright when my tummy gurgled. As a nurse, though, she really ought to know that it's just air I've got in my tummy, not anything dangerous that's going to make me sick. But I don't think she was listening properly when I tried to explain to her why your stomach rumbles and what it means. Instead she just kept apologising for not having given me anything to eat till now, even though I've been here for several hours.

'There you go,' she says, putting the plate in front of me, right on top of the picture I drew of my family. Only Papa's head with the red patch on the side is peeping out from beneath the plate, because he's the biggest of us. The rest of us have disappeared beneath it.

'The cafeteria opens at seven, we can get something else then. On Saturday they always have fantastic apple cake. You've got to try it.'

I say thank you. You always have to be polite.

'Go on then, tuck in, Hannah,' Sister Ruth says.

I pick up the folded slice of bread and nibble it. Papa always gets bread when he goes shopping, but only ever one loaf because bread soon goes mouldy and mould isn't good for your health.

Sister Ruth stands beside the table, watching me eat.

'When you're finished, you should have a little lie-down,' she says, nodding to the bed on the left-hand wall beside the big metal cupboard. 'You've had a long night. A little rest would do you good.'

'But I thought we were going to see Mama,' I say, putting the bread back on the plate.

'Yes, of course we will. But I want to talk to the policemen first.'

'Because of Grandad?'

Sister Ruth picks up the bread on my plate and puts it back in my hand.

'That too. Please try to eat something, Hannah. I know you're probably too upset to get much down you, but have a few mouthfuls at least, hmm?'

I take five mouthfuls, because I reckon five's a good number. One for each member of my family. One for Mama, one for Papa, one for Fräulein Tinky, one for me and an especially big one for Jonathan because he's got to clean the carpet.

'Can't you manage any more?' Sister Ruth says.

I shake my head. The bread has now got the outline of Africa. After Asia, Africa is the second largest continent on earth. Lions, zebras and black-backed jackals live there.

'Come on, then,' Sister Ruth says, pulling my chair back so I can get up.

The bed in the staffroom is nice and hard. It just has a sheet. Sister Ruth fetches a pillow and a rolled-up duvet from the metal cupboard and tucks me up. My eyes close at once, but I don't want to sleep or I might miss going to see Mama when it's finally time. Sister Ruth sits next to me on the edge of the bed. I feel her stroking my hair and I imagine she's my mama.

LENA

It's 16 September, Cham replies to my question about the date.

Four months.

Your husband kept me captive for four months, Lena. Maybe you think that's nothing. You stuck it out with him for years. Bore him children and played family.

I remember that first evening, sitting beside him on the sofa, rigid with disbelief. Peering at him from the corner of my eye, unable to do anything but admire his disguise. A good-looking man who'd got changed for 'our special first evening', no longer in jeans and faded T-shirt, but dressed smartly in dark trousers and a light blue shirt. He looked as if he'd just come home from the office or was about to go out on a date. This was no dishevelled, stinking monster from a horror film. I also remember gazing at your children, who also looked normal, totally normal and at the same time not. How could they chatter away so cheerfully as they sat by the stove, warming their hands? Even the girl, who earlier had stood in the door frame, staring suspiciously with narrowed eyes, was now cackling gleefully as she put her cat on her brother's bare toes.

'Bite him, Fräulein Tinky!' the girl called out, and all I kept thinking was: this isn't possible. This can't be happening. This isn't real.

I remember mourning for you too that evening, Lena. Mourning for the woman whose shoes I now had on. The poor woman from the cabin, who must have been here before me. Who, so far as I understood, was now dead, her skull bashed in, *bam!* Your shoes were the starkest warning. And yet I knew at once that I wasn't going to go along with his crazy, sick game. I had to compose myself and summon all my strength, recover from his attacks, his kicks and punches, and then find a way out of here. Him or me. One of us – the inevitable end was probably clear to me that first evening.

I'd already discovered the exit. The door in question was made out of wood and secured with two locks. There was a metallic jangling in his trousers whenever he moved, so I assumed he kept the keys on him the whole time. The door was to my left, just a few metres from the sofa we were sitting on together. There was no hallway or separate entrance area; the door opened straight on to the room we were in, a mixture between kitchen and sitting room. On the other side, further into the cabin, I imagined there was a hallway leading to the bedrooms and storeroom where I'd woken up after having been abducted. There was probably a bathroom too, or a toilet at least. Although I couldn't wait for him to show me the rest of the rooms, so I could get a better idea of the layout and look for other escape possibilities, I also had a strong inkling of what would ensue when he brought the evening to an end and took me to bed. I briefly harboured the foolish, slight hope that he'd simply take me back to the storeroom and bind me to the sink overnight.

From the word go I had to exclude the windows as an escape opportunity, at least those in the sitting room. They were boarded up with insulation panels. He created day and night. Like God. The very idea of it made me taste bile. From the corner of my eye I'd counted the number of screws – more than forty per window. Without the appropriate tool I'd never manage to get them out.

The door on my left – so far that seemed the only possibility. It led out, to wherever. All that mattered was it led out. I had to get my hands on the keys. Or kill him. But for that I'd need some sort of weapon. My eyes darted over to the other side of the room, to the dining area. The four chairs arranged around the table seemed to be made of solid wood. And they were screwed to the floor with metal brackets. The wall behind was taken up by a galley kitchen. I noticed the empty work surfaces and the padlocks, padlocks on every fucking cupboard. I briefly put my hopes on the drawers, imagining myself taking out a knife, preferably one of those really sharp knives that cut through everything, including meat. But in truth I already suspected that they were empty.

I heard myself sigh.

'Are you tired, Lena? Would you like to go to bed?'

I flinched.

'No, no. I'm fine, thank you.'

He lifted his heavy arm from my shoulder and checked his watch. I glanced at the face. Just after half past seven.

'Children, Mama's right. It's late. Time for bed.'

The children moaned.

'No buts! When your mama says something, you have to listen.'

The girl turned her head to me and scowled.

'They could stay up for a while longer if they want,' I said cautiously.

'No, it's late.' He got up from the sofa and shooed them away with his hands. 'Go and brush your teeth!'

The children obediently got to their feet.

'Can Fräulein Tinky sleep with us, Papa?' the girl asked.

'No, she stays in the sitting room, otherwise you won't sleep again.' Turning to me, he said, 'Are you coming?'

Somehow I managed to stand up, to manoeuvre this outsized wound which was my body into a vertical position. Your husband reached for my arm to support me. Walking carefully I followed the children out of the sitting room and into a narrow hallway.

The children stopped beside a locked door on the right. He squeezed past me, reached for the key on top of the door frame and unlocked the door. The children hurried in. He turned to me, grinning, slipped the key into his trouser pocket, then gestured with his head for me to go in.

The bathroom was very narrow, barely big enough for all four of us. To the left, a washbasin was fixed to the wall, beneath which a water canister was standing ready. Straight ahead was the toilet, which looked like a small, white barrel, and to the right stood an old zinc bathtub with no taps. Above the tub, just a few centimetres below the ceiling, I noticed a fist-sized hole in the wall, into which a section of tubing had been inserted. I suspected this was some sort of vent, but it didn't seem to be working particularly well as the air was sticky and musty. There was no window and, as in the storeroom, a bare bulb just dangled from the ceiling.

The children reached for their toothbrushes, which were in two colourful plastic mugs on the shelf above the basin. I found the sight of these two mugs perverse. As I felt with my tongue the new gap between my teeth, I imagined this man, your husband, like thousands of other customers, standing by the toiletries and lovingly choosing designs that would appeal to your children. On the boy's blue mug, a knight on a horse, and on the girl's pink mug, a princess dancing in a meadow full of flowers. I pictured this man standing at the checkout, paying for the toothbrush mugs and nobody suspecting that they weren't destined for a normal home, but for this hole where the inhabitants were locked up.

'Cleaning the bathroom is, of course, the housewife's job. But no worries, I'll see to the toilet myself.' I only realised later what he meant by that. As there was no running water in the cabin, we used a compost toilet where the faeces went straight into a container filled with bark mulch, which had to be emptied from time to time – *outside*. Obviously he couldn't leave this task to the housewife, because *outside* didn't exist for her anymore.

'Right,' he said, looking at his watch. 'The three minutes are up.'

As if on command, the children spat froth into the basin in sync. Then, one after another, they washed their faces with water from the canister.

'Mama's going to take you to bed tonight,' he told them with a lavish smile.

'Yay, finally!' the boy beamed, patting his cheeks dry with a towel.

Your husband led me outside into the hallway. The girl followed us, closing the door behind her. I had no idea why we were waiting until the boy came out and the girl took his place in the bathroom. I realised he was allowing them to go to the loo unsupervised, and this gave me the whiff of another escape opportunity. Even though all I could think about was the toothbrush mugs with the childish designs. If I could break them somehow. Broken plastic can be very sharp – a weapon.

The children shared a tiny room with just about enough space for a bunk bed. The wooden walls were filled with paintings and spidery drawings the children had done themselves. I tried to make out the subjects of these pictures, but the light, again coming from a single bare bulb, was too dim. A window: boarded up, of course. The boy climbed up a ladder to the top bunk; the girl crawled into the bottom one.

'You have to sit here,' the girl said rather robotically, patting a space beside her. 'That's what you always do.'

I looked over my shoulder at your husband, who leaned

against the door frame, his arms crossed and a smile on his face. Tentatively I approached the bed and sat down, my head bowed and back bent, so as not to hit the top bunk.

'And now you're going to tell us a story. As always.'

'I –'

'Look, Mama!' The boy's head suddenly appeared beside mine. He was dangling head first over the wooden board that prevented him from falling out at night. 'I can fly!'

'Stop it, Jonathan,' the girl hissed. 'That's dangerous. And we want to hear a story now.'

'Okay,' he grumbled, swinging his torso back upwards. Above me the mattress bulged through the slatted frame as he got himself into a comfy position.

'I want to hear something about aeroplanes!'

The girl clicked her tongue.

'It's not your decision. I'm the older one, I get to choose.'

'You always get to choose!'

'Yes, and it's only fair –'

'Enough!' All three of us flinched. Your husband. 'No story tonight now. Get up, Lena.'

'But Papa,' I heard the boy above me say.

'No. You two have no manners. Get up, Lena!'

I don't know why I stayed sitting down. Maybe it was his abrupt change of mood that paralysed me, or perhaps the overall situation, the shocking normality of an argument between siblings in these shockingly different circumstances. But I sat there, just staring.

'Get. Up. Now. Lena.'

I couldn't breathe. Every word, and the way he emphasised them, felt like the stab of a knife into my lungs. I went flaccid, started breathing shallowly, almost panting. Then I noticed a gentle touch on my knee. Your daughter's hand. I looked at her.

'You have to get up now,' she whispered, barely audibly. For a fraction of a second we looked each other in the eye. Then she swiftly rolled over, so I could only see her narrow back, and pulled the duvet over her shoulders. I stood as if in a dream, as if hypnotised by her voice.

'Say goodnight to the children, Lena,' your husband said, now smiling again.

'Goodnight, children.'

'Goodnight!' came the reply in unison as he closed the door behind us. As with the bathroom door earlier, he took a key from the top of the frame and locked the door. He was locking the children in overnight. I put a hand in front of my mouth to stifle a gasp.

'Right, then,' he said with a smile once he'd replaced the key. 'Now to us . . .'

I give a start. There is a loud ringing, which for a moment goes unnoticed by the others. Then Cham, who seems lost in thought, gives a slight start too, and his notebook and pen slip from his lap to the floor. He leaves them where they are and pats feverishly at his jacket, then puts a hand inside and fishes out a mobile.

'Giesner,' he grunts. I try to make out the fragments on the other end of the line, but the disruptive beeping of the ECG machine makes it difficult. He says, 'Okay, wait a moment,' takes the phone from his ear and gives me a penetrating look. 'Our people have found the cabin. Is there anything they should be prepared for when they go in?'

I shake my head. 'I hit him, with a snow globe. I . . .' I pause, grabbing the back of my head.

'You knocked him out?'

I nod.

'Go in,' Giesner orders into the phone.

I sink back into the pillow and close my eyes. In my mind I hear a voice that says, 'Can you see how nice it is here?'

'Yes, darling, it's really nice here,' I reply silently and smile.

LENA

'Lena?'

'Hmm?'

'Do you think you could tell us more?'

I open my eyes and try sitting up again. At once Munich leaps up from his seat to arrange the pillow behind my back so I'm comfortable.

'Just give me a moment, okay?'

He gives a sympathetic nod and Cham says, 'Take all the time you need.'

I ponder where I could begin again. I think about the things that can't be said, Lena. I have to put brackets around those things that the policemen don't absolutely need to know about. But you, Lena, you should know what he did to me.

I look from Munich to Cham. Munich is rubbing his hands together awkwardly. With a sigh, Cham leans forward in his chair and picks up the notebook and pen which slipped from his lap when his mobile rang. I reckon they're now expecting to hear about a rape, a really rough, brutal episode. It would be perfectly understandable if I had to compose myself before talking about it. What they can't imagine are those other things.

This is just for you, Lena.

'Right, then,' he said with a smile once he'd replaced the key. 'Now to us . . .'

My shoulders tense, my back stiffens and I clench my fists. My expectations now were no different from those of the policemen who'd listened to my story up to this point.

I thought of Kirsten and how she came back home last year, at that hazy, grey time between night and morning when everyone is in bed. Nobody hears your stifled screams, nobody crosses your path by chance, and there's nobody to wrestle the beast from you or offer any help. I thought of how she slid down the wall in our hallway, with a deathly pale, bruised face and torn dress, and how I squatted beside her, but not daring to put my arms around her.

'Why didn't you fight back?' I asked, because I was too stupid, or just too tired, not yet clear-headed, having been jolted out of my sleep when I heard Kirsten come crashing into the apartment. Because I'd been sleeping like everyone else, while Kirsten was attacked in a rear courtyard.

Kirsten turned her ashen, unfamiliar-looking face to me and said, 'Because at that moment, I was dead. I didn't have a body anymore. No arms to thrash about with. No legs to kick him with. And my mind was elsewhere.'

That's what I was banking on, Lena. That beneath his body I would be dead at once, just hoping that it would be over quickly. I stood tall, clenched my fists and arched my back, even though it still ached after the pummelling and kicking your husband had inflicted on me earlier that day. I raised my chin and looked him in the eye. I thought of Kirsten, who had survived her own death. Who was so strong. I would be strong too. Even if he took my body, he wouldn't have my soul.

'Okay, then,' I blustered in a mixture of defiance and wantonness. 'Let's get it over with.'

I could see his face crumple, Lena. The features just slipped away, the entire construct collapsed and it took him a while to reassemble it. I'd caught him off-guard. His left eye twitched and the smile he assumed looked uncertain. But he was still stronger than me, he was the man who didn't joke, he was God and I a mere worm, something he needed to prove to me. Grabbing me by the arm, he dragged me down the hallway back to the bathroom.

'Your times for using the toilet are seven o'clock in the morning, twelve-thirty, five in the afternoon and eight in the evening,' he said again, fumbling for the key in his trouser pocket. 'It's eight o'clock now.' I could see his fingers trembling, only very slightly, but they were trembling. It was a blessed moment, Lena.

He unlocked the door, I stepped in and turned around in the expectation that he would close the door again behind me. After seeing him let the children go to the loo on their own, I didn't entertain the possibility that he might do any different.

'Go on then,' he said, motioning with his head. I staggered over to the toilet. This had to be a test, a trial of strength in return for the mini triumph I'd just had.

'Do it!'

I teetered backwards. Your husband stood in the doorway with repulsive nonchalance, his left hand propped against the frame, his head cocked, and wearing a smile from which all the uncertainty had disappeared.

'No,' I said.

'Go to the toilet, Lena.'

I pursed my lips and slowly shook my head.

'I said, go to the toilet.'

'Then get out of here. I'm not going to do it with you watching me.'

'Oh yes, you will, Lena. Because you're going to do everything I say.'

When he took a step towards me I threw my hands up in the air and panted, 'Wait. I'm sorry. I'm sorry.' I wanted to fight, I wanted to be strong, I really did. But I couldn't risk him giving me another beating today. He stopped and eyed me suspiciously.

'I . . . I don't need to.'

No movement, just his gaze. I tried to hold it.

'I said, your times for using the toilet are seven o'clock in the morning, twelve-thirty, five in the afternoon and eight in the evening.'

I dropped my hands and nodded vigorously.

'I know. I heard what you said. Seven in the morning, twelve-thirty, five and eight in the evening. But I don't need to.' I felt a passable smile dart across my lips. 'I don't need to,' I said again. 'We can go to bed straightaway.'

It all happened so quickly that I didn't have time to step out of the way, raise my arms, or even breathe or blink.

Do you want to know, Lena? Do you want to know what your husband does when you refuse to go to the loo in front of him? Did this ever happen to you, perhaps?

If so, then you know what it's like to be wrenched to the ground. To curl up into a ball on the floor, your hands up to your face to protect the sore stitches on your forehead. You will have tried to take one last deep breath before he starts kicking you in the stomach. You will have screwed up your eyes in anticipation of a dreadful pain. But it doesn't come. You will have taken another deep breath because it's coming now, now, the pain . . . but no. No kicking, no pain, just a strange, rasping sound. You will have dared to take a peek through your splayed fingers and you'll have seen him, your husband, standing over you, legs apart, his hand on the zip of his trousers. In fear, you'll have forgotten to breathe for a third time, and now it's essential because you've got to hold your breath as he relieves himself above you, over you, and it's warm and burns your skin, seeping through your clothes; your clothes and your hair soak it all up. You know what it's like to struggle but there's no hope of getting away. The sensation as the last splashes hit you right in the face, you feel a drop on your tightly pursed lips, you hear that noise again, *zzzzzzip*, then he, your husband, says calmly, 'I hope you now understand why it's so important to stick to the times for using the toilet, Lena. Otherwise, you see, something might go wrong.'

After that you were probably sick, Lena, and your husband made you clean the bathroom, unconcerned by how much you were trembling and retching in disgust. You cleaned the bathroom, on your knees, with wet hair and soaked clothes while he sat watching on the edge of the zinc bathtub, his legs crossed casually. Perhaps it took hours before he was satisfied with what you'd done. Afterwards you had to get undressed and stand in the bathtub. He washed you; you were dirty, after all. 'Oh, Lena, how come you're so dirty again?' Then he dried you and took you to the bedroom.

If these things happened to you too, Lena, then you'll know that you can't simply talk about them, because what they do to you is very different from the rough, brutal things which are awful, but not new. The police know about these things. They've heard about them often enough now to be sitting here beside me, their eyes lowered and rubbing their hands. Although they feel moved, such things are part and parcel of their job, and once they've jotted down the word 'rape', they're done. No further details needed. A man lies on top of a woman and she probably feels pain. I can be one of these women, Lena. I will be one of them once forensics have combed their way through the cabin and inspected the sheets. There's nothing I can do about that.

But I definitely won't be the woman who crawled around a bathroom on my knees in a pool of urine and vomit. I have put that in brackets. They are fixed and non-negotiable.

The policemen, meanwhile, are still waiting patiently for the inevitable part of my story. I nod as a sign that I'm ready to resume talking.

'After he'd locked the children up for the night, he took me into the bedroom. A set of handcuffs hung from the right-hand bedpost. I wasn't going to be getting out of there.' I pull up the sleeve of my hospital gown and hold out my right arm to Cham and Munich in turn. There's still a pale red ring of chafed skin around my wrist.

'He shackled me to the bedpost, always. Even when we went to sleep. I think he did it to stop me from secretly getting up to look for the keys. Or trying to smother him with a pillow.'

Cham jots something in his notebook.

'So . . .' he starts hesitantly, '. . . he, erm . . .'

'Yes,' I reply.

Just 'yes'. That's enough to confirm the roughness, the brutality, Lena. It's that simple. Maybe at a later date a policewoman will try to find out the exact details. That's what happened to Kirsten after she was attacked in the rear courtyard. They send the female officers because they think it's easier to discuss this sort of thing with women. But ultimately all the female officers do is ask which orifice was involved and whether the woman conveyed clearly enough that she didn't agree to the 'intercourse'.

'Did you say no?' the policewoman asked Kirsten. This was enough for Kirsten to ask back, 'Are you being serious?'

For a short while I have a bit of peace.

Until Cham's mobile rings again. I can't make out what's being said so I turn over and drift off. No handcuffs tonight . . . I smile, no handcuffs.

Cham clears his throat. The hand holding his mobile is now in his lap. The conversation is already over. Either it was very quick or I must have nodded off briefly.

'What?' I ask, trying to sit up again. This time Munich doesn't help me with the pillow. I bet he's thinking I'd rather struggle with it myself than have to be so physically close to a man, especially now.

Cham waits until I've made myself comfortable. Then he says, 'They've got the man. The boy too.'

'Is everything okay?'

'They've got them,' Cham says again, as if that were an answer.

I nod all the same, say, 'Thank God,' and then, because it's over, because it really is over for good, I add, 'Jasmin Grass. My name is Jasmin Grass. I was born 28 March 1983 in Regensburg. My mother's name is Susanne. She's Grass too. Could you call her?'

Cham looks surprised, but only momentarily.

'Of course, not a problem.'

'Thanks.' I smile.

'But there's just one more thing, *Jasmin*.'

My smile falters. The way he emphasises my name. His face. The beeping of the ECG machine takes on a new rhythm.

'What?' I ask cautiously.

'You told us earlier that you knocked your abductor out.' He glances at his notebook. 'With a snow globe.'

'Yes.' I nod vigorously. 'Why?'

Cham says nothing, looks at Munich, looks at me, looks back at Munich and then hands him his mobile. Munich takes a close look at the display and then fixes his eyes on me.

'What?' I ask to the millisecond beat of the ECG machine. 'What's wrong?'

MATTHIAS

For a moment there was peace, an unfamiliar acceptance, just Karin and I and the sky, where the new day was taking hold. This moment, as we clutched each other, was like an island, a tiny, welcome refuge. No doubt we wouldn't be able to stay where we were for ever; soon the door would open and someone would come in – Gerd or Giesner, or one of their men, to jolt us back into reality. I realised this, but I tried so hard not to think about it that of course I couldn't help thinking about it. And then it was Karin who completely ruined the moment.

'I think we should let Mark know,' she said into my chest.

'Over my dead body,' I said.

That was that, the peace was shattered, the sky no longer full of hope, but grey, sombre and hanging heavily over the black silhouettes of houses in the distance, which looked like paper cuttings. There was light in the odd window. Early risers beginning their day and giving the unmissable sign, by switching on lights, that the world keeps turning inexorably. You can't stop it or escape. There wasn't any island, not really.

'What do you want to say to him?' I asked her, trying to manoeuvre myself out of a looming discussion on fundamental principles. Karin had always liked Mark. 'He'd never have laid a finger on Lena' – this was the position she'd steadfastly maintained, whereas I'd immediately mentioned his name when we were making the missing person's report at the police station. 'Has your daughter ever had trouble with anyone?' they'd asked us.

'Mark Sutthoff,' I spat out.

'Matthias,' Karin said at once, elbowing me in the side.

Mark Sutthoff, in his own little world a model-cum-actor-cum-singer, in reality a conceited second-hand car dealer we'd bought Lena's old Polo from. Lena must have just turned twenty at the time; she was definitely still living with us and hadn't yet moved into her apartment in Haidhausen. It had completely escaped me that he'd been hovering over her in the showroom and had talked her into giving him her number behind my back. One evening he turned up at our door to fetch Lena and she said, beaming, 'Papi, you remember Mark, don't you? He sold us the Polo.' That's all he should have done and no more. That was all we'd wanted from him, that silly little blue Polo. Nobody had mentioned that included in the delivery was a drama that would go on for years. Lena and Mark Sutthoff together, Lena and Mark Sutthoff split up. 'Can you believe it? Mark's been flirting with another girl!' 'Mark can go fuck himself.' 'But Papi, I love him so much!'

Lena couldn't see what I saw. He simply wasn't good enough for her, not good enough.

'You're not prepared to give him a chance,' was Karin's way of dismissing my reservations. She said it with a sigh and a shake of the head.

Nobody could see what I saw.

And now, in the hospital, we were clearly heading yet again for this self-same discussion. Karin wanted to call Mark Sutthoff and tell him what had happened overnight.

'But we don't know a thing,' I said between gritted teeth, hoping that Karin would leave it at this.

'I don't mean now, and certainly not at this ungodly hour. But afterwards, later –'

'My arse!' I rudely interrupted her, but immediately had second thoughts when she freed herself from our embrace and shuffled back to the bed. 'I'm sorry,' I muttered over my shoulder. 'I just don't understand what the point would be. He's got nothing to do with Lena anymore.'

'He's suffered just as much as we have.'

'From what? The uncertainty?' I puffed angrily. Barely a year after Lena disappeared Mark Sutthoff moved to Paris with his new girlfriend. 'It didn't take him long to get over her, don't you remember? She wouldn't want that.' I faltered, and Karin noticed.

'We have to wait for the time being anyway. But when we know something concrete we ought to call him, we really should, Matthias. We've got to do that, it's only fair.'

I could literally see my face distorting in the reflection of the windowpane.

'I said no,' I growled to the face in the window.

'It's all right.' Karin sighed. 'Calm down. I didn't mean to . . .'

Her words hung unfinished in the air, making it dry and thick.

We haven't said another word about it since. The air is still thick, the silence is pressing on our heads. Inside them scenarios are playing out that are even worse if you don't share them.

'So far we've only got some pieces of the puzzle,' Giesner said. Abduction, cabin, a woman who looks like Lena, little Hannah. I try to arrange the pieces, but the meaning defeats me. So I start prowling around the room like a caged tiger. Karin has put her feet up on the bed and is now lying, staring at the ceiling, with her hands folded on her tummy. I tell her she should try to get some sleep.

'I can't,' she whispers back.

It feels as if we're waiting for the results of a serious operation. I can't take it any longer.

'I'm going to see what's happening.'

Karin props herself up on her elbows.

'They must still be in the middle of their interrogation. They would have already come and told us otherwise.'

'Maybe I can help.'

'With what? The interrogation?' Karin laughs softly. 'Oh, Matthias.'

'No, I'm being serious. What's taking so long? Maybe they just need to twist her arm. I bet she knows exactly what's happened to Lena.'

Karin's eyes are like saucers.

'Do you think so?'

'Of course! Why is she making out that she's Lena? Why is she making out to the girl that she's her mother?' I point vaguely to the door. 'The girl out there is Lena's daughter, a blind man could tell you that! There's no need for any DNA test.'

Karin's feet swing over the edge of the bed.

'Do you think that woman's involved somehow?'

'Surely you must have realised that something's not right here?'

There is a knock at the door.

In a flash Karin leaps down from the bed and reaches out for my hand. Her fingers are flapping frantically in the air, as if she's playing a wild piano piece. I grab her hand and pull her beside me. We stand like that, hand in hand, shoulder to shoulder, when a moment later Giesner enters the room to give us an update on the investigation.

HANNAH

It's really dark outside. The trees are black and their branches are like ossified monsters' fingers. 'You can't catch me!' Mama cries out.

As I run there's a loud cracking beneath my feet, and the same with Mama too. That's how I know which direction to go in, even though I can barely see her anymore in the darkness. Only when the trees are very far apart can I sometimes see a corner of her beautiful white dress that shines like silver in the light of the moon.

Suddenly there's a lot of light, a really yellow light, like a bright stream. I see the black tree trunks and between them the outline of Mama, which is black too. Her arms are outstretched like an angel about to fly. Then there's a huge bang and I stop. That's what a shock feels like. I can't see Mama anymore, only the yellow stream of light. I'm walking on tiptoe now; the light's getting brighter and I have to put my hand in front of my eyes because they're starting to fill with tears. I push away branches until the wood comes to an end and suddenly turns into a road. Mama is lying in front of a car. I can see her face in the headlights. Her eyes are closed.

I hear a crack behind me. I turn around and see Papa. He runs past me on to the road, to Mama, who's lying there. 'You lost!' he cries out. 'Ha ha!'

Mama opens her eyes and laughs.

'That was unfair, you two!'

She holds her hands up to Papa. He pulls her up and wipes the red stuff from her face.

'Now it's your turn, Hannah,' Papa says to me. 'Try your best.'

I squeal and turn around to run back through the wood. After a few paces there's something tugging at my sleeve. It's Sister Ruth, who pulls me behind a thick tree trunk and says, 'This is a good hiding place, Hannah . . .'

'. . . Hannah?'

The wood fades away and only Sister Ruth's face is still there, right beside mine.

'Hannah,' she says. 'Wake up, Hannah.'

I yawn and blink.

I'm not in the wood at all, but in the staffroom, in bed.

'Wake up, Hannah,' Sister Ruth says once more.

'Can we go and see Mama now?' I ask. My voice is still really tired and croaky.

Sister Ruth doesn't say anything at first, but then she asks me if I slept well.

'Yes,' I say, 'and I had a dream.'

'Was it a nice dream?'

I nod.

Sister Ruth does her silly half-smile. I know that something's not right.

'Is Mama not well?'

Now Sister Ruth looks at the floor. 'I have to take you to see Dr Hamstedt.' For a few seconds I've no idea who that is, but then I remember. The tall, thin woman with short brown hair, who came into the staffroom with the policeman. The doctor who forgot her coat.

I want to ask why I have to see her, but Sister Ruth beats me to it and says, 'But you can say goodbye first.'

JASMIN

Dr Schwindt came, despite the chaos of the shift changeover. Even I could see it was necessary.

'It wasn't me! It wasn't me!' I cried over and over again, thrashing about with my arms and accidentally ripping out the intravenous line. That shouldn't have happened, but it did, like all those things that happened which oughtn't to have. And certainly not –

'Try to breathe as calmly as you can, Frau Grass,' Dr Schwindt says, emphasising my name as if it's something precious. The ECG has gone blank; Dr Schwindt has to restart it. 'Technology,' he says laconically, as he presses the relevant buttons. I reckon the machine has just about had enough of me and my unreliable heart that's linked to my mood.

'In a moment you're going to feel a little tired,' Dr Schwindt says when the machine starts beeping regularly again. I've decided to like him, simply because right now I feel alone and without any allies. He's an elderly gentleman with an elaborately waxed beard and glasses with half-moon lenses. I wish my father were here. Or anyone, for that matter.

'You might also feel a numbness in your arms and legs. But that's completely normal, no cause for concern, okay?'

'Dr Schwindt?' I say, my voice already slightly feeble. 'Could you do me a favour?'

'What's that, Frau Grass?'

'Could you check something in my medical file?'

Dr Schwindt turns around as if he's looking for something, then says, 'Hmm, I think the police are examining it at the moment. What would you like to know?'

I swallow; my throat is dry.

'I need to know if I'm pregnant.'

Dr Schwindt pushes the glasses back up his nose. They'd slipped forwards when he was fiddling with the ECG machine.

'If you have any concerns about the sedative, then I can tell you it's not harmful – '

'My concerns are more general,' I interrupt him.

'No problem, Frau Grass. I will check for you.' He nods and I like him all the more now because he doesn't ask any further questions.

'Thanks.'

'And now you should get some sleep, okay?'

He says he hopes I get better soon and puts the little box with the emergency button within my reach before leaving the room.

Now I'm lying here and the sensation of numbness starts to tingle in my fingers and toes. But my mind doesn't feel a thing. It's wide awake; the adrenaline must still be having an effect.

'There's just one more thing, Jasmin,' Cham had said after his phone conversation and handing the mobile to Munich.

'What?' I asked. 'What's wrong?' My heart was pumping in panic.

They've got the man. Those were Cham's words. So what was it? Had your husband resisted arrest? Escaped, perhaps? Was he on his way here? That wasn't possible, totally impossible. I'd hit him with the snow globe, really hard. He'd fallen to the ground. He'd collapsed and lain there without moving.

Munich sighed and looked from the screen back to Cham.

I couldn't take it any longer.

'Just tell me what's wrong!'

They conferred about whether to show me the photo that Cham had been sent by his people from the cabin.

'It's not good enough for an identification,' Munich crowed.

I wiggled my hand impatiently in the air.

Cham looked at me through narrowed eyes.

'Show it to her, Herr Brühling. She'll cope.'

I nodded my affirmation.

But what I saw, when Munich gave me Cham's mobile . . . the photograph . . . your husband.

'It wasn't me! It wasn't me!' I started to scream, dropping the phone in the process. It lay there, in the hollow of the duvet between my outstretched legs, the screen glowing, glowing red, everything was red. I turned my head away. His head wasn't there anymore, or at least not really, his face, shreds, red, everything red.

Munich leaped up from his chair, grabbed the mobile, pressed the button at the top right to switch off the display and handed it back to Cham, who retrieved the photo.

'We need to check whether these injuries really are the result of a snow globe,' he said soberly. 'I mean, at first glance, it looks as if, well — '

'No, no, no!' I screamed again. 'It wasn't me! Only once . . . the snow globe . . . I only hit him once . . .'

My voice caught in my throat in mid-scream. Now I was completely quiet. It only dawned on me slowly.

I'd broken your husband's skull.

Broken every bone in his face.

Shredded his skin.

I must have flailed the snow globe against his face countless times, as in a frenzy. *Bam!* it went, just as he had said.

Bam! Like dropping a watermelon on the floor.

Nice, calm breathing, Dr Schwindt said.

Nice, calm breathing, I repeat to myself and my eyelids are heavy. I feel myself sinking, sinking deeper and deeper into a dull tiredness; it's gradually getting colder and colder, and the cold is creeping into my limbs, making them numb. Dr Schwindt said that too, a numbness in my arms and legs, completely normal, no cause for concern. It's just that I feel dreadfully cold.

Are you freezing, Mama? I hallucinate and nod weakly.

Yes, Jonathan, I'm freezing, really freezing.

Something went seriously wrong. I killed him, Lena. I killed your husband. I slaughtered him so wildly as to make him unrecognisable. *Bam!* it went. *Bam!* again and again.

My head tips heavily to the side. Was that a knock at the door? My eyelids open sluggishly.

A woman appears, either in my dream or for real; I'm too far gone to be able to tell the difference.

'Hello,' I think I hear the woman say. 'Here's someone who wants to see you.'

A movement behind her back, I blink, dream or reality. Hannah steps forwards, approaches my bed, everything in slow motion. She feels in the left-hand pocket of her dress. I realise I'm beginning to roll my eyes. Under Hannah's touch I feel my hand ball into a feeble fist. Hannah carefully prising open my fingers again, one after the other. Putting something in my palm, then just as carefully pressing my fingers back into a fist. My eyelids flickering and Hannah's tender kiss on my forehead, right on my scar, her voice whispering, 'I remember every detail.'

I slump and fall into a deep sleep.

Woman escapes after being imprisoned in cabin for four months

Cham/Munich (MK) – It is verging on a miracle. After four months of captivity, the advertising consultant from Regensburg, Jasmin G (34), missing since mid-May, has escaped from a remote cabin in the woods near the German-Czech border. The details of her imprisonment, which are slowly emerging, are beyond belief. The 34-year-old lived with her abductor, about whom the police have not yet released any information, and his two children in an enforced family unit. Initial sources are also suggesting the incidence of deviant sexual and psychological abuse. G is said to have been chained up for weeks and fed from a dog bowl. On Tuesday Jasmin G finally succeeded in escaping her tormentor, killing the as yet unidentified man in the process, Chief Inspector Gerd Brühling announced early on Wednesday morning. He also said that this kidnapping was directly connected to the Lena Beck case, the 23-year-old girl from Munich who went missing after a party in January 2004.

Like the two children of the alleged abductor (a girl, 13, and a boy, 11) Jasmin G is currently undergoing therapy. One of the two children is said to have suffered physical injuries in addition to their psychological problems, possibly abnormal development. As yet there has been no confirmation that the children also suffered the sexual abuse which Jasmin G was subjected to.

TWO WEEKS LATER

JASMIN

The sequence is three short ones, followed by two long ones.

Knockknockknock knock – knock.

I creep across the floor, but I wait another moment to be safe. A floorboard creaks by the door to my apartment. *Go on, go on;* I growl silently at the thought that Frau Bar-Lev might have an ear pressed to the other side of the door, to listen for any noises inside my apartment. *Not today, you old cow.*

Yesterday I was so hungry that I opened the door too quickly and offered her a view of the tragic curiosity. Since then I've been picturing her serving coffee to a reporter in her apartment. 'The poor girl's in a terrible state. She's much too thin. She's stopped washing her hair, she's wearing a T-shirt with stains on it and baggy tracksuit bottoms. You can see she's not right.' You can see what she's been through, she's saying, nibbling on a biscuit with her false teeth. The reporter is busily writing. About kisses and caresses that stick to my face and body and cannot be washed off. He writes that I've given up showering and scrubbing my skin sore because I've lost the energy and, in any case, I'll never rid myself of the cold sweat of fear. A tiny residue of logic inside my head tells me that Frau Bar-Lev would never do anything of the sort, but the images are vivid and persistent. She's only got a small pension, so a little pocket money would surely be welcome. *Stop it.* In today's paper: an exclusive interview with the neighbour of the cabin victim. *Stop it!*

My tummy is rumbling. The smell of freshly cooked food wafts under the door; I bet it's stew. The floorboard creaks again, then I hear footsteps on the stairs. Frau Bar-Lev walks slowly; she's got a bad hip. Momentarily I feel really bad. Every day since I got back home this wonderful old woman has been climbing the steps up to my apartment, which to her must feel like she's conquering Kilimanjaro. She could have chatted to reporters all this time, but instead she's been standing with her dodgy hip by the stove in her kitchen, cooking for me. *You should be ashamed.*

I wait until I hear the door click shut two floors below, then wait a moment longer to be sure that it's absolutely silent in the hallway outside. I turn the key, press down the handle, pick up the pot from the doormat, close the door and turn the key again. My best time so far – under three seconds. With the pot in my hand, I briefly lean with my back against the locked door and breathe as if I'd just completed a marathon. *Everything's fine, calm, stay totally calm*, I implore the thumping in my chest. Then I lift the lid. Goulash. I could have sworn I smelled stew.

I could have sworn I only hit your husband once.

I take the pot into the kitchen and put it on the cooker.

I'd arranged him in such a way that at first glance it wasn't clear whether the murder weapon really could have been a snow globe. The police officers must have searched for other potential murder weapons in the cabin, but there was no hammer that could have accounted for the violence of the blows, nor any knife that could have been responsible for the deep cuts. Well, they did exist, of course, hammers and other tools, knives, even really sharp ones, like the knives they use for gutting animals. But they were locked away and plainly out of access to me. It was only when the full forensic report came in that the snow globe was confirmed beyond doubt to have been the murder weapon. Apparently they even put it back together again, almost in its entirety. Only one piece is missing, they can't find it.

Your husband is dead, Lena.

Your children are in the loony bin.

I should feel better, as a survivor, the victor, grateful and eager for the life I doggedly fought for over four whole months. The reality is different, however. My apartment is darkened. The sky I longed to see for so long, the sun, the tweeting of the birds – I can't take any of it. My doorbell is switched off; I react to sequences of knocks. I've even disconnected my landline. I only leave my mobile on so the police and my therapist can get through to me. I respond to police queries in dribs and drabs, matters that seemingly refuse to come to an end, and my therapist says I'm doing well. I'm praised because I made it to the supermarket around the corner today, all on my own. Because I'm about to cook something delicious and then catch up on the last season of *Gilmore Girls*. Because I won't be able to make my next appointment as my mother or some close friends are coming round. My mouth is already parched from utter lies.

Do you want to know what my daily routine really looks like? I still wake punctually at ten to seven, my right arm beneath my head, the only possible sleeping position in the cabin when I was tied to the bedposts. Occasionally I try to be rebellious and close my eyes again. I change position; I just want to turn over and continue sleeping. But it doesn't work. I have to get up and make breakfast for the children. It has to be on the table at half past seven on the dot or they start getting nervous, chasing each other around the sitting room like bouncy balls out of control and squealing until my head's about to burst – *please, children, not so loud!*

It has to be on the table at half past seven on the dot or he'll scream at me. *What kind of mother are you, Lena? What kind of monster are you?*

He's not here, I know that for sure. He's dead, I killed him. The police found his body. But I still can't feel it yet. When I told my therapist this, all she could come up with was, 'That's totally normal. It takes time.' Let me tell you, she doesn't listen properly. Time doesn't play a part in my life anymore. I lost it that first day I entered the cabin. Only his time exists. He creates day and night. Like God. Still.

I don't make breakfast, of course; there aren't any children, only me in my apartment, in – ha ha – freedom. Nonetheless I'm in the kitchen at half past seven. Even if all I do is hold on tight to the work surface and try to breathe away the voice raging inside my head.

You're an ungrateful woman, Lena. An ungrateful and bad woman.

I'm good, I retort pathetically. I'm good at moving from the bed to the sofa or to my worn-out reading chair. I'm good at reading books I don't understand. 'The river was there. It was a hot day,' Hemingway writes. That much I can understand. Then the letters start to dance before my eyes and the river he talks about takes a bend, becomes wild, an uncontrollable current tearing me away while the hot day becomes an unbearable furnace, driving the sweat from my pores and tears from my eyes. I'm good at clapping books shut and tossing them away. I'm good at stuffing down the food which old Frau Bar-Lev leaves outside my front door, then bringing it up again in jets. And I'm good at attending to my needs according to his daily schedule, still, still, still. *Your times for using the toilet are seven o'clock in the morning, twelve-thirty, five in the afternoon and eight in the evening.*

What remains of an individual when they deny themselves a shit because it's only half past four? What remains of me?

I often stand by the knife block in the kitchen and sometimes my hand grips a handle all by itself. It's not the largest knife in the block, but it is the sharpest. My mother gave it to me one Christmas. 'It cuts everything,' she said. 'Vegetables, bread, meat.' Meat, Lena.

I'm empty, apart from this one, very certain feeling. It has planted itself inside me and I simply can't be rid of it. It burns in my stomach, it presses against my temples like a vice that tightens by the day. My therapist reckons this is normal too. She says it takes time to process what's happened, first to order it in my head, then to understand that it's really over.

I think she's mistaken. But I don't dare say that I feel sure she's wrong. The police know nothing about this either. It took so much energy and all my acting skills to get myself discharged from the hospital. I'm worried that they'll think I'm mad and lock me up again.

You have to know that after the first two nights in casualty I was transferred to the secure unit. That's the ward for patients who pose a risk to themselves or others. There, the door handles can be removed with a simple flick of the wrist. I don't know whether they were seriously worried that I might harm myself or someone else. And if so, then I wonder why nobody thought of taking a look inside my overnight bag which my mother brought to the hospital for me. I could have done it, Lena. Thanks to your daughter, I had everything I would have needed. But I'd rather believe that my transferral to this room was – as the hospital staff maintained – to give me security and keep unwanted visitors away. Overzealous journalists, for example. I probably don't have to tell you what effect this supposed safe room actually had on me. How in the footsteps of the security personnel who wandered up and down outside my room in the first week I thought I heard other footsteps. Someone coming to get me, to punish me. How in this locked room I felt captive again, while everyone around me was talking of 'freedom', the end of my ordeal: a paradox. The freedom didn't make up for the fact that I was imprisoned. My therapist said it was important for me to see your children. But I can't do it. I can't look them in the eye, having killed their father.

Is that what it is, Lena? The feeling gripping me like a vice. Is it guilt?

I'm taking painkillers for the three ribs I broke in the car accident. I still take half a tablet more than necessary in the hope that this will dull another pain. I'm so alone, Lena. And yet I can't bring myself to pick up the phone and ask for some company. I think of my father and Kirsten and how nice it would be if one of them were outside my door and knocked. Three short ones, two long ones. But that's not going to happen. They're gone, both of them, and are never coming back. My father died in a car accident when I was seven. In death he took my mother with him, albeit in a very complex way. She lives in Straubing, less than fifty kilometres from here, and is in rude health. But when my father died she never again sat on my bed and sang to me about spiders. And when she came to collect me from hospital last week she merely offered me her hand in greeting. Kirsten, meanwhile, couldn't stand the sight of me any longer, even before I was abducted. As you can see, Lena, your husband couldn't have chosen anyone less suitable than me for his little, sick, make-believe family. I was the worst possible person for the role. Even though these past few days I've kept wondering whether your role was really that clear. I'm not talking about what your husband forced you to do. No, I'm talking about you, Lena. I've started reading the online articles relating to your disappearance. I can't take it for long, the dancing letters, the bright screen that brings tears to my eyes, never-ending photos of you, the similarity between us that tastes like bile. Who are you, in fact? Who are you, Lena Beck?

MATTHIAS

Dear Herr Rogner,

I've tried calling the editorial office several times, only to be told that you are unwell. In my view this doesn't, however, absolve you of the responsibility for the content of your newspaper, which, as editor-in-chief, you ought to bear even in your absence. How can you allow your staff to submit articles like that? How can you permit such rubbish to be printed for the umpteenth time? I'm seriously disappointed in you, Herr Rogner! You ought to know exactly what it feels like to suffer such a loss, and yet, having dragged my daughter through the dirt, you now dare do the same to my granddaughter? Furious as I am, I would like to make one thing perfectly clear, and feel free to quote me on this: given the circumstances Hannah is in pretty good shape, both physically and mentally. She is just somewhat smaller than most children of her age, due to a lack of vitamin D over many years. Believe it or not, Hannah is a perfectly normal child! She can hold a soup spoon without making a mess. She doesn't dribble. She knows how to go to the loo and even washes her hands afterwards. Moreover, she shows no signs of physical abuse. Her teeth are impeccable. The doctor treating her even gave her a star sticker. Have you any idea what a star sticker means? Only those children who clean their teeth thoroughly get one. Hannah doesn't communicate by means of animal noises. On the contrary, she has an impressive vocabulary, which in any case is far superior to that of your rag. She can also speak four foreign languages, in case you're interested: English, French, Spanish and Italian. So please choose which one she should use to tell you and your colleagues to stop printing your bloody filthy lies! Although nothing could compensate for my personal despair about the articles over the past few days, I beg you urgently to make the writer in question see reason. Should further unethical and plainly untruthful articles appear in your newspaper again, I reserve the right to take legal action.

Yours emphatically,
Matthias Beck.

I hesitate to press 'send' for a moment, probably because of Karin. She said I shouldn't start trying to take on the media. After all, I know from experience what they're like, those vultures. She also said I should go easy on my heart. That I've got better things to do than entrench myself in my room, working on angry and, as Karin says, 'pointless' emails.

But how could I? The press has called Hannah 'zombie girl' and 'ghost child'. There's one photo of her, just a single photo, but on the internet you can find it with captions even in Chinese and Cyrillic. I'm glad I can't read what these say. 'Zombie girl' is enough for me. You miserable hacks! Haven't we been through enough already?

'Precisely,' Karin said, when straight after breakfast I was about to disappear back into my study to boot up the computer. Between the two plates with nibbled slices of toast and jam lay the daily paper. Its headline had ruined our appetites. 'Zombie Girl from the Cabin of Horrors!'

'That's precisely the point: we *have* been through enough already.' Karin's tone was gentle, although the accompanying expression on her face told me what my wife actually wanted to say: you're going the wrong way about this. We have a daughter we ought to be grieving for. Because that's what you're supposed to do, or because after all these years of waiting and not knowing, we've simply deserved it. First of all we had to get over what happened that night two weeks ago. The merciless emotional rollercoaster, when for a few moments we got our Lena back, only to lose her again straightaway.

'Lena would want me to.' That's what I said to Karin, that's the karate chop to her neck, every time. She can't argue against that; that phrase silences her. Lena left behind a gift for us, the most precious gift possible. And that's exactly why I now press 'send', firing off my rant to the editor-in-chief of the daily paper.

What a gruesome miracle life is.

A miracle that Lena perfomed.

Hannah. Our little Hannah –

'Matthias,' Karin calls out from downstairs in the hall, as if I could have possibly failed to hear the bell. Gerd called to say there were developments in the case, but he wouldn't say any more than that to Karin over the phone. He must have learned from the chaos he unleashed on the night in question.

'Matthias!' Karin's voice rings out from below once more and I sink slightly lower in my desk chair. They still haven't found Lena's body.

'Gerd's here!'

I place my hands on the desk and haul myself up with difficulty.

It's important to Karin. She'd be happy with a few bones that were definitely Lena's. She'd just like to have something to bury, and a place where she could shed tears and plant flowers. I, on the other hand, don't know how I'd cope if somebody showed me a bone and said, 'That's your Lena.'

Gerd and his colleagues are working on the assumption that her abductor buried her somewhere in the woods near the cabin. But they're no longer expecting to find her in one piece. Apparently there's a large wild boar population in the area. It's not nice to be told, when it's a question of your own child, that wild boars are omnivores and sometimes drag their spoils for kilometres.

'Apart from the skull,' Gerd told me. 'They leave that behind. It's too big for them.'

Thinking about this, I can barely make it down the stairs. My knees are trembling and my heart is having convulsions. Down below, Karin has just put a foot on the first stair, obviously to come up and see what I'm doing.

'I'm on my way,' I say feebly.

Karin nods vigorously. I can see nervous red blotches on her face and neck.

Gerd is already sitting on one of the two-seater sofas in our living room. There's a cup of coffee on the table in front of him. Karin has used our best crockery, the white china with the golden rim.

'Don't get up,' I say when he makes to stand. I go to the sofa opposite and Karin sits beside me on the armrest. 'So? What's new?'

Pompously, Gerd takes a deep breath.

'We're now able to prove beyond any doubt that Lena spent time in the cabin.'

I wait for the climax. It doesn't come.

'Is that it? We already knew that.'

'No, Matthias, we suspected it. There is a difference. Knowledge is based on facts and evidence. We were able to recover two strands of hair with their roots and draw up a genetic profile from them. It matches the sample we took from Lena's toothbrush all those years ago.'

I sigh and look at Karin, who has one hand pressed to her chest and does actually look impressed.

'With your DNA kit have you been able to pin down the identity of the abductor too?'

'No,' Gerd says, his jaw visibly tensing. 'I'm afraid we've got nothing to match it against. He doesn't correspond with any profile in our database, which means he's never had a criminal record, or at least has never been involved in anything serious. We don't store data for lesser offences, such as common theft.'

'Or maybe he was just shrewd enough to avoid being captured by you.'

Karin lays a hand on my arm to try to placate me.

'Matthias . . .'

I gesture towards Gerd. 'What about the cabin? It must belong to somebody! The owner will be in the land register.'

Gerd gives a tense sigh when he turns from Karin back to me.

'It's unclear whether the land where the cabin stands is still in Bavaria, or whether it's on Czech soil. It's the border area, at any rate. No man's land. Officially, nobody built a cabin there. And nobody appeared to have noticed either. The surrounding area is so overgrown that you can barely get a car through.'

'For Christ's sake, Gerd!' I bellow, leaping to my feet. 'Why don't you bloody well tap that Grass woman up! She's supposed to have spent four months in the cabin with that guy and she doesn't even know his name? She's taking the piss!'

Gerd gets up too. Now we're standing facing one another, with just the coffee table separating us and Karin's pitiful efforts to keep the peace.

'Matthias, they're doing all they –'

'Frau Grass told us,' Gerd interrupts her attempt, but unlike me he strives to keep his cool, 'that the abductor didn't mention his name. We have no reason to doubt her statement. And as far as the children are concerned, he's just *Papa*.'

'Let me talk to her! You'll see how quickly she remembers the name!'

'You know that's nonsense, Matthias.'

'Oh, nonsense, is it?'

'Of course we wouldn't allow you to harass a witness.'

'Lovely witness.'

'You're best placed to know how something like that can turn out,' Gerd says with a meaningful look.

I open my mouth to say something, but then drop it.

'Listen, Matthias. I'm sure we'll find out the abductor's identity very soon. That doesn't automatically mean that we'll discover what happened to Lena. You have to realise that.' Turning back to Karin, he ventures a smile; a moronic, patronising smile. 'But we'll do our best.'

I clutch my chest; the pain tempers my tone.

'*I'll bring your Lena home*. Your words, Gerd. Your words.'

I cross the living room to the hallway with small, cautious steps. I mustn't break down, not here, not in front of Gerd.

'At least fathom some explanation as to why he took our girl away,' I say over my shoulder when I get to the hallway. 'And bring my wife a bloody bone so she can finally plant a few flowers.'

'Matthias!' Gerd calls out as I'm already by the stairs. 'By the way, the DNA kit has also confirmed that Hannah and Jonathan are Lena's biological children. Which means you're officially a grandfather now. Congratulations!'

'Idiot,' I mutter as I carefully climb the stairs to my study.

HANNAH

Sometimes I lie in bed at night and wish I could have my starry sky back. I stretch my arm as far as I can towards the ceiling and wish I could touch them, the stars. Like before. I imagine Mama's hand on mine, moving my index finger from one star to another until they've all been joined up by invisible lines. 'That's a very well-known constellation, Hannah. The Plough,' she says, smiling at me. I smile back, even though some time ago I read in the fat book, which is always right, that the Plough isn't a real constellation, but it's made up of the seven brightest stars of the Great Bear. When I think about my mama and the stars, my heart aches from the sadness gnawing away at it.

I don't like the children's clinic. I miss my family and my little Fräulein Tinky with her sweet, clumsy paws and her soft coat.

I don't like my room. The ceiling is far too tall. I'll never be able to reach it, no matter how far I stretch out my arm. There aren't any stars up there. And I can't see anything through my first proper window either, because the blinds have to be closed all the time. I threw a chair against the windowpane, but it just made a noise. And got me into trouble. Frau Hamstedt is still saying she's a doctor, even though I haven't seen her in a white coat yet. She's the boss here. I've told her I'm not sick and so shouldn't be in a children's clinic, but I'm not allowed home. I can't even go to the toilet when I need to and I just have to keep saying what I'm afraid of. But I'm not afraid of anything. I simply don't like it here. And that's why I don't want to wait any longer; I want to go home, right now. When I tell her that, she just says 'Hannah' in such a funny way as if I were a little bit stupid. But I'm not stupid! And I'm not afraid either. There's a boy here who sometimes has serious attacks just because he's afraid. One moment he's sitting at lunch perfectly normally, and the next he sweeps his plate and cutlery on to the floor and starts banging his head on the table. I secretly count the number of times he does it. His record is twelve before someone intervened. I asked Frau Hamstedt why the boy does that and she says it's called 'post-traumatic stress disorder'. You can get it if you've been through a terrible experience, she told me. Like an invisible injury that's very slow to heal.

But I don't believe they can really help the boy. They just stick a plaster on his head, give him the blue pills and send him off to do some drawing. All he ever does is black scribbles, even though I've told him a thousand times, 'Jonathan, you can't just do ugly black scribbles all the time. You have to make an effort with your pictures.' You always have to make an effort with everything. But the boy just stares at me with funny eyes, which come from the blue pills, and then I think: this isn't Jonathan anymore. This isn't really my brother anymore. Frau Hamstedt and her helpers have destroyed him.

I've got to get away from here. This isn't a children's clinic at all. They're just saying that, but it's not true. Nothing that they say is true. They're liars and wicked people. This is a really bad place.

My grandfather thinks so too. He visits me every day and also comes with me to my appointments. We've already been to the dentist, who gave me a star sticker because I've got such good teeth, and to other doctors who said I need lots of vitamin D. Vitamin D is important. You don't grow without it. You get vitamin D from sunlight. In spite of this, I'm not allowed to have the blinds open in my room. I asked why, but the only answer I got was, 'It's very complicated, young lady.' But it's not complicated at all. Grandad was able to give me a very simple explanation: 'Your eyes have to get used to the light slowly, Hannah. Otherwise you might get a detached retina.' The retina is the nerve tissue that lines the inside

of the eye. If the retina becomes detached, the eye is no longer sup-
plied with the information it needs and can go blind. That's why I
always have to wear sunglasses when we go to my appointments.
But I don't like the sunglasses. They make the whole world brown.
The trees, the sky, everything brown. Whereas the sky's supposed
to be a canvas, with snowy-white clouds against a blue background.
The city looks completely different from behind the brown lenses
too, and it smells bad. The houses are tall, brown boxes. If you
look right up at them your neck starts to ache. Sometimes, when
we're on the way to an appointment, Grandad asks if he should
drive slower to give me time to have a good look at the city. But I
tell him to drive faster instead. Paris would be more beautiful. I'm
not missing anything here.

My heart has been aching quite a lot recently. Every day and
every minute, in fact. I'm sad, but I think Grandad is the only
one who really understands. Yesterday he promised he would
take me home. He also said I should just answer the questions
to satisfy Frau Hamstedt, her helpers and the police, and I'll
be able to get out of here sooner. Jonathan can't answer any
questions anymore. The blue pills have made him so stupid
that he's forgotten how to speak. He doesn't say a single word
anymore, not even to me. My grandfather says, 'Now it's all up
to you, darling Hannah.' I would answer the questions, but all
they ever want to know is what happened to Mama and where
she is. I can't think of an answer. The last time I saw her was
that night at the hospital. It's just that when I say this, they
merely shake their heads and act as if I'm lying. They think I tell
a lot of lies. Once Frau Hamstedt almost got cross with me. She
didn't have a go at me, but I could see it in her face. She said I

was living in two worlds. One inside my head and the real one. She also said that wasn't a bad thing, but she frowned and her eyebrows went into such a funny position that it looked as if she had a big brown 'V' right above her eyes. I shouldn't have told her anything about our trips. Because unlike Sister Ruth she snitched on me to the police and the man in the grey suit came back and asked me about them. He had a big 'V' above his eyes too and lines on his forehead. He doesn't believe all the lovely things I did with Mama. He believes we were locked up all the time like animals in a zoo.

'You're a smart girl, Hannah,' he said. 'Perhaps the smartest girl I've ever met. That's why I believe you know very well what went on at home. And I'm certain you also know that the woman in the hospital can't be your real mama, can she? Her real name, by the way, is Jasmin. Pretty name, don't you think? Why don't you tell me how you met Jasmin?'

'I prefer Lena,' I told him, then said nothing else. I don't talk to people who think I'm lying.

JASMIN

It's Tuesday or Wednesday or some other day. All I know for certain is that it must be after twelve-thirty, because I've already been to the loo. Frau Bar-Lev hasn't come yet. My stomach is gurgling.

What I also know at once is that the knocking, which makes me jump from my reading chair, is wrong. The sequence isn't right, it's not three short knocks, followed by two long ones: *knockknockknock – knock – knock.*

I wipe my eyes – I barely slept last night – and listen. The tap is dripping in the kitchen. In the street below, the traffic is rumbling and a pneumatic drill is whining away.

More knocking at my door. It's too hard and the wrong rhythm. *Knockknockknockknock.*

Four short ones. I cross the sitting room cautiously in my thick woollen socks. The dim light coming from the small lamp on the side table next to my reading chair distorts my shadow, making it absurdly long.

Knockknockknock. Three short ones. I pause. Can that be Frau Bar-Lev?

I creep onwards, knowing I mustn't make a sound, creep along the hallway, my shadow out in front like a sombre advance guard, sidling its way along the bare laminate towards the front door, and me behind.

Knockknockknockknock. Four short ones.

My eyes dart towards the bedroom door to make sure it's closed.

Outside my apartment the floorboard creaks several times, as if someone is impatiently shifting from foot to foot. I hear a woman's voice utter a tentative 'Hello?' and then she says, 'Frau Grass, are you in?'

That isn't Frau Bar-Lev.

When I get to the front door a current is surging inside my chest. Through the peephole I see the distorted image of a woman. A policewoman, perhaps, who's been sent with another query? A keen reporter who's found out where I live and wants to make me an offer for those things that can't be said? Both possibilities only give rise to a more intense surge inside my chest. I'm going to ignore the knocking. I've already turned away and have my back to the door when the voice speaks again: 'Frau Grass, if you're there, then please open up. Frau Bar-Lev has sent me.'

My entire body is seized by the feeling that something's not right, more than just the sequence of knocks. I reach out behind me to a cabinet on the left-hand wall of the hallway and, without taking my eyes off the locked front door, grope along the surface in a pointless search for a weapon. A picture frame clatters to the floor. Startled, I pull back my hand.

'Frau Grass? Are you in?' asks the woman, who must have heard the giveaway sound of the picture frame.

I exhale, turn the key in the lock and hesitantly open the door, just a crack. The woman, who's about my age, has dyed hair, tomato red, with a slanted fringe on one side that falls down her face. She smiles sheepishly.

'Oh good, I thought you weren't in.'

I size her up, note that she's wearing jeans and a T-shirt, and also see the pot she's holding in front of her tummy.

'I've brought your lunch, Frau Grass.'

'Who are you?'

The woman gives a vague nod back towards the stairwell.

'Oh yes, well, hello. I'm Maja, Frau Bar-Lev's neighbour, her next-door neighbour. I live on the second floor too. Frau Bar-Lev went to see her son today and asked me to bring you this.' She points her chin at the pot in front of her tummy. 'She cooked this for you specially. Oh, and here,' she says, tipping her head on her left shoulder. Beneath her crooked arm she's carrying a few envelopes, a rolled-up newspaper and some leaflets. 'I've brought your post too. Frau Bar-Lev says you're recovering from a major operation and you're not so steady on your feet yet.'

'Yes,' I say with determination, at the same time wondering whether she really doesn't know who I am. Hasn't Frau Bar-Lev already whispered to her about the tragic curiosity living on the fourth floor?

Frau Bar-Lev herself knew at once. With her crooked back and cumbersome movements, she was sweeping her doormat when, almost a week ago, just discharged from the hospital, I trudged up the steps to my apartment, accompanied by my mother and a policeman. I was walking with a slight stoop and breathing shallowly. As far as the doctors were concerned, my broken ribs were healing beautifully, but the stabbing pain still occasionally brought tears to my eyes, especially when I put any strain on my body. The cuts on my face were now just small, brown-encrusted triangles, and in some places there was still a slight yellow shimmer beneath the healed bruises.

Frau Bar-Lev put down the hand brush when she saw me and said, 'Good God.' Quite apart from my appearance, the presence of police officers, who must have been in my apartment several times while investigating my disappearance, and who no doubt questioned the neighbours, would have definitely set her thinking. Then there were the reports in the media. I was the woman from the cabin, it was as clear as day. Even if the press, for the sake of victim protection, had only printed my face with a black bar across my eyes or pixelated it, putting two and two together can't have been that difficult.

'Well, I'm sure you know that Frau Bar-Lev's hip means she has difficulties with the stairs,' the woman says. I'm still trying to work out if she's actually been oblivious to the news these past few months, or if she's just sensitive enough to hold back those things that people apparently say and do when they come face to face with the tragic curiosity. The 'Good God', the 'You'll be all right', the sympathetic but fervent gaze that goes right through my clothes like an X-ray, intent on dissecting me for traces of some hellish abuse.

I nod and say, 'Yes, her hip. It's been bothering her for ages.'

That's why Frau Bar-Lev only brings my post on the days when she's obliged to leave the house herself, to go shopping or visit the doctor. Otherwise she doesn't subject herself to the strain of going down all those steps to the mailboxes in the entrance to our building. Or, to be more precise, she doesn't put herself through it just for my sake.

'I recently noticed that your mailbox was overflowing, so I thought –'

'I've never seen you here before,' I state.

'Me? No. I mean, I haven't seen you either, but I've only been in the apartment for a few weeks.'

'Next to Frau Bar-Lev?'

'Yes.' She nods, giving me another smile.

'But there's a family living there.'

'The Hildners, yes. They moved out.'

'I didn't know that.'

'Yes.' The woman shrugs. As she moves her arm the post falls to the floor. 'Shit,' she laughs, and holds out the pot to me. I take it and watch her sink to her knees to gather up the letters. 'Not the best multitasking, eh?' She giggles.

'Wait a sec,' I say, and step back behind the door to put the pot on the cabinet so I can help her.

'It's fine, I've done it.' She hands me the pile of post through the gap in the door.

'Oh yes, Frau Bar-Lev also asked for her dishes back from the past few days.'

I think of yesterday's pot with the stew. The small, fireproof dish with the potato bake and the bowl with the pasta salad that stood outside my door, right on the mat, its inviting logo – *Everybody Welcome* – now very much obsolete. I appear in the door once more. Maja is still smiling.

'I'm sorry,' I say with a slightly forced smile. 'I haven't yet managed to wash the things up.'

'Don't worry, I can do that. Just give me it all.'

In my mind I see myself pottering in the kitchen, ashamedly scraping a few leftovers into the bin, while my front door stands wide open and standing there is the stranger supposedly sent by Frau Bar-Lev. Who now has access to my apartment. I feel a gentle panic well up inside me, a silly panic certainly, but I can't comprehend it with logic and reason. The woman is supposed to bring me food and fetch dishes. What did she want inside my apartment? What did she intend to do to me?

My mind is working feverishly, but I can't come up with any reason to shut the door in her face while she waits outside. No reason that wouldn't make me look like a complete idiot.

'I don't know, I really ought to –'

'Honestly, I don't mind.'

Maja, smiling. Maja, sent by Frau Bar-Lev so I don't starve. She has no reason not to think of me as what I'd sworn I wouldn't be: the poor woman from the cabin, traumatised for the rest of her life, sensing danger in everything and at every turn. It was bad enough that I couldn't bring myself to invite my new neighbour into my apartment while she waited for the dishes. Before, when

Kirsten used to live here, we always had people over we hardly knew. They were just people others had brought along, and who liked to party as much as we did. 'Fewer than a dozen and it's not a party,' Kirsten always said, laughing. *Everybody Welcome* back then, in another life.

I nod decisively, turn around as if being pulled on a string and hurry along the hallway to the kitchen.

My front door, open.

My heart is in my mouth. With jittery movements I stack the baking dish and little pot into the large salad bowl, in which streaks of dried mayonnaise draw accusatory patterns. How can I possibly let the elderly woman cook for me and not even wash up her dishes? *You should be ashamed, Lena. Don't you have any manners?* There must be some Tupperware too somewhere. I turn right around, my woollen socks sliding over the tiles, and reach out for the edge of the work surface to give myself some support. My front door is open. Maja, who I've never seen here before. Who supposedly moved in only recently. Her voice: 'Are you okay, Frau Grass? Do you want any help?'

'No, no,' I call out.

The Tupperware container, the fucking Tupperware, where is the Tupperware? I yank the handle of the dishwasher. Somehow the Tupperware container has made its way into the dishwasher, although it's still waiting there, dirty, alongside a few cups and some cutlery, for me to turn the dial to the right programme. I take the container from the rack and keep the stack of dirty dishes balanced as I carry them through the kitchen and hallway back to my front door. Which is still open. Giving a view of the stairwell. The pile of dishes clunks in my shaky hands.

No Maja. Maja has gone.

You're mad.

Maja was never here, she doesn't exist.

There's just us now. We're your family.

I shoot an uncertain glance at the cabinet. The pot and the post prove she was here. With a clatter, I put the stack of dishes on the floor and venture a peek outside my door. Nothing, just the stairwell in complete silence. Not a trace of Maja. I listen out for footsteps – none. I close the door as gently as possible and tentatively turn my head to peer over my shoulder, while my heart beats in an ominous rhythm.

Why should she have slipped into my apartment? logic and reason ask. There is a reason, panic screams.

JASMIN

The apartment I moved into more than three years ago had the following listing:

Flatmate (M/F) sought for three-room apartment in Regensburg old town. 74m² in building with twelve apart-ments, balcony with mostly good view. Preferably a smoker because I smoke too. Love of animals would be an advan-tage because apart from me, an employee in the hospitality industry, the apartment is also home to a cat. You will have exclusive use of the 12m² bedroom. Kitchen and bathroom shared. We have a dishwasher, fridge, microwave and washing machine. Monthly rent: 310 euros including bills.

The accompanying photographs showed a home, that was my immediate impression. Not a home in the purely architectural sense of four walls and a roof over the head, but clearly a place where someone lived. The rooms looked colourful and slightly haphazard, a collection of furniture from flea markets and little treasures. A dreamcatcher by the bedroom window, a mattress for a bed, above it, in a chunky, ornate golden frame, a kitschy picture of the Virgin Mary with her baby Jesus, and a chandelier with colourful glass beads. In the kitchen, a large, rustic wooden table, its scratches and blemishes visible even from a distance, and one of those large, pink, American-style fridges. Piles of books towered behind the worn-out reading chair in the sitting room, metres of them covering the entire wall. Vast quantities of books, just on the floor, without any shelves. That alone would have driven my mother crazy, and it made me crazy too, but in a completely different way. I was electrified, I simply had to live there. Especially once I'd met Kirsten, who'd posted the ad. Kirsten, who seemed from a different world, who could have lived on Ibiza or another hippy island with her long, brown hair that looked as if it had been tangled by salt water and the wind and not brushed properly for years, in a flowery dress, countless necklaces and brown moccasin boots that were laced up to her knees. Kirsten, who was so cheerful, so full of life and only ever laughed. I was late moving out of home, but that was down to circumstances and probably a misplaced sense of responsibility towards my mother too. After my father's death we only had each other, even if our relationship was more a matter of principle than anything to do with love or affection. Here, in this apartment, I was happy, strong, boisterous. Until Kirsten and Ignaz, a fat black tomcat, moved out about two months before I was kidnapped. I wanted to stay here just as fervently as I'd wanted to move in. I wanted to look after the apartment and the memories associated with it like a legacy, like a witness of an era, a brave remnant defying change; like a plant which grows through grey tarmac that you can pull out as often and forcefully as you like, but you'll never get to its roots. Like the weeds in my parents' drive that my mother never stopped complaining about.

I creep into the kitchen and take a knife from the block. The sharp one that cuts everything, including meat. I search every room, every one of the seventy-four square metres of this former home. I pay attention to the blind spots behind the doors and the floor-length curtains. I even check behind the shower curtain. There's nobody here, the apartment is empty apart from me and my ghosts. For a moment I had been absolutely convinced that Maja had slipped in the door and was waiting in a quiet corner just to pounce on me.

Exhausted, I slump back into my reading chair and pull my knees up to my chest. My right hand is still clenched around the knife. Maybe it's true, maybe I am going mad, properly mad in the clinical sense. Maybe I have been for a while and I really ought to go back to hospital, to a room with a door handle that can be removed for safety reasons. I rest my broken head on my knees and start sobbing. I'm trapped; freedom hasn't changed this one bit. I smell goulash in a stew, and in a person who means me well, I smell a danger that I'm prepared to overcome with a knife. And even now, as I'm feeling mad and stupid, my thoughts cling to the question of why Maja vanished so abruptly. She went without saying goodbye, without a 'I don't want those dirty dishes anymore. I've thought it over and I'd rather you washed them up yourself'. Not even a 'Sorry, I've got to go'. No explanation.

I put the knife down on the side table and struggle out of the armchair. I want to check the door again, to see if I locked it properly. The doctors and my therapists advised me not to be on my own to begin with, seeing as I was leaving the clinic at my own discretion and refused to be admitted to any other specialist institution. I told them I was going to stay with my mother for a while and must have sounded convincing enough.

The door is locked, twice. You can't turn the key any more than that. I take a picture frame from the cabinet and balance it on the door handle. Nobody's going to get into my apartment without the sound of breaking glass acting as a warning. I take a step back and look at the picture: Kirsten and I, our shoulders touching, our heads leaning in slightly to each other. Between us is Ignaz's big black head. Kirsten is holding him under his armpits towards the camera. His front legs are hanging limply, his yellow eyes have narrowed to surly slits. Seconds after the photo was taken he took a swipe at Kirsten. 'Our moody child,' we often said. I sigh. The pile of mail on the cabinet catches my attention. On the top is a newspaper folded in half, yesterday's edition. The front page has a picture of Hannah. She looked pale enough under the gloomy forty-watt bulb in the cabin. Here in the colour photo, which is the size of my hand, she appears almost unreal with her white skin, watery eyes and light blonde hair. With my finger I trace the line of her lips, which curve upwards but almost imperceptibly. Hannah's way of smiling.

Zombie Girl from the Cabin of Horrors!

Cham/Munich (MK) – Two weeks after the spectacular escape from the cabin (as reported here), our editorial team has been anonymously sent a photograph of the daughter of the abducted woman, Lena B. The girl (13) and her brother (11) are currently in therapy. B has been missing since January 2004. According to Chief Inspector Frank Giesner, her whereabouts are unknown, as is the identity of the abductor. The police hope to obtain new clues and information from a three-dimensional facial recon-struction of the man who was fatally injured during the course of Jasmin G's escape. He is believed to be the abductor of both Lena B and Jasmin G. G was kidnapped in May this year and kept captive in the cabin for four months until her escape in September. Only a few, shocking details have come to light about the circumstances of her imprisonment and the state of health of the two children . . .

My concentration wanes, the letters start to swim. Only Hannah's photo remains in focus. I wonder who took it. Who Hannah was smiling for. And then I realise that since I was discharged from hospital I haven't asked after her once. Nor after Jonathan. The vice around my skull tightens.

What kind of a mother are you, Lena?

What kind of monster are you?

The newspaper rustles as it flies into the corner. I massage my temples. To distract myself I grab the rest of the mail and take it into the kitchen. I sit at the table and skim through the letters.

One from my health insurance, probably about them paying for the therapy which I'm not actually doing. A letter from my mobile phone provider and one from the water company. I leave them all unopened apart from one letter from an anonymous sender. A plain white envelope with just my name on it, Jasmin Grass, written in black felt tip in capital letters. Just my name, no address. I tear open the envelope and take out a folded piece of white paper. It has just two words on it: *FOR LENA*.

MATTHIAS

'No, Matthias!'

Shit, I knew it.

'Just no.'

'Darling – '

'No!' Karin's knife and fork clatter on the rim of her plate. I've lost my appetite too, but I'm trying not to let it show, so I cut an especially large piece of my steak. It would be the most normal thing in the world, I tell myself, completely normal, and absolutely no reason to interrupt our dinner.

'Karin, I beg you – '

'I said no.'

She pointedly picks up her napkin and dabs her mouth. Then she gets up from her chair, grabs the plate with her steak, potatoes and beans, which she's barely touched, and takes it into the kitchen. I hear the lid flip up and her dinner being scraped into the bin.

'Karin!' I shout above the noise. 'Let's at least talk about it!'

All I get by way of an answer is the bin lid again and the door of the dishwasher. I try to resume eating. I find the meat tough.

'Are you being absolutely serious?' Karin says, when she reappears a moment later in the doorway between the kitchen and dining room.

I swallow a mouthful of beans and say, 'Of course I'm being serious. It would be the most normal thing in the world to bring her home, to her family. I've already spoken to Dr Hamstedt and she's got no objections. On the contrary, she thinks that it might be of great help for Hannah's therapy.'

'When?'

'Well, as soon as possible. Tomorrow.'

'No, I mean when did you thrash this out with Dr Hamstedt?'

Now I reach for my napkin too and dab the corners of my mouth.

'A few days ago,' I say softly. 'Which, by the way, you would have known if you'd come to visit her.'

'Matthias, don't.'

'But it's true. I mean, you are her grandmother.'

Karin disappears into the kitchen without another word. This time I hear the fridge, then a drawer and finally the plop of a cork.

'Get me a glass too, would you?' I ask her.

I'm going to bring Hannah home whether Karin agrees to it or not. I promised her.

'Grandad,' the little one said. 'I don't like it here. It's a bad place. I can't sleep at night because I'm so sad. I want to go home.' *Grandad*. That was the loveliest thing I've heard in ages.

'Cheers,' Karin snarls when she comes back into the dining room and hands me a glass of red wine. 'Here's to you and your solo efforts.'

'Oh, Karin, please stop that now.'

I watch her wander stiffly around the table back to her chair.

'No, Matthias, I'm not going to stop, no way. You talk with Dr Hamstedt behind my back and then present me with a fait accompli. That's not fair, do you hear me?'

'I just wanted to find out first if in theory it was possible to have Hannah discharged, for a few days at least. And then Dr Hamstedt needed to think about it. But it hasn't escaped her notice that Hannah has been very resistant since she was admitted to the trauma centre. Therapeutically she's not going forwards or backwards. Do you understand that, Karin? They have no idea how to get her started! They can't even make a diagnosis! They can treat the boy, but Hannah, Karin. Hannah . . .' I put down my wine glass and throw my hands in the air. 'For God's sake, that girl is our granddaughter! We have to help her!'

'And how do you suppose we're going to do that? I mean, we're not psychologists! If they don't know what to do with her, how are we meant to cope?'

'Hannah is desperate for a family, for family life, for normality and –'

'Normality!' Karin cuts in. 'She doesn't have any idea what normality is!'

'In that case it's even more essential for us to show her. Look around!' I wave my arms theatrically. 'This! All this! Our house! This is where her mother grew up!'

Karin takes a sip of her wine.

'So how's it going to work?' she asks when she puts her glass back down. 'Are we going to make up the bed in Lena's old room for her?'

I ignore the hint of sarcasm in her voice and nod eagerly.

'And absolutely we have to get her some books, Karin! She's

missing those too. She can't learn anything in the trauma centre. She urgently needs a few schoolbooks.'

'And what, next year we're going to send her to school? Like a perfectly normal child?'

'All I'm saying is that she'll be delighted if we get her a few books. She's so thirsty for knowledge and she really does know a huge amount already. You should hear her, Karin. She's very well educated.'

I can't help smiling when I think of Hannah telling me what 'grandfather' is in Spanish.

'It's not going to work, just think about it.'

Abuelo, that's the Spanish word. *Abuelo* —

'Matthias!'

'Hmm?'

'I said it's not going to work. We can't simply play family.'

'Play, Karin? For God's sake, we *are* a family! She is our grand-daughter, our daughter's child.'

Karin rubs her brow.

'Just for a few days to begin with, darling,' I try. 'That's what I agreed with Dr Hamstedt. And I'll still be taking Hannah to her therapy sessions at the trauma centre. It's just about giving the poor little girl a bit of respite.'

Silence. I know I've almost won Karin round, I know it. She doesn't want to be the heartless grandmother, and she isn't. She's just scared and she wants to do everything properly. Leave Hannah to the professionals. The 'professionals', who themselves don't know what to do with her.

'There's not a huge amount I can tell you at this stage,' Dr Hamstedt said during our last conversation.

We were sitting in her office on either side of her desk. Hanging in frames on the wall behind her were countless accolades identifying her as a 'professional', while on the windowsill to her left, a spider plant with limp, yellowed leaves proved that this supposed 'professional' wasn't even capable of looking after an undemanding houseplant.

'But it's already striking how differently the children seem to be processing what has happened. The way Jonathan is dealing with it is not really surprising; in fact it's,' she said, pausing slightly to make air quotes, '*normal*, even if in these circumstances that word might appear a little strange. Jonathan has nightmares, he screams, he refuses to talk to us. We often find that those who've been through traumatic experiences start by sorting things out for themselves, or at least they try to. We're assuming, however, that over time he will open up. But first he has to feel he can trust us and realise in the longer term that we're all on his side and that he's secure here.'

I started jiggling my leg. Hannah must be waiting for me.

'Well, that sounds encouraging.'

'Hannah,' Dr Hamstedt said emphatically.

'What about her?'

Dr Hamstedt smiled as if she'd caught me doing something.

'We're seeing a completely different pattern with Hannah.'

I stiffen my back and shift on to the edge of my chair.

'And?'

'Her behaviour.'

'What about it?'

'Well, it would be easiest if I tried to explain it using Jonathan as a comparison. That boy has spent his whole life inside the cabin. In cramped, makeshift surroundings, locked away without any windows or contact with the outside world.' She gave an affected pause and only started talking again when I glanced at my watch.

'This world here in its entirety, the hustle and bustle, all these people, the noise, all the things he'd never experienced in the cabin, he finds them completely intimidating. The lift? A disaster! If we want to take him to a different floor we have to use the stairs. And because of his anxieties, even that proves to be a challenge each time. Quite apart from the unfamiliar physical movements. Do you understand, Herr Beck? We're teaching him how to climb stairs like a little child. Of course he finds it frustrating as well. Sometimes he crawls under the table and stays there for hours, or at night he'll pull off his bedclothes so he can sleep on the floor. In this way he's giving us a very clear signal that he's hopelessly out of his depth at the moment.'

I had no idea what she was going to tell me next, but I felt under fire. 'Hannah isn't particularly happy here either,' I said. 'She's sleeping badly, so she tells me every time I come to visit.'

Dr Hamstedt let out a lengthy sigh.

'That may well be, Herr Beck. All the same, she seems to be coping astonishingly well in a world that is alien to her. Or does she appear horribly frightened to you?'

'She's strong,' I say, not without an element of pride.

'Herr Beck, there is a particular neurological disorder we call Asperger's syndrome. Maybe you've heard of it. It's a form of autism and it influences the way in which those affected process stimuli and interact with other people —'

'Hannah's not ill.'

'I wouldn't necessarily describe it as an illness,' Dr Hamstedt said, cocking her head. 'More a disorder. And we're not even certain that Hannah has this disorder, but we'd like to continue examining her.'

I checked the time again.

'All right, Herr Beck. As to your request to take Hannah home with you for a few days, I'm prepared to take the risk. But I must insist that certain conditions are met.'

'No problem.' I nodded and started to get up, finally. Hannah was waiting.

'One second, Herr Beck. I'd also like a quick word with you about your daughter. Lena.' The way she stressed her name made the anger boil inside my chest. As if I could have forgotten it, my only child's name.

'Dr Hamstedt, I really must –'

'I can't begin to imagine how difficult it must be for you still to be without the answers you've been so desperate for.'

I bit my lower lip as a precaution. She was right. Neither of the children had yet made a helpful statement in this regard. It was as if they hadn't even noticed that one day this Frau Grass had appeared in the cabin in Lena's place.

'It must be very frustrating. So I'm all the more pleased by the commitment you're showing as a grandfather. And to support you in this, I'd like to quickly go through the psychological aspects one more time.'

I let go of my lip and sighed. I'd heard it all before. For ever labouring the same comparison. Hannah and the boy, who till now had only been able to view the world as if through a keyhole. Locked up all their life in the cabin where there were only two other figures to relate to: their parents. An environment in which children were required to love their parents unconditionally. An isolation which precluded any possibility of comparison. If they knew nothing else, how could they realise that something very wrong, something terrible was happening around them? How could they learn to differentiate between good and bad? And then their dependence on the father, the bondage developed since birth. They didn't see him as a monster who was keeping them locked up. They were grateful to him for giving them food so they didn't starve, and for lighting the fire so they didn't freeze. And hovering above this all the while, still hovering even now, was the word 'normal'. For Hannah and the boy, the cabin had been normal, their normality. And people rarely questioned their own normality.

'I've already grasped that,' I said, trying to bring Dr Hamstedt's lecture to a swift conclusion. Hannah had now been waiting for me for a quarter of an hour.

'When their father told them to go to their room, in a way this was no different from his saying they now had a new mother,' Dr Hamstedt continued, unperturbed. 'His word was law. It's crucial you don't forget that, Herr Beck. Even if right now you think you can cope with the fact you still don't know what happened to your daughter, the longer this goes on, the more frustration you'll probably feel. A frustration that might escalate rapidly.'

'Please don't take offence, Dr Hamstedt, but right now it's my impatience that's escalating, and extremely rapidly. My granddaughter has now been waiting for me for a quarter of an hour.'

Dr Hamstedt gave a knowing smile.

'Then I shan't hold you up any longer, Herr Beck.'

*

'Has it ever struck you that you only ever talk about Hannah?' Karin says, breaking the lengthy silence between us.

I sigh when I anticipate what's coming next.

'I don't want to talk about Lena now.'

'I don't mean Lena. I mean Jonathan. You called him *the boy* earlier. You said they're able to treat the boy. Didn't you notice?'

'I don't get what you're trying to say.'

Karin sits up in her chair; her back is perfectly straight now.

'Is it because he's got the wrong colour hair?'

'What?'

'Because in your eyes he doesn't look enough like Lena?'

'What are you talking about?'

'You don't see any father in Hannah, just Lena.'

'That's absolute bollocks, Karin.' I try to dismiss her objection with a wave of the hand, but catch my wine glass by accident. The bowl breaks from the stem when it hits the hard wood of our dining table. In a split second a pool of red seeps into the light tablecloth. I leap up, as does Karin.

'I'm sorry, darling,' I say, clumsily dabbing the red patch with my napkin. Karin lifts the edge of the tablecloth to prevent the wine from running on to our beige carpet.

'These things happen.' She looks up. 'But have you considered all the consequences of bringing Hannah here? Can you imagine those journalists and photographers besieging our house again, like they did when Lena disappeared?'

'Oh –'

'The phone keeps ringing all the time as it is. Frau Beck,' she says, imitating a honeyed voice, 'do you still have any hope that your daughter will be found? How are your grandchildren, Frau

Beck? Just a short interview, Frau Beck, we won't disturb you for long.' Shaking her head, she starts clearing the table. 'I don't want to have to go through all that again, Matthias.'

'I know, Karin. But I don't believe that will happen. Why would they hang around here? Why would they waste their time? They won't get an interview, not with us and certainly not with Hannah. And they've already got a photo of her. Why should anyone take the trouble to lie in wait here with a camera? They're calling her the zombie girl, Karin! You've seen for yourself!' I shake my head in disbelief. 'Zombie girl. But she looked so pretty in the photo.'

Karin freezes.

'Matthias, no.'

I lower my eyes. Karin can read me. She's known me for almost forty years. She knows. Her 'no' has got nothing to do with my desire to bring Hannah here. I can sense that Karin understands something bigger.

'You took that photo of Hannah and gave it to the press,' she says eventually. 'You've done it again.'

JASMIN

So far as the pain of my broken ribs will allow, I sit huddled in my reading chair. My fingers clenched around the letter. Trembling.

Are you freezing, Mama?

Be quiet, Jonathan!

I love you, Mama.

Be quiet, both of you! You've got to leave me in peace, do you hear me? I don't feel so well today.

I close my eyes and count my breaths, just as my therapist

advised in the case of a panic attack. 'The voices aren't real, Frau Grass. They're just inside your head. Let them pass over like clouds you watch in the sky. Don't try to banish them, nor the images in your memory. Let them come and pass over; everything is all right, breathe. Breathe, deeply and calmly, breathe in, breathe out . . .'

I breathe.

The voices, they're here. The memory floats upwards, breaches the surface. But it doesn't pass over, it grabs me by the scruff of the neck and drags me down, right into the depths where it's dark, dusky at forty watts. I'm back in the cabin and it's cold, so terribly cold. My breath makes little clouds in the air as I sit at the dining table with Hannah and Jonathan. English is on our timetable today.

'You have to concentrate, Mama. Learning is important. It's important not to be stupid.'

I can't concentrate. The cold. The clouds of breath which remind me how time is passing and I still haven't found a way to escape from this hole. I don't even know if I've been here for days, weeks or months. It could be just a cold summer's day, or winter already.

'Are you freezing, Mama?' Jonathan asks with the naïve sincerity of a child who knows nothing apart from all this here. Your husband has been leaving us on our own more often during the day recently. Supposedly he goes to work, an absurd thought. A monster with a job, possibly a very normal, structured job; a monster with a payslip and insurance cover.

'Mama, I asked if you were freezing?'

Don't call me Mama.

I'm not your mama.

'Yes, Jonathan, I'm really freezing. It's cold today.'

He leaps up from his chair, darts to the sofa, where a woollen blanket is folded over the armrest, and brings it to me.

'Thank you, that's very kind of you,' I say, wrapping the blanket around my body. For the past couple of days all I've been wearing is a thin, ankle-length satin nightie, as a punishment. While I was doing the washing under *Papa*'s supervision I spent a fraction too long with the detergent bottle, scouring the information on its contents. Poison, a possibility.

No possibility.

'You could drink that stuff for breakfast, Lena. It's organic.' A short, horrible laugh. 'You don't appreciate just how much freedom I let you have.'

'Oh, I do appreciate it very much.'

No, I didn't, God decided, and he punished me. No clothes, no stockings, no shoes, just my thin nightie. By now my feet feel like two lumps, foreign bodies that no longer belong to my body, and my fingers are numb. The cold has eaten its way inwards from the goose pimples on my skin, right through my bones. I'm stiff all over. I even find sitting down difficult.

'Next word!' Jonathan calls out, beaming.

'Summit,' I read out robotically. This isn't a textbook in front of me, but a general dictionary. 'Basic English Vocabulary'. We're merely working our way through the alphabet, from beginning to end. Robotically, we do everything robotically.

Jonathan's index finger shoots in the air straightaway; Hannah's doesn't, which is unusual. Instead she's thrown her head back and is letting her gaze wander across the ceiling.

'What's up with you, Hannah?' I ask cautiously.

It seems to take an eternity before she looks at Jonathan, then at me, and says, 'The recirculation unit is broken.'

'Don't worry. I'm sure Papa will be back home from work soon and he'll fix it in no time,' I say.

But I'm wrong. Nobody comes.

A quarter past six – a quarter to seven – half past seven – almost eight o'clock.

We're going to get tired – sleep – suffocate. Jonathan's already yawning.

'Don't worry,' I keep saying.

The air seems to be getting thinner; I can't differentiate anymore between fact and imagination. The ticking of the kitchen clock begins to sound like the beating of a heart, a heart with a loud, muffled, sluggish beat – loud, muffled, sluggish – louder, more muffled, more sluggish. The children, both yawning now, behind their hands at first, then with wide-open mouths. Jonathan, his eyes already closed. Hannah, with Fräulein Tinky on her lap, me reassuring her time and again that she doesn't have to be afraid.

I brace my cold hands on the table and push myself up from the chair. I stagger through the sitting room, stagger to the front door, shake the knob pathetically until I've no more strength and I slump to the floor.

'I'm very tired, Mama,' I hear Hannah say softly.

'I know,' I reply.

Reaching out for the doorknob, I pull myself up on to my weak, cold, stiff legs, and go back to the children, the table. I glance at the kitchen clock, its heartbeats echoing inside my head, almost eight o'clock. I put my hand on Jonathan's shoulder, *wake up, stay awake*, and hear myself say in a surprisingly calm voice, 'Children, it's time for your bath.'

We wander down the hallway, Hannah in front with Fräulein

Tinky, then Jonathan and I, hand in hand. We take turns to go to the loo and clean our teeth, maybe for the last time. I suggest to the children that they sleep with me tonight, in the big bed.

'Can Fräulein Tinky come too?' Hannah asks.

I smile. 'Yes, of course.'

We lie down close together; they mustn't be alone now, that's all I can do for them, be there for them right now; it's not enough. I cry silently. When Jonathan breathes, there's a rattling in his chest.

'We'll definitely wake up again tomorrow morning,' Hannah whispers. 'You don't die that quickly, do you, Mama?'

'That's right, darling,' I say with a smile and kiss her cold forehead. I avoid asking her how long the extractor hasn't been working for, how long ago she stopped hearing the humming. In any case I'm far too tired to utter so many words.

'I love you, Mama,' Hannah says, but I can barely hear her now. 'For ever and ever and ever.'

'I love you both too. Goodnight.'

I wrench open my eyes and gasp for air. I'm back in my sitting room, huddled in my reading chair. In my hand the letter is quivering. The piece of white paper with the accusatory letters on it. *FOR LENA*.

It's not possible.

Is it?

JASMIN

I forced myself to call Kirsten, who is outside my apartment less than half an hour later, knocking just as I instructed her to do over the phone: three short knocks and two long ones. *Knockknockknock – knock – knock.*

'I've been meaning to get in touch,' she says, closing the door behind her. I just nod. I'm mesmerised by the sight of her. She looks so good, tanned. I wonder if she went away on holiday in summer. If she went away while I was locked up in the cabin.

'What a fucking mess, Jassy.' She strokes my hair, which was brown last time we saw each other; it was always brown, but now it's blonde. Light blonde, with brown roots. When I was in the cabin I sometimes imagined us seeing each other again. Only in my imagination she said, 'It's great you're back.'

'In the beginning, when you'd gone, I thought   ' she begins, once we've sat on the sofa in the sitting room.

'I can imagine,' I interrupt her as soon as I can. I don't want to hear that my disappearance could have easily been a melodramatic ploy to get her attention.

Just a few days away, mobile switched off. *Go on, start worrying about me, look for me, find me, take me back home.*

'Is it all true? I mean, what I've read?'

She takes a packet of cigarettes from her handbag and offers me one.

'No thanks, I've given up.'

'How stupid of me. I don't imagine you had any in the cabin.'

'No, I didn't.' I start biting my thumbnail, another annoying habit I ought to have given up a long time ago.

'Well, what about the rest? I mean, what it says in the papers?'

Her lighter clicks. She bends down to the ashtray, which is on the shelf of the coffee table, and puts it on the top.

'Do you mean that we were tied up and had to eat out of dog bowls?' I shake my head. 'We had cutlery and crockery.'

It takes Kirsten a few seconds to decide she can chuckle at this. Much has been written in the papers these past few days; some of it accurate, but a lot of it far-fetched. Sometimes I wish I could bring myself to agree to an interview, to put them right. But I'm scared of the questioning, of some pedantic, overambitious, suspicious reporter trying to dig ever deeper. My brackets are fixed, even if this means that the poor woman from the cabin was fed from a dog bowl.

I show Kirsten the letter.

'This came in the post today.'

Kirsten inspects the piece of paper, far longer than necessary to take in the two words written on it. When she finally looks at me again, I detect a hint of doubt in her eyes.

'It must just be some nutcase who's followed the reports in the media and wants to scare the living daylights out of you. You hear about this all the time.' She puts her head to one side and gives me a searching look. 'Or who else do you suppose wrote it?'

I keep biting my thumbnail.

'Your abductor? Jassy, he's dead. You killed him.'

'I know. But . . .'

Kirsten shakes her head ignorantly.

'What, then? Go on, tell me.'

I take a deep breath.

'The children.'

'What?'

'The children have every reason to be angry with me.'

Kirsten's eyes get bigger, practically bursting from their

sockets. This is what people look like when they come face to face with madness.

'The children? Jassy, what on earth are you talking about?'

I ought to laugh to cover up my silly little outburst, but instead I grab the armrest and try to get up. I can't: the pain.

'There's something else,' I pant. 'In the bedroom. In the chest of drawers, second drawer, in a rolled-up pair of socks.'

Kirsten nods.

'It's okay, Jassy. I'll go take a look, you stay here.'

She gets up, bends down to my legs and lifts them carefully on to the sofa.

'Have a rest,' she says. I close my eyes gratefully.

Soon afterwards I hear the wonderfully familiar sound of her heels on the laminate in the hallway and then a jarring squeak: the handle of the bedroom door. We oiled it hundreds of times, but just couldn't get rid of the squeaking. I don't know how often it woke me at night when Kirsten tried to slip into the bedroom after her shift at the club. At some point we got used to just leaving the door open . . . I tear my eyes open in horror, but I can already hear Kirsten's voice, shrill with shock. 'Jassy! What the . . . ?'

MATTHIAS

Student, 23, missing in Munich

Munich (LR) – The Munich police are searching for clues relating to the whereabouts of Lena Beck, 23, from Munich-Haidhausen. According to eyewitnesses, the student was at a party on Tuesday night in the Maxvorstadt district until around 5 a.m. On the way home she telephoned a friend. Her mobile phone has been switched off ever since. A police search of Munich on Friday produced no leads. Lena Beck is 1.65 metres tall, petite, and has blonde, shoulder-length hair. She was last seen wearing a silver top, black jeans, black boots and a dark blue coat.

That was it, the first article of many – as I so naïvely thought – that would keep appearing until we'd found Lena.

It was the first article of precisely four: four articles over all the years she remained missing. Four serious articles, to be precise. The second one mentioned the police divers sent to check whether Lena might have fallen into the Isar and drowned. Witnesses who were at the party with her said she'd consumed 'large quantities of alcohol and other unspecified intoxicants'. The third article then went off on a completely wild tangent. The *Bayerisches Tagblatt* had interviewed a girl, supposedly a friend of Lena's, who had spoken to her on the phone just before she disappeared. The supposed friend, Jana W ('the name has been changed') was quoted as saying, 'Lena is a girl with a lot of problems.' Apparently she'd been on the verge of abandoning her studies. She'd taken drugs, not just at this party in Maxvorstadt, but at many parties, everywhere. She'd been 'one of those', 'one of those' who'd go off with someone at the drop of a hat. An easy girl: you just had to buy her a beer, it was claimed. By the time the fifth article appeared, the 'Munich student (23)' had become the 'Munich party girl (23)'. At the time I agreed to every bloody request for an interview, even though I already suspected that the press's interest was no longer in finding Lena, or at least helpful witnesses.

I'll never forget the day I met a journalist in my office.

'Lena is a model student,' I said, showing him her semester reports as proof. 'Even as a young girl she wanted to become a teacher. And so her studies are her top priority – besides her family, of course. Our relationship is very close.'

A photographer the journalist had brought along took pictures of her reports and of me sitting upright in my chair, upright in every respect. Matthias Beck, then forty-eight, independent tax adviser with a successful practice, starched shirt and pinstripe suit, neat parting, rational, strong-minded.

'We don't know what's happened to my daughter, but she's already a victim in some way. So I'm not going to allow her to become the victim of a media smear campaign too.' I'd specifically jotted down some notes beforehand, prepared in advance the sentences I was determined to say so I wouldn't forget anything. 'The way she's presented in the media doesn't reflect her character at all, and this type of reporting is also, in my opinion, hampering the police investigation.'

'How are you coping with all of this?' asked the journalist Lars Rogner, a smooth type with dark, gelled hair and a turned-up collar. This was a question I hadn't prepared an answer to.

'It breaks my heart,' I said quietly, a lump in my throat.

Rogner nodded sadly.

'I can well understand that, Herr Beck. Terrible.' Then he cleared his throat and asked, 'How old was Lena when she started taking drugs?'

A question like a fist, a hard right hand that hit me square on and made me slump into my chair.

The following day, of course, Rogner's paper didn't publish the picture of Lena's reports or a determined father sitting upright.

It showed the heap of misery slumped in his desk chair. *Father of missing party girl (23) from Munich: I knew nothing of her double life*, ran the headline.

Karin belted me when she read that. It took her almost a week, and half a packet of opipramol, before she finally believed me that I'd never said those words. After that I would get up earlier every day and get the paper from our mailbox before Karin did. I read it secretly in the garage, sitting on my fishing chair in case my legs gave way as I browsed all the rubbish about my daughter. When I was finished I waited a while for my circulation to return to normal. Then I would fold up the fishing chair, leave the garage and put the paper in our neighbour's bin. I would force a smile on my face, go back into the house and make breakfast. Karin and I came to an understanding that I'd learned something.

'At least she's still in the papers,' we persuaded ourselves. However painful it was, we shouldn't care whether the police and people out there were looking for a model student or a wild party girl. The key thing was that they were still looking for her. The key thing was that she didn't fall into oblivion. Nonetheless Karin made me promise that I'd keep my distance from journalists in the future.

But now she'd found out that I'd intervened again. That it was me who'd passed Hannah's photo to the press. It was a snapshot she'd let me take last week on one of my visits to the trauma centre after I'd shown her my camera.

'Why the hell did you do it?'

Karin is standing beside our dining table, her arms spread wide. I pick up the dishes she has already stacked and take them silently into the kitchen. Karin scurries after me.

'Have you forgotten what happened the last time you got

mixed up with those vultures? How first they tore Lena to pieces, then us?'

'All I want is for them to keep away from Hannah,' I say, making a pitiful attempt at an excuse as I run water into the sink to wash up. Karin's incomprehension moans over the rushing of the water. Me of all people, who ought to have known better.

'And I can't believe you sent the photo to Lars Rogner!'

Yes, Lars Rogner. It had to be him. After all, he was the only one who occasionally filed reports about the case once the world started turning again without Lena.

'Look, he's a father who's experienced tragedy himself. If anyone understands what we're going through, it has to be him.'

Karin gives me a weary chuckle.

'Are you talking about the story he told you back then? That his son supposedly died at the age of eight? Please. I bet that was just a ruse to win your confidence. Lars Rogner wasn't thinking for one minute about Lena, or about us. All he's ever been concerned about are his circulation figures, just like every other rag. And you can't even see it.'

'He didn't just lose his son. His wife suffered severe depression and she killed herself and their child! It's true. I read about it – '

'You're just saying that now because you don't want me to ask you how gullible I think you are. If there were any truth to the story, he wouldn't have done anything like that to us.'

I sigh.

'Come on, Karin, it's okay. Maybe I didn't think the photo thing through particularly well. But all I wanted was for people to see that Hannah's a perfectly normal child. Not a zombie or the daughter of a monster. She's Lena's daughter.'

I turn off the tap, roll up my sleeves and start scrubbing the pan Karin fried the steaks in.

'Glasses, plates and cutlery first,' she says, shoving me aside. 'Pots and pans always at the end, otherwise the water gets filthy right away. Give me that.' She puts her hand into the water to get the washing-up sponge in my hand. 'I do understand, Matthias. You want to protect her, just as you wanted to protect Lena. But this isn't the right way. You're just going to cause more harm. And didn't you say yourself that the little girl needs peace and quiet? So why drag her into the public spotlight? And, if the worst comes to the worst, us too?'

I take the small kitchen towel from the oven handrail and dry my hands.

'Rogner doesn't know that the photo's from me, if that makes you feel better. I created a new email address specially.'

Karin chuckles again, but she still doesn't sound amused.

'Of course you did. Because you knew full well that if I found out you'd got involved with that riff-raff again you'd spend the rest of your days sleeping on the sofa.'

'Do I have to?'

'I'll think about it.'

I hang the towel back on the rail and roll my sleeves down.

'Everything's going to be fine. I'll make sure of that, I promise.'

'That's something else I've been worried about,' Karin responds, sighing. 'But please promise me that you won't make any solo efforts in the future . . .' She breaks off when there's a ring at the door.

'Who can that be at this time of night?' she whispers, then slaps a hand over her mouth, opens her eyes wide and gives the answer herself. 'Gerd!' she gasps. 'They've found Lena's body.'

162

For a few seconds my senses fail me; the finality makes my chest constrict, blood rushes in my ears. My wife's eyes are like saucers. They're glassing over. The hand in front of her mouth is starting to tremble.

The path from the kitchen through the hallway to the front door becomes contorted in slow motion. I sense Karin at my back, I can hear her breathing heavily. It's a long way to the front door, and it's strenuous. I try to comprehend that these will be the final steps I take as the father of a missing daughter. That the steps I will take in future will be as the father of a dead one. Gerd was right: there is a difference between conjecture and knowledge.

 JASMIN

I press my lips together and stare at the ceiling. I hear Kirsten's heels again, this time at small, jittery intervals. I don't have to turn my head to know that now she's standing in the doorway, staring at me incredulously. She didn't make it as far as the chest of drawers.

I picture her placing her hand on the squeaky door handle less than two minutes ago, the bedroom door handle, the door which for good reason is always open and has been closed recently for an even better one. I picture her face and how her heart must have burst when she entered the room.

The white walls papered with you, Lena. With your story.

The walls papered with all the articles I could find about you on the internet. Three hundred and twelve articles. That represents almost an entire packet of printer paper, a change of cartridge, my work for the whole of last night.

I blink weakly when I hear Kirsten's footsteps, now getting closer, tentatively, circumspectly, as if approaching a dangerous animal.

'Jasmin,' she says again.

What else should she think, Lena? How can she not think I'm a madwoman, an obsessive? How could she avoid thinking I was wallowing in my misery? I've locked out the sun, freedom, the world. I ought to take a shower. Go to the dentist because of the hole in my jaw where I'm missing a molar. Go and have my hair dyed. Or at least ask Kirsten to get me a colourant from the chemist's. All her life Jasmin had brown hair. Jasmin ought to open the windows to take a glimpse at the sky, any sky. After her escape from the cabin Jasmin ought to be alive. That's what all the papers are saying. *The victim, Jasmin G, survived her four-month ordeal.*

Survived.

'Jassy?'

Kirsten sits on the edge of the sofa. I make no attempt to look at her; my gaze is fixed stubbornly on the ceiling.

'Why did you do that? Why have you stuck up all those newspaper articles? What are they for?'

I close my eyes.

'Jassy . . .' Kirsten sounds as if she's started crying. I feel her hand on my cheek. 'You're not well. You need help.'

Scream as loud as you like, Lena. Nobody's going to come and help you.

'You need to go back to hospital, Jasmin.'

They've forgotten you, Lena. You've just got us now.

For ever and ever and ever.

A shudder shoots through my body when Kirsten grabs my shoulders and begins to shake me.

'Open your eyes, Jassy! Look at me!'

Open your eyes, Lena. I know you're awake.

I obey.

'Can you hear me, Jassy?' A pale horror has bleached Kirsten's healthy glow, leaving just the ample rouge marking her cheek-bones like a failed attempt at warpaint. 'Can you hear me?'

I nod feebly. A single tear uses the momentum from this move-ment to free itself from the corner of my eye.

'It's my fault,' I whisper.

'Nothing that happened is your fault.'

I shake my head. Another tear is released.

'It's my fault, that's what they're trying to remind me. Because of me the children don't have a father anymore. Nor a home.'

'Yes, right, the letter.'

A second later Kirsten leaps up from the sofa. 'Chest of drawers,' I hear her murmur, before her heels fly across the laminate again. I wipe my eyes with the heels of my hands and sniff. For a while this remains the only noise, no footsteps, nothing suggesting any movement in the bedroom, no drawer being scraped open. Fleetingly I wonder if Kirsten's actually here or whether her pres-ence might have just been another trick played by my deranged mind. I struggle to my feet, breathe away the pain that's flared up again and shuffle into the bedroom.

No trick, she is here, really here. Only she hasn't made it as far as the chest of drawers. Instead she's sitting on the mattress, head back, her gaze sweeping the walls. With difficulty I sit down beside her. It's pointless to deny how I feel. The walls are papered with my state of mind, it's so obvious.

'He never told me the reason,' I begin, my voice cracking, once

165

I've sniffed again and wiped my eyes. 'I mean, I can imagine why he chose me. I just happened to be in the wrong place at the wrong time, and was unlucky enough to look a bit like her.' I gesture with my head at all the photographs. There's barely an article which didn't include a photo of you, Lena, and it's almost always the same one, a snapshot. It looks as if you'd just turned around, as if you'd spun around a millisecond before the shutter was pressed. You're brushing a few blonde hairs from your face and laughing; everything about you is laughter and so carefree. Last night, when my printer was working, whirring away non-stop, I even fancied I could hear your laughter, very quiet to begin with, like a breath. Then each time the printer spat out another image, it seemed to be closer and louder, as if you were here, with me in the same room.

'Why did he choose her, Kirsten? Did she remind him of somebody too, just as I did? But in that case, how come she was allowed to keep her real name and I wasn't? Or did he actually know her?'

'Maybe she was just a coincidental victim, just like you in the wrong place at the wrong time. Do you think you'd feel better if you knew the reason?' She shakes her head. 'After I was attacked in that courtyard, I asked myself this same question a thousand times over. Why me? Why did it have to happen to me? I imagined the man watching me in the club. Maybe he was sitting in the bar, smiling at me as I served him a drink. And maybe I even smiled back in the hope of a decent tip. I really convinced myself that this is what happened, but as you know, I was completely wrong. The guy who raped me was never in the club. He didn't wait until my shift was over and then follow me. He was just a guy I bumped into on the way home. As the police established later, he'd been partying in a different club and was drunk.'

'Yes, I know.'

'He could have met anyone that night, or no one. He met me. Fate.' She shrugs. 'Sometimes there simply isn't a reason, Jassy. Sometimes two people cross paths in a most unfortunate way and all you can do is accept this and somehow carry on.'

'But they caught the guy who raped you. You had the opportunity to ask him why he did it. Even if all you found out was that there was no real reason.' I stretch out my legs and wiggle my toes through my thick socks. My feet are cold, just as everything about me is cold and refuses to get warm again.

Are you freezing, Mama?

'I can't ask my abductor because he's dead. I don't even know his name.'

'The police will find that out soon enough.'

'Do you know how long the police have been investigating this case? And no matter what they believe they've found out, all of it will still just be conjecture. He's dead. Don't you get that, Kirsten? She was his original victim, his reason, his motive.'

'Jassy—'

'How will I ever get closure if I don't know the reason for it all?'

Kirsten nods at the wall opposite. 'Do you think the answer you're looking for is in those newspaper articles?'

'I don't know. I think I just want to know who she was.'

Kirsten laughs. I haven't even mentioned how weirdly comforting it feels to be surrounded by your story and your photos. How it makes being on my own bearable because I don't have to go through it on my own anymore. You went through the same thing, there are two of us. You're here, Lena. You understand me.

'Half of it is nonsense anyway. Just think about it, Jassy. They're now writing that you were tied to a leash and fed from a dog bowl. Do you in all seriousness believe that by reading a few articles about Lena Beck you'll know more than the police?'

'Probably not,' I say quietly.

Kirsten makes a vague gesture with her hands. 'You might as well pin up the articles relating to your own case, but you don't! Because you know damn well how much of it is rubbish.'

'Yes.'

Kirsten gets up, shaking her head, and goes over to the wall opposite.

'Leave it!' I shout when she takes out the first drawing pin. 'Please, Kirsten. It helps me.'

'No, Jassy. It doesn't help you, quite the opposite. You won't ever make any progress if this is the first thing you see when you wake up in the morning.'

'Please,' I say again.

Kirsten sighs and pushes the drawing pin back into the wall. 'Are you going regularly to your therapist?'

'I'll call her tomorrow, I promise.'

Kirsten lowers her eyes and rubs her forehead again with a sigh. Then she looks up again suddenly, as if she'd remembered something important.

'Chest of drawers, you said. Second drawer.'

MATTHIAS

It's not Gerd outside our door. It's Mark Sutthoff, and now everything happens in quick succession. I try to close the door

again, but he's got his foot in, and in the background Karin bel-
lows, 'Matthias!'

Mark Sutthoff in my house.

Mark Sutthoff hugging my wife. My wife hugging Mark Sutthoff.
As I stand in the hallway it feels as if I'm swaying.

'What do you want?'

'Matthias, please,' Karin says.

'I'm sorry to turn up so late and without letting you know, but
I've tried ringing several times and never got an answer.'

'We unplugged the landline,' my wife explains, now with a
hand on Mark's back, leading him into the living room. 'Those
people from the press. The phone wouldn't stop ringing, it was
unbearable. When did you get back to Germany, Mark?'

I follow the two of them like an abandoned dog.

'I just landed. I hired a car at the airport and drove straight
here.'

Mark, taking off his coat and throwing it over the armrest of
the sofa as if he were at home here. Making himself comfortable
on my sofa, his legs crossed casually. Requesting a glass of water,
or a tea – but only if it's no bother – when my wife asks him if
he'd like anything. I start grinding my teeth when Karin scuttles
into the kitchen to put the kettle on: 'It's no trouble at all, Mark.'

'We've been meaning to ring you,' she calls out from the kitchen.

'But then we thought there wasn't any reason to,' I explain when
Karin turns on the tap, crossing my arms in front of my chest.

'Do sit down, Matthias,' Mark says unperturbed, a smile on
his face. His dark brown hair is shorter than it used to be, while
his face – his physique as a whole – looks fuller than the last
time we met, back at police HQ. At the time he was as thin as

a rake, almost emaciated, which emphasised his swollen nose, encrusted with blood, even more. He couldn't really blame me, he said in Gerd's presence; he understood the state I must be in. I just wanted to spit in his face, and in Gerd's too, who was also taken in by this rotten bit of play-acting. In the end Mark collected seven thousand euros for his performance.

'Thanks, but I'd rather stand,' I growl.

'How are you, Mark?' Karin says, coming back into the living room with a tray. Three cups, my cups. I always suspected that Karin had kept in contact with him, but I never asked. I imagine her response would have been to add up the number of times she'd gone to the chemist with prescriptions for opipramol and other sedatives because of me and my solo efforts.

'Yes, Mark,' I say with a smile. 'How is the second-hand car business going?' From the internet I already knew that he'd started up a stage school after moving to France, but it went bankrupt after a few months.

Mark smiles too.

'We don't live in Paris anymore, we've moved to the country. The Marne Valley, it's a beautiful area, incredible countryside. We're making wine. I'll send you a crate, Matthias.'

'Very kind of you.'

Karin, who's now sitting down, clears her throat and puts the tea bags on a separate saucer.

'Here, Mark,' she says, gesturing to him to take a cup. 'How are your wife and daughter?' Mark has a daughter. First he had mine, now he's got one of his own. I feel a throbbing above my left eyebrow.

'Fine, fine,' he says, sipping his tea.

'How old is the little one now?' Karin asks.

'She's nine. Time flies.'

'Yes,' Karin says wistfully. 'Sometimes.'

'Any new developments about Lena?'

The throbbing above my eyebrow gets worse when he utters her name.

'Since when has that interested you?'

Mark noisily puts his cup down and looks at me. If I didn't know him I'd think this comment had hit him hard, a good shot, accurate. The corners of his mouth sag and I even think I can detect a slight quiver around his chin.

'It always interested me, you know that perfectly well.'

Karin gives his knee a pat of encouragement and he takes her hand. Mark Sutthoff and my wife are holding hands. I imagine what those hands might have done to my daughter. Grabbed her, strangled her, dug her a grave.

'Mark Sutthoff has an alibi,' Gerd revealed to me at the time.

I shook my head.

'Alibi, what does that mean? People lie to give alibis.'

'Matthias, he wasn't in town during the week before Lena's disappearance.' Gerd threw his hands in the air when he saw I was still shaking my head. 'For Christ's sake, Matthias, he wasn't even in the country! He was in France! We've got his plane ticket, the hotel reservation, statements from the hotel staff and his companion!'

'What companion?'

Gerd stared at me for a moment.

'A woman.'

'A woman?'

'Herr Sutthoff said that he and Lena had already split up several weeks before. We found text messages on his mobile which prove this, but also suggest that they were staying in contact and planned to meet up when he got back. They wanted to make another go of it.'

I look away.

'I know we've had our difficulties in the past, Matthias,' I hear Mark say. I nod feebly, a memory. My hands on his collar, his back against a wall, his face lobster-red. *Where is she, you bastard?*

'But, like you, I was always hoping that what happened to Lena would come to light. I never forgot her.' When he laughs it almost sounds bitter. 'Just ask my wife. She's fed up with hearing stories about Lena. But what can you do? Your first major love never goes away.'

Karin sighs, sounding almost ecstatic.

'That's why,' Mark continues, 'I jumped on the next plane when the police contacted me.'

The throbbing above my eyebrow stops all of a sudden.

'The police?'

Mark nods.

'Yes, that Bernd Brühling called me yesterday. It seems like they need my help.'

'Gerd Brühling,' I correct him. It's a silly, automatic response, but my mind is trying to get to the bottom of this. 'Your help? With what?'

'I don't know yet for sure. But,' he says, taking a deep breath, deep and dramatic, 'I hope you realise I will do everything I can to help find Lena.' He turns to Karin, who looks touched. 'I have a daughter now myself. I don't know how I'd have got through these past few years if I'd been in your shoes.' Now he looks at me. 'I'd have probably gone mad.' I ignore his suggestive gaze.

'But Gerd Brühling must have said something to you on the phone.'

Mark shrugs.

'Only that I might be of some help now that they've found the other woman and have a new lead. How are the children, by the way? A boy and a girl, wasn't it? Good God,' he says, smiling and deep in thought. 'My Lena, a mother, unbelievable.'

'*Your* Lena –'

'The children are as you might expect given the circumstances,' Karin says hastily. 'But I wouldn't call it good. Jonathan is severely traumatised, while the psychotherapists suspect that Hannah has a mild form of that . . . Darling, what's it called again, that syndrome?'

'Asperger's,' I grunt.

'Asperger's, exactly. It's a type of autism that makes interaction with other people difficult for those affected. In communication, for example. They have a tendency to take things literally and not really understand the context in which something is said . . .'

'Sure, but it's hardly normal for a child to spend their whole life isolated in a cabin. How is that poor girl supposed to relate to other people? She's got no experience of it.'

'My words exactly!' I exclaim, sticking my finger in the air. 'My words exactly, Mark! They can't diagnose a disorder so quickly! You should see how clever Hannah is!'

'But Matthias, Dr Hamstedt explained it to you,' Karin interjects. 'Many people with Asperger's are of above-average intelligence. It's far more about how they experience the world . . .'

Mark shakes his head.

'Maybe the girl just needs to get used to everything.'

'Exactly my point,' I say, clapping my hands.

Karin sighs.

'We'll see what happens. At least in Regensburg they're in the best possible hands. The therapist treating them is totally committed.'

'Something Karin can only guess at,' I say to Mark. 'She doesn't come with me when I go to visit the children.'

'No?' Mark gives Karin a look of surprise. She lowers her eyes.

'I've got to get used to everything too,' she says.

'I'm sure it'll all be fine in the end,' he says, reaching for her hand again.

'When are you meeting Gerd?' I ask.

'As soon as possible, I suppose. I couldn't tell him on the phone which plane I was taking. So he doesn't know I'm already in Germany. But I'll give him a call first thing in the morning.'

'Will you keep us updated?'

'Of course, Matthias. Of course I will.'

Father of missing Munich party girl found guilty of assault

Munich (LR) – Matthias Beck, the father of the Munich party girl, Lena Beck (23), who has been missing since January, was yesterday found guilty of assault. Munich District Court sentenced the 48-year-old to a fine of 70 days' salary, after he was found guilty of assaulting his daughter's ex-boyfriend, up-and-coming actor Mark S (26). According to his own statements, Matthias Beck was convinced that S was responsible for the disappearance of his daughter. When handing out the fine, the court took into consideration Matthias Beck's psychological condition at the time of the assault, based on an expert testimony. The judgement is final. The victim, Mark S, seemed happy with the proceedings. 'When Herr Beck went at me like a wild animal I feared for my life. I'm pleased that the court hasn't let him get away with it. While I sympathise with his grief, Herr Beck's explosive behaviour must be checked to protect not just me, but the public as a whole.'

JASMIN

Chest of drawers, second drawer down. I'm still sitting on the mattress, watching Kirsten feel for the right pair of socks, then unroll it. I gaze at her face. Her eyes, usually so clear, now cloudy. Her lips thin and drawn. With shaky fingers she's taken the shard of glass, still with dried, brown streaks of blood on it, from the tangle of socks.

'Was this . . . ?'

'That is the piece of the snow globe that the police didn't find.'

'Why did you take it with you from the cabin? Surely not as a souvenir?'

I shake my head.

'Hannah gave it to me. In hospital. The doctor had administered a sedative and I was fairly out of it. Then Hannah came into my room and put the piece of glass in my hand. She said: *I remember every detail.* I thought I'd dreamed it when I first woke up, but then I realised I was clutching the piece of glass.

'But why did she give it to you?'

'I couldn't find an explanation for that, either, at first. But after seeing that letter, I think she was trying to remind me of my guilt.'

I think back to the ambulance and the strange feeling I had when I heard the voice. *Her name is Lena*, she said, the voice, which at the time I didn't think could be real, but must be a result of the sedative or the shock. The strange feeling, which was even stronger later when I learned from Cham and Munich that Hannah had actually come with me in the ambulance and was now here in the hospital, probably just a few rooms away, one floor at most. The strange feeling that something wasn't right. Hannah would never have left the cabin. Even though I'd screamed at her only a few hours earlier. I'd screamed at both of them to follow me. *Come on, children! Let's go!* But they didn't come. Jonathan was whimpering quietly as he kneeled beside the lifeless body on the floor. Hannah was standing beside him, staring at me in disbelief. I'd just struck their father, with full force, with an archaic cry, with the snow globe.

'They're blaming me for their father's death.'

'Jassy, they're little children.'

'Hannah's thirteen already and Jonathan's eleven.'

'They're children.'

'The shard is a sign.'

'Oh, please.'

'And the letter was meant as a reminder. I should never forget what I did to them. They wanted to keep me as their mother for ever and ever and ever. And I destroyed everything for ever and ever and ever.' I lower my voice to a whisper. 'She remembers every detail.'

176

'Jassy, the letter doesn't even have a sender. It must have been put straight into your mailbox. You don't seriously believe that two children being treated in a psychiatric institution were allowed out to roam Regensburg and deliver letters?' She twiddles the bloody piece of glass in her fingertips. 'Why didn't you hand this over to the police?'

'I don't know. I think I just didn't want to have to do any more explaining. So I hid the glass in the gap between my bed and the mattress, then in the overnight bag that my mother brought to hospital for me.' I pause to read Kirsten's face, a face that was once so familiar. In which the twitch of an eyelash contained an answer and pursed lips an entire discussion. The face that's so alien to me now, just as mine must appear alien to her. As everything about me must appear alien.

'You don't understand,' I tell her.

Kirsten doesn't respond.

'It's okay. You don't have to.'

'But I'd like to, Jassy! It's just so bloody hard to follow you.'

I give a feeble smile. He was right.

You don't have anybody anymore, apart from us. You'll feel better when you understand that.

HANNAH

I liked it better here in the beginning. In the children's clinic, I mean. It wasn't that good, but it was better. Jonathan and I could sleep in the same room. We were allowed to eat together there too, just the two of us, rather than go to the big hall with the other children. Frau Hamstedt and her helpers left us in peace. Although they came to check on us regularly, that was all right. We were allowed to go to the toilet punctually and they kept asking us if we needed or wanted anything. I said I wanted Fräulein Tinky, but Frau Hamstedt said the police hadn't found her. I think she escaped when Mama and I ran out of the cabin that night. Or when the police went into the cabin. I bet they didn't close the door properly. I imagine Fräulein Tinky getting very scared of all those policemen she'd never seen before and running off into the woods. And now she's sitting somewhere in the dark undergrowth, scared because she's hungry and can't find her way home. Or, worst of all, she has found her way back to the cabin, but now she's even more scared because none of us are there.

'I'm sorry, Hannah,' Frau Hamstedt said when I wept. 'I know how important your cat is to you. I'm sure she's fine.' Then she said that animals weren't allowed in the children's clinic anyway. That was what made me think this couldn't be a particularly nice place.

And after a few days I knew I was right.

They said it was better if Jonathan and I had our own rooms and ate in the big hall with the other children. They also stopped asking if there was anything we wanted and they locked the toilet. I was pretty good at holding it in, but Jonathan wet himself three times. It was then that they gave him the yellow pills and they were okay. At least he made an effort with his drawings and talked to me. Not to the others, but he did talk to me. Once he said we had to be here as a punishment. 'That's not true,' I said and told him not to worry because someone would pick us up soon. A promise is a promise and promises don't get broken. He didn't believe me.

178

Shortly afterwards he started hitting his head on the table whenever we were eating. Then they gave him the blue pills. Now he doesn't talk anymore and just scribbles when it's drawing time. I've told him he needs to make more of an effort, but he simply won't listen to me. His scribbles are so ugly that we're not even allowed to have drawing time together anymore. His drawing time is always earlier than mine. I hardly see him any longer, only when he comes out of drawing from Frau Hamstedt's office and I'm waiting in the corridor to go in. Like today.

I don't like his stupid eyes. I know that it's the blue pills making him stare so idiotically, but it's making it harder for me to love him. He doesn't say 'hello' either when he sees me. You always have to be polite and say 'hello'. Frau Hamstedt pushes him out the door and then it's just a few steps along the corridor to the helper who brought me here and who's waiting for him.

'Would you look after the young man, Peter?'

'Okey-dokey,' the helper replies, which isn't a proper word. Then to Jonathan, he says, 'So, little man, how are you today? Have you been drawing with Dr Hamstedt?' Jonathan shuffles beside him without giving an answer. 'Great,' the helper says anyway. 'Now we can take you back to your room, mate.'

I watch them wander down the corridor. Apart from his stupid eyes, Jonathan looks completely different in other ways too. Even from behind I can see that his hair hasn't been combed. In the middle, where he laid his head on the pillow last night, his hair has gone flat on both sides, while the funny grey trousers they've given him almost hang down to his knees. I've been given some trousers like that, but mine are pink. I'd rather have my own things from home.

'So, Hannah,' Frau Hamstedt says when Jonathan and the helper are almost at the glass door which leads to the stairwell. 'It's your turn now, hmm?'

'Yes,' I say and slip past Frau Hamstedt into her office.

The window is open. Frau Hamstedt always airs the room in between drawing times. I like it when the window's open. Because it means the blind's up too and I can see the sky. Sometimes it's really blue, sometimes grey, but it's never brown because I don't go into Frau Hamstedt's office with sunglasses on. I don't like the brown sky at all. I wait until she's closed the window and pulled down the blind. Then she tells me to sit. My seat is at a children's table where the drawing pad and sharp pencils are ready. Further back in the room is Frau Hamstedt's large desk. It's got chairs too, but I've never sat there.

'Two things are different today, Hannah,' Frau Hamstedt says, sitting at the children's table with me. I pinch my lip as I don't want to laugh at her because her long legs don't fit properly under the low table. You must never laugh at someone, even if the way they're sitting looks funny.

'Would you like to know what?'

I nod.

'First, I've got some good news for you. Would you like to hear it?'

I nod again.

'Your grandfather's coming to fetch you.'

My heart is beating faster.

'To take me home?'

Now she's nodding.

'Are you pleased?'

I want to nod again, but I leave it because I think it'll look stupid if the two of us keep taking turns to nod. In any case her question is a stupid one, because I've already told her a hundred times that I want to go home. So of course I'm pleased. 'Right now?' I ask instead.

'Later. I need you for the time being,' Frau Hamstedt says. She sounds very important.

'Why?'

'This is the second thing that's different today.'

With her long legs she gets up awkwardly from the little chair and walks over to the large desk. I can only see her back, but I hear her rustling paper. When she turns to me again she's holding a drawing. I know at once that Jonathan did it: black scribbles. Frau Hamstedt returns to the table and squeezes herself back into the chair. Only now do I realise that he actually drew something different under the black scribbles.

'Go on, you can have it,' Frau Hamstedt says, waving the piece of paper at me. I take it and put it on the table in front of me. Since we stopped drawing together Frau Hamstedt hasn't shown me any of Jonathan's pictures.

'I need your help, Hannah, to work out what it is he drew there.'

I trace my finger over what remains of her face below the scribbles. He did it well; just for once he's made a real effort.

'That's your mama, isn't it?'

He's given her a long dress. But her feet must be cold because he's forgotten to draw her any shoes, the silly little boy.

'Hannah?'

'Yes, I think so.'

181

'And that's your real mama? I mean, the woman who gave birth to you and Jonathan? Or is it the woman who came to the cabin after her?'

'Papa said that's not important.'

'Not important?'

I shake my head.

'It doesn't matter whether she gave birth to us or not. What's important is that she behaves well and loves us.'

'That's what your papa said?'

I shrug.

Frau Hamstedt looks at me as if I ought to say something else, but I don't. Eventually she's had enough of waiting for an answer and starts speaking again herself.

'Take another look at the picture, Hannah. A close look.'

I look. Mama's holding something in her arms, a bundle with a face.

'I can see a baby in her arms.' Frau Hamstedt taps the bundle. 'Is that Jonathan?'

I shake my head.

'Or you, Hannah? Is that you?'

'It's meant to be Sara, but Jonathan hasn't drawn her particularly well, do you see?' I point to the mouth. 'Here she's smiling, but in fact all she ever did was howl.' When I look up there are red blotches on Frau Hamstedt's face and neck.

'Who is Sara?'

'Our sister.' I scratch my neck, which has started itching as if I've been infected by Frau Hamstedt's blotches. 'But we didn't keep her for very long because she was nothing but trouble.'

MATTHIAS

After an initial examination at the hospital in Cham, which the police had ordered, the children were taken to Regensburg. Although Cham has its own psychiatric clinic, it doesn't specialise in treating children. I'd have preferred them to be admitted to an institution in Munich, but as I didn't yet have any DNA proof that I was the grandfather, they ignored my requests. For two weeks now I've been driving between Munich and Regensburg every day. An hour and a half if the traffic's good. Karin thinks that's too long. Too much time which could be put to better use. She keeps asking me when I'm going to re-open my office, and even says it would do me good to work on tax documents with other people again. But both of us know that ever since Lena disappeared, and the mud-slinging in the press that followed it, I've hardly had any clients. Since the night of the accident two weeks ago a sign has been hanging on the door that says: *Closed due to family emergency*. Karin pops in occasionally to listen to the answerphone messages and water the plants. I used to be able to afford two assistants, back in the day when my clients saw me as a meticulous tax advisor rather than the violent criminal who'd badly beaten up the nice up-and-coming actor. What Karin doesn't yet know is that I'm considering closing the practice for good. I am, after all, sixty-two now. The mortgage has been paid off and we have some savings. I could retire and be a grandfather. *Abuelo* . . .

'No, I don't want you to,' I told her at breakfast when she said she was thinking of coming with me today to fetch Hannah from Regensburg. 'The drive is too long, you're right. The section on

183

the A9 is usually congested. You know how long it always takes me.' So many dinners have gone cold over the past two weeks.

In truth I'm looking forward to picking up Hannah on my own. The idea of being able to drive home with her feels like a celebration. Lena loved going in the car when she was a little girl. Occasionally, when it was a long drive, she made me stop en route. Once, when she spotted an entire field of sunflowers, she grabbed my headrest with her little hands and shook it until I gave in. We parked at the first opportunity and went back to pick sunflowers and gaze at the cloud formations. Sometimes our reason for stopping was just a service station with the prospect of an ice cream. I think Lena told Hannah about this, and in great detail too. She told her everything. For example, Hannah knows what our garden plot looks like as if she'd been there hundreds of times herself. Our plot is just outside of Germering, where we live, not far from Munich. It's an idyllic spot right on the edge of the forest. I inherited it from my mother, Lena's grandmother. We used to spend many a weekend there. Lena loved the hydrangeas. Once Hannah's settled in with us, I'm going to take her to the garden as soon as I can, before the hydrangeas wither.

So now I'm sitting in our old Volvo, the back seat still empty. It's another twelve kilometres to Regensburg. My mobile buzzes inside my jacket pocket. I leave it, not because you shouldn't use a mobile phone while driving, but because it strikes me that it might be Dr Hamstedt calling to say she's changed her mind, I can't pick Hannah up. Or Karin. Karin might say the same thing, but for other reasons. I turn up the radio. The weather report is promising an absolutely gorgeous late summer's day. I'm not going to let anyone ruin that for me.

It's almost half past eleven when I turn into one of the visitors' parking places behind the large building. I'm really early – we'd agreed twelve o'clock. I turn off the engine and take the mobile from my pocket. I've missed four calls. All from Karin. She's sent me a text message too, but I'm careful not to open it. There is no way back. This is the most normal thing in the world. Hannah belongs to us. I put the mobile back into my pocket and get out.

The district clinic consists of several buildings dotted around the campus like a small village. Every day I walk past the unmissable sign pointing the way to the 'Clinic for Paediatric and Adolescent Psychiatry, Psychosomatic Medicine and Psychotherapy' and look at the ground. 'Psychiatry' is an ugly word. For Hannah it's a 'children's clinic', for me a 'trauma centre'.

I enter the building, which reminds me of a huge, multi-storeyed version of Lena's old primary school: lots of glass and colourful steel struts. The woman on reception knows me by now and raises her hand.

'Good morning, Herr Beck!'

'Hello, Frau Sommer. I'm quite early.'

'That doesn't matter. Please go up. They're already waiting for you anyway.'

I realise at once that it's Frank Giesner, even though he's got his back to me as I walk along the second-floor corridor towards Dr Hamstedt's office. It seems as if he only has that one suit, mouse-grey; it's too broad at the shoulders and makes his back look bigger than it really is. With him is another policeman, in uniform, and Dr Hamstedt. They talk in hushed tones until Dr Hamstedt notices me and pauses, and a second later all three of them have turned in my direction.

'Ah, Herr Beck, it's good you're here,' Giesner says.

I begin to shuffle. It briefly crosses my mind that for some reason Dr Hamstedt has called for police support to stop me from taking Hannah away. I square my shoulders and jut out my chin. Hannah is my granddaughter, I'm her *abuelo* and I'm taking her home.

'Dr Hamstedt, Herr Giesner,' I say curtly. I give the uniformed policeman a nod.

'Herr Beck,' Dr Hamstedt says with a smile. 'I'm glad you're here.'

'Is there something wrong with Hannah? Where is she?'

'Don't worry, Herr Beck. She's waiting in my office with a nurse.'

'Is there a problem?'

Giesner puts a hand on my shoulder and sighs. 'There's been a new development,' he says. 'Dr Hamstedt called me earlier to tell me about a therapy session she'd had with Hannah. Apparently, Herr Beck, there's a third child.'

'Sara,' Dr Hamstedt adds.

'Sara,' I repeat inanely.

Dr Hamstedt nods.

'We need you now, Herr Beck. Help us to talk to Hannah.'

HANNAH

Mama's screaming made me worried. Worry isn't really fear, but it's not good either. I leaped up from the edge of the bed and squeezed myself up to Papa, who was standing beside the bed. It was lucky he was there because he could make the cabin warm and cook for us. Now he held me very tight. His large, warm hand was over my right ear and I could hear the sea. I'd pressed my left ear against his chest. On one side the sea was roaring, on the other his tummy was gurgling.

'Don't worry, darling,' he said, stroking my hair. 'The pain is a good thing. It means the baby's on its way.'

I turned to look at Mama who was writhing on the bed. Her face looked really ugly. The sheet made waves beneath her convulsions. Her chunky silver bracelet clattered against the bedpost and her legs were tangled up in the duvet.

'It's fine, Hannah, it's all fine,' she blurted out between two screams.

'Shall we help Mama by holding her hand?' Papa said.

I wasn't sure at first, but then I nodded. Everything was fine. The pain was good. The baby was on its way.

But that wasn't the case. They were wrong. The baby wouldn't come.

Mama had been screaming since yesterday.

I didn't want to hold her hand anymore, none of us did. We were tired, nobody could sleep with all that screaming and we were all nervous. Even Fräulein Tinky. She'd knocked over my cup that morning. My hot chocolate had spilled all over the table and floor. She knew she wasn't allowed on the table. Papa came. He'd probably heard me giving Fräulein Tinky a telling-off. He agreed with me that cats weren't allowed on the table. Fräulein Tinky tried to hide under the sofa, but he found her, grabbed her by the scruff of the neck and took her outside, outside the front door.

I thought that was okay at first; after all, she had to learn. But no sooner had Papa locked the door again than I started getting scared. It was dangerous outside. What if Fräulein Tinky got lost and couldn't find her way home? If she got frightened? If she thought we didn't love her anymore? Now Mama's screams were really horrible. Papa was going to check on her, then get a bucket and a cloth so I could clean up the mess Fräulein Tinky had made.

'Papa?' I managed to say just before he left the room.

He turned around.

'Is there something you want to tell me, Hannah?' He smiled, went on one knee and held his hand out to me. Our eyes were at the same level. Papa always says that if you can't look someone in the eye they've got something to hide.

'We have to let Fräulein Tinky back in. It's far too cold for her outside.'

'She needs to be taught a lesson, Hannah,' Papa said, giving me a kiss on the forehead. 'Now I've got to check on Mama, darling. She needs me.'

I nodded.

I heard Mama screaming. And Fräulein Tinky outside, scratching the door and meowing woefully . . .

'Hannah?' It's Grandad. He must have realised I was lost in thought.

In turn I see him, Frau Hamstedt and the policeman in the grey suit. They're sitting with me in Frau Hamstedt's office, waiting for me to tell them something about Sara. But I don't want to talk about Sara. I told Frau Hamstedt about her this morning. Surely that's enough. I told her that Sara was our sister and we didn't keep her for long. Frau Hamstedt wanted to know more. 'What do you mean by that, Hannah?' 'What does that mean?' 'Would you like to do a drawing?'

I said 'no' in my lion voice and told her I wanted to go back to my room. I wanted to have a rest because you always have to have enough rest before you do something special. And today I was going to do something special.

My grandad's going to take me home. I'm his favourite grandchild, I've known that for a while. He doesn't go to appointments with Jonathan, but that's not Grandad's fault. Jonathan doesn't want to leave the clinic. That's why he hasn't been to see the dentist and hasn't got a star sticker either.

'Hannah?' Grandad says. 'You can tell them. I'm here too, there's no need to worry.'

I'm not worried, I just don't want to talk about Sara anymore. The world doesn't just revolve around her. There are far more important things.

'Has anyone found Fräulein Tinky yet?' I ask. 'I bet she's really missing me.'

MATTHIAS

Giesner wants us to go on a little stroll around the grounds of the clinic. I'd have rather left with Hannah right after the conversation in Dr Hamstedt's office. We could have been halfway down the motorway by now. But, with a doubtful glance at Hannah, Giesner said, 'Dr Hamstedt has told me about your plans.' At least he had the decency not to discuss these in front of the girl. He nodded towards the door.

'Let's go and stretch our legs, Herr Beck.'

Hannah stayed with Dr Hamstedt. I promised I wouldn't be long and thought I could see a fleeting smile dart across her lips. Her smile is really enchanting.

'I can understand that you want to take the girl back with you,' Giesner says the moment we step out of the large glass door and on to the gravel path that runs around the clinic.

'Dr Hamstedt is in favour of the idea,' I say cautiously. If Hannah and I were to set off in the next half an hour we'd be able to stop once or twice on the way. Otherwise it'll be too late; Karin was right about that. She said it would be better if Hannah got to know her new home in daylight. Although Karin's reasoning was that if Hannah didn't feel comfortable at our house I'd be able to drive her back to the clinic in time for dinner. I said, 'That's what we'll do, darling,' and smiled.

'Yes, I know,' Giesner says, putting a cigarette between his lips. I didn't know he smoked. 'Want one?'

I tap the left-hand side of my chest and say, 'My doctor would tear strips off me. It was a close-run thing on two occasions.' I've no idea why I'm telling him about my dicky heart. Maybe it's to make him feel sympathy – *just let the sick old man have his granddaughter, he's not got long to go.* And indeed, there is a hint of concern on Giesner's face.

'I'm sorry,' he says, blowing the smoke from his first drag over his shoulder, away from the sick old man. 'Would you rather I . . . ?'

'No, no, it doesn't bother me. You wanted a word.'

'Yes. As I say, I can understand you want to take Hannah back with you. The question is – and I've put this to Dr Hamstedt too

– is there any way we can use the situation for our investigation? Dr Hamstedt thinks there might be a chance.'

'I don't understand.'

Giesner points to a bench a few metres away on the edge of the gravel path.

'Let's sit down over there for a moment.'

We wander over in silence, our shoes crunching on the gravel.

'Herr Beck,' Giesner begins again when we're sitting, 'Hannah is an important, but also very tricky, witness. I don't understand much about psychology, but it makes sense to me when Dr Hamstedt warns us against putting her under pressure. On the other hand, she hasn't been particularly helpful for our investigation so far.'

'Aren't children always tricky witnesses?'

'Hmm, you might be right.' Giesner takes a puff on his cigarette. 'When we question children we usually come up against two types of reaction. It takes some of them a long time to start talking because they're intimidated, and then they only say the bare minimum. By contrast, others are talkative from the start and just keep babbling away as if they'd been waiting for their cue. Along with a description of the perpetrator, you get details of what they had for lunch and what Ernie said in the last episode of *Sesame Street*.' He smirks, I don't. When he notices the lack of any change in my expression, he clears his throat. 'Well, what I'm trying to say is that these children, some of them quite a bit younger than Hannah, at least understand why we need their assistance and make every effort to help solve the case.'

'To be perfectly honest, I still have no idea what you're getting at.'

Giesner bends down to the side of the bench to stub out his cigarette.

'Hannah doesn't obviously belong in either of these two categories, which makes the whole thing even more complicated.' When he sits up again I notice a strange expression on his face. 'She's got a really enquiring mind, don't you think?' he says with a frown and searching, narrowed eyes. 'For example, she was able to tell me how the blue lights on a police car work. But when I ask her for her father's name, I only ever get "Papa" as an answer, or nothing. And I wonder why. This is a girl who seeks answers to everything. Has it never surprised you that Frau Grass suddenly appeared in the cabin as a replacement for Lena? Did she accept her mother's disappearance just like that?'

'Please,' I say, waving my hand in the air in annoyance. 'You're not seriously saying that Hannah might be deliberately holding back information?' I laugh. 'It's called *trauma*, Herr Giesner. And who knows what that monster might have done to her if she'd dared ask the wrong questions?'

Giesner looks at the ground and starts scraping at the gravel with the tip of his shoe.

'But now the monster is dead,' he says after a while, looking me straight in the eye. 'I've questioned Hannah nine times over the past fortnight, Herr Beck. Nine times.' He shrugs. 'At least I now know how tall the Eiffel Tower is, which she claims to have visited with her mother. Three hundred and twenty metres.'

'Three hundred and twenty-four,' I correct him and begin shifting around uneasily on the bench. The hard wood now feels very uncomfortable. 'With all due respect, Herr Giesner, I don't think that either you or I are in a position to appreciate just what happens to the human psyche in such extreme situations. But at least you have the cabin, a dead body and the DNA kit. So why don't you solve the case without Hannah's help? And find my daughter's body.'

'That's exactly what we're trying to do, Herr Beck! And I believe that Hannah could be a real help in this. It's just that she seems to be holding something back from us. What could that be, Herr Beck?'

'Why don't you just leave my granddaughter in peace and turn your attention to Frau Grass instead? You want me to question Hannah, don't you? That's what you meant at the beginning when you said: *is there any way we can use the situation for our investigation?* You say you don't want to put her under pressure. No, because you want to leave that job to me, don't you? You want me to solve your case, that's the long and the short of it!'

'For heaven's sake, Herr Beck, nobody has said that. All I thought was that you've developed a rapport with Hannah, and so there's every chance she might open up to you and tell you things which might be helpful for the future course of our investigation.'

'Investigation,' I mutter.

'I'm simply asking for your help. You want to find your daughter and so do we.'

'I'll give you some help: Frau Grass is a liar. You're very welcome.'

'Do you have any concrete proof? What makes you think that? Has Hannah by any chance said anything –'

'What makes me think that? Common sense, Herr Giesner! You don't just get abducted and live for months with a family, playing mother and wife . . .' Giesner opens his mouth to interrupt, but I hold up my hands defensively. 'Yes, yes, I know, she was forced. But did she never try to find out what was really going on there? What happened to the woman who must have been there before her? Did she never try talking to the man who supposedly abducted her? Surely you can't believe all that, Herr Giesner!'

'Herr Beck, Frau Grass is a victim, just like your daughter.'

'But unlike my daughter she made it out of the cabin alive.'

'I understand your anger. But don't take it out on Frau Grass. That's unfair, don't you think so?'

I sigh.

'Besides, Herr Beck, you said yourself that neither of us is in a position to appreciate just what happens to the human psyche in such extreme situations.'

My heartbeat, which has substantially accelerated over the past few minutes, prompts a well-known tugging in my chest. Then there's the hard wood under my buttocks. I turn my head away from Giesner and look over the back of the bench to the large building where Hannah is waiting for me. I try to think of her, of the fact that the two of us will soon walk out of that building together and drive away, away from here, back home. But my thoughts keep drifting to Jasmin Grass. That woman. How I'd like to have spoken to her and asked the probing questions myself. Grabbed her by the collar if necessary and shaken the answers out of her. *Where the hell is my daughter? What do you know? How did you manage to get back home, but not my daughter?* But not a chance. After I wasn't able to identify her as Lena on the night of the accident, they wouldn't allow me to talk to her. *For your own good*, as Gerd put it. They stationed guards outside her room.

'It's just a hunch, Herr Giesner,' I say as calmly as possible to slow my heartbeat down to a healthier rhythm. 'There's something about that woman that isn't right. She's not telling you everything she knows.'

Giesner lets out an absentminded 'Hmm' and then pulls a folded piece of paper from the inside pocket of his suit jacket. He straightens it out and passes it to me.

'Do you recognise this man?'

I take my reading glasses out of my coat.

'No,' I say eventually. 'Who is it?'

'This is a facial reconstruction by the forensic department of the male whose body was found in the cabin.'

'The man who abducted my daughter?'

'That's what we're assuming, yes.'

Normal, that's my first thought. He looks completely normal. That's what shocks me most of all. If I keep focusing on his face, maybe I'll find some abnormality that might be weirdly comforting. Lena would have fallen victim to a monster, some creature whose gruesomeness would have been apparent kilometres away. Against something like *that* she wouldn't have stood a chance. But the picture in my hand doesn't depict a *that*, it depicts a *someone*, a human being. A man who could have lived in our neighbourhood. Could have been one of my clients. Someone who could have been a lawyer or a car mechanic. A man who could have appeared at our front door to pick Lena up for a date and I would have wished them a nice evening. Maybe I might have even liked him on first impression. More than Mark Sutthoff, in whose smile I thought at first glance I could detect a slyness. For a moment I don't know whether to be disappointed that the reconstruction doesn't show Mark's face or relieved, because yesterday evening when he agreed with me about Hannah, I thought for the first time that I might have been wrong about him. Perhaps I'd been unfair on Mark after all.

'Are you sure, Herr Beck?' Giesner says, his voice mingling with my thoughts. 'Have a good look at the man. Take your time.'

I nod. The man who abducted and probably killed my daughter. This quite normal, unremarkable man.

Without taking my eyes off the picture, I shake my head.

'I don't recognise him, no.'

Giesner sighs, I look up.

'Have you shown this to Hannah?'

'Yes, this morning before you arrived. She looked at it and congratulated me on my drawing skills.' Giesner gives another sigh.

'You need to get that picture in the media! It should be in every paper and TV news bulletin!' My hands, which are holding the piece of paper, start shaking with agitation. 'Surely someone knows the bastard.'

'Hmm,' Giesner says again, then, 'We'll consider it, Herr Beck. Only in our experience, when we publish something like that, it seems as if half the world claims to know the person. You get people ringing up saying, "That's my neighbour, my children's teacher, my dentist." We would have a flood of leads and it would take us ages to work through them all without any guarantee of a result.'

'You're not seriously telling me that this is too much work for you, are you, Herr Giesner? That's your job!'

Giesner doesn't reply.

My heart starts racing again.

'So nothing's going to happen? You're just going to let the matter rest?'

'No, no, Herr Beck, on no account.'

He takes the piece of paper from my hand, folds it up again and slips it back into his jacket pocket.

'We're going to start by asking people personally connected to the case.'

'But that includes me! And I tell you, I don't know this man!'

'Herr Beck, I know you had a close relationship with your daughter, but . . .' He falters. I have an idea what he's going to say next as he chews over his words so they don't upset the poor, sick old man too much. Of course he's read the old files. Of course Gerd has briefed him about the investigation into Lena's disappearance. Of course he's familiar with the newspaper articles. The lies he possibly thinks are the truth merely because they seem so weighty when printed in big, bold letters. Parents who didn't really know their own child. I can recall every single article, every single word . . .

Friend of missing Munich student (23): Lena had problems

Munich (LR) – Jana W (her name has been changed) sits on the windowsill in her sitting room on the fourth floor and gazes out at the city. 'Where are you?' is the question that this friend of student Lena Beck (23, as reported here), who disappeared almost a week ago, keeps asking herself. W was the last person Lena Beck was in contact with before she vanished. 'She called me on her way home from the party,' W recalls, trying to retain her composure. 'I should have realised that something was wrong, but I was annoyed that she'd woken me up with her call.' As to the details of this last telephone call, W says, 'Lena told me she wanted to change her life, things couldn't go on as they were.' But W didn't hear this as a cry for help. 'She sounded as if she'd had a lot to drink. Besides, Lena was often in the mood to want to change something. She'd already contemplated abandoning college, which would have been a sensible move. She was never really interested in her studies, and was more often to be seen at parties than in lectures. As a result she was probably going to flunk her exams this semester.' Like Beck, W is in her fourth semester of a teaching degree at Ludwig Maximilian University in Munich. 'But I think she was worried about disappointing her parents. The Lena her parents know is a very different person.'

Could the 23-year-old possibly have been so desperate that she was contemplating suicide and jumped into the Isar on the night she disappeared? Jana W won't rule this out. 'But I can also imagine her absconding with some guy. She was always telling me about new male acquaintances. In the worst-case scenario, maybe this time she hooked up with the wrong one.' W says, however, that she hasn't given up hope of seeing her friend again soon. With tears in her eyes, she begs, 'Lena, if you're out there somewhere, please come home. We miss you.' Just before midday, police divers resumed their search of the river. 'So far we haven't come up with anything that has any bearing on the case of the missing woman,' Chief Inspector Gerd Brühling said. He refused to comment on Lena Beck's current psychological state. Nor would he go into any more detail about the statement given by a woman who claims to have seen the student in the company of a man at a motorway service station near the Austrian border. But he insisted, 'Of course we're taking every piece of information seriously and following up every lead.'

*

'Herr Beck?' Giesner says.

'Okay,' I say wearily. 'Ask those people' – I do air quotes – '*personally connected* to the case. The friends who apparently knew Lena far better than I did. Ask them if this man might have been one of the allegedly vast number of male acquaintances my daughter had. Give them a good grilling.' I reach for the back of the bench as support and groan as I haul myself up. 'Maybe unlike Herr Brühling, you'll realise how many people back then spread lies about Lena just to make themselves feel important. Lifting the lid on that would be worthwhile in itself. Oh yes, and please don't forget Frau Grass.'

Giesner, who has got up from the bench too, gives me a searching look.

'You have no cause to doubt yourself as a father, Herr Beck. Parents want to protect their children, that's only natural. It's just that sometimes they forget that their children are independent people –'

'Yes, yes, okay,' I growl and point at his jacket. 'Could I take the reconstruction with me to Munich to show my wife? After all, she's *personally connected* to the case too.'

'Inspector Brühling can do that. He's right there.'

'Herr Giesner, I don't want to upset my wife any more than is necessary.' I clutch my chest. 'These interrogations are arduous for all of us.'

'I'm very sorry, Herr Beck, but I can't give it away, I really can't.'

The hand sitting flat on my chest clenches to a fist and I grimace.

'Maybe you could just look away for a second while I take a picture with my mobile,' I pant, short of breath. 'Then I'll show it to my wife and we'll get in touch immediately if the man is familiar. I mean, we just decided we were going to do our best to work together, didn't we?'

Giesner gives a subtle shake of his head. 'Even if you don't believe me, Herr Beck, I understand you. But this doesn't mean I'm going to do you this favour. Let me do my job and you look after your granddaughter. That way we're all best served, trust me.'

HANNAH

My grandfather went outside with the policeman but he promised me he wouldn't be long. Which also means it won't be long until I'm back home.

Frau Hamstedt suggested that we should do some more drawing in the meantime. I pointed out to her that it's lying to say *we* should do drawing because in truth it's only *me* who would draw. But I don't want to draw anyway. I think I should use the time to say goodbye to Jonathan. You always have to say goodbye before you go. Not saying goodbye is impolite. Frau Hamstedt let me.

We go out of her office and down the corridor to the glass door. To the left is the lift, to the right the stairs. I ask Frau Hamstedt if we can take the lift. She looks at me like Mama sometimes does when we're doing lessons and my answer's not quite right. As if I hadn't thought something through properly.

'It's only a cable system,' I tell Frau Hamstedt, after by accident I briefly show my annoyance. I can't tell Frau Hamstedt she's an idiot or she definitely won't let me go home. 'And the doors have to be shut otherwise you could fall out of the compartment.'

Frau Hamstedt is silent to begin with. The lift gives a ding when it arrives and we get in. The silver doors close behind us. Frau Hamstedt pushes the round button with the number two on it. There are three round buttons in total, one above the other like a traffic light. This is how you tell the lift which floor to go to.

'Why didn't you ever take Jonathan with you when you went on your trips?'

The corners of my mouth twitch as there's a tugging in my tummy. The tugging feeling in my tummy is what I like most about going in a lift.

'Hannah?'

I make a cross face again.

'Because I'm her favourite child.'

I don't know how often I need to say this until she understands. There always has to be a favourite child you can rely on.

It's dark in Jonathan's room because the blinds are down. The retina problem must be in our family. It smells bad in his room too, of stale farts, which isn't surprising as nobody's put a recirculation device in here. In my room too they only tilt open the window when I go to eat or to do drawing or go with Grandad to the appointments. I've asked why, but nobody's given me an answer. I think it's because the handles on the windows have a little lock on them and they have to be unlocked before you can tilt the windows open. There's probably only one key and Frau Hamstedt's helpers have to look for it each time. I told them to do it like we did at home. We never had to think where the key might be or spend ages looking for it because Papa looked after it.

I told Frau Hamstedt's helpers that they should choose someone to be in charge of the key. But of course they don't listen to me. They probably think I'm just a child and so I'm not particularly clever. But I'm much cleverer than them.

Jonathan is sitting on the floor in the far corner of the room, his knees up to his chest. 'Hello, Jonathan,' Frau Hamstedt says. She opened the door especially quietly so he wouldn't get a fright, but I think Jonathan is taking so many of the blue pills that he doesn't care if someone comes into his room. He doesn't even lift his head from his knees.

'Would you like me to wait outside?' Frau Hamstedt asks me. I nod. *Outside* means, however, that she'll wait in the open doorway, with her back to us. I approach Jonathan on tiptoe, although I don't think he's dangerous. He isn't anything anymore. I sit very close to him so he can hear me properly when I whisper. Assuming he can hear at all.

'Why did you draw Sara?'

I think he flinches very slightly.

'Have you forgotten how dreadfully Mama screamed because of her? Have you really forgotten it all?'

I remember every detail. The dreadful screaming. The ugly face that Mama pulled. How she kicked and tossed and turned so much that her bracelet cut her wrist and blood ran down her forearm. Then there was more blood and much more screaming, which meant nobody could sleep. *And* the Fräulein Tinky business. If Mama hadn't screamed so dreadfully because of Sara, Fräulein Tinky would never have knocked over the cup of hot chocolate in fright and Papa wouldn't have put her outside as a punishment. She wasn't allowed back in until the evening. She'd turned very cold and stiff, and it took ages to warm her coat up again beside the stove. All because of Sara.

She was a very funny colour. She was purple and slimy, smeared with yellow and red. I wouldn't touch her until Mama had cleaned her up. Everything was filthy: Sara, Mama, the entire bed. I pulled the sheet off the mattress. Papa said that Mama lost far more blood than when Jonathan and I were born. The stains were really big. Papa also said there was no point in washing the bedclothes. He brought a roll of big rubbish bags into the bedroom, then the three of them went into the bathroom. I was just unbuttoning the pillowcases when Mama came back with Sara. Mama was moving very strangely and slowly, as if she was worried her bones would break with every step. She sat on the bed. The baby looked better now, clean. Mama said it was perfect. *She* was perfect, Sara. The name means 'princess'. Now there was nothing better than Sara. I was so tired. First Mama's screaming, now Sara's whining. I stuffed the bedclothes in two loads into the rubbish bags, like Papa had told me.

'When are we going to go away again, Mama?'

Mama didn't hear me at first, so I had to ask her again.

'We can't just at the moment, Hannah,' she said, without taking her eyes off Sara, who she held in her arms. That dreadful whining. I wouldn't have even been able to tell if the recirculation device was working properly.

'She can come with us,' I said, even though I didn't really want that to happen. 'She can come with us,' I said again. Mama ought to look at me, I was talking to her. 'Mama?' It was impolite not to look at me. 'Mama!'

'For goodness' sake, Hannah,' she hissed. Now she looked at

me, but only briefly, because Sara immediately began whining again, this time even louder.

'Shh, shh,' Mama said, stroking her head. 'She's still so little, Hannah. You can't go away with such a little baby. It would be far too exhausting.'

'But Mama . . .'

'Not now, Hannah,' she just said.

'What not now?' Papa said, standing in the doorway. I'd just taken a breath when Mama said, 'Nothing.' As if our trips were worthless, as if from one moment to the next they'd never happened. Now that Sara was here.

'I think Mama loves Sara more than us,' I said to Jonathan. I'd told him to wait by the front door because of Fräulein Tinky, who was still having to sit outside. It would be good for her to hear a familiar voice, even if it was just through a closed door, so she didn't get even more frightened and run away into the woods. Jonathan sat on the wooden floor, his back against the door. The crying was upsetting me so badly that it brought tears to my eyes.

'What do you mean, Hannah?'

'Mama hasn't said it directly, but I don't think they want us anymore. They've got Sara now and they say she's perfect.'

'They don't want us anymore?'

I shake my head.

Jonathan can't have forgotten that. And I know he hasn't because although he doesn't give me an answer, he flinches. I think he might even be crying, but I'm not sure because I can't see his face.

'You drew Sara so I would get into trouble, didn't you? Because I said I couldn't stand her.'

Now Jonathan makes a noise that sounds like a grunt.

'Everything okay?' Frau Hamstedt asks from the doorway. Her head is turned towards us.

'Yes,' I say, then go on whispering to Jonathan. 'I kept saying I was sorry. Don't you remember? When Papa cried so badly. I knew at once that it was my fault Mama had gone away with Sara. But you couldn't stand Sara either. That's how it was, Jonathan.'

He grunts again.

'It was pretty stupid of you to draw her. But even though you're an idiot, you're still my brother. That's why I'm going to tell you something nice now. Our grandfather is really kind. He's taking me home today. So it's true. I told you, but you wouldn't believe me. A promise is a promise and promises don't get broken.'

Jonathan turns his head towards me, only slightly, and without lifting it from his knees. All I can see is a silly eye, but it's huge with surprise.

'You have to try hard to be normal again. Do you understand, Jonathan? If you're not normal we can't come and fetch you. Then you'll have to stay here, all on your own.'

He turns his head back, but he nods. That's a definite nod.

JASMIN

The first time I awoke this morning it was ten to seven, as ever. The voice inside my head was urging me to get up and make breakfast for the children. It had to be on the table at half past seven on the dot. I turned to Kirsten, whose face lay in the muted light of the streetlamp that seeped into the bedroom through the narrow gap beneath the roller blind. Her eyes were closed and her mouth slightly open. I listened as she breathed calmly, in and out. The voice in my head got louder. The children must have breakfast, now. Half past seven: breakfast. What was so difficult to understand about that? The children needed a structured day. I began copying Kirsten's breathing, in and out, setting it against the coercion and the voice inside my head. Just breathe, in the same rhythm, in and out. I must have actually nodded off again. It had worked, for the first time. I'd just lain there.

It's Kirsten's soft voice that wakes me now, her voice and an unusual brightness I'd long forgotten. I blink. Dust particles are dancing in the sunlight. I sit up. Kirsten has raised the roller blind. Early autumn floods the room. My heart beats wildly. I smile. You smile from the walls, Lena. I let my gaze wander across the newspaper articles and wonder at how different that familiar picture suddenly looks in the light. It takes me a moment to focus my attention on Kirsten, who's on the phone in another room, the kitchen probably. I hear her cancel her shift in the club today; she explains it's a private matter. Her boss seems to be understanding because she thanks him heartily. It's the same boss she had before she was attacked in the courtyard, the same club where she works behind the bar, the same working hours, the same clientele. After the rape it took Kirsten less than a week to go back and continue working, defiant and determined. At first she would take a taxi home after work, at that uncertain, grey, dangerous hour. But soon afterwards she started walking back again, past the same courtyard. I still don't know how it all pieces together. On the one hand, this strength, this defiance, this determination to carry on. And on the other, the end of our relationship. After the attack I'd asked her why she hadn't put up a fight – that was stupid and not particularly sensitive, of course.

'It was like a slap in the face when you asked me that, Jasmin. At that moment something broke between us.'

I assured her a thousand times that I'd just been tired and overwrought, but Kirsten wouldn't believe me, even when she smiled and said, 'Fine.'

We bumbled on for another few months, then she moved out.

'I can't live with you anymore, Jasmin. I've tried, but it just doesn't work.' And: 'We can stay friends.'

The last time I heard that was on the night I disappeared. *We can stay friends.* And yet, judging by the look on her face, she just wanted to close the door again when I turned up that evening, an idiot with bread and salt and an overnight bag. Bread and salt as a moving-in present, even though that had already been a few weeks earlier and I was still waiting for an invitation to come and see her new apartment. So that evening I'd just turned up unannounced. With the essentials in my overnight bag. I could have stayed the night with her. Or, if we'd got into another fight, jumped on the next train to spend a few days away, get some distance, take a step back, mobile off, *come to terms with it,* just as Kirsten wanted me to.

'You've got to come to terms with it, Jasmin! I don't want any more calls or messages from you. And I certainly don't want you just turning up outside my front door, okay? I need some time to myself at the moment. Please understand that.'

I shake my head to banish the memory of that terrible evening. That evening doesn't matter anymore. What matters is that she's here now. She's come back to me and I'm no longer thinking about the circumstances. She's here.

A clatter of crockery comes from the kitchen, while a strong whiff of coffee wafts through the open bedroom door, a strong whiff of normality. I lean back against the pillow and close my eyes. I'm probably just dozing because for a while I've been hearing the irregular knocking at my front door, whereas Kirsten only stops what she's doing when the knocking becomes constant. I hear her footsteps cross the laminate in the hallway, the click of the lock as she turns the key and then the surprised 'Oh, hello, good morning' of a man's voice I recognise at once.

'Frank Giesner, Cham police,' the voice says.

'Kirsten Thieme,' says Kirsten, who also seems to have registered Cham' surprise that a stranger has opened the door. 'I'm a friend of Frau Grass,' she explains without being asked.

'Frau Thieme, oh yes. Your name is familiar from Frau Grass's case notes. You were the one who reported her missing.'

'Yes, that's right.'

'Well, I'd like to speak to her, please.'

I carefully lower my head into the pillow and close my eyes. I don't want to talk to Cham now, certainly not in Kirsten's presence.

'I'm afraid she's still asleep.'

'Maybe you could tell her that it's really very important.'

'I understand, of course. But she's not feeling particularly well. She had a difficult night and is in urgent need of rest. Would it be possible for her to call you later?'

Cham is hesitant to answer.

'Of course. But perhaps you might be able to spare me a minute of your time? You're very close to Frau Grass, aren't you?'

I freeze. Everything in me freezes.

'Yes . . .' Now Kirsten sounds surprised. 'Do come in, Herr . . .'

'Giesner. Thank you.'

I feel sick. Cham is inside my apartment. Cham, who wants to talk to Kirsten. Kirsten, who now pushes down the squeaky door handle to close the bedroom door. Because the poor woman from the cabin needs her rest, or because the police inspector mustn't get a glimpse into a room where the walls are for some sick reason covered in newspaper articles about Lena Beck. I know I ought to get up, but instead I pull the duvet over my head, screw up my eyes and breathe, in and out.

I must have fallen asleep again. Kirsten was right: I'm in need of sleep as well as peace and quiet. I still haven't recovered from the night before last in particular, when I'd researched and printed out the articles. I wake with a start and listen. I can't hear anything, neither Kirsten nor Cham. Awkwardly I haul myself out of bed and plod over to the bedroom door. Before pressing the squeaky handle, which would give a clear sign that I'd woken up, I put an ear to the door to make sure, but still I can't hear anything. It's silent in the sitting room.

I find Kirsten sitting at the kitchen table, painting her nails dark red.

'Hello, Sleeping Beauty, you're awake!' she says, smiling and looking up at me. 'Fancy some coffee? There's still some in the pot. But you'll have to help yourself,' she says, holding up her left hand with its freshly lacquered nails by way of explanation.

I fetch myself a mug from the cupboard.

'What was so urgent?'

'What do you mean?'

My hand, which has just grabbed the coffee pot, pauses in mid-air.

'I heard a knocking at the door, but then I fell asleep again.'

I turn around to Kirsten and raise my eyebrows.

'Oh yes. That was your neighbour. Maja, I think. From the second floor. Nice girl.' Kirsten gestures towards the cooker before resuming painting her nails. 'She brought you lunch.' I spin around and see a little pot on the cooker. 'Chicken noodle soup,' Kirsten explains. 'I told her she doesn't need to come anymore now that I'm here to look after you. She left her mobile number anyway, in case there's anything she can do. It's on the fridge.' And there it is: a pink Post-it with Maja's name, a sequence of numbers and a smiley face she drew beneath. 'Oh yes, she brought the post too. It's on the cabinet.'

The coffee pot now feels heavy in my hand. I put it down on the work surface.

'No, Kirsten, I'm talking about Frank Giesner. He was here. I heard him.'

Kirsten looks up again and sighs. It might only be a matter of seconds but these stretch into infinity, as I start to feel a burning behind my forehead. The heat trickles out through my pores, covering my face with a damp, hot film. My apprehensions create bubbles. Kirsten, who's about to tell me that I merely imagined Giesner's visit, his voice; I just imagined it again. It was Maja knocking at the door. The pot on the cooker and the phone number on the fridge are proof.

'Yes, he wanted to talk to you about the facial reconstruction,' Kirsten says eventually, and I laugh with relief before I understand. My abductor has a face again now and they want me to look at it. Identify him. Reanimate the pictures inside my head. Look into a pair of eyes that are accusing me. *What kind of a monster are you?*

'Why didn't you say that straightaway?' I ask to drown out the other thoughts.

'Because I didn't want to upset you again. Come on, have some coffee and let's wait until you're properly awake.' It doesn't escape my attention that she sounds slightly irritated. I pour myself a mug of coffee.

'Did he show you?'

'The picture? Yes. But I couldn't be sure if I'd ever seen the man before. I mean, we used to have a lot of people over here, do you remember?'

Yes, I do. People others had brought along, and who liked to party as much as we did. *Fewer than a dozen and it wasn't a party.*

I suppress the wistful feelings welling inside me and nod.

'I reckon you need to take a look at it yourself, Jassy. There's nothing for it.' Kirsten looks concerned. 'Do you think you'd be up to it?'

I manage a smile at least, even though it feels slightly artificial.

'I don't really have a choice, do I?'

I take a few sips of my coffee. Swallowing is difficult. With another sigh, Kirsten screws the cap of the nail polish back on with her fingertips. I wonder if she regrets coming back to look after me. Whether she can put up with me.

'Giesner's waiting for you to call to fix an appointment for the identification. He said you don't have to go to police HQ if you don't want to. He'd be very happy to come back here. Any time, even after work if necessary.'

'That's nice of him,' I say hoarsely.

'I'm wondering whether it might not also be a good idea to

make an appointment with your therapist now. Who knows how you'll react when they show you the picture of your abductor?'

'She can't help me either.'

'Well . . . you have to want to.'

'You think so too, do you?' I say softly, putting my mug down on the work surface. 'If I'm getting too much for you, feel free to tell me. I'd understand.'

Kirsten rolls her eyes.

'Come on, Jassy. Don't be like that. Really.'

'You don't owe me a thing.'

'Just stop, would you? This isn't about us, it's about you coming to terms with things.'

'Coming to terms.'

'Learning to live with what happened to you. It's not going to work if you keep on like this. You need professional help.'

'I feel better with you here.'

Kirsten clicks her tongue. I see her chew her bottom lip for a few seconds before deciding to resume the conversation.

'You wet the bed.'

I think I've misheard her at first, perhaps I'm even laughing.

'I . . . ?'

Kirsten slides back in her chair to get up. Then she stands beside me with sad eyes and her head angled to one side.

'You wet the bed,' she says again slowly. 'Last night. You must have been dreaming. You were kicking with your legs and thrashing about with your arms. And you were screaming. *That's not a bracelet, Hannah! Those are handcuffs! Open them, for God's sake!* I tried waking you, but you were out of it.'

I shake my head. I didn't dream last night.

'Yes, Jassy, that's exactly what happened. When I realised the sheet was wet I pulled you out of bed. I was going to put you on the sofa in the sitting room so you could continue sleeping while I changed the bed. But you held on tight and screamed at me not to leave you alone and you were terrified that some sort of machine might stop working again.'

'I don't remember that.'

'Well, you slept.'

I shake my head again, while Kirsten's sad eyes widen with concern and she just keeps nodding, as if hypnotised.

'That's what happened, Jassy. Just that. And it's a sign that you're not actually much better. Don't you understand? I can be here. I can go shopping for you and change the bed. I can hold you in my arms and listen to you when you need to talk. But I'm no therapist.'

I push past her without saying anything. I go out of the kitchen, away from her concerned look, her closeness that now pains me. My goal is the sitting room, to be alone there, just for a moment, to be able to think, to try to reconcile the feeling of peacefulness I felt when waking up with the terrible night I'm supposed to have had.

'I don't mean any harm,' I hear behind me, and I turn around. Kirsten has followed me into the hallway and is now facing me, both hands up, her fingers waggling in the air. The nail varnish isn't yet dry. 'But we're not going to manage it alone.' She puts out her arm to touch my shoulder, but then thinks better of it, presumably because she doesn't want to smudge the nail varnish. 'Please let's call your therapist.'

I turn away.

'Come on, Jassy. Why are you making it so difficult for me to help you?'

My gaze alights on the post piled on top of the cabinet. I see it at once.

'Do you think you deserve to suffer like this?'

A plain white envelope without a stamp.

'Nobody deserves this.'

It's half concealed beneath yesterday's newspaper, which means I can only see part of the address. But it's the same hand-writing, I'm sure of that.

'Okay, fine. I'll call her right away,' I say in a monotone voice. 'Could you see where I left my mobile? I think it's in the sitting room.'

Behind me I hear Kirsten give a sigh of relief before she shuffles off.

'I'm just popping to the loo!' I call out, grabbing the letter.

I steal into the bathroom, lock the door and lean against it. I pull at the flap of the envelope with trembling, sweaty fingers, but then am briefly distracted by the rattling of the washing machine. When I realise that it must be the soiled bedclothes from last night going around and around, a lump forms in my chest. I take the piece of paper from the envelope.

The same large, black, bold, accusatory letters. But different words, three this time.

TELL THE TRUTH.

MATTHIAS

The conversation I'd had with Giesner I could have had with Gerd, only we would have been on first-name terms, and afterwards he would have called me an ass and I would have called him an idiot.

Policemen are all the same, interchangeable, templates. They all say the same things. *Personally connected*. I just can't get over this. The expression accompanies Hannah and me on our drive home. It has filled the car like the sticky, stale, heavy air, and it's squashing my skull. None of them believe I ever really knew my daughter. They think I closed my eyes and spent the last thirteen years – perhaps even longer – in a semi-doze, lulled by my love for my girl. But I do know my daughter. I knew her very well.

I sniff noisily and glance in the rear-view mirror. I can only see Hannah's eyes and her hairline: they could be Lena's. Right now I could be driving my little Lena to gymnastics or to a friend's house.

'Papi,' the squeaky voice would come from the back seat. 'Shall we stop quickly and get an ice cream?'

'Sounds good. Who's paying?'

'You are, of course, Papi! I'm still little and I don't have a job.'

'Yes, of course, I'd totally forgotten. Okay, Lena. But only because it's you.'

One day Hannah might ask me the same question: 'Shall we stop and get an ice cream?' What I would give to see this day.

'Shall we have a quick stop at the next services, Hannah?' I say into the rear-view mirror, a hopeful smile on my lips. 'It's still another half an hour's drive. A short break would be a good idea, what do you think?'

Hannah looks out of the side window, without giving me an answer. Trees and uncultivated fields fly past on either side of the motorway. The weather report was wrong; a sad, grey veil has now covered the sky which was still blue a few hours ago. I wish I could look inside Hannah's head. I wish I had the courage to ask her what she's thinking about right now as we tear along the motorway at 130 kph. Whether she finds it frightening or exciting. Whether she's looking forward to getting home. But it is as it always is when we're alone. Something inhibits me from asking about the really important things, maybe for fear I'll upset something.

A BMW that rudely pulls in close to me tears me from my thoughts. A sign to the right announces a service station in five kilometres.

'Hannah?' I try again. 'What do you think? A short stop?'

'I'd rather go home without a short stop, Grandad.'

'Okay, that's fine,' I say as cheerfully as possible to conceal my disappointment, then mutter unwittingly to myself, 'Probably a stupid idea anyway. Someone's bound to whip out their mobile and take the next photo of zombie girl.'

'What did you say, Grandad?'

'That you're absolutely right, Hannah,' I say louder, smiling at her again in the mirror. 'Let's hurry home instead.' I crane my neck so I can see the whole of Hannah's face in the mirror. Now she's smiling too. My little Lena . . .

My heart is pounding when I turn our old Volvo into our street, which is in a traffic-calming zone. On either side of the street, separated by neatly trimmed hedges, stand lovingly-cared-for houses, their front doors hung with clay tiles bearing greetings and the name of the family that lives there. Each house has its own little front garden with climbing frames or rose bushes like little islands in the lawn. *The perfect environment in which to raise a child.*

I steer around the bend that takes the road to its end, and I've just caught my breath to tell Hannah that we're here, when I see them. Around a dozen people on the street outside our house. Half a carpool lining the pavement.

'What the . . . ?' I say, bringing the car to a stop.

Behind me Hannah sits up, slides forwards on the seat and clutches the headrest of the passenger seat.

'What's wrong, Grandad?'

The mob has spotted our car. Heads turn in unison to the Volvo, which has come to a halt in the middle of the street about twenty metres away from them. My jaw clenches. My shoulders tense. My entire body becomes painfully wooden. My hands are holding the steering wheel so tightly that my knuckles stick out white beneath the skin. I hold my breath.

'Grandad? Who are all these people?'

My right foot twitches above the accelerator. An idea briefly flashes in my mind: foot down, straight into the crowd, peace at last.

'Grandad?' Hannah's voice has lost some of its usual monotony; she's almost sounding slightly tearful now. *Can't you see you're frightening the girl?* I want to shout, but then I think of my granddaughter, who doesn't need any more cause for alarm at the moment. It's obvious that this bunch of people are all journalists. I can see clipboards and cameras, even a television camera and boom mic. A red-haired woman in a light blue coat breaks away from the pack and takes a few tentative steps towards us.

'Fucking Rogner,' I snarl, but Lars Rogner doesn't appear to be amongst them. Not in person, at least, but I bet he's sent one of his people. Maybe the woman in the light blue coat who's approaching our car, slowly but steadily. A few others follow her. Now they're about ten metres away.

'Hannah,' I say as softly as I can. Without taking my eyes off the journalists, I've swiftly removed my coat and tossed it behind me. 'Lie down flat on the back seat and cover yourself with this.'

Hannah doesn't object and I hear the click of her seat belt. Just to be sure, I glance behind me briefly and see she has actually curled herself up into a bundle beneath my coat. I reach behind and pull the coat up where a few blonde locks are still sticking out above her head. Then I turn back, place my hands on the steering wheel and drive forwards carefully. My heart is in my mouth. I'm almost expecting the mob, now only five metres away, to cluster around the car on every side. In my mind I see the woman in the light blue coat throw herself on to the bonnet while her colleagues shake the car doors and pound at the windows, screaming. But I'm wrong. The crowd parts and even keeps at a safe distance as I drive towards them at walking pace. I have no trouble turning into our property as my right hand takes the small remote control from the centre console and activates the automatic garage door.

'Stay down, Hannah,' I say, waiting for the door to close completely behind us before I switch off the engine and find myself able to breathe normally for the first time in what must be minutes.

'It's okay.' I give Hannah the all-clear and lift the coat from her delicate body. 'We made it.'

Hannah sits up and blinks.

I open my door, get out, then help Hannah out of the car. From the boot I take the small bag they packed with things from the clinic's clothes bank for her visit. We'll have to go shopping, tomorrow if we can. I don't want to see my granddaughter in other people's shabby clothes.

From the garage we go through a heavy metal door, then up a few steps to the back of the hallway. Karin's waiting for us there, her face as white as a sheet.

'Thank God,' she says with relief in her voice when I push Hannah into the room. An unusually dim light is evidence that Karin has lowered all the roller blinds in the house to protect us from prying eyes. Her knees clicking, she squats right beside Hannah, but keeps her eyes on me. 'I tried calling your mobile about half a dozen times! How could this happen?' Her voice is shrill with anxiety. 'Where are all these people from? How do they know you picked Hannah up today? What are we going to do now?'

'Just calm down,' I say, raising my hands aloft to placate her.

'Calm down? You've seen what's going on outside, haven't you?'

'I'm on the case.'

'What? We can't even call the police to get them off our backs! Not one of them has put a foot on our property! You know the rules from when they came because of Lena. So long as they're just hanging round in the street, there's nothing we can do. That's public space.' She puts her arm out and points to the front door. 'They could quite happily stay there for days undisturbed!'

'Karin . . .' I gesture towards Hannah, still standing rigidly and silently beside her.

Karin sighs before finally turning her attention to our grandchild.

'Hello, Hannah,' she says with a smile. 'I'm so happy you're finally here.'

When Hannah fails to react, Karin looks back up at me, slightly at a loss. I'm about to say something to break the ice when Hannah turns to me. She looks disappointed.

'But Grandad, I thought we weren't going to have a stop.'

'No, we . . .' I stutter. 'We're here, Hannah. We're at home.'

Hannah pulls a face.

'But this isn't my home, Grandad.'

JASMIN

'I'm sorry I haven't been able to see you until this late, Frau Grass,' Dr Hamstedt says, closing the door behind her. Our appointment was for half past eight, but I've been sitting waiting for her in her office for a while now. 'It's been a busy day,' she adds with a smile. The psychiatric clinic in Regensburg, run by Maria Hamstedt, is the only one in the area that specialises in children and adolescents. I don't want to spend any longer thinking about what 'busy' means in a place like this, because my mind is immediately filled with images of teenagers flailing and kicking epileptically, their arms wrapped tightly around their bodies in straitjackets. I also hear screams echoing down the clinic's long corridors, which give me goosebumps.

Smiling back at her, I force out a 'That's okay'. But nothing's okay. The whole situation, the thing with the letters. My little excursion to the psychiatric clinic, the venturing-back-outside, at this time of the evening too, when it's already dark and the streetlamps cast yellow cones of light which distort everything into long, ghostly shadows. All this presses down on my chest and wrenches at my limbs as if a heavy cold were brewing.

Dr Hamstedt gives me a brief look of suspicion before wandering around her desk to sit down.

'To be honest, I was surprised when you called me to request this meeting, Frau Grass.'

Just as it surprised Kirsten that I didn't go on shouting and screaming, refusing to call the therapist. That instead, I was almost zealous in repeatedly calling her number, which was engaged for half a day, until I finally got her on the line and persuaded her to see me today, in spite of how *busy* she was.

'Especially,' Dr Hamstedt continues, folding her hands on the desk and leaning towards me, 'as you're no longer being treated by me, but by my colleague Dr Brenner in Schützenstrasse.'

I steal a furtive glance at the door to check that it really is closed. Because sitting out there in the corridor is Kirsten, who accompanied me here. To see – as she thinks – *my* therapist. But I've only met Dr Hamstedt once before. For my psychological anamnesis at Cham hospital right after my escape from the cabin.

'Yes, I bet. That you were surprised, I mean,' I say in hushed tones, even though I can't imagine Kirsten listening at the door. In any case she's probably got her iPod earphones in or she's buried in a magazine. Kirsten isn't very good at doing nothing; she's got a low threshold for boredom.

Dr Hamstedt appears to be waiting for more, an explanation of why I've asked to see her rather than Dr Brenner, and why I sounded so urgent on the phone. Earlier, on the way here, I worked everything out and rehearsed the words in my head. But suddenly they've all gone.

Dr Hamstedt leans further forwards.

'Do you not get on with Dr Brenner?'

I shake my head resolutely. 'No, no, it's not that. She's very nice. I think.'

'Are you not going to her sessions regularly?'

'Not that often, no.'

'You ought to, Frau Grass. It's important.'

'I know. It's just . . .' I pull my head back and stare at the ceiling. The frayed, brown contours of a water stain up there start fraying even more, become diffuse. *Don't howl*, I urge myself. Just don't start howling again. Not here, not now. I haven't come here to have Maria Hamstedt poke around my wounds. I'm here because I need information. And her opinion.

'You find it difficult to talk about what happened to you,' I hear Dr Hamstedt's sympathetic voice say.

'Yes.'

'Perhaps you even think there's a reason for you to feel ashamed.'

'Perhaps.'

A scratching sound makes me flinch. I turn my gaze from the ceiling to Dr Hamstedt, who has pulled a paper tissue from a cardboard box on her desk rather too hastily and is now offering it to me. I take it and wipe my eyes before squaring my shoulders and clearing my throat.

'Thanks.'

'I've known Dr Brenner for many years, Frau Grass. She's a terribly good listener. And as far as you're concerned, you have absolutely no reason to feel ashamed. You are a victim. That's not something anybody chooses to be.'

'Yes, that's what people keep telling me,' I say with a slightly daft smile, as I think of how to change the subject.

'And it's true, Frau Grass,' Dr Hamstedt replies, giving me an encouraging smile. 'Nevertheless, if you don't feel comfortable as Dr Brenner's patient, obviously I'd be happy to help find you another therapist.'

'No, it's not that,' I say quickly, when I realise that she must think this is the reason for my visit. 'I don't need a new therapist. There's something else I urgently wanted to talk to you about.'

'Oh, all right then. So, how can I help you, Frau Grass? If this is about how the children's treatment is going, please remember that medical confidentiality means I cannot discuss anything with you, seeing as you're not a – '

I shake my head.

'I need to know whether the children are being let out.'

'Let out? Are you asking whether they leave the clinic from time to time?'

'Exactly.'

Dr Hamstedt looks slightly confused.

'Yes, of course. As you know, we are a psychiatric institution and obviously limited in what we can do as far as general medical examinations are concerned. So the answer to your question is yes. Hannah has been to visit other doctors.'

'Hannah has been out of the clinic?'

'To see the dentist and several times to the district clinic, yes. But given the circumstances, she's in good physical shape, in case you were worried about that.'

'Hannah has been out of the clinic,' I repeat to myself, and the picture forms in my mind of the girl spookily wandering the streets on her own, coming to my street, to the building where I live. I see her barefoot, in a white nightie with Fräulein Tinky under her arm. 'I remember every detail,' she whispers. Then she adds, 'For ever and ever and ever.'

'Not on her own, of course. She's always been accompanied by a member of staff or her grandfather, who's been going with her more often recently,' Dr Hamstedt says, dispelling my vision as if she'd read my thoughts. 'Why do you ask, Frau Grass?'

Rather than say anything, I start picking the paper tissue in my lap to pieces.

'Frau Grass?'

Hannah's grandfather. Your father, Lena. The man shouting beside my bed in hospital.

'Frau Grass?'

'What about on her own? I mean, do the patients have a sort of free time here when they can go out unsupervised?'

'As I said, Frau Grass, this is a psychiatric institution for minors. Obviously we can't allow most of our inpatients to wander around outside unsupervised.'

'Not even in the grounds?'

'No, of course not,' Dr Hamstedt says very definitely.

'And it's not possible for someone to slip outside unnoticed?'

Dr Hamstedt sighs and says very clearly, 'No, Frau Grass, that's absolutely impossible. May I ask what this is about?'

I'd intended to tell her about the letters. I've even got them on me, in my handbag, which is on the floor beside the chair. Suddenly, however, I'm no longer sure it's a good idea. What if she reacts like Kirsten did? *You're not well. You need help.* I think of the rooms where the handles can be removed with a flick of the wrist. *For your own security, Frau Grass.* I swallow hard; my throat feels sore. I imagine nobody would be quicker to commit me to this psychiatric clinic than its director, who's looking at me expectantly.

'Frau Grass?'

'Erm . . .'

I now feel really stupid for not having combed my hair, let alone changed my tracksuit bottoms and stained, sweaty top before coming here. Everything about me must be screaming *cause for concern!* As if on cue, a greasy hair falls down my forehead. I hastily sweep it back.

'Listen, Frau Grass. Medical confidentiality extends to this conversation here,' Dr Hamstedt says, and I'm receptive to her deep, velvety voice and sincere expression. 'So, if there's anything you want to get off your chest . . .' The rest of her sentence, her invitation, hangs in the air and I take a deep breath.

'Someone's been sending me letters,' I begin circumspectly as I watch for the tiniest changes in Dr Hamstedt's facial features. For narrowed lips, raised eyebrows or a wrinkled nose. 'And, well, I know this must sound silly, but I was wondering whether they might be from the children.'

'The letters?'

I nod.

'What's in them?'

So far I can't detect anything in her features to alarm me, so I bend down and take the two envelopes from the side pocket of my handbag.

'*For Lena,*' Dr Hamstedt reads out loud, then, '*Tell the truth.* What does that mean, Frau Grass? And what makes you think they could be from the children?'

'Because they must hate me after everything I've done. They can't do anything but hate me. Especially Jonathan.'

Now I do notice a change in Dr Hamstedt's features: her eyebrows, which have shot up her forehead. Fortunately I detect honest surprise in this expression rather than doubt towards me.

'Jonathan?'

I nod apprehensively.

'I hurt him very badly.'

'I don't understand.'

I nod again, but now avoid looking at her.

'On the day I escaped from the cabin . . .'

JASMIN

By now I was familiar with the restrictions of daily life inside the cabin. I'd found my footing and had fallen into line as far as possible. When your husband kissed me on the lips before going to work that morning, Lena, I didn't even retch. But then he said, 'I'm going to bring a test home this evening,' and beamed.

Over time I must have merely suppressed the fact that I hadn't had a period in quite a while. It could have been my body suffering from stress. It could have been my weight loss, which was readily apparent in my shoulders and hips that stuck out sharply. But it hadn't crossed my mind that I could be pregnant until he said these words. *I'm going to bring a test home this evening.* Everything collapsed, the ground broke up, gaped open and swallowed me into a huge, jet-black hole. When he was out the door, I summoned the last of my strength to drag myself over to the sofa and on to it.

I knew from a conversation we'd had earlier that he'd always wanted three children. A little brother or sister for Hannah and Jonathan. We'd even toasted me getting pregnant as soon as possible. Every day I took the vitamin pills he gave me, which were supposed to increase fertility, and I'd nodded in agreement when he thought up names. Matthias if it was a boy, and Sara if it was a girl. Matthias, he explained, meant 'gift from God', Sara 'princess'.

There was no reason to doubt that he meant all of this seriously. No, he didn't joke. Now it was all over, everything was black, inside I was dying from the realisation that I would be bearing his third child. And if the test wasn't positive today, it would be tomorrow, next week, or in a month. It would be my fault that another child had to endure this terror. I would give birth to a prisoner, someone who would be dead as soon as they were born. I cried so bitterly that it felt as if my face was going to burst.

The children were used to me having bad days, or at least a few bad hours in which my mood would swing violently and I would scream at them or pulverise some of their illusions out of sheer rage. I'd bawled at Hannah when she tried to persuade me to go on a trip which was never going to happen anyway. I'd kicked Fräulein Tinky and hissed at Jonathan, who loved pretending he could fly, that he would never, ever in his life get on a real plane. I'd yelled, 'I'm not your mama!' and yelled it even louder when they appeared to ignore me. But my cruel outbursts never lasted much longer. I usually felt ashamed immediately afterwards, or at least terrified that they might tell their father, and so I would apologise.

Today I wasn't mean, wasn't angry – I wasn't anything anymore.

I sat on the sofa, my arms around my torso, rocking back and forth listlessly for hours on end. Both Hannah and Jonathan had made a few attempts to get through to me. They asked when lessons were going to begin. They urged me to join in with exercises at least, reminding me what could happen if you didn't exercise your muscles regularly. They offered me something to drink and a bit of energy bar. Each of them brought me a picture they'd drawn to try to cheer me up. But I didn't even look at their pictures, which were just stupid, pointless scribbles. At some point I was distantly aware that Hannah was reading to Jonathan from the big book.

'Depression,' she read out in the monotone typical of her voice, 'is a psychological disorder, characterised by despondency, negative thinking and lack of motivation. Joy, productivity, empathy and a general interest in life are often lacking.'

'Does that mean she doesn't care about us anymore?' Jonathan asked.

'Idiot,' Hannah retorted. 'It means she doesn't care about anything.'

'Including us,' Jonathan noted and started making funny noises. This was probably the only reason I took notice. I'd never heard these noises before, neither from him nor from Hannah. And yet, despite their strangeness, there was also something familiar about them. They reminded me of the pain after my father died, when I locked myself in my room for days on end and cried. They reminded me of the hurtful feeling which engulfed me each time Kirsten insisted she was serious about the end of our friendship and there was no way back.

Jonathan swallowed.

I blinked my tears away. He had in fact started crying and was sobbing so intensely that his little chest rose and sank as if being given electric shocks. I looked at his pale, tender face, distorted by pain, until I could no longer bear the sight of it and I offered him my hand. Rather than take it, the boy dived on me, almost pulling me off the sofa. I was completely rigid in his clutches to begin with. I hadn't seen either of the children cry before, ever. Maybe I'd assumed by now they weren't capable of showing emotion, or even feeling it. Yes, there had been that day when the recirculation device had stopped working and we'd lain in the big bed together, me with my arms around both of them. 'I love you, Mama,' Hannah had said. 'For ever and ever and ever.' And I'd said, 'I love you both too. Goodnight.' Now I can see another significance behind it, but at the time I thought she'd only said that because it made the horrific episode slightly more bearable. Mitigated the fear slightly. At least that's why I'd done it. Sure, I had feelings for the children. But was there ever anything more than pity there? I shuddered at the thought that the children had already started feeling love for me, real love, and I hadn't noticed or returned this love. That everything I'd ever done for them was merely part of my role. That I'd only done it because I was worried their father would punish me if I didn't play this role properly.

I hesitantly placed a hand on Jonathan's back, and stroked his head with the other, feeling his soft hair. Felt his warm, nervous breathing on my neck and the spasms his body made as he sobbed. I felt his fluttering heartbeat, I felt the same pain which had afflicted me after my father's death and my break-up with Kirsten. He had the worst pain possible, the pain of love.

I looked over to Hannah, who was standing beside the shelves, still holding the big book. I was expecting to see her staring at me with those defiant, ice-blue eyes. But she kept her eyes fixed downwards, making her appear embarrassed. This was an emotion I hadn't come across either. Hannah had never had a problem looking me in the eye when a fresh, unmissable bruise decorated my face following another assault by her father. Sometimes she would even smile and say, 'It's not so bad, Mama. It was just a silly accident.' With her words she wasn't trying to excuse her father's violent outburst, but *my* behaviour. *I* had done or said something silly by mistake, for which her father had beaten me. A pure consequence of my own stupidity.

'I know!' Jonathan exclaimed.

He leaped off my lap and raced out of the room into the hallway. When he came back his face was still red from crying, but he was beaming. He was holding something hidden behind his back.

'I've got a present for you,' he said solemnly and brought it out.

The snow globe.

Inside it I could see a tiny house with a brown door, red shutters and a pointed roof. On either side of the house stood two Christmas trees.

'Look, Mama.' Jonathan shook the globe and thousands of tiny, artificial snowflakes flew up and swirled around, before landing on the roof, the trees, or the ground. 'Look at the snowflakes dancing! And we're in here.' Jonathan smiled, pointing at the tiny house.

'Can I hold it?'

Jonathan held it out to me.

230

'But be careful. It's made of real glass and it's very heavy.'

'Very heavy,' I repeated as if in a daze. He was right. The snow globe was really heavy. Fantastically heavy.

'Where did you get this?'

'Papa gave it to me. He gave Hannah Fräulein Tinky and me the snow globe. It's my most precious treasure.'

'Where have you been hiding it?'

'In our bedroom. One of the floorboards in our room is loose and there's a hole beneath it.' He grinned. 'Fräulein Tinky hides in there sometimes too when she's eaten something.' He turns to Hannah, but she doesn't grin back.

'In your room,' I repeated, still weighing up the snow globe in my hand. The room I'd been into hundreds of times to make the beds or tell goodnight stories.

'Yes,' Jonathan said, sitting beside me on the sofa. 'But now I want to give it to you.'

'You want – ?'

'Yes, because you're so sad, Mama.' He took the globe and shook it again. The snowflakes scattered around the little house. Jonathan smiled dreamily. 'That's our cabin. We're sitting inside, nice and warm.'

He gave me the globe back.

'Can you see now how nice it is here?'

'Yes, my darling, it's really nice here.'

'Next time you're sad you can just shake it.'

'Yes, darling, I'll do that.'

Tears were in my eyes when I gave Jonathan a tight hug. The wonderful little boy who wanted to cheer me up and gave me his greatest possession, his only possession.

'Can we maybe do some lessons now?' Hannah said grouchily in the background. She'd been astonishingly quiet.

I kissed Jonathan on the head, said, 'Thank you,' glanced at the kitchen clock – almost four in the afternoon – and got up from the sofa.

'All right then, children. Get your books and crayons. Today we're going to do dictation . . .'

It was late now, almost eight o'clock. I didn't think he'd be coming back home today and I was going to send the children to the bathroom to get ready for bed. During our lesson the snow globe had stood on the dining table. My eyes kept wandering to it and I couldn't resist smiling. Jonathan smiled too when he caught me doing it. Presumably he was a very happy, proud child who felt he'd done something very important. He'd cured his mama of pathological sadness. He had no idea.

Finally I could hear footsteps outside, heavy footsteps on wood, steps that must lead up to the cabin. The children leaped into position in the middle of the room, clearly visible, holding out their hands. I put the snow globe on the seat of my chair, so he wouldn't see it the moment he came in, then stood beside the children and held out my hands too. At that moment the key turned in the lock.

I watched his back as he locked the front door again from the inside, and the movement of his hand as it took the key, which was on a bunch, from the lock and slipped them jangling into his pocket. Everything was as normal. Apart from the fact that my heart was beating all over my body; I was one big pulse as he inspected the cleanliness of my fingernails, coming so close that I could feel the cold that lingered on him from outside. He'd been shopping to cook something delicious for us in honour of the day. And he'd also got hold of a pregnancy test kit, which would provide the reason for our celebration. Even the children were allowed to stay up later this evening, all in honour of this day. He seemed very sure of what the result would be.

'Everything okay with you, Lena?' he asked as he wandered past me to put the shopping bags down on the work surface.

'Yes, yes,' I said hastily, placing myself between him and my chair to shield the snow globe with my body. Today was crunch time. Either I'd be free or I would die; I could feel it, I felt it in every heartbeat. And I was scared, terrifically scared. Fear enveloped my body like cling film, something impervious, constricting me and making me numb.

From this point everything runs on automatic. I swear I cannot remember exactly when I grabbed the snow globe. Is he emptying the shopping bags? Or poking at the ashes in the stove? I see him before me, his back to me, bent forwards. I step up to him from behind. The globe in my hand weighs a tonne, I can barely hold it and yet I manage to take a big swing.

Where are the children at this moment? Is it Hannah, less than a metre from me, who screams a warning, which I don't hear because nothing can get through my cling film? Yes, I can see it's her from the corner of my eye, but her mouth is closed. Hannah watches silently and idly as I execute the snow globe's dangerous, wide arc through the air.

What about Jonathan? Jonathan must be somewhere here, too. I'm sure he hasn't left the room. Maybe he's run around the sofa, babbling away with excitement. He's happy that Papa's back. Papa will heat the stove and make it nice and warm in the cabin. Papa will cook something delicious for us. What luck that Papa's back.

At that moment your husband makes to turn around, but he's too late, there's a crack, it goes *bam!* like when you drop a watermelon on the floor. Does he make a sound? Does he groan in pain or even scream? I don't hear anything apart from the blood rushing in my ears and the muffled *bam!* that shakes everything. I've struck him, I've hit him once, hard, hard enough to make his body double up, as if a puppet's strings had been cut. That strike was enough, now he's lying on the floor, but it seems as if I just can't stop. I hit him and I hit him and I keep hitting him until the glass of the snow globe shatters on his skull. I must be kneeling over him, hitting him again and again, the glass shards shredding his face. Blood, blood must be everywhere now.

I stagger backwards, the murder weapon in my hand. The children come into my field of view. They stand there as if rooted to the spot. Hannah, her expression unmoved, empty. Jonathan horrified. Tears are running down his cheeks, his mouth is wide open with shock. His arms hang limply either side of his little body. His eyes, his stare. The snow globe was his present to me, the greatest, most important act of his life, his proudest possession. His snow globe has killed his father. *He* has killed his father because he gave it to me. His lips form a silent 'Mama'.

I drop the globe. In my head it crashes on the floor. In my head it only breaks now. The noise makes its way through my cling film, alarming me. I sink to my knees beside the inert body and fish the bunch of keys from his trouser pocket. Oh God, did he move just then? No, impossible, he's dead, as the police will corroborate later on. I stagger backwards again. The keys jangle in my hand. I run to the front door; my trembling fingers try key after key in the lock until one finally fits. It fits! The door, open!

'Come on, children!' I shout. 'Let's go!'

But the children don't move. They stand frozen beside the motionless body of their father.

'Come now! We've got to go!'

I see Jonathan sink to his knees beside his father as if in slow motion. His torso leans forwards, jerkily. He's sobbing, quietly, with pain, with love.

I shake my head in disbelief. Look at Hannah who's still standing there, frozen, her face devoid of expression.

I pant. There are no more thoughts in my head, apart from one, maybe: *get away from here!* My legs start moving. I stumble down wooden steps that lead to a narrow veranda. I'm hit by the darkness and ice-cold air. For a moment I forget to breathe; my lungs seem almost blocked by the strangeness of this air, real, fresh air.

I run. Across the grassed plot of land that surrounds the house and into the neighbouring woods. Branches scratch my skin, I can barely see anything in the darkness and I hear loud, dry cracking beneath my feet. I flail about, knocking branches to the side, sometimes flailing into thin air too. I stumble and fall, pain. I pick myself up again – *go on, keep going, get away from here.*

There, suddenly, behind me. Was that a crack? Has he got up again, is he behind me? *Faster, run!*

I run, falter, slip, crash into a tree.

Keep going, don't stop!

That's a crack behind me.

Up ahead, some distance away between the trees, is that a light?

Two lights, only tiny, but they're there. They're moving. Car headlights?

I run towards them. *Keep going, just don't stop!* A road, there's a road! I hold out my arms and wave. A car, it really is a car coming! I run towards it, wave, the car is close now, closer – and then . . . a deafening crash. Bright colours explode before my eyes. My eyelids flutter. I'm lying on the cold, hard ground. It's so dreadfully cold. I detect a movement above me. Someone's there. He bends over me. The driver of the car. His voice doesn't match his face when he calls out, 'Frau Grass? Frau Grass! Nice and calm, now, Frau Grass!'

MATTHIAS

I'm desperate to fall asleep quickly so it'll be morning sooner: a new, better day. But I have a very restive night. I can hear Karin beside me, breathing through her nose. She's unsettled too as she tosses and turns repeatedly. But at least she's sleeping, lucky woman.

I'd been expecting a different reaction, of course I had. When Hannah said, 'But this isn't my home, Grandad,' it was as if an invisible axe had split my ribcage and someone was removing my heart while I was fully conscious. And how disappointed she looked. She'd obviously thought I was taking her back to the cabin. While words failed me to begin with, Karin managed to improvise.

'You're right, Hannah,' she said calmly. 'This is our home, mine and your grandfather's. Your mama lived here with us for a long time. That's why we thought you'd like to visit us. Would you like to see her old room?'

'Yes.' Hannah nodded and let Karin take her upstairs by the hand. I trudged behind, keeping my distance.

To be precise, it's just a shell of Lena's old room. The pine-wood bed, the wardrobe, the chunky stereo that was a Christmas present when Lena first discovered music for herself, the desk and its accompanying swivel chair are all in their usual places. And the star stickers that glow in the dark are still on the ceiling above the bed, a sentimental relic of Lena's time at primary school. She'd made her own starry sky. 'It's silly that you can only see the stars when you're outside at night, isn't it, Papi? It's much nicer to sleep beneath the stars, isn't it?'

'Yes, Lenchen, it is,' I'd agreed, and stuck up the stars on her instructions because she couldn't reach.

All the posters that used to cover the walls were put in the recycling long ago. The photos and the pinboard with its colourful jumble of polaroids and concert tickets were taken down. The clothes that used to hang in the wardrobe have been discarded. The chest of drawers and bedside rug were new purchases, Karin's attempt to set up a guest room, or at least a bedroom without ghosts. Just like the curtains and the white orchids in a pot on the windowsill, which Karin lovingly nurtures.

Hannah stepped hesitantly into the middle of the room and allowed her gaze to roam.

'It's very big,' she said, then walked back to the door and started to measure the room by putting one foot in front of the other, heel to toe.

'Twenty-eight steps,' she declared when she got to the wall opposite.

'Do you like it?' I asked hopefully; she just shrugged.

When I showed her the desk I must have looked as desperate as a furniture salesman who's yet to make a sale that day.

'Look! This is the perfect place for studying. And the chair is very comfortable. Do you want to try it out? Go on, sit down. And look at this! We specially got you a drawing pad and colour pens, and if you like, we'll buy you a few books too, tomorrow or the day after. Or Karin, I mean your grandmother, could have a look in the cellar to see if some of your mama's old schoolbooks are in a crate somewhere, and then – '

'Matthias,' Karin said from the door, waving me over. 'Just leave her in peace for a little while.'

With a sigh, I obeyed and stood beside her. 'What were you thinking?' she hissed from the side.

She was referring to me telling Hannah I was taking her home. But nobody was more disappointed by the misunderstanding than me.

'The stars,' Hannah said out of the blue. Now she was standing beside Lena's bed, her head back, smiling. Her smile gave me heart.

'Yes, your mama was so desperate for her own starry sky that we stuck one up for her. Karin, turn off the light and close the door for a sec.' Because the roller blinds were down in Lena's bedroom too, as protection from the reporters outside, the stars shone as soon as the switch clicked, a sea of neon-green above, large ones, small ones, stars with tails and others without.

'Mama made a starry sky at home too, but the crayon doesn't glow.'

'Did she draw you stars?' A warm feeling flooded my chest, my broken ribcage seemed to heal for the time being. What a wonderful, loving mother my Lenchen must have been.

'Yes, on the slatted frame under Jonathan's bunk. When I lay in bed I just had to reach up and I could touch them, the stars. They're even beautiful when they don't shine. They're blue and green and red. It's only the yellow ones that are hard to see on the wood, but I still know they're there.'

'Listen, would you like to sleep in this room tonight? Beneath your mama's shining stars?'

Hannah said nothing, but in the residual light seeping into the room under the door from the hallway I saw her nod. I thought that this was the moment, the moment when we'd bond, when the loose strands would come together. The stars on the ceiling, which her mother had left behind like a sign. The stars, which in their own, silent way had to prove to Hannah that this was where she now belonged.

But I was mistaken. It was during dinner that she asked, 'How long do I have to stay here before I can go home?'

I put my hope in Karin again, but even she seemed to be at a loss on this occasion.

After a moment, therefore, I had a go myself. 'Hannah,' I said, 'the police have sealed off the cabin. They've stuck something on the door which means you're not allowed in there anymore.'

Hannah put down her bread, having taken a few bites.

'Never again?'

'I don't think so, no.'

'But why not?'

239

'Hannah –' I began without knowing what I actually wanted to say, but was interrupted by Karin.

'Because terrible things happened there.'

I tensed up and gave Karin a reproachful look. Until Hannah's able to understand for herself what really happened in the cabin, I believe we ought to leave it to the professionals to explain things carefully to her. The fact that they hadn't yet been successful in this showed me even more clearly how sensitively we had to treat her. But I couldn't have said this to Karin, of course, for she would have immediately reminded me of how often I'd recently described the specialists as incompetent idiots.

To my surprise, however, Hannah nodded at once.

'I don't think Jonathan will have managed to get all those stains out of the carpet anyway.'

An audible intake of breath from Karin.

'We have to go there anyway, Grandad. Because of Fräulein Tinky. You see, she doesn't know that the cabin can't be our home anymore.'

'We'll do that, Hannah. No problem,' I say, earning a reproachful look myself from Karin.

I don't doubt that Hannah will feel happy with us. That everything will be fine in the end. And yet the night refuses to give me any peace. I refuse to dwell for a second on that tiny, nagging doubt. Ultimately Karin's doubt that we'll succeed in being a family must be proved wrong.

I've got used to Karin not sleeping through the night. She hasn't done it for years, not since Lena disappeared. At some point in the middle of the night she wakes up and gets out of bed. She'll go to the bathroom or down to the kitchen to have a glass of water or a cup of tea, or she'll go into the living room for a bit of a read until her eyelids feel heavy again. After all these years, the footsteps on the stairs and the sound of running water have just become background noise. I barely open an eye anymore; at most I'll turn over.

But now I wake with a start.

Screaming.

My hand reaches for the switch of the bedside light.

Screaming. Karin's voice.

My body shoots upwards; my circulation can barely keep pace. My feet feel for the floor.

The screaming's coming from downstairs. Something clatters, a chair perhaps. Dining room, I think.

I make it to the bedroom door, my legs like jelly.

Someone's in the house, I think. Someone's got Karin. A weapon, I need a weapon, but I don't have one. All that comes to mind is the poker, which is in its stand beside the fireplace, but the fireplace is in the dining room where I suspect Karin to be.

Stumbling across the landing, I'm briefly tempted to pop into Lena's old room when the thought of protecting Karin is displaced by the thought of little Hannah. Nothing must happen to her.

I hear Karin again and pause.

'What the hell were you doing?' she shouts. And gets a soft reply: 'It's impolite not to wave back.'

Hannah! That was Hannah replying.

I hurry to the stairs, then down the stairs, through the hallway and into the brightly lit dining room, where Karin is holding tightly on to Hannah's arm.

'What's going on?' I ask, looking around incredulously. No burglar, no struggle, just Hannah and Karin.

'I saw them from the window!'

When I see Hannah wince in Karin's firm grip, I leap forwards and release my wife's clenched fingers from Hannah's thin arm.

'I didn't know I wasn't allowed to go to the window. I'm sorry.'

'Of course you are, Hannah,' I say, trying to put some distance between the two of them by holding on to Karin's shoulders and pushing her away. 'What happened?'

'When I came downstairs for a glass of water I heard her by the roller blinds. I thought it was a burglar,' Karin says breathlessly. I take her to the dining table and lower her gently on to a chair. She's trembling. 'She says someone was throwing stones at her bedroom window.'

'It's true. I'm not lying,' Hannah interjects. 'I couldn't really see who it was so I came downstairs. You get a better view of outside from here.'

'How fortunate that you only looked out of the window rather than unlocking the front door,' Karin says sarcastically, propping her elbows on the table and putting her head in her hands.

'Is there someone outside the front door?' As if on autopilot, my body turns to the fireplace, to the poker.

'No, there's nobody there,' Karin interrupts me mid-movement. 'Hannah must have scared him off when she gave him such a friendly wave.'

'Oh, Karin, stop it, please,' I say, nodding towards Hannah. She looks pitiful enough as it is in her nightie from the clothes bank, which is far too big but also far too thin for the autumn weather. Her head hangs heavily and sadly on her narrow, limp shoulders.

'Hannah,' I say, stepping over to her and struggling to bend down on my old knees. 'Will you tell me what happened?'

'Someone was standing in the garden and threw something at my window. I thought at first it had started raining. It sounded just like it, a small, gentle tinkling. But then I thought I'd better check, though all I could see was a shadow. So I went downstairs into the other room.'

'And there was someone standing at the window?'

She nods.

'We waved at each other.'

'Did you see who it was?'

'It's still very dark outside.'

I stroke her arms to comfort her.

'No need to worry. I'll have a quick check. Go back upstairs and lie down, okay?'

Hannah nods again and says over her shoulder to Karin, 'I'm sorry. I promise I'll never go to the window again without permission.'

When Karin just sighs, I say in her place, 'It's all right, Hannah. You've done nothing wrong. Everything's okay. Go back to bed, now. We'll be up in a sec.'

I keep my eyes fixed on Karin as I listen to Hannah's cautious little footsteps. When I think she's out of earshot, I launch into Karin: 'How could you?'

'Please!' she snarls, taking her hands from her head.

'She might have just had a bad dream. And you get at her like that!'

'Or it's just as I feared.' Karin gives the tabletop a feeble thud. 'One of those press vultures set up camp outside overnight.'

243

'Rubbish. They all left just before nine o'clock. We heard the cars drive off. And when I went to check a little later there was nobody there. They realised there's nothing to be had here.'

Karin ignores my objection.

'And then Hannah's encouraging these people by giving them a jolly picture of her waving! I told you, Matthias! I said right at the start that I didn't want any of that again. I don't want to see myself in the paper every day.' Karin jumps up so abruptly that her chair almost topples over. She catches the backrest just in time and pushes the chair to the table.

'I'm going to take a look just to be sure,' I say, turning to the fireplace and taking the poker from its stand. 'If anything needs sorting out, I'll sort it out. And you're going to go back up to Hannah. But be friendly, Karin, okay?'

Outside it's completely silent save for the birds who've started chirruping away in the dawn light. Poker in hand, I stand on the top of the four steps that lead down from our front door. My gaze flits across the front garden. The garden gate is shut and there's no sign that anyone was on our property a few minutes ago. And apart from the rose bushes, there are no shrubs or trees with large trunks, behind which an intruder could hide. Even in the grey dawn light, I have a good view of our small front garden, which sits there in peace. Just as I suspected, Hannah must have had a bad dream.

MATTHIAS

I don't know what's up with Karin. It begins at breakfast. Hannah only eats a slice of bread with butter, just like yesterday evening.

So what? Well, Karin thought she was giving her a treat – *offering* her something – when she brought a jar of Nutella from the kitchen and placed it on the dining-room table.

'So far as I know, all children love Nutella,' she said, giving Hannah a conspiratorial wink.

But after studying the ingredients on the jar, Hannah pushed the Nutella away.

'You mustn't eat too much sugar. The excessive consumption of sugar and sugary foods can lead to the following symptoms: tiredness, lack of motivation, anxiety, digestive problems, flatulence, diarrhoea or constipation, nervousness, sleep and concentration disorders, as well as tooth decay.'

Karin's lips formed a half-baked smile, then she picked up the jar, took it back into the kitchen and stuffed it into the larder, with all the chocolate bars, bags of gummy bears and packets of biscuits she'd bought specially once we knew for sure Hannah was going to stay with us. I can understand her disappointment. She meant well. But couldn't she have been happy with taking the jar off the table?

No, now she starts sniffling too. I can hear it from the dining room. I've already braced my hands on the table to push myself up and follow her into the kitchen. But then I think better of it. Hannah is sitting opposite, looking at me. On the plate in front of her is a plain slice of bread she hasn't touched since Karin shot off into the kitchen.

'Just butter?' I ask.

Hannah nods.

I reach across the table and pull her plate over so I can butter the bread.

'Thanks,' she says very politely when I give her back the plate. 'Do start, Hannah. I'm just going to check on Grandma.'

'Can't we just have breakfast in peace?'

I try to whisper so Hannah won't hear, but even at this low volume there's an unmistakable sharpness to my tone which surprises Karin as well as myself.

'I don't want to live like this, Matthias,' she says, pointing vaguely upwards. Unusually for this time of day the ceiling lamp casts a cold white light into the room. In all rooms, to be exact, for the roller blinds are still down throughout the house.

'There aren't half as many as yesterday, Karin,' I say, referring to the journalists who are kicking their heels pointlessly on the pavement outside. When I went to fetch the newspaper from the mailbox at half past six this morning nobody had turned up yet, and I almost thought it would stay that way. The first car finally arrived around eight o'clock.

'Yes.' Karin laughs scornfully. 'They got their photo of Hannah last night.'

'Don't start again, please. Nobody was here last night. Hannah had a bad dream. And you've seen today's paper. There's no picture of Hannah waving, just . . .' I hesitate when I realise. But I don't want any discussion now about whether the article in the *Bayerisches Tagblatt*, attacking the police's handling of the case, is justified or not. 'Listen, Karin,' I say instead. 'It's not easy for me either. But all that matters at the moment is that we find out who this guy was and what he did to our girl.' My throat turns dry. 'And where he took her.'

'That's what this is about, is it?' Karin's eyes are still shimmering with a film of moisture, and now there's a disconcerting, sinister note to her expression.

'Yes, of course. What did you think?'

'You haven't even asked Mark if he's met Gerd.'

'Gerd would have told me.'

Karin throws her hands in the air.

'You don't even see that!'

'Don't be so loud,' I hiss, peering around the corner at Hannah. She's staring straight ahead of her as she chews thoughtfully on her bread. Fortunately she's sitting side-on to us, which means her vacant gaze passes us by and perhaps alights on the fireplace.

'What don't I see?' I say, turning back to Karin.

'Gerd doesn't talk to you unless he absolutely has to. And today's newspaper article gives him even more reason not to.'

'Gerd doesn't talk to me? Really? Then maybe there's something wrong with my memory. I must have imagined him calling me in the middle of the night when Frau Grass was admitted to hospital.'

'He called *us*, Matthias. And I'm sure he regrets that now. He didn't want us to go to the hospital in Cham. That was *your* decision.'

'No, it was *our* decision!'

I shake my head wearily.

'Why are we talking about Gerd, anyway? I was asking you why you were making such a fuss over a jar of Nutella.'

Karin's chin is quivering.

'Because you claim this is about Lena. But that's not true. Not anymore. Now it's all about Hannah, isn't it?'

I can barely believe what I'm hearing. How can she have the

nerve to talk like this? My Lenchen, my everything . . . Only the thought that this is Karin, the woman I've been married to for almost forty years, prevents me from turning abusive. Had it been Gerd, Giesner or Mark, I'd have grabbed them by the collar for being so offensive.

'Hannah is all we have left,' I say instead, then in the same breath add, 'and Jonathan,' to avoid giving her more ammunition in this dreadful conversation.

But it seems that Karin refuses to accept this.

'How do you know that?' she shouts, keeps shouting, while I say 'Shh!' and peer around the corner again to see if Hannah is listening. 'They still haven't found Lena's body! What if – ?'

'Karin. We know she's dead,' I interrupt, when I see that Hannah's still sitting unfazed at the table like a good girl, eating her bread.

'But how? When Gerd called us a fortnight ago on the night of the accident, neither of us doubted that Lena might be still alive, did we?'

'Karin, please – '

'And you're doing nothing to help!'

'What?'

'You could ask Hannah about her!'

'I'm not a psychologist, Karin! You can't predict what you might unleash if you – '

'Wasn't it you who said the so-called professionals haven't got a clue? And yet you seem to feel you're enough of a psychology expert to bring her home to us,' she interjects.

'Karin, it's all right.' I take a step towards her and take her shoulders. 'I promise I'll give Mark a call later. Gerd too. In return you're going to join Hannah and me at the table and have breakfast with us. Okay?'

Karin opens her mouth, but then appears to change her mind and just nods weakly. I take her hand and pull her into the dining room. But Hannah's no longer in her chair.

'Where is she?'

'In the loo, probably,' Karin says, but I know at once that can't be the case.

'Hannah!' I race into the hallway.

'I'll look upstairs,' Karin says, scurrying up the stairs.

The guest loo at the back of the hallway is empty. I close the door I just opened a second ago. Of course she didn't go to the loo. It's not Hannah's time for the loo, and she wouldn't go without asking permission first. She probably did hear Karin and me arguing and got a fright. I can't help thinking of Lena, who also hated it when we argued. She always hid, usually in the big cupboard in the hallway. She would sit there, her knees up to her chest, waiting for us to look for her and eventually find her. It was as if she was trying to distract us from arguing. About the household goods we had difficulty paying off every month, my practice, which wasn't going so well, parenting, the washing, which I had promised to do but forgot, and all those tiny things that blow up from time to time.

I carefully approach the antique fir wood cupboard beneath the stairs, where Karin keeps the jackets and coats we don't use every day. A memory . . .

Found you! Finally!

Were you worried about me, Papa?

249

Terribly worried, darling!

That's good . . .

I'm just about to open the cupboard door when Karin calls out from upstairs, 'She's in her room!' In a flash my heart returns to normal and a smile darts across my lips. I'm relieved, but slightly disappointed too. Maybe I wanted to find Hannah in the cupboard.

Were you worried about me, Grandad?

Terribly worried, darling!

'Would you come up, Matthias?' Karin says.

When my foot is on the bottom step I detect a movement from the corner of my eye: a shadow darting about behind the pane of frosted glass in the front door. I don't think, I make straight for the door and yank it open at the very moment a woman puts a large cardboard box sealed with packing tape on our doormat.

'Herr Beck . . . hello,' she stammers, clearly as flummoxed as I am, and takes a step back in shock.

At the same time the small bunch gathered outside our gate has been stirred into a frenzy of activity. Cameras click like keys on a typewriter and questions are shot at me like missiles.

'How's the girl, Herr Beck?'

'What about the boy, Herr Beck?'

'Any news on the whereabouts of your daughter, Herr Beck?'

'Is it true you feel let down by the police?'

My eyes flit between the brown cardboard box by my feet, the woman who's going unsteadily back down the steps to the front garden, and the bawling mob on the other side of the garden fence.

'Is Hannah going to live with you permanently now, Herr Beck?'

'Are you going to bring Jonathan back here too?'

'Herr Beck! Herr Beck!'

Then everything erupts, a sudden explosion of sheer despair. 'Piss off!' I bellow. 'Piss off, you bastards, or I'll call the police and sue you for harassment!' I kick the heavy box on our doormat, kick it towards the woman who has now negotiated the last of the four steps and is continuing her retreat on the flat, tiled path. I know her. I recognise the red hair and light blue coat. She was here yesterday when I came back from the trauma centre with Hannah. 'Just leave us in peace,' I growl at her before going back inside the house and closing the door noisily behind me.

'So that's the headline we're going to be reading tomorrow.'

I hear Karin's grim voice coming from the top of the stairs. I turn my head feebly towards her.

'I'm sorry.'

My wife rolls her eyes.

'You're always saying that. By the way, Hannah has locked herself in her room. Maybe you can try.'

'She's – ?'

'Locked herself in. Voluntarily.'

JASMIN

I wake up. It's not ten to seven and I haven't got his voice inside my head, but I do have a hangover-like feeling, which immediately reminds me of yesterday evening. I feel beside me, where Kirsten ought to be, but then I remember she'd planned to go home this morning to feed Ignaz and then do some shopping for us. She must have already left, for I can't hear any sounds coming from the bathroom or kitchen. Maybe it's a good thing that I'm on my own, a sort of grace period. When she comes back we're going to call Cham. I need to look at the facial reconstruction. I have to, of course. Especially as since yesterday evening there's now another urgent reason why I should meet him.

'That could be an important piece of information, Jasmin,' Dr Hamstedt had said. 'It may even help establish the identity of your abductor and his motive. It sounds very personal somehow, don't you think?'

'Or maybe he just read the reports in the newspaper and was having a bit of fun.'

'Possibly. But I think you should talk to Inspector Giesner as soon as possible.'

The very thought of it makes me want to turn over and go back to sleep. But how could I, Lena, with you staring at me from the walls a hundred times over? Encouraging me, urging me, smiling from all those photos in the countless newspaper articles I stuck up on the walls? I concede defeat and get up.

My apartment is indeed empty, Kirsten already gone. I toddle into the kitchen, still feeling sluggish, fill a glass with water from the tap and take my painkillers, half a tablet more than necessary, as ever. Yesterday evening is still playing as a loop inside my head. My meeting with Dr Hamstedt. I'd never intended our conversation to go the way it did. I just wanted to tell her why I'd hit on the idea, which must have sounded utterly ludicrous at first, that the letters might be from the children. I didn't want to come across as crazy, not like someone who for good reason would be better off in a room without a door handle. All I wanted to tell her was that the children, especially Jonathan, had very good reason to be disappointed in me. Hate me. Send me letters reminding me of my guilt. I had abused Jonathan's loving gesture, the greatest act of his life, his gift and his trust, to kill his father. Then, without looking back, I'd run to my freedom – in front of a car, perhaps – but I'd run away. First I'd taken everything from the children – their father, their mother, who they'd accepted me as, their home – and then I'd abandoned them.

As I told Dr Hamstedt of my escape, I drifted ever further away. I'd become so drawn in to my own story that I felt as if I were experiencing the whole thing again. I ran through the woods. I felt the uneven ground beneath my feet, which made me stumble, the branches hitting my face and scratching my skin. I could hear the cracking of the undergrowth, my own, laborious panting, and everything was so real. The moment when I emerged from the woods on to the road. The car that hit me. The bright flashes exploding before my eyes. The hard, muffled thud when my body landed on the tarmac. I blinked when I heard the voice of the driver, bent over me, as if I were under a bell jar.

'Frau Grass,' I heard him say several times before realising that there was something not right about his voice. Of course he couldn't have called me by my name. The person really talking to me at that moment was Dr Hamstedt, trying to haul me back to reality.

'Frau Grass! Nice and calm, now, Frau Grass!' I heard her say emphatically, and felt her hands around my shoulders. I hadn't even twigged that as I was telling my story she'd got up from her chair on the other side of the desk. 'Are you all right, Frau Grass?'

'Yes,' I gasped. 'Yes, I . . .' I grabbed my head and realised I was burning hot. 'I'm sorry, I don't know what got into me.'

'No need to apologise, Frau Grass. Would you like a glass of water, perhaps?'

'No, thanks. I'm better now.' I hardly dared look her in the eye, so I searched for another, more innocuous object to focus on. The notepad, which lay on Dr Hamstedt's desk beside the two letters. But then I realised what I was staring at. Dr Hamstedt had been taking notes.

'You've been writing?'

'Yes.' She nodded, but she was smiling. 'You were incredible, Jasmin. I know similar things from therapies that work with hypnosis techniques. But you went back of your own accord and without my help, and relived the day of your escape. And you mentioned something . . .' She picked up her notepad and tapped with her finger on a particular place. 'Here,' she said, looking almost excited. 'You said your abductor wanted your baby to be called Sara or Matthias. Do you know that Lena Beck's father is called Matthias?'

'Yes,' I said, but neglected to tell her that I had my extensive research to thank for this detail, the research that covered the walls of my bedroom. Dr Hamstedt didn't appear to think I was crazy and I wanted it to stay that way.

'That could be an important piece of information, Jasmin. It may even help establish the identity of your abductor and his motive. It sounds very personal somehow, don't you think?'

'Or maybe he just read the reports in the newspaper and was having a bit of fun.'

'Possibly. But I think you should talk to Inspector Giesner as soon as possible.'

'Do you really think it might be so important?'

Dr Hamstedt nodded.

'Why should the abductor want to call your child after the father of his first victim?'

'I don't know. Maybe he was a sick bastard?' With the tip of my tongue I felt for the hole in my jaw, which had healed, but was still there. 'You're the expert. So, what was he? A sadist?'

Dr Hamstedt rocked her head from side to side and said, 'For Lena Beck, Matthias would have had a significance. It would have probably been torture for her, having to call her child by her father's name all the time, a constant reminder of the life she'd had. But for you, Jasmin, the name would have had no meaning at all during your time in the cabin. You only found out that Lena's father was called Matthias after your escape. So as far as I'm concerned, there's definitely a personal aspect here. Even if he couldn't torture *you* with the name, it must have satisfied him in some way or other.'

'Well, he did think I was Lena.'

'He tried to turn you into Lena. There's a difference.' She pursed her lips pensively. 'Maybe he knew him.'

'Who did he know?'

'Lena's father. Although . . .' she said, still thinking this through. 'So far as I know, Herr Beck didn't recognise the perpetrator from the facial reconstruction. But you'd best discuss these things directly with Inspector Giesner.'

The facial reconstruction. All at once I felt sick, the same feeling that's overcoming me now. I try to convince myself that it's just a picture, a piece of paper, but that doesn't help. My stomach cramps; my cheeks suck inwards at the sour taste in my mouth. I slam my water glass on the kitchen table and hurry into the bathroom, where I kneel beside the toilet bowl, my fingers clutching the rim. I kneel there for a while and the reflex won't come to an end, although by now my stomach's empty and all that's coming up are deep, hollow sounds.

'I beg you, Jasmin,' Dr Hamstedt said, picking up the letters from her desk, folding them and slipping them back into the envelopes. 'Do call Inspector Giesner. Talk to him. Tell him about the letters too,' she said, holding them up pointedly. 'Although it's out of the question that the children could have been involved, I think Inspector Giesner ought to take a look at them.'

I nodded.

'Okay, yes. I promise I'll give him a call in the morning.' I got up from my chair and offered her my hand to say goodbye, but noticed a hesitation in her movements which unsettled me fleetingly.

'There's something else, isn't there?' I said.

'For the time being I've left Hannah in the care of her grandparents.'

'She's . . . out of the clinic?'

My heart started racing. Dr Hamstedt realised that I was worried by what she'd said.

'Please give Dr Brenner a chance, Jasmin. I'm sure it'll be of help.'

She's out of the clinic . . . I crawl over to the sink and pull myself up weakly. There are still cramps in my stomach; I try to breathe. I turn on the tap and wash my face. The woman in the mirror looks sick. Her complexion is grey, dark shadows circle her eyes. Nonetheless she nods at me determinedly. *You should ring Cham.*

I know. *He can check the letters for fingerprints and then you'll have certainty.* But he'll take the opportunity to show me the facial reconstruction too, and I'm not sure I'll be able to take that. What if I lose control like with Dr Hamstedt yesterday evening? The last morsel of control I still possess? What if I see the reconstruction, then everything surfaces and I simply start talking, telling him everything, unable to stop? I shake my head. I will ring Cham, but not till later and only when Kirsten's here. *Kirsten, who thinks you're sick.* Who's right. *For whom you're a burden.* I slap the side of the sink and breathe out the resulting pain through clenched teeth. All of a sudden the woman in the mirror looks up. *Someone's here.*

JASMIN

I dash out of the bathroom and into the hallway. I know at once that it's not Kirsten. She must have taken the key because it's not in the lock. And the knocking on the door isn't our signal. I'm expecting it to be Cham, who must have taken the decision of whether and when I'm going to talk to him out of my hands. But then I hear the voice in-between the knocking.

'Frau Grass? It's Maja here. I'm a bit early with lunch today!'

I pause.

'Frau Grass?'

As I quietly approach the front door, Maja starts knocking again.

'Frau Grass, it's Maja here!' The floorboard outside my apartment creaks several times. Maja's getting impatient. I take a deep breath and open the door.

'Did I wake you, Frau Grass?'

'No, it's fine.' I sigh.

257

Maja holds out a Tupperware container with a green lid. There doesn't seem to be any post.

'I'm afraid I wasn't able to warm the food today,' she says. 'My microwave is broken.'

'That's fine, don't worry. Thanks.'

I take the container and am just about to turn around to put it on the cabinet when Maja pushes the door and is now inside my apartment.

'No, Frau Grass, it's not,' she says so firmly that I flinch. 'I gave Frau Bar-Lev my solemn promise that I'd look after you, and now I'm bringing you cold food. She'll kill me if she finds out.'

'I won't tell her,' I say briskly, still trying to comprehend that Maja has just entered my flat and right now is shutting the door behind her as if it's completely normal.

'No way.'

She grabs the container from my fingers, which are still stiff with fear, and hurries past me. 'I'm just going to quickly heat this up for you. You've got a microwave, haven't you?'

My eyes, which can't believe what they're seeing, are fixed on the doorway to the kitchen where Maja has just gone. A moment later I hear her call out, 'There you go.'

When I enter the kitchen she's turning the timer on the microwave, which starts humming.

'I hope you're hungry, Frau Grass. It's vegetable gratin today. I chose it myself, I hope it's okay.' She spins around and gives me an overly sweet smile. 'In my freezer there's still a pasta bake and something with mince. At least I think so. Frau Bar-Lev's handwriting isn't that easy to decipher. So you can decide what you'd like tomorrow.'

'Thanks, Maja. I think I'll manage now.'

'I could wash up if you like?'

'That's not necessary. My friend will do it later.'

'Oh yes, Kerstin. I met her yesterday. I hope you liked the chicken soup.'

'Kirsten. Her name's Kirsten. She told you she's moved in here temporarily. She's a very good cook, so I won't starve.' I turn to the hallway, encouraging her to leave. 'Well . . . I don't mean to throw you out, but I'd really like to have a lie-down. I don't feel so well today.'

Maja is still smiling, though now there's something stiff and unnatural about her expression. As if she were a sculpture created by an artist who'd never seen a real smile and had fashioned it merely on the basis of what they'd heard and using their own imagination. As if Hannah had done it.

'But first you've got to eat something, Frau Grass.' The microwave beeps as if on cue. 'Ping!' Maja says, imitating the sound. 'Look, it's already done.'

She turns her back to me and I watch her open the kitchen cupboards and drawers in the search for a plate and some cutlery. She's too close, I think. Too close to the knife block. It would take a single swish of the hand. I carefully take a step backwards.

'Where did you vanish to so quickly last time, Maja? When I came from the kitchen with the dishes you were gone.'

Maja darts to the other side of the kitchen, to the microwave and away from the knives.

'Smells delicious,' her cheery voice says.

I take a further step back and bump into the kitchen door.

'Maja?'

'Last time? Oh yes. I remembered I had a pizza in the oven and there's nothing worse than burned pizza. Although that's not true, is it? There's much worse, isn't there, Frau Grass?'

I grab my throat, which suddenly feels constricted.

'My friend's going to be back soon.'

Unfazed, Maja empties the contents of the Tupperware on to the plate.

'Sit down, Frau Grass.'

The kitchen door is pressing into my back. Just one step to the side and I could back into the hallway, but my body's not working; it seems to be uncoupled from the synapses inside my head, it just stands there rigidly. I stare and croak, 'She's just gone to fetch a few of her things. She'll be back any minute.'

'I'm sorry, Jasmin.' With the plate in one hand and the knife and fork in the other, Maja turns around to me. 'I'm afraid there's only enough lunch for one.'

HANNAH

Some things aren't right. The garden, for example. It's not huge, it's not at least five hundred steps in every direction. And there aren't any hydrangeas, either, with flowers as big as cabbages. I know, because I've peeked through the gaps in the roller blinds. All that's outside in the garden are a few thin, crooked rose bushes and people with cameras.

Grandma's not right either. She's not that nice and she hasn't told me a goodnight story yet..

Only Grandad is right, exactly right. He's very polite when he knocks on the door to Mama's room.

'Hannah, open up, please,' he says. You always have to say please and thank you. You always have to be polite.

I turn the key and he comes in. 'Why did you lock the door, Hannah?' He looks really horrified.

'Because you forgot to, of course,' I say. 'The adults always have to lock the children up before they argue.'

'Oh,' Grandad says. He puts a hand on my back and pushes me over to Mama's bed. 'Sit down, Hannah.' I obey him, even though I'd rather sit on the swivel chair. It's very comfortable, Grandad was right. And you can roll on it from one end of the room to the other.

'Listen, Hannah,' Grandad says. The mattress bounces when he sits beside me. 'Your grandmother and I weren't really arguing. We were just discussing something we have different opinions about. That's perfectly normal and there's nothing bad about it. You don't need to be afraid.'

I look up to the stars on the ceiling. Usually this makes me think of when I used to lie in bed at home with Mama beside me, moving my finger along the slatted frame of Jonathan's bunk from one star to another until they were joined up by invisible lines. Mama would smile and say, 'That's a very well-known constellation, Hannah. The Plough,' and I would smile back, even though some time ago I'd read in the fat book, which is always right, that the Plough isn't a real constellation, but it's made up of the seven brightest stars of the Great Bear.

'I'm sorry,' I say.

'For goodness' sake,' Grandad says, looking even more horrified. 'You don't have to be sorry, Hannah, my love. Your grandmother and I, both of us are delighted to have you here with us. Grandma just got a bit upset because there are so many people outside the house.'

'But there aren't that many. Only six. Yesterday there were many more.'

Grandad coughs but I think it's meant to be a laugh.

'Hannah . . .' he says, but then pauses until he's taken a tissue from his trouser pocket and wiped his nose. 'You can't choose your family. And you can't replace anyone either.' He scrunches up the tissue untidily and puts it back in his pocket. 'But believe me when I say that your grandmother, Karin, is the best grand-mother you could hope to have. She just has to get used to everything first.'

'That's what Papa always used to say.' I smile, although I feel slightly sad when Grandad makes me think of Papa. Grandad appears to be sad too. He presses his lips together so tightly that all I can see of his mouth is a thin line.

'Do you know what, Hannah?' he says after a little while. 'How about we go back down and see Grandma? I bet she's calmed down now and is wondering where we've got to. We could have a look at some photos of your mama when she was a little girl.'

I nod.

'Just one more thing, Hannah. Please don't shut the door any-more. Leave it just a tiny bit open so I know you're all right. Okay? Promise, Hannah?'

I nod again.

Grandad smiles, first at me, then up at Mama's stars. 'You got a star sticker from the dentist. You can put it up there if you like.'

I shake my head.

'That wouldn't work, Grandad. The constellation wouldn't be right.'

'I see,' he says. 'Oh well, it was just an idea.'

When Grandad and I come down the stairs, there's a large package in the hallway and Grandma is closing the front door.

'They've gone,' she says, sounding cheerful. She's holding a letter. 'That was outside the door.'

'Yes,' Grandfather says, taking the letter from her. 'One of the journalists put it there earlier. But I thought she'd taken it away again after I kicked it down the path.'

'What's in it?' Grandma asks.

'No idea.'

There's a *rrrrip* when Grandad tears open the letter.

'Aha,' he says when he's skimmed the note. 'They're things for Hannah and Jonathan. It says:

Many of our readers are concerned about your grandchildren and would like to help. We've put together the things they've sent to us over the past few days or dropped off at our offices. Best regards, the editorial team from Bayerisches Tagblatt.'

'How lovely!' Grandma says, tearing a length of brown sticky tape from the box. 'Come over here, Hannah. Let's take a look.'

I step closer.

Grandma takes items of clothing from the box one by one.

'Look,' she says, holding up a dark blue knitted jumper. 'Do you think Jonathan would like that?'

'He likes blue. His favourite trousers are blue.'

'He'll definitely be pleased about the jumper then.'

'More charity stuff,' Grandad says, scrunching up the letter in his hand. 'Great,' he adds, although it doesn't sound as if he really thinks it's great.

'Matthias,' Grandma says, still taking things from the box, having a look, then sorting them into two piles on the floor. One pile for me, one for Jonathan. 'That's really nice, don't you think? And the clothes are in such good condition . . . Oh, Hannah, look! This is perfect for you.' She holds up a dress; it's white with flowers. 'That's just your dress!'

I'm about to ask her how she knows that when she says, 'And look! Toys too!'

First she takes out an orange plastic digger with a black bucket, but then . . . I immediately drop my dress and put out my hand. Grandma smiles and hands me the small, red-and-white spotted bundle, then turns back to Grandad, saying again how nice the readers of the *Bayerisches Tagblatt* are. Meanwhile I hold Fräulein Tinky to my chest as tightly as I can.

'I've missed you, little one,' I murmur, burying my nose in her soft coat.

JASMIN

My stomach jerks, as if I'd missed a step going downstairs. The key scraping in the lock, the door handle being pressed down several times, the resistance arching my back. Only when I hear the occasional swearing from the other side of the front door do I get up and open it. I've been sitting in front of the door, my back leaned against it, knees up to my chest, my bodyweight acting as a doorstop to defend the apartment against possible intruders.

'What's going on?' Kirsten asks when I pull her into the apartment, snatch the key from her hand and lock it twice from the inside.

'Jassy?'

'She was here!'

'Who?'

'That Maja. You know, the woman who moved into the Hildners' apartment on the second floor. It was creepy.'

Kirsten gives a drawn-out sigh, then takes off her coat.

'I'm here now,' is all she says, without reacting to my behaviour. She reminds me of myself. When I used to live with my mother. When I thought I was there for her even though every moment it felt as if my guts were filled with lead.

'I coped fine while you were away,' I tell Kirsten, who's just hanging her coat up on the rack. I don't want to be a burden on Kirsten, like my mother was a burden on me. 'Really, I did. If you'd rather go home, that's not a problem. And I'm sure you've got to get back to work. Surely they need you at the club, especially now it's the weekend.'

'I get it, Jassy,' she mutters, then turns around to me. 'So? What about Maja from the second floor?'

I hesitate.

'Jassy?' Kirsten strokes my cheek. 'My God, you're all hot again.' Her face takes on a serious, concerned expression. 'Did you get upset?'

I nod.

'Maja. She came and brought me lunch.'

I tell Kirsten about Maja's strange behaviour, her unpleasant pushiness. The moment when she said, 'I'm sorry, Jasmin. I'm afraid there's only enough lunch for one.' And how I just wanted to run away, get away from this woman. I stumbled backwards out of the kitchen, while Maja put the plate of food on the table and came after me. She didn't rush at me, she came slowly, sedately, holding her hands up to reassure me.

'Don't be afraid, Jasmin. I know you've been through a terrible time. Things nobody seems to understand. That's right, isn't it, Jasmin?'

I'd made it into the hallway and had to decide. Right, into the sitting room where my mobile was and I could call for help? Or left into the bedroom where I could lock myself in?

'It's very lonely if nobody understands you, isn't it?'

Left, I decided.

'What do you want from me, Maja? What's this all about?'

'I'd like to listen to you, Jasmin.'

I crashed backwards into the shoe cabinet.

'Talking helps, Jasmin. Trust me.'

*

Kirsten shakes her head, barely able to believe what I'm saying.

'What then?'

'I ran into the bedroom and locked the door. She knocked a few times and tried to convince me to come out. I shouted at her to leave or I'd call the police. All she said was, "That won't help you, Jasmin." Then I heard the front door. She'd gone.'

'She'd gone,' Kirsten repeats in a monotone voice, narrowing her eyes. 'Are you sure it all happened just like that?'

'Of course I'm sure!' I snap, but Kirsten just raises her eyebrows. 'I'm not mad,' I say more calmly. 'Okay, it may have been ridiculous to think that the children wrote those letters. You were right, it must have been some nutter trying to put the wind up me. But the thing with Maja . . .'

Kirsten looks up.

'What do you mean *letters*? There was only one.'

'No,' I say quietly. 'A second one arrived yesterday.' I fish my handbag from the rack and take both envelopes from the side pocket to give them to Kirsten. The first one she opens contains the letter she's already seen.

'Tell the truth,' she reads from the second one, then raises her eyebrows and adds, 'How appropriate.' She gives me back the letter and envelope. 'Why didn't you show me?'

I say nothing.

Kirsten laughs, slightly bitterly.

'Do you realise just how much you're expecting from me?'

'I just didn't want you to worry anymore. So I thought it might be better to discuss it with Dr Hamstedt first. And she assured me it was absolutely impossible for the children to have written them.'

Kirsten sighs.

'And the reason she knows this is because she's the children's therapist, not yours as you told me.'

'Yes,' I say hesitantly.

'I went with you yesterday because I thought you were on the verge of a nervous breakdown.' Kirsten shakes her head. It's silent for a moment before she says, 'Jassy, it won't work like this. If you don't trust me, I can't stay here.'

'It's not that. I do trust you.'

Kirsten laughs again.

'No, you don't! You keep the uncomfortable things to yourself. But I'm not stupid, Jassy. Don't underestimate me.'

I instinctively take a step backwards.

'I remember it exactly when you disappeared. We happened to have had an argument just beforehand. You had an overnight bag on you, I haven't forgotten that. The black one with the silver clasps. I didn't tell the police about it when I reported you missing a couple of days later, because I wanted them to take the search for you seriously. Because I thought it might be salutary if they, the police, discovered you in some hotel room, rather than me finding you, which was what I imagined you were expecting.'

'What are you saying, Kirsten? That I planned my disappearance?' My mouth goes dry. *Go on, start worrying about me, look for me, find me, take me back home.* 'It certainly wasn't my plan to be locked up in a cabin and tortured by a psychopath for four months!'

'I didn't say that.'

'What are you saying, Kirsten? That I'm a liar?'

'That your penchant for drama keeps getting you into trouble, that's what I'm saying. And that you don't realise how ludicrous it makes you look. First you accuse two little, disturbed children of threatening you, and now it's the neighbour from the second floor harassing you.'

'But that's exactly what happened! Maja was here and she harassed me. Yes, she did, she harassed me.'

Kirsten makes an indeterminate gesture with her head. Then she hurries to the door, turns the key in the lock, yanks the door open so hard that it bashes into the cabinet and rushes out of the apartment.

My heart misses a beat.

'No . . . please . . . don't go,' I stammer almost silently. The shock has stolen my tongue, and when I hear Kirsten's footsteps clattering at short, determined intervals down the first flight of stairs, I realise it isn't true what I thought. I can't cope without her; I need her.

I set off after Kirsten. With every step, the pain in my ribcage explodes in my body. I pant.

You're ungrateful, Lena.

'Kirsten, wait . . . I know you only mean well! I'm sorry! I'm really so sorry!'

When I catch up with her on the second floor I realise she had no intention of leaving. She's standing outside Maja's apartment and she gives me a resolute nod before pressing the bell.

'Let's ask her what all this nonsense is about.'

The bell rings. I can hear movement behind the door.

'Frau Grass! Frau Thieme! I haven't seen either of you in ages!' It's not Maja who says this, but Frau Hildner, who never moved out of her second-floor apartment.

JASMIN

I can practically see the cogs setting in motion inside Kirsten's head, turning until they're out of control and Kirsten's eyes open wide. Notwithstanding Frau Hildner, who's still standing in the doorway, Kirsten turns on her heels and races back up the stairs without a word of explanation. Confused, Frau Hildner takes a step forward to see where Kirsten's going, then draws back again and looks at me expectantly.

'We . . . I . . .' I stammer.

'Who is that, Mami?' a little voice in the background asks. It's the Hildners' young son, who appears in the doorway too and clings to his mother's knee.

I'm just about to ask about Maja, but without Kirsten by my side I find it embarrassing to stand here. At once I feel non compos mentis again and mentally ill. What's Frau Hildner going to think of me if I ask her about Maja? No Maja lives here, that's obvious. I fumble around for an explanation, something about my washing machine being broken and wondering if I might be able to use Frau Hildner's over the coming days.

'I just wanted to ask . . .'

Frau Hildner's face suddenly brightens.

'Are you here because of that König woman who's always hanging around here at the moment?'

'That . . . ?'

'Go on, ask me, Frau Grass!' She almost sounds aggressive now. 'Ask me if I talked to her! Of course I didn't! Nor my husband! We'd never do that! She hasn't got a single word out of us, even though she's been doing her darnedest to get us to speak.' She smiles and I'm sure there's a hint of pride in it. 'She's even offered us money, but she's not going to buy us! You've really been through enough already, Frau Grass.' The pride in her smile now gives way to a touch of sympathy.

'Mami? What are you talking about?' the son says, tugging her trouser leg.

'Let go, Lenny. Please. Mami's having a word with Frau Grass.'

Lenny moans something incomprehensible before letting go of his mother and plodding back into the apartment. As she watches him go, Frau Hildner tells him to tidy up his toys.

'I don't understand . . .' I say to turn her attention back to me.

'Yes, that König woman! She had a right tough time with us. But I expect she found another victim after that.' She grimaces. 'I'm sorry. *Victim* isn't a good word. Anyway . . .'

'Kirsten!' I call out a couple of minutes later, and her name echoes in the stairwell. The blood rushes to my head when I run up the stairs. 'Kirsten!' I hold the banister with one hand and the other is gripping my side, my injured ribs throbbing painfully with all this exertion. 'Wait!' I know exactly what's happening two floors above me right now. I can see Kirsten mouthing ugly words of abuse, clattering around the apartment in a blind rage, as aimlessly as a headless chicken, until she remembers the Post-it on the fridge.

And indeed, when I'm back inside the apartment, she's tapping the number on the small, pink note into her mobile.

'No, Kirsten, don't!'

I fly at her and tear the Post-it from her hand.

'What are you doing, Jassy? Give me the number – I'm going to call that woman and ask her what the hell she thinks she's playing at!'

She tries to reach around me and get back the note I'm concealing in my fist behind my back.

'Wait, Kirsten,' I pant. 'I understand it all now! Just listen to me for a minute!'

'Frau Bar-Lev?'

Kirsten's eyeballs seem to bulge in their sockets and her mouth is open. Her expression gives my feelings a face, a terrified, bewildered face. And yet . . . didn't I think precisely this some time ago? Frau Bar-Lev serving coffee to a reporter in her sitting room. Nibbling on a biscuit with her false teeth, casually dropping comments about the poor woman from the fourth floor, who's way too thin, who's stopped washing her hair and is wearing dirty clothes. You only have to look at her to see it, you can see it *all*. Frau Bar-Lev, who's been given the opportunity to top up her modest pension with a little pocket money.

'Are you saying Maja's a journalist?'

I nod.

Sonja Hildner told me about the woman who, going by her description, has to be Maja. Roughly mid-thirties, dyed red hair and a slanted fringe. In search of someone suitable to talk to, she'd obviously rung bell after bell in the building, encountering the resistant Sonja Hildner before coming across the amenable Frau Bar-Lev.

Kirsten is busy with her mobile again, but this time to look up Maja on the internet. Feverishly almost, a fever compared to which my alleged penchant for drama seems to fade into the background, I note with relief.

'That's her,' she says, waving her mobile in excitement. 'Maja König, *Bayerisches Tagblatt*, Munich office. Munich, Jassy! Has she seriously come from Munich to Regensburg every day to bring you lunch? She must be completely obsessed with you!' Kirsten hands me her phone with Maja's picture on the screen. 'We should give Frau Bar-Lev a talking-to, then notify the police.'

'According to Sonja, Frau Bar-Lev is staying with her son at the moment,' I say abstractedly as I gaze at Maja's photo. Maja König, a woman in a white blouse with the collar turned up, smiling coquettishly into the camera. '2004: internship, 2005–08:

traineeship, 2008–11: junior editor, since 2011: "people and current affairs editor".' I read out the short CV below the picture.

'Good, now let's call the police,' Kirsten says. 'Lying to people to gain access to their home must be a criminal offence. And anyway, don't journalists have a sort of professional code of honour too?'

'I don't know, Kirsten. After all, she hasn't written any articles yet. But what will happen if we get the police on her back?' I draw an invisible headline in the air with my finger: *Victim uses police to obstruct journalistic work. Does Jasmin G have something to hide?'*

'But it won't happen like that! Surely she's not going to –'

'The letters!' I blurt out.

'What?'

'They were from Maja! Letter number one arrived on the same day that Maja first came to my door with food. She even brought it up for me, supposedly from my mailbox.' I slap my hand over my mouth. 'What does she want from me?'

'An interview, obviously!'

'All that trouble for an interview?'

Kirsten shrugs.

'You haven't got a clue what an exclusive interview with you would be worth right now. Maybe this is her attempt to break you down, to get you to give her the sensational story.' She shakes her head. 'Honestly, Jassy. Let's call Giesner.' She takes my hand. 'We've got to anyway, you know that.'

I nod.

'The facial reconstruction.'

Kirsten nods too.

'The longer you put it off, the more difficult it's going to be for you.'

'No, we're going to do something else. We're going to call Maja. We're going to find out what she wants.'

'Jassy.' Kirsten sighs.

'And then we'll call Giesner, okay?'

Maja answers after the second ring.

'Hello?' says a very friendly voice.

'Maja? It's Jasmin Grass here.'

'Frau Grass! What a surprise! Is everything all right? Are you feeling better? I think I should apologise for this morning. I must have given you a fright –'

'It's fine,' I interrupt. 'It wasn't your fault. You were just trying to be nice and I overreacted. *I* ought to be apologising to you.'

Kirsten, sitting cross-legged on the sofa beside me, rolls her eyes.

'You know I'm not in a good way at the moment.'

'Yes,' Maja says, sounding concerned. 'My offer still stands, Jasmin. If you need someone to talk to . . .'

'Yes, Maja. I do need someone to talk to.'

'That was quick,' Kirsten says when I hang up soon afterwards. 'What did she say?'

'That she's still at work, but she can come over this evening. Around nine, half past nine.'

'Which means right now she's swanning into her boss's office, bragging that she's clinched the exclusive interview,' Kirsten says. Her grin tells me she is quite keen on my idea after all. Her plan was to call Maja and confront her, and I know she would have done this for me. She'd have been happy to act as an outlet for all the pressure of the past few days and the situation as a whole. But I didn't want to give Maja the opportunity to hang up. Extricate herself from the matter with the push of a button. Not after she'd gone so far and even entered my apartment under false pretences. Not after I had barely any space left in this world, and she'd infiltrated the last few square metres that gave me some inkling of protection and control. Kirsten had to understand this.

'Probably,' I say, returning Kirsten's grin, although I don't really feel like it.

Kirsten reaches for my hand.

'And now . . . ?'

And now.

I take a deep breath.

HANNAH

Grandad is down in the cellar, looking for the old photo albums.

He and Grandma have been arguing again. It didn't bother them that I was standing next to them, listening. Grandad was cross because Grandma had put the photo albums in the cellar. He doesn't think that the pictures of my mama as a girl should be banished to some old crate, and certainly shouldn't be in the cellar, because the cellar's a bit damp and that might ruin the pictures. Grandma said he ought to make his phone calls like he promised he would.

'I'll ring Mark later,' Grandad said, then disappeared into the cellar.

Grandma is in the laundry room.

She told me that you always have to wash other people's clothes before you wear them, and that she's going to wash the donated things in the cardboard box right now so I might be able to put some of them on tomorrow. She wanted to take my dress too, but I held on to it tightly. When she made a funny face, I wanted to tell her that the dress didn't belong to anybody else and so it didn't need washing, but then she said, 'Fine, you can try it on and we'll wash it later.' Probably because she didn't want any more trouble with Grandad. He now knows that Sister Ruth can be my grandma too, if necessary, so Grandma Karin has to pull her socks up and behave well. I think she realises this because I only had to scream once when she was about to take Fräulein Tinky to the laundry room as well. 'But that creature's totally threadbare and filthy . . .' She didn't get any further; my lion voice saved Fräulein Tinky. Although I think that Grandma's not completely wrong, Fräulein Tinky's far too weak for the washing machine. So I had to be there for Fräulein Tinky and save her from being washed. Just as Fräulein Tinky was there for me, so often taking the blame when something fell down or tipped over at home, or when something else stupid happened. She spent a whole night sitting outside our front door for me.

Grandad's in the cellar, Grandma's in the laundry room and I'm in Mama's bedroom. The door is slightly open, as Grandad told me it should be.

I've already got changed and I look beautiful. I turn around in front of the mirror in the door of the wardrobe. Fräulein Tinky's lying on Mama's bed, behind me. 'Look, Fräulein Tinky,' I say, spinning around again especially fast just for her, so the bottom of my skirt flies outwards.

But Fräulein Tinky just rocks her head wearily from side to side. I sit down beside her and lift her on to my lap.

'This is how we always sat by the wood burner at home. Do you remember, Fräulein Tinky?' I ruffle her head. She's still very cold and stiff, but that's no surprise. Maybe she had to sit outside for hours in the box of donations before Grandma finally brought her in. 'Have you seen the pretty stars up there?' I say, pointing to the ceiling. 'Mama did those for us. She knew we'd come here.' I close one eye and with my finger draw the invisible lines for the Plough in the air.

I pull my legs on to the bed and curl up into a ball with Fräulein Tinky in my arms.

'Don't worry,' I whisper to her. 'It won't be long now.'

JASMIN

It's almost seven o'clock already. I don't open the door until the knocking becomes persistent and I recognise Cham's voice calling out, 'Frau Grass? This is Chief Inspector Frank Giesner.'

He's brought with him the policeman who took me home last week with my mother. I invite them in.

'Hello, Herr Giesner,' Kirsten says, stepping out of the bathroom and offering her hand to Cham and the other policeman.

Cham says hello to Kirsten and thanks me for having called him and being prepared to see him today. I apologise for not having made myself available yesterday, and I'm grateful when he doesn't say in front of Kirsten that he tried to reach me on my mobile several times throughout the day. This is another reason why I've forced myself to see him today after all. If I continued to ignore him, I reckoned it would only be a matter of time before he turned up at my front door unannounced. Likewise it could only be a matter of time before Kirsten caught me fiddling with my mobile in an attempt to reject his calls. I doubt she would have understood how I could be so determined to lure Maja to my apartment and cut her down to size, but weasel out of assisting with the police investigation. Because the case is me, it's both of us, Lena. I wish it could just be about you. I want to help you find peace. Help find you. I know you're counting on me, and I'm trying to draw strength from this. I think of your smile, your photo, that carefree moment when you were happy and had no idea what the two of us would have to go through.

'Let's sit down,' Kirsten says, making for the sitting room. When Cham follows her and walks past me, I notice the thin green cardboard folder under his left arm. That must be it, the piece of paper with the facial reconstruction.

'It'll all be very quick, you'll see,' Kirsten assured me earlier on, to give me the last bit of courage, the spark of effort I still needed to dial Cham's number. 'It's purely a formality. You'll look at the picture and identify the man. It's quite simple: yes, that's him. And finished. You don't have to say any more. You put up with that face for four months, Jassy. And you made it. You'll manage the few seconds Giesner needs for his files.' I really wanted to believe her, but I probably didn't appear especially convinced, so she added, 'Trust me, you'll feel a good deal better afterwards. This is the first step forwards for us.' What I heard most clearly in that was *for us*.

'I'm sure this isn't easy for you, Frau Grass,' Cham says as he sits beside Kirsten on the sofa and puts the cardboard folder on the coffee table in front of him. I try to ignore him sizing up my dishevelled appearance, the same stained sweatshirt and tracksuit bottoms baggy at the knees, which I wore for my meeting with

Dr Hamstedt and which at best seemed to confirm that I couldn't be expected to make much of an effort at the moment. 'But I hope you appreciate that we can't spare you this, unfortunately.'

'It's all right,' I say, stifling a cry of pain as I sit in my reading chair. 'Let's get it over with, then,' I say, looking at Kirsten who's giving me nods of encouragement. Cham nods too, then takes the piece of paper from the folder and holds it out to me. I take a deep breath; I breathe to calm my increasing heart rate, my heart that pumps and pushes, expanding its power until I feel it in my whole body rather than just my chest. Then I'm holding the paper in my hands, studying the face, his features. I'm both amazed and terrified. My index finger traces the lines. His picture flashes in my mind, overlapping almost uncannily with the image of him on a sheet of A4 paper, and then everything blurs before my eyes, the image blends with the three-dimensional reality, scraps of memory flare inside my head like shots, tearing me away. It's a vortex, sucking me in, taking me with it; I screw up my eyes and when I open them again I'm back in the woods.

The accident. Bright colours explode before my eyes. Pain. The ground where I'm lying is cold and hard. Someone is bent over me. His voice: 'Shit, are you hurt? Can you hear me?'

I blink weakly, there's blood in my eye. His face keeps blurring.

'Can you hear me? I'm going to call an ambulance, okay?'

I want to nod, but I can't. My eyelids flicker.

'You've got to stay awake, okay? Hello? Can you hear me?'

'Frau Grass?' a distant voice from another reality asks. It's Cham.

'Just give her a moment,' another voice urges: Kirsten.

The headlights, they're blinding me, the pain makes me feel drunk. The man, the driver of the car, is leaning over me. I can vaguely see him put his hand in his coat pocket. 'I'm calling for help, okay? The ambulance will be here soon.' I can relax for a moment. If I die now, I'll be dying in freedom. And this man will have saved me. And I worship it, the face of my rescuer . . .

'Is that him, Frau Grass?'

Suddenly I notice something else too. A sound, like a swishing through the air. I know this type of sound. I heard it earlier, I made it myself when I took a backswing with the snow globe and sent it flailing through the air. And I know the sound that comes afterwards too. Like dropping a watermelon on the floor – *bam!* *That's what it sounds like when you bash someone's head in.* I blink in horror. At first the driver is still kneeling over me, but when I blink again he collapses. Now his face is right beside mine, so close that I ought to be able to feel his breath on my skin. But I don't feel anything; he's not breathing. His eyes are wide open and frozen. I want to scream, but I can't. Not here, not right now. Somewhere else, yes. The scream echoes around my sitting room, mangling the images. I curl up on my reading chair, twitching as if suffering an epileptic fit, everything in convulsion. Kirsten leaps up from the sofa, takes me in her arms. I'm kicking my legs, my face is hot and wet, my skin is burning.

'Jassy! Everything's all right, you're safe. You're at home and I'm here with you. Can you hear me, Jassy?'

'Do you recognise him, Frau Grass?'

Yes, I do recognise him. And I scream – in fear. And I cry – for my rescuer. And I kick – against what this means. And Kirsten holds me tighter.

'Just leave it, Herr Giesner! Can't you see the state she's in?'
You're not well. You need help.

Back. I run. Across the grassed plot of land that surrounds the house and into the neighbouring woods. Branches scratch my skin, I can barely see anything in the darkness. There, suddenly, behind me. Was that a crack?

'Is that the man who abducted you, Frau Grass?'

I could have sworn I smelled stew.

I could have sworn I only hit him once.

His face, shreds, red, everything red.

A room without a door handle. For your own security, Frau Grass.

'Breathe, Jassy, nice and calm. I'm here, everything's all right. Try to breathe.'

It's purely a formality. You'll look at the picture and identify the man. It's quite simple: yes, that's him. And finished. You don't have to say any more.

'I'm here with you, Jassy. You don't have to be afraid. It's over.'

I blink. I feel Kirsten's heartbeat, strong and reliable. Her arms holding me tightly. Her warmth. And then I hear my own voice, saying, 'Yes, that's him.'

MATTHIAS

Hannah's lying on her bed, asleep. She looks like an angel, like my Lenchen. What a picture, spoiled only by the old cuddly toy in her arms, donated by some *Tagblatt* reader, and the faded dress she's got on. We didn't manage to go shopping today, but tomorrow I intend to go to town with Hannah, get her some new clothes and a new toy. Okay, maybe without Hannah, to avoid a scene in the shopping centre. But I have to be confident that Karin will be on top of things if I leave the two of them alone at home for a couple of hours. I carefully spread the bed cover over Hannah's delicate body and whisper, 'Goodnight, my darling.'

I cast a final glance at the little sleeping angel, then leave the door just slightly ajar. Karin has gone to see a friend of hers from her yoga course in Gilching, just down the road, presumably to rant about me.

I'm just going down the stairs when I hear my mobile ring from the living room, reminding me that she may have good reason for her resentment. I've forgotten to call Mark. I hurry down the last few stairs so the insistent ringing doesn't wake Hannah.

The screen reads: *Gerd Brühling, office*.

'Hello?' I say. But before I can get any more words out, Gerd lets rip. He talks of screws loose, lost marbles and me not being all there anymore. I'm a silly old ass, unhinged, useless and dangerous even. I understand the words he's saying, but not what Gerd's problem is.

'I assume we're now over the part where you insult me?' I ask, using the first pause for breath he seems to have taken in his tirade. 'So would you be so kind as to tell me what this is all about?'

'You've been sounding off to the newspaper about our work!' Gerd pants; his outburst has made him run out of steam. I see him before me, sitting behind his desk, his belly tight beneath his wrongly buttoned-up shirt and his fat face bright red. 'The article in today's *Bayerisches Tagblatt*!'

'And?'

'For God's sake,' Gerd snarls, before quoting from today's paper. '*Given that the fruitless combined effort of two police authorities,* open brackets, *Cham and Munich,* close brackets, *continues to grope sedately in the dark, almost three weeks since the escape of Jasmin G, the woman who was abducted, we regard it as our responsibility as an informative and responsible newspaper to make the public aware that a photofit already exists, which could help identify the suspected perpetrator. The authorities are withholding this, however, for they seem to be shying away from the workload that would result if the public became involved in the process of identifying the hitherto unknown man. An unnamed witness recalls a comment to this effect made by one of the investigating officers: "We would have a flood of leads and it would take us ages to work through them all." For this reason no attempt is being made to consult the public, even though this may delay the solving of a case, one of the most sensational of the past decades, for the victims and their families.*

'The unknown man, who was beaten to death by Jasmin G during the course of her escape, is also said to be connected to the case of the Munich party girl, Lena Beck, open brackets, then 23, close brackets. We, the Bayerisches Tagblatt, strongly disapprove of the decision taken by the authorities to withhold important information from the public, which with your help could ultimately lead to the discovery of Lena Beck . . . Can you imagine what it's like here? Our phones won't stop ringing – not because some freaks claim to have recognised the guy, but because they want to complain! It's been like this all day long! Do you think I've got nothing better to do? Shouldn't I be looking for your daughter? Wasn't that what you wanted me to do? Instead I've got to sort this shit out! Look at the time! Can you see how late it is? And I'm still sitting in my office, fielding pointless calls.'

'Somebody's got to do something – ' I growl, but Gerd doesn't seem to be finished.

'We're doing everything, Matthias! We're doing everything we can to find Lena! But it won't work if you hamper our investigation by turning that tabloid, and with it the whole of Bavaria, against us!'

'What do you want me to say now, Gerd? That I'm sorry you've got to do a few hours of overtime just for once? No, I'm not sorry! It's high time someone gave you lot a kick up the arse! Now you've got to deliver, you see, to prevent the public from losing faith in you and the system as a whole!'

'Tell me, is this about your daughter still, or are you just trying to make some sodding point?'

'How dare you?' I bark down the phone. 'Shouldn't you have been round already and shown Karin the photofit, like Giesner said? Shouldn't you have been outside our front door at eight this morning to' – I give a disdainful sniff – 'question *people personally connected* to the case? Where were you then, eh? If you're taking the case as seriously as you claim to be? What if Karin had recognised the man? We might know by now where to start looking for Lena!'

Gerd grunts.

'Just tell me one more thing, Matthias. So I can brace myself. Did you also let that fucking editorial team know that Mark Sutthoff came in for a DNA test?'

'He did . . . what?' I slump on to one of the sofas in our sitting room, by coincidence exactly where Mark sat on Wednesday evening and was given a cup of tea by my wife.

'Well, that's good.' Gerd sighs with relief. He says goodbye.

'Gerd, no, wait, don't hang up! I'm sorry I complained to Rogner about you. But you have to tell me why you gave Mark a DNA test.'

'Like hell I do!' Gerd laughs.

'No, Gerd, really! I swear on my granddaughter's life, I won't mention it to anyone!'

Gerd says nothing; all I hear for a moment is a slight crackling on the line.

'I'm already regretting having trusted that Rogner again. In gratitude he set a mob of reporters on me when I came home with Hannah from the trauma centre.'

Gerd's still saying nothing; more static on the line.

'Please,' I try again. 'Mark paid us a surprise visit two days ago. Although he told us you'd requested his assistance, he didn't say anything about having to give a DNA sample.'

'Hmm, *requested* is relative,' Gerd says. After another short pause, he adds, 'Swear to me, Matthias. Not a word to anyone.'

'Yes! I mean, no. Not a word, I promise. Now, tell me.'

Gerd sighs once more and for a few seconds I honestly worry that this time he won't give in, seeing as after that article was published, my trustworthiness must appear about as steadfast as newspaper ink you touch with damp fingers, sweaty with rage. Yes, it's true. After my conversation with Giesner outside the trauma centre, I really had nothing better to do than to call the editorial office of the *Bayerisches Tagblatt* and air my grievances to Rogner's assistant about the police's unsatisfactory efforts. But far too many things have gone wrong in the thirteen years during which the search for Lena ought to have been carried out thoroughly and consistently, especially now that all the pieces of the puzzle are on the table. No one seems to be prepared to make the effort to put them together, and I can't accept that. How is it possible to have a perpetrator and a crime scene and yet fail to find the victim? How can it be that the most important witness, Frau Grass, has not been interrogated so she finally says what she knows? Why has the hit-and-run driver still not been found, and why have they dug only a metre and a half around the cabin – a pathetic radius – in the hunt for Lena's body? They ought to have excavated the entire fucking wood! I am actually expecting Gerd to snub me this time. I bet he's learned something from his obstinate colleague, Giesner, who wouldn't let me take a picture of the photofit for my wife, not even when I dropped hints about my dicky heart. But it wouldn't have made much difference in the end. One way or another, I'd have got in touch with the newspaper. The only difference is that I'd have sent them my picture of the photofit rather than whining down the phone. They'd have printed it in today's edition and maybe the public would have come up with some useful leads.

Fortunately for me, however, Gerd isn't the stubborn Giesner. Fortunately for me, Gerd is still Gerd, the man who used to be my best friend, my fishing chum, my daughter's godfather. And so he stumbles again and says, 'Okay, then. As you know, as part of our investigation we're obliged to test for blood relationships, even if the case appears obvious. Just as we had to prove the relationship between Lena and the children. But, you see, there's a discrepancy.'

My chest tightens and a ridiculous thought comes to mind: Hannah isn't my granddaughter. It was all a big mistake. I realise I'm shaking my head. *Don't worry, it's not possible. Hannah is your granddaughter. She looks just like your Lenchen.*

'The thing is, Matthias . . .'

She looks just like your Lenchen.

'We haven't been able to establish any blood relationship between the body in the cabin and the children.'

My heart sinks towards my stomach in relief. Of course Hannah is my granddaughter, it's all good.

'That means . . .'

'That means the body in the cabin isn't the biological father of the children. The DNA evidence means it's not possible.'

'Mark Sutthoff,' I pant down the telephone, without really understanding the significance of what I'm saying.

'My colleague, Inspector Giesner, came up with the idea of testing Herr Sutthoff, because Lena had got back together with him shortly before she went missing. Although officially they were separated at the time of the abduction, if you remember, her text messages from the time revealed that the two were back in contact and were planning to make another go of things just as soon as Mark came back from his trip to France.'

'Go on,' I say, grinding my teeth.

'Well, we just did some calculations! We don't have the exact birthdates of the two children, so we have to rely on their statements and the doctors' educated guesses. If Hannah is indeed thirteen years old and Lena disappeared thirteen years and nine months ago, there are only two possibilities. Either Lena fell pregnant immediately after her abduction and Hannah was premature . . . or Lena was already pregnant at the time of her abduction.'

'By Mark Sutthoff,' I say, putting a hand to my mouth.

'Yes,' Gerd says, though he doesn't sound particularly convinced. 'It's just that the corpse's DNA doesn't match Jonathan's either, and he's roughly two years younger than Hannah.'

'Well, is there a match with Mark's DNA?'

'We don't know yet. The laboratory won't have the results until Monday at the earliest.'

'For Christ's sake, Gerd! If Mark is the father, then . . .' Words fail me as the significance of this sinks in, sinks deeper, burying me beneath its immense weight so I can hardly breathe.

Good God, I had him. I actually had him.

My hands on his collar. His back pressed up against the wall. His face as red as a lobster.

Where is she, you bastard?

I had him at a time when Lena must have still been alive.

'Yes,' is all Gerd says.

'But who's the guy in the cabin, then?'

'Hold on, Matthias. Until we have the lab results, everything's just theoretical, do you understand? Until we have the results, Mark Sutthoff remains a witness who's kindly helping us rule out one particular line of enquiry. And, to be honest, I don't think we're going to get a positive result from the lab. He loved Lena, and he's actually a rather nice guy, don't you think? He even asked me for Jasmin G's address because he wanted to send her a get-well-soon card. I couldn't give him the address, of course, but it just goes to show what sort of a person he is.'

'But if—'

'And it's a very big if,' Gerd says. 'Then the corpse in the cabin would be the wrong man. Or there was more than one man involved.'

'One of whom was Mark Sutthoff.' The agonising throbbing above my eyebrow that I'd felt when Mark visited us a couple of days ago begins again.

'We'll soon know. But . . .' Gerd hesitates.

'But what?'

'Listen, Matthias. I want you to get Karin on the phone for me now.'

'I can't. She's out with a friend.'

'Okay, call her then, would you? Tell her to come home. I don't want you to be alone now and do something rash that would end up getting us all into trouble again. You swore on your grand-daughter's life . . .'

Gerd keeps on talking: don't do anything stupid, wait for Karin to get home. I stare into space; his words fly right past me. Even though I'm sitting with my back to the hallway, I can sense it. A shadow in the corner of my eye, at that moment scurrying towards the front door.

JASMIN

Part of me has shut itself off, huddled in a confined, black room with thick, impenetrable walls, while the rest of me is still sitting in my apartment with Giesner and Kirsten, who I've just lied to. Giesner's sheet of paper doesn't show my abductor but the driver of the car that hit me. And slowly, very slowly, drop by drop, the significance of this is trickling into my consciousness.

'There's something else I'd like to discuss with you, Frau Grass,' Cham says, clicking the nib of his biro back into the casing. He's just noted, witnessed by the other policeman, that I've identified my abductor beyond doubt.

My abductor who isn't dead. I realise that what I'd thought when I was admitted to hospital was what actually happened. I hit him only once, not several times, as the police believe, and so furiously that it shattered the snow globe. Just one futile time.

'Just a moment,' Kirsten intervenes. 'With all due respect for your work, Herr Giesner, I think Jassy has done her bit for today. She ought to get some rest now.'

The snow globe only broke when I dropped it on the floor.

Come on, children! Let's go!

'It's fine, Kirsten.'

'Are you sure, Jassy?'

Now I am. I didn't imagine the cracking in the undergrowth as I was running through the woods. He followed me, killed the driver of the car and then stuffed him in the cabin in his place. That's exactly what must have happened. Then he cut up his face until it was unrecognisable, while Hannah went in the ambulance with me.

'Yes, I'm sure.'

Once again I'm seized by that strange feeling I had in the ambulance when I heard Hannah's voice. Hannah, who didn't belong there. And I ask myself why. Why did he let the ambulance take me away? Why didn't he kill me along with the driver of the car? In his eyes surely that was the least I deserved after my attack on him and my escape.

'Excellent, Frau Grass.'

But no, he didn't drag me back to the cabin or into the woods to let me die. He even sent Hannah with me.

'Just let me know whenever you want a break.'

I nod absentmindedly.

Why? Why didn't he just grab the kids and run? Surely he must have realised that the police would launch an investigation, whether I succumbed to my injuries or pulled through. He must have known that the police would find the cabin, of course he did, otherwise he wouldn't have put the driver of the car there in his place. So why? Why?

'Okay, let's go on, Frau Grass. You're almost there.' I think Cham is smiling, but I can't smile back because my features are numb. 'Does the name Sara mean anything to you?'

So there had already been a Sara. The third child your husband had always wanted. You'd given birth to her. The assumption is that she's dead. He wanted to replace his third, dead child, just like he wanted to replace you. Thoughts shimmer in the part of me that's huddled in the confined, black room. The rest of me, sitting with Cham and Kirsten, is completely empty, just a shell, like a dummy standing in for me, giving monotone answers to questions, incapable of telling the truth. Of course I know why. I mean, it's not that hard. Your husband is alive. Your husband let me live. Your husband has a plan. Cham begins talking about the latest DNA results, which effectively prove beyond any doubt that they've got the wrong man. Only they can't work it out, of course they can't, because I'm still keeping my mouth shut. Maybe Cham thinks it's an accident, a contamination in the laboratory that's led to an inaccurate result. His words swirl, surrounding me, becoming more oppressive by the minute. My breathing gets shallower, ever shallower. As if simply by panting I could dismiss the realisation that is so horrific. For a moment it works. But then the heat surges in me again, a merciless, scorching heat. I'm suffocating.

You have to tell them. Open your mouth. The police can help you.

Nobody's going to come and help you. You've just got us now.

For ever and ever and ever.

Your husband's alive. Your husband let me live. Your husband has a plan. And he's coming to get me. At that moment the dummy in my reading chair slumps.

Papa! Mama's had another fit!

MATTHIAS

A shadow flitting across our hallway.

As if in slow motion I turn my head, but I can already hear the door click shut. My mobile slips from my hand and lands with a thud on the living-room carpet. I leap up from the sofa. My footsteps, which ought to be rapid, are heavy. What this means. My heart. My hand reaches for the handle. I wrench open the door. It's already dark outside, only the streetlamps providing yellow islands of light on the black tarmac. My eyes scope the scene. I glimpse her. Hannah, getting into a car about three hundred metres away. And the large, black figure slamming the passenger door behind her. As if paralysed, I watch the man hurry around the car to the driver's door.

'Hannah,' I croak.

The engine starts. The car gets moving. Drives off. It's only now that my paralysis from the shock abates. I rush down the steps, through the open garden gate and into the street and bellow, 'Mark! No!'

But all I can see of Mark and Hannah are two little red taillights in the darkness.

JASMIN

It's too dark. Ever since I was discharged from hospital I've had to have a light on somewhere. Kirsten knows that. Darkness is the storeroom in the cabin, it's the feeling of my arms being painfully stretched, wrists shackled to a waste pipe; it's the terrifying black sphere where my thoughts cannot anchor, it's the fear and the waiting for him to come back and kill me. I blink, but it's still dark. I try to quickly recap what's happened. Cham was here. He showed me the facial reconstruction. I lied, I identified the wrong man. Cham said the children's DNA didn't match that of the body they'd found inside the cabin. He asked me if I could explain that. I could explain it to myself, of course. But not to him. I was too worried he might think I was mad. Too worried that I might actually be mad after everything that's happened. And how would Kirsten react if I came up with the next melodramatic story? How much longer could I punish her? I must have passed out, something inside me must have shut down and sought the easiest route to a short-term blackout. Like back in the cabin. How often did the ceiling tilt, the floor ripple and the room spin as soon as I felt unable to cope? And how grateful I was each time to slide into the redemptive blackness, surrendering to what Hannah called a 'fit'.

I can feel the pillow beside me. Kirsten must have taken me to bed after I collapsed in front of her and Cham. So that's where we're at, and it speaks volumes. Nobody considered calling a doctor or even an ambulance. Because nobody takes me seriously anymore. Because I'm not ill, but at most hysterical. I picture Kirsten panting from the exertion of heaving me up from the sitting-room floor, having assured Cham that there's no cause for concern. It's just nerves, after all, I'd spent two days fretting about the moment when I'd come face to face with the picture of my abductor. Besides, I'm short on sleep, and need peace and quiet. *She's not well. In fact, she's been wetting the bed recently.* And I imagine Cham's reaction. The obligatory comment about the importance of regular visits to the psychotherapist, the universal remedy for someone in my situation.

And am I doing it again or not? If right now what I'm most worried about is what other people might think about me, then that's ludicrous, a shabby attempt to escape inside my head. I *am* doing it again, trying to suppress what's going on here, trying to ignore the panic drumming inside my chest, the fear of the blackness all around me.

I blink again. Black is still black, shapeless, pitch-black. I reach for the bedside light switch. I find it, press it. It clicks, but the room remains black. An unfamiliar sound rises from my throat, not powerful, not loud, but strained; a short, forgotten breath, desperate to catch up. I sit up and look where residual light from the streetlamp should leak into the room through the gaps in the roller blind. No light, just blackness and my heart pounding.

'Kirsten?' I call out and wait for an answer. It doesn't come. I listen out for any sound. But there's nothing. Silence, blackness and my pounding heart. I think I'm dreaming – I know I'm dreaming. And yet I find it hard to calm myself. To resign myself to this oppressive blackness, this sheer disorientation which reminds me of the storeroom, on the day I was abducted. I sink back, close my eyes, breathe in the familiar smell of home, a trace of Kirsten's perfume, the hint of freesias still on the pillow. I can cope with this dream.

But I can't. I open my eyes, again in hope, again in vain. Everything is black. I sit up once more. Feel my way to the edge of the mattress, crawl across the floor to the bedroom door, one arm outstretched. I carefully get up, now feeling for the door handle. I press it down. It squeaks as it always does. Once, again, and many more times in quick succession until I realise that the door won't open. I'm locked in. I feel beside the door frame for the overhead light switch. A click, but it's still black. Click again, still black. I hammer my fist against the door. 'Kirsten!' I shout. 'What's going on? Let me out!' I hammer, I shout, unable to believe this. It's a dream, a bad dream. My breathing is fitful, I'm panting. Then I hear a gentle laugh from the other side of the room. His laugh.

And the question.

'How are you, Lena?'

MATTHIAS

Drive faster. Drivedrivedrivedrive.

The speedometer is quivering at 180. The old banger can't go any faster.

Where's he taken her?

Gerd! flashes in my mind. Gerd's words on the telephone earlier.

He even asked me for Jasmin G's address because he wanted to send her a get-well-soon card. I couldn't give him the address, of course, but it just goes to show what sort of a person he is.

A person who was definitely in a position to get hold of Jasmin G's address, even without Gerd's help. Anyone can do it; it just takes a few clicks on the internet. I narrow my eyes to help me see better in the distance. But the motorway is empty and black. No taillights, not anywhere.

What if he's taking her somewhere else?

I lost valuable time running back into the house to fetch the car keys. I lost years while waiting for the garage door to open, and even more years as I was reversing the car from the garage into the street. More than thirteen years.

I won't be able to catch Mark up.

I didn't lose any time grabbing a coat or putting on shoes. I'm operating the pedals in my slippers.

I ought to have lost time getting my mobile phone, which is now lying uselessly on our living-room carpet.

No mobile. No possibility of calling for help. No support.

I'm alone.

I had him.

My hands on his collar. His back pressed up against the wall. His face lobster-red.

Where is she, you bastard?

I let him go.

In my mind I hear him talking about the Marne Valley, *a beautiful area, incredible countryside* – liar. He was making fun of us. He even admitted to having a daughter. Hannah. How come I didn't see through him?

'Papi,' comes the squeaky voice from the back seat. All I can see in the rear-view mirror is her forehead and her shining eyes standing out against the darkness behind me. 'You've got to help me, Papi.'

'I know, my darling,' I answer, my voice choking.

'This time you've really got to help me.'

'Yes, Lenchen, I know.' I wipe my eyes with the back of my hand when the road ahead starts to blur. 'I'm on my way to help you. This time I won't let you down, I promise.'

'But you've got to hurry, Papi.'

The speedometer is trembling at 200; the old banger is careening.

JASMIN

'Where's Kirsten?' I croak.

'She's not coming,' his voice says. 'No one's coming.'

I slap the door and scream, 'Kirsten!' and 'Help!'

'Shut up!' the voice hisses. 'You wouldn't want to worry the neighbours, would you?'

I keep hammering against the door, banging it, shouting louder, pulling and shaking the handle, which squeaks and squeaks and squeaks. A moment later his hand is there. It takes him a few attempts – in the pitch-black of the room he must be just as disoriented as I am – but then the hand finds what it's looking for, now over my nose and mouth, tight, too tight, I can't breathe. His body pushing firmly against my back, his hand on my face. I start thrashing my legs, I kick the door, am wrenched back, I fall, a hard landing, he's flung me to the floor. I scream in terror and pain and disbelief.

'Please unlock the door.'

Silence.

'Please turn the light on.'

Somewhere in the darkness the voice says, 'I'm afraid it's not so simple, Lena. You see, I flipped the fuse switches.'

I scrabble backwards until I feel the wall at my back. I carefully pull myself up, groping for the wall with my hand. There's a rustling, paper: one of the articles I stuck up. I stick out my other hand into the void. Where is he?

'How did you do this? Who helped you fix it all?'

'Helped? Me?' He laughs; it's coming from my right. 'Nobody, Lena. I'm God, I don't need anybody's help.' Footsteps slowly getting closer, a whisper: 'I can even rise from the dead.'

I push myself along the wall, away from him, the newspaper articles rustling behind me.

'If it's any consolation, you gave me a right proper whack with that snow globe. I had concussion and was even written off sick.' I tremble, he laughs. 'But let's see the positive side. At least I had a bit of time to prepare everything else.'

'You killed the driver,' I pant into the darkness.

'What about you? You would have killed me. Which means you're no better than I am, are you? But, to be honest, I'm surprised you haven't understood all of this until now. I thought you were smarter, I really did.'

'Hannah . . .' I whisper. My legs are weak, *pull yourself together*, keep going, along the wall, it can only be a few more steps. 'You sent Hannah after me.'

'No, actually she went with you of her own accord. And you also had a big head start. Especially as the blow to my head meant I wasn't in the best state to catch you up. Fortunately, however, you ran straight in front of that car.' There is a brief silence in the darkness, then I hear him chuckle. 'But I can see you're keen for the denouement. Like in films. At this point, what happened after the accident would be shown as a flashback from the baddie's viewpoint. It would show him slashing the face of his stand-in, packing the essentials, instructing his son to wait and clean all the surfaces while the baddie himself drives the car involved in the accident across the Czech border and hides it. Grinning, because he knows full well that by the time the police find it he'll be long gone.' He laughs again, from my right, too close. I swing my hand, but into thin air. 'But you can dream up a scenario like that yourself. We don't have much time, my darling.'

'Because now the baddie has come to bring the story to an end and kill the main character.'

'The main character?' Right in front of me. I freeze. His breath on my face. 'Full of confidence, I like that. Believe it or not, I always liked it when you put up some resistance. But no, don't worry. I could have killed you long ago if I'd wanted to. Even at the site of the accident. Why do you think I called an ambulance? You survived because I wanted you to.'

My hand makes a grab to my left, finds the cord for the roller blind and gives it a forceful tug. A gap, the width of a hand, perhaps, and, in the light of the streetlamp, his smile.

'Or, more precisely, because your daughter wanted you to.'

HANNAH

Papa said I should draw something. So I don't get bored while he wakes Mama up. He's brought me a drawing pad and crayons in a metal box, all new. They're really long, longer than my index finger, and there are even three different shades of red: carmine, vermilion and claret. He also gave me a cereal bar in the car, and for the first time ever I was actually pleased to have one. I was so pleased, it made the cereal bar taste a bit better than usual. But I was hungry. At my grandparents' house all I ever had was bread and butter to eat. Papa praised me for remembering everything so well. Better, in fact, than he'd hoped. He says he finds it astonishing. I like being praised. I can be proud of myself now, I think. Although I wonder whether Papa may have doubted me too, because 'astonishing' doesn't just mean 'impressive', it also means 'unexpected'. And that wouldn't be right, seeing as the whole thing was my idea. I mean, he couldn't have had any ideas in his head when he lay on the floor as if dead, soaking the carpet in blood, after the really silly thing Mama did. Mama had opened the cabin door and said in her lion voice, 'Come on, children! Let's go!' But Jonathan and I were still thinking about it. 'Come now! We've got to go!' Jonathan sank to his knees beside Papa, on the carpet soaked in blood. Mama ran outside.

I told Jonathan we ought to split up. The carpet was dirty and had to be cleaned. Cleanliness is important. But Mama had said we should go with her, and you always have to do what grown-ups tell you.

'But look what she did, Hannah!' Jonathan whined as I was deep in thought. I didn't know if he was talking about Papa, who was still lying motionless on the floor, or his broken snow globe, a bit of which he held in his hand.

'Give it to me!' I took the glass shard and put it in the pocket of my dress to stop him hurting himself. Sharp objects can be very dangerous, and there were enough stains on the carpet already. Then I told him I'd made my mind up. He should clean the carpet and I would follow Mama.

Although I was quick, I didn't catch her up until after I heard the big crash. She lay there in the middle of the road, her eyes closed, and a stranger was kneeling over her. I heard him talking to her.

Suddenly there was a crack behind me. It was Papa, who had a red patch on the side of his head. And he was holding our poker. He put a finger up to his pursed lips and went, 'Shh!' Then he held my shoulder and whispered into my ear through the secrets funnel, 'Sit here and close your eyes, Hannah.'

So now I was sitting there in the undergrowth with my eyes closed, just like Papa had told me to. Although I blinked sometimes. I blinked after the *Bam!* and I blinked when there was a rustling and cracking beside me, and Papa laid the man down in the undergrowth. But then I opened my eyes properly again. I wanted to see what was going to happen to Mama.

Papa had grabbed her under the armpits; her head was wobbling loosely on her neck and her legs scraped along the tarmac as Papa dragged her towards the undergrowth too. I leaped from my hiding place and said in my lion voice, 'The ambulance!'

Papa gave a start, almost dropping Mama.

'The man said he was going to call an ambulance. The ambulance won't find her if you take her away!'

'Hannah.'

Papa put Mama back on the road and came over to me. He squatted down and stroked my face. His was completely wet, beads of red sweat rolled from his forehead to below his chin. His collar had turned red too.

'Darling, you don't know what you're talking about.'

'Yes, I do!' my lion voice said. 'An ambulance is a vehicle specially equipped for emergency medical care and is used to administer first aid to sick or injured people and to take them to hospital.'

'Yes, Hannah, that's true, but – '

'And a hospital is a building where diseases or injuries are treated by medical specialists!'

'It's not that simple, my darling – '

'The ambulance has to come!'

'Hannah, you can see what she did.' He meant the red sweat on his face and the thing with the snow globe.

'That was just a silly accident. Please, Papa.' You always have to say please and thank you.

Now Papa went back and forth, rubbing his brow, which smeared the red sweat all over his face. 'Okay, then,' he said eventually. 'Let's get her to a hospital.'

The stranger had a mobile in his coat pocket. A mobile is a cordless and wireless telephone that works almost everywhere. 'I'll call the emergency services now, but then we've got to quickly pop back to the cabin to pack our things.'

But I didn't want to pack my things. And certainly not go *away*, as Papa said. I told him that if we went away, it would be pointless if the hospital made Mama better, because we wouldn't be able to have our better mama back. I almost thought Papa was a bit of an idiot if he hadn't understood by now that I wanted to keep Mama. And I'd have never thought myself that I'd want to keep this mother. When she came to us, I was worried she'd just be another of those who didn't work out. But she did look really good as a mama: she had the scar, the beautiful long, blonde hair and a very white face. Papa had made a real effort with her, because you always have to make an effort, especially for your children. Maybe he'd just got a bit irritated, because Jonathan and I kept telling him we wanted a new mama to stop us feeling so alone at home when Papa went to work. Being a bit irritated doesn't mean you're really angry and you go shouting your head off and punish people, but you don't like it when nobody talks to you anymore. Especially as we'd really deserved a new mama by now. We'd been very good children, Jonathan and I. We'd always done our homework well and I was being serious when I swore I'd learned something from the business with Sara. But when Papa finally saw our point and the new mama lay on our sofa, she didn't seem at all happy to have been chosen. Even though children are the greatest gift there is and you have to be grateful for them. I don't suppose she realised this until the day when the recirculation device stopped working and we almost suffocated. But that didn't matter. At least she'd finally understood. It takes some people a little longer, which doesn't make them a bad person, only a bit of an idiot. They learn slowly, just like Jonathan who didn't learn how to read properly until he was four.

'Okay,' Papa said when he'd finally understood. 'But then I'm going to need your help. Concentrate, Hannah. Will you cope? You will cope, won't you? You're a big girl now. So, listen to me very carefully . . .'

He took off the stranger's coat and put it round my shoulders to stop me freezing in the cold night. You can't concentrate properly if you're freezing. Then we discussed what I had to do and I really tried my best, which wasn't always easy. After all, you mustn't lie. But nor must you be like Jonathan and just say nothing, otherwise people think you're ill and give you pills, or they think you've got something to hide. Then they get suspicious and end up spoiling the entire plan. Even though I knew I was doing everything right, I sometimes worried that Papa might have changed his mind. Then I thought he'd changed the plan without letting me know but had told Grandad, because Grandad kept talking about taking me home. Unfortunately I was wrong and got into all of a muddle. I wasn't even sure if it really was Papa in my grandparents' front garden yesterday evening, throwing stones at the window of Mama's old bedroom. It could have been one of the people who'd been standing outside with their cameras since the day of my arrival – 'hanging about', as Grandma called it. But the very next day – today – the package with my dress and

Fräulein Tinky arrived, and I knew the time had come. Finally we were going to be a family again and have a new home. Papa said Mama was already waiting for us. But the waiting seems to have made her tired, I think, and she had to lie down for a while. That's all right because you always have to have a good rest before doing something special. So Papa brought me to the kitchen in Mama's apartment, took a candle from the windowsill and lit it so I'd have enough light to draw with while he went to wake Mama. He said he had to turn off the light fuses for a while so she doesn't have any problem with brightness when she wakes up. Because the retina problem is in the family. It's very gloomy in the kitchen now, and it's black in the rest of the apartment. It would have been better if Mama had just used dimmer bulbs for her lights. But at least the candlelight is good enough for me to be able to see the difference between the three reds in my box of crayons. After all, I'm drawing the woman lying on the kitchen floor and I definitely need carmine for her. It's not true that this colour is made of cochineal blood. It's more an acid produced by these insects to defend them against their predators. To get the colour, the cochineals are dried and boiled in water with sulphuric acid. But it's always the best colour to use for drawing fresh blood. Claret's fine for old blood, and for really old blood the brown crayon is best.

JASMIN

It's a strange, cement-like layer of horror and affection that covers my face and makes it rigid.

He notices.

'In spite of all that you've done, the children still love you.'

I nod. I understand. The glass shard that Hannah gave me in the hospital. I now realise it wasn't intended as a threat, but as comfort. Her assurance that she'd remembered everything in perfect detail. And by that she meant what Papa had instructed her to do.

'Why didn't you just take the children away? Why did you expose them to this world which they're not capable of understanding?'

I think of Hannah, the zombie girl, whose smile nobody understands. Those terrible faces in the newspaper, the truth and the lies. The scrutiny which the children are also subjected to. Two more tragic curiosities. And tears flood my eyes. Tears of shame, of sympathy, of all the emotions washing to the surface at that moment. I'm crying for all of us.

He puts his hand out to my face and wipes away a tear with his thumb. I cope with it.

'I know it wasn't ideal. But somebody had to look after them in the meantime, didn't they? I've got a life outside of the cabin. What explanation could I have given for suddenly having these two children? I needed time to get everything prepared, too. Give up my job and the apartment. Look for a new home for us. What would it have looked like if I'd vanished from one day to the next? What would people have thought?'

I try to picture him leading his other life, as part of normal society, as a man who buys colourful toothbrush mugs and nobody bats an eyelid. I can't, I still can't.

'What now? What are we going to do now? Are we going to get the children and just disappear?'

'I've already got Hannah. We just need to go and pick up Jonathan.'

'And how are we going to do that?'

'You probably haven't heard of the heart-warming campaign launched by the *Bayerisches Tagblatt*. Two large cardboard boxes full of clothes, books and toys donated by readers. One of them went to the psychiatric clinic. Jonathan will have recognised his favourite trousers and the red T-shirt. He'll know we're coming.'

'But you can't just march into the clinic and take the child away.'

'I didn't have to go into the Becks' house. Hannah came out.'

'Hannah,' I gasp. 'Where is she? I want to see her.'

He cocks his head – that look of his.

'Please,' I say when I think I've grasped the implicit request. You always have to say please and thank you. 'Please take me to my daughter.'

Another moment in which he just stares at me, scrutinises me, his head cocked, that look. Then he bursts out laughing, a laugh that is pure cruelty, a laugh I know from him. One second later he grabs the cord for the roller blind beside me, I hear a crash and it's black in the room again, pitch-black.

'You're so pathetic,' he hisses. 'Pretending all of a sudden to show an interest in the children.' Footsteps, I hear footsteps crossing the room slowly and then something metallic thrown to the ground. The key to the room.

'But in truth you don't give a toss about them.' I slide on my knees, feeling the floor with small, panicky movements. 'You let the newspapers write those lies. You let them say Hannah is malformed. You could have given them an interview to put things right. You could have at least complained to the paper.'

I've got it, the key. I keep crawling, the key tight in my hand.

'Sexual abuse – just that phrase in connection with the children! Just the speculation! I never touched them! You know that full well! I'd have never done that!'

His voice thundering over me, his footsteps that seem to come from all directions. I reach a wall, but I don't know which one.

'What kind of a mother are you who allows something like that to be written? What kind of a mother are you who doesn't stand up for her children? You haven't even gone to visit them!'

The wardrobe, I can feel the wardrobe. Now I know where I am. Where I need to get to.

'You're no mother at all!' the voice booms.

The door, the lock. I fiddle the key in, it slips and falls to the floor.

'A woman who's not good enough for any of this!'

While my mind is snatching scraps of what's happening here – flipping the fuse switches, the circle that's now closing, waking up to him and the darkness, as I did that time in the cabin storeroom, the black room as a warning, a demonstration of his absolute power that still lets him play God, still lets him decide over my life, over the day and night, even here, in my own apartment, in the real world, the freedom that is no more than an impression while he, God, is still alive – I pick up the key and make a second attempt. It goes in, I turn it, I yank the handle, which squeaks, the door opens, I stagger out into the dark hall, close the door, brace myself against it, and now try to lock it from the outside. Resistance pushing against the door from the other side, the key falls to the floor again. I leave it, so what, I just have to get out, out of this apartment, into the refuge of the stairwell. I've almost made it to the front door, just a few more steps, when the voice says behind me, 'Are you really sure you want to go without your friend?'

MATTHIAS

The old banger clatters on to the pavement outside Jasmin Grass's building. One hand is already on the door handle, while the other is switching off the engine. I jump out of the car and run to the entrance. An elderly lady has just gone inside and gives a terrified shriek when I squeeze into the hallway behind her, almost tripping over the suitcase she's put down right behind the door.

'Call the police!' I bark at the woman, grabbing her shoulders. She's shaking. 'Did you hear me? You've got to call the police immediately!'

I leave her and bluster up the stairs. As I know from looking at the bells outside, Jasmin lives on the third or fourth floor.

What if you're mistaken?

What if he didn't bring her here?

Then I'll have let him get away again.

I banish all doubts and focus instead on the stairs.

On the third floor there's no bell with Jasmin Grass's name, so I have to keep going, up another floor. The sweat runs into my collar, and my stiff old body is groaning under the strain. I reach the fourth floor. The first two bells I check rapidly aren't the right ones. Then I do find the right apartment and for a second go completely stiff. It's open a crack. Hannah, I think at once.

'Please don't shut the door anymore,' I asked her only this morning, when she'd locked herself into Lena's old room. 'Leave it just a tiny bit open so I know you're all right.' Hannah, that gorgeous, good girl who always does what you tell her to. I take a deep breath, then cautiously open the door and slip inside the apartment.

The hallway is dark, but I can make out a light from one of the rooms. And I can hear muffled voices. I creep further into the apartment, my entire body pounding. This time I'm going to get Mark. The pain simmering in my chest says it might be the last thing I ever do, but that doesn't bother me. This time, Lenchen, I'm not going to let you down. For the last few steps I try to stay as close to the wall as possible to avoid casting a warning shadow which would alert Mark to my presence. The voices are clearer now.

'We can still be a family.' That must be Jasmin Grass.

Someone gives a drawn-out sigh, a man. Mark.

For a second it is totally silent. Then, without warning, so sudden that my legs almost give way in shock, there's a clatter, a shrill scream mingles with a crash and I leap out from my hiding place, ready to take Mark down.

JASMIN

This is the end, we all know that.

My kitchen, our kitchen, which used to be a place of laughter, conviviality, the heart of our home, has become a site of pain, a sphere full of anger and fear and despair and sorrow. There's no longer any way out, not the one envisaged by God when he

309

intruded into my apartment tonight to take me away. It's as if this moment has become disconnected from the normal course of time; inside this room the world stands still.

It all happened in quick succession.

He shoved me from the dark hallway into the kitchen, where Hannah was sitting at the table, drawing by candlelight. A still life – Kirsten, silent, contorted and motionless on the kitchen tiles. With a checked drying-up cloth gagging her mouth and blood on her face. Blood running from her temple and across her closed eyelids. She could have been dead or unconscious. As I know from experience, you can't always tell by first glance.

Hannah, by her standards sounding jolly when she greeted me with a 'Hello, Mama!' Me, rigid in the door frame, my entire body quivering, shuddering as if in extreme cold, a cold that would not allow me to breathe, gripping me tightly and shaking me.

'Sit down,' he said, before disappearing around the corner. I heard him at the fuse box, returning the little levers, one after the other, back to their original position.

'Kirsten,' I whispered.

Kirsten didn't react.

'I told you to sit!' He came into the kitchen, praised Hannah for her drawing and switched on the light above the cooker.

'I'm not going to tell you a third time.'

I hesitantly went over to the table and sat down. To my left, at most half a metre away, lay Kirsten, contorted, motionless, bleeding.

'That's a good girl,' he said with a smile of satisfaction.

I tried holding his gaze, not to allow myself to get distracted by the knife block on the work surface behind him. Not to allow myself to get distracted by Kirsten, whose pulse I ought to have checked, who I ought to be saving or mourning. She must have unsuspectingly opened the front door to him while I was asleep in my bed. And he'd struck her down.

'Nobody had to get injured,' he said, as if reading my thoughts.

'I know. It's my fault.'

'Absolutely right.'

'It's not so bad, Mama,' Hannah said, looking up from her pad. I could see the almost imperceptible upwards curve of her lips – Hannah's way of smiling. 'It was just a stupid accident.'

I sniff.

'Yes, Hannah, it was.'

A soft groan: Kirsten.

'You see.' He'd heard it too. 'The tough little cookie's still alive.'

'Please, leave her alone,' I said with difficulty. 'This is about us. I made a mistake, lots of mistakes.' From the corner of my eye I detected a movement: Kirsten, lying no more than an arm's length from the doorway to the kitchen. I shifted around on my chair to conceal her from him.

'I disappointed you all. I'm sorry.'

'Is that so?'

'Perhaps I can make it up to you. We can still be a family.'

I don't know when he noticed Kirsten trying to crawl out of the kitchen. Whether he'd been watching her pitiful attempt the whole time, maybe even secretly having a good laugh about it. Whether he'd just been waiting for the right moment when her trembling fingers touched the threshold. Or whether the realisation was sudden, because he'd been focusing not on Kirsten, but on my blatant attempt to play for time. In the blink of an eye he dived around the table, pounced on Kirsten and dragged her by the hair back into the middle of the room. In the blink of an eye I'd jumped up from my seat and was pounding my fists on his back, kicking his legs, screaming. In the blink of an eye I was lying beside her, simply shaken off like a bothersome insect. Only now did I notice the second man collapse to his knees in the doorway, his hand clutching his chest, eyes wide open, his face like colourless wax with deeply etched features distorted by shock. This man hadn't been attacked, there had been no need for that. It was the realisation that had wrestled him to the floor. 'Rogner?' he gasped.

A feeling washed through the room and hit me like a huge, icy wave. I recognised the name, but couldn't remember where from.

'Herr Beck,' was all Rogner said, then, 'Oh well.'

This is the end, we all know that.

Probably even Rogner himself, who now opens the top button of his shirt, as if the collar has become too tight. Matthias Beck, Kirsten and I are sitting in a row along the left-hand wall of the kitchen, all three of us impotent, passive, weak. Rogner doesn't even have a weapon to keep us quiet. He doesn't need one. Matthias Beck is feeling faint; I'm worried it might be his heart. His face is still as white as a sheet and pinched, while he has clenched his right hand into a fist and is pressing it to the left of his chest. Kirsten, who was struck down by Rogner, has a head injury that won't stop bleeding. I press the cloth which was gagging her mouth to the wound, while her head rests wearily on my shoulder. And me, the cause of all of this, the cause of all the pain, I'm not in any state to rise up and launch myself at him, do something, try at least. After Rogner threw me to the ground in both the bedroom and the kitchen, my ribs are as sore as they were after the car accident, the pain as acute; every breath feels like I'm being stabbed by a knife. And I hate myself for it. I should be the one rescuing us, even just for the sake of making amends, even if it means me sacrificing my own life.

Rogner is pacing up and down. I can tell he's thinking. He's thinking about the end. He will have to kill Matthias Beck and Kirsten, there's no other way out. As for me, I'm not sure. Maybe he still intends to take me with him, for Hannah. I ought to have known. I can't help thinking that I ought to have known. That I wasted precious time feeling sorry for myself and suspecting the children. I ought to have known, everything. After all, I know this man.

'Listen.' I try again. 'I'll come with you, okay? I can be your wife and a good mother. But in return you have to let Kirsten and Herr Beck go.'

Rogner spins around. Gives a joyless, dry laugh.

'Don't be so ridiculous. Of course you'll come if I want you to.' He wanders over and looks me in the eye. 'The question is whether I still want that, *Jasmin*.'

I swallow hard several times while Rogner continues his brooding stroll around the kitchen. From right to left and back again, time after time, a caged tiger, an unpredictable wild animal. My gaze remains fixed on the microwave. Maja, I suddenly think. Maja, who I'd completely forgotten. Maja, who was going to come after work. Who will come, because she has no idea that the point of my telephone call was merely to lure her into my apartment to tear a strip off her. She must think I was intending to pour my heart out, provide her with the material for the article of her life. Although she's late – she mentioned nine o'clock or half past nine, and it must be almost eleven by now – she will come, absolutely, she just has to. Maja, who can save us. In my excitement my breathing gets shallower. The moment I hear her at the door I will have to scream, scream at the top of my voice. I realise I'll only have seconds before he beats me or shuts me up some other way, maybe with one of the kitchen knives. But I'll make use of those few seconds. I'll direct all my strength into this cry for help and hope that Maja's reaction is the right one and she alerts the police. I'm startled from my thoughts when Rogner's hand suddenly grabs my chin and moves my gaze from the clock to him.

'I'm sorry, Jasmin,' he says, grinning. 'But she's not going to come.'

I try, but fail, to grasp the sense of what he's saying. He appears amused by the confusion on my face. He lets go of my chin and pats my head as if I were a stupid little puppy.

'I know you had an appointment with Maja. But I'm afraid you're going to have to continue to make do with me.'

'I don't understand . . .'

'Oh dear, such a disappointment, isn't it? And I thought you were smarter than that. But if it's any consolation, Maja didn't understand to begin with, either. She had, after all, been allowed to stand in for me when I was unwell. Apart from some articles – which, by the way, I disapproved of just as much as you did, Herr Beck, but which I'm afraid slipped through somehow – I have to say that she's done a really good job. Under my guidance, of course. First she made friends with your neighbour. Old . . . what's she called? Oh well, it's not important. She was very chatty and immediately told her that she was cooking for you because there was nobody else looking after you. When she'd arranged to go and see her son she was worried about you. Who'd cook for you now? Well, of course Maja was only too happy to take on the responsibility.'

This is like a torrent of cold water right in my face. He'd set Maja on me. Remotely, he knew how I was all the time. Had a laugh at my expense.

'Are you saying – ?'

'Lars Rogner,' he says very formally, not without a hint of disappointment. 'Editor-in-chief, *Bayerisches Tagblatt*. You really ought to read the papers more, Jasmin.' He grins again and now I realise where I know his name from. He wrote lots of articles about you, Lena. Perhaps even most of them. What a gruesome pleasure it must have been for him.

'In Maja's defence,' he continues, 'she thought the whole time it was about getting an interview. It was her job to get friendly with you, win your trust and keep an eye on you. When you rang up today and asked to meet her, the sweet little mouse was so excited. But in the end she had to appreciate that this was a job for the boss.'

I imagine an open-plan office with people behind thin, grey partitions, telephoning animatedly. I can hear the noise of all those fingers clattering away feverishly at the keyboards. I see Maja in her starched white blouse with its raised collar, which she was wearing for the photograph on the online editorial page, and can scarcely believe that Kirsten and I would have just had to click a few more times before stumbling upon a photo of Lars Rogner. We'd have notified the police and now he'd be handcuffed in the cells. Then I picture him in my mind, slinking down the corridors of the editorial offices, on the hunt for someone he could set on me, selecting Maja because she's dedicated, ambitious and, to cap it all, perhaps susceptible to his charm. And she has no idea that rather than furthering her ambitions she's just part of his game. And I fear she's delighted, she feels honoured. He has chosen her.

'Did you . . . ?'

'Oh, please!' He raises his hands defensively. 'Right now Maja's in the office doing overtime. Unfortunately she wasn't the only one at the Becks' house yesterday after Hannah was discharged from the psychiatric clinic. And once you've lost the exclusive claim to a story, you then have to make a bit of an effort if you're going to distinguish yourself from the competition. I suggested she get in touch with your ex-boss at the advertising agency. They met this afternoon. As I hear, you were sacked three weeks prior to your disappearance because one day you failed to turn up to work. He said you didn't get over the break-up with your friend. Or maybe your problems go back further, they're deeper-rooted. You didn't have an easy childhood, did you? After your father died, you lived in a home for a few years until your mother came and took you back in. Nice woman, by the way, your mother. Nice, but quite damaged. You really were – how did she put it? – a *difficult* child.' Rogner clicked his tongue disapprovingly, while I gasped for air a few times. 'A good upbringing is so important, isn't it? Anyway, the article is scheduled to appear in tomorrow's edition, so I imagine Maja's still got quite a bit to do. Let's say she sends her apologies.'

'If I were you, I'd bugger off as quickly as possible,' Kirsten says soberly. As injured as she is, she's still strong and defiant – nobody can change that. Not even an angry god. 'Because if Maja knows you're here . . .'

He waggles his hand grumpily.

'And? Who's saying I did the interview with Jasmin this evening? Perhaps in the official version of events, I don't turn up here till tomorrow morning and find a few corpses. I've got lots of options.'

'You're going nowhere until you tell me what happened to my daughter,' Matthias Beck growls. It's the first thing he's said since he recognised Rogner and slid limply down the wall. Your father, Lena. I can't begin to imagine how painful this discovery must be for him. He's quoted in many of Rogner's articles and must have been in permanent contact with him, his daughter's abductor, unaware, unsuspecting, full of hope.

'Quiet!' Rogner thunders, before immediately regaining his composure. With a sigh he moves his chair and sits facing us, like a ruthless general who's taken three prisoners. There's a furtive expression on his face. 'I've always had respect for you, Herr Beck. Respect of the highest order. I might even go so far as to say I've admired you. The way you fought like a lion for Lena and your family. You failed, obviously, and often what you did was nothing short of idiotic.' He laughs. 'But you never gave up. How I enjoyed reading your emails, the anger in them, the determination. The threat, repeated a hundred times over, that you'd never talk to me again. But then you had no choice. You kept coming back to me, with complaints, with information, clues, always in the hope of some development. You're a father, Herr Beck, a real father. You must understand me, surely? A real father doesn't have a choice.'

'You are perverted,' Beck pants, clutching his chest again.

'And you are here, Herr Beck! What does that say about us? You know full well that you won't get Lena back. But now you've replaced her with Hannah.' Rogner salutes him. 'We're not that dissimilar, Herr Beck.'

'Tell me what you did with my daughter, you monster!'

One side of Rogner's mouth twitches into a smile.

'You have no idea, Herr Beck. The daughter you spent all those years defending never existed. We had an affair. Your daughter was that kind of girl. She had an affair with a married man.' His smile becomes broader, provocative. 'What do you think about that, Herr Beck?'

'That's a lie!'

'No lie,' Rogner protests. 'It's the truth. Can you cope with that, Herr Beck?' He puts his head to one side in feigned sympathy. 'Can your sick heart keep up?'

From the corner of my eye I see Matthias Beck grinding his teeth.

'Well?' Rogner bares his teeth. Then, as if at the flick of a switch, his face darkens. I know this look. It's the last thing you see before his fist slams into your face, his foot starts kicking you mercilessly; before the pain explodes and everything turns black. 'A lying, spoiled brat, stuffed with Papi's cash like a plump Christmas goose. Irresponsible, fickle, lacking any respect. That was the daughter for whom you beat up a man so badly he had to go to hospital and whose reports you faked.' Now he leans his head on the other side to see what effect his words have had. 'Surely you remember our first meeting, Herr Beck? How proudly you showed me Lena's reports. A straight "A" student! My photographer even took pictures of them and I didn't doubt her achievements for one second until I had an interview with her tutor. Your daughter's average grade was a "C" bordering on a "D". But you knew that, didn't you?' Rogner shakes his head, smirking. 'You lied for your daughter from the beginning. And so I suspected we'd have great fun together, which we did, didn't we, Herr Beck? I mean, I had a lot of fun at least.'

'Go on,' Beck growls. 'I want to know it all.'

Rogner mutters something. Looks at Beck. Seems to be thinking.

For a moment I feel a spark of hope. I pray his next reaction will be the right one. Someone intending to escape doesn't have time for long stories. Someone with something to lose keeps the unsayable things to themselves.

'So be it, Herr Beck,' I hear him say and close my eyes.

This is the end.

'We met when Lena was in her second semester. When she turned up at our office enquiring about an internship. Maybe she was motivated by the fleeting desire to stand on her own two feet, or at least to escape her mother's pesky criticism. In the interview, I already guessed that Lena was no journalist. There wasn't a world *around* Lena Beck. Lena Beck *was* the world. Or at least so she thought. Nonetheless I gave her a chance. I asked her to write an article on a particular topic by the following week.' He laughs. 'She didn't, of course. When I called her, she said she'd changed her mind and wanted to concentrate on her studies instead. What a dreadful girl, I thought. And yet I just couldn't get her out of my mind. Her lightness, like a delicate little bird. Her carelessness, which both fascinated and repelled me.' Rogner shakes his head again, this time deep in his memories. 'One thing led to another. But we had to be careful – after all, I was a married man. I'd been married to Simone for twelve years and had never been unfaithful. I'd pledged my life to her and I meant it. Until Lena came on the scene. In the beginning we'd just meet for a few hours, but soon that wasn't enough. So we started spending weekends together. I told Simone I was away for work. As a journalist you spend a lot of time away, so there was no reason for my wife to doubt me. I took Lena to the cabin, which had existed when I was a child. I originally come from near Cham, you see. The cabin . . . I'd played there as a child. Pretended I lived there. It's really lovely. Sadly, you've never seen it by day,' he says to me. There's a hint of melancholy in his voice, but I don't buy it. 'The cabin is at one with its surroundings, it exists outside of time and space. You can't get there by car. At least you couldn't until the police came and made access paths that nature had never intended. Before, you had to park a good half kilometre away, near a footpath, and walk the rest of the way through the woods. There was always something so primordial about that for me. Something romantic, even, when I walked hand in hand with Lena, when we made our own paths to the secret, enchanted place that belonged to just the two of us. Here we existed only for each other; we were secure and far away from the world. Back then the cabin was really run-down. Together we renovated and furnished it.' He looks at me and grins. 'Lena chose the carpet in the sitting room.'

You helped build your prison, Lena.

I peer over at Matthias Beck, a vein protruding on his forehead. He's totally silent, mesmerised. But I suspect it's just a matter of time. He won't be able to stick this out, not for long.

'I lived for our weekends in the cabin. And I thought she felt the same way.' Rogner runs his hands roughly through his dark hair. When he jerks his hands back down, it's now all shaggy where it was neat. 'But I was mistaken. After a while she came up with more and more excuses as to why we couldn't meet. She didn't have time, she had to revise for exams. She had to go to a birthday party. Father, mother, grandmother – all of a sudden there were these endless birthdays. She also stopped answering the mobile phone I'd bought for her. For both of us, as I didn't want Simone to get wind of anything.' He snorts, sounding both scornful and perplexed. I sense him getting ever more caught up in his story, this story becoming an experience he's now reliving. 'Who does she think she is?' his voice now drones through the room. 'Who does she think I am? I'm the best journalist in the country, I know when someone's lying to me. She's lying. So I follow her. And I'm right. She's meeting her ex-boyfriend again. Just when I've told my wife about us. I finally told her, just as Lena wanted. She wanted me to decide. So I told Simone I was leaving her. That I wanted to live with Lena.' He breaks off. At this moment, something happens; I can feel it. All of a sudden he looks unbelievably old. It may be just my imagination, or the unfavourable angle at which the gloomy light from the cooker hits his facial features and distorts them.

'That's why,' Matthias Beck says, clearly having twigged something.

Rogner nods.

'I couldn't stop some papers writing about it. Luckily, people in our business tend to be concise when reporting on suicide, to avoid encouraging other poor, desperate souls.' He rubs his brow, wearily, perhaps in the hope of banishing the images from his head. But in vain.

'Carbon monoxide poisoning. She took our barbecue into the bathroom, sealed the room completely and then lit some charcoal. It's me who finds them when I come home from work. They're lying in the bathtub, Pascal in Simone's arms, almost like they're asleep. But they're not. They're dead.' He takes his hand from his head. The expression that now flashes across his face suggests he's come up with an idea. 'Lena's all I've got left now. I'm never going to relinquish control again. No more disasters like that again, I promise you, Pascal. From now on, Papa's always going to take good care.'

It's silent for a moment, and the silence assumes a tension that's almost unbearable. As if an invisible, deadly gas were swirling around this room, just as it had in Rogner's bathroom. Then Rogner clears his throat, and he appears to have returned from the past, he's back with us, in the kitchen where the inevitable end is being played out.

'Lena wasn't even startled when I intercepted her on the way home from a student party. *Hey, Lars*, she said and laughed. She stank of alcohol and grass. *Haven't seen you in ages.* It had been precisely thirteen days. Thirteen days during which I'd buried my family and converted the cabin. She thought I was joking at first when I took her there. She thought it was a game, even something sexual, perhaps. A little goodbye game. Until I told her about Simone and Pascal. Then it dawned on her. She was never going to leave the cabin. For the first time in her life she was going to take on some responsibility, I'd make sure of that.'

'You . . . you wrote articles about her,' Matthias says, unable to believe what he's hearing.

When Rogner looks at him I can see that the pain has vanished from his face at a stroke. He's grinning again.

'That was my way of letting you know what sort of a girl your daughter really was. Besides, it meant I was always close to the investigation. That's quite important when you've committed a crime and are not particularly keen on the truth coming to light.'

I can see Matthias Beck struggling. The vein on his forehead is throbbing; his lips are moving without any sound. And yet the question, this one question, comes out – probably all of us suspect it's going to be the last one.

'Why did Lena have to die?'

Rogner sighs as he leans back in his chair and puts his head back.

'You think I killed Lena,' he begins cautiously. 'But that's not the case. It was an accident, not long after Sara was born. Our little one. In the beginning she just screamed . . .'

HANNAH

You always have to listen carefully, especially when Papa's talking. I put the red crayon away some time ago. But that's partly because my subject has moved. The woman's not lying on the floor anymore, but sitting by the wall between Grandad and Mama. The carmine crayon won't work for those patches on her face anymore. I'd need the claret one. Papa slammed her head really hard against the wall in the hallway. So hard that it went *Bam!* But no matter how big the wound is, blood generally dries very quickly. Speedy clotting of the blood raises the chances of survival when you're injured. Once we had a mama at home who had a bleeding disorder. She bled a carmine red colour for almost three days non-stop. Cleverly we laid her on a plastic tarpaulin, otherwise she'd have probably

323

made everything dirty. Anyway, Papa's just been telling the sad story about the boy in the bathtub. He was my brother, just like Jonathan's my brother. I listened carefully, even though I know the story. Papa told it to me after the thing happened to Mama and Sara. He cried and said you always have to protect your family, otherwise you lose them. I bet he said that because I couldn't stand Sara and felt very ashamed of this. Now he's telling Grandad, Mama and the woman about Sara and how she did nothing but cry when she was born. Soon after that the coughing began too. Luckily, though, that didn't last long. I remember how happy I was the first time she was quiet, because I thought we'd finally be able to sleep through the night again. 'It's not good,' Mama said, but she was wrong. Sleep is very good, and most of all, it's important, as it allows the body to regenerate. 'She needs to go to hospital!' She'd been saying this to Papa for a few days now, but Papa said, 'It's nothing, it's just a minor cold. She'll get better again soon.' Usually such words would satisfy Mama, but not that evening. She insisted that Sara had pneumonia. Pneumonia is an acute or chronic inflammation of the lung tissue, caused by a bacterial, viral or fungal infection. Papa said she wasn't a doctor. And not a good mother either if she couldn't make Sara better again. Mama cried, loudly.

Grown-ups always have to lock children in their room before they start arguing. Probably they hadn't planned to argue and besides, Papa had already said, 'That's enough!' But Mama still cried, and she got louder and louder.

'What's wrong?' whispered Jonathan, who was also hiding behind the bedroom door. We'd just finished brushing our teeth when we heard the agitated voices.

'Sara's causing trouble again,' I whispered back.

'I've said that's enough!' Papa's lion voice. Jonathan ducked.

'Please! I don't have to go with her,' Mama howled. 'I'll stay here. Just take her to hospital.'

Papa grabbed Mama's arm.

'If you don't stop right now . . .' he hissed at her.

'She's got a temperature!'

'She's getting better.'

Mama spat in Papa's face. And she had a lion voice too.

'You are a vile human being! You're allowing your own daughter to die! She's not going to survive the night!'

Papa tried to calm Mama down. She'd never had a fit as bad as this. He held her by the throat, which he'd often done when she had a fit.

Turning to Jonathan, I said, 'Let's go to bed.' We really wanted to stay up until Mama came to read us a goodnight story. But as soon as we were in bed, we fell asleep. We were so tired because we'd slept badly all those nights when Sara just screamed. But that night it was nice and quiet.

Papa is talking about this right now: 'But that night . . .'

JASMIN

'. . . it's terribly quiet.' Rogner sighs sadly then pauses for a moment. 'I know it shouldn't have happened,' he resumes. 'Not again. Once again I didn't take enough care. I failed. Just like you failed, Herr Beck. Just as all good fathers fail from time to time.'

'Don't you dare,' Matthias Beck snarls, in pain, it seems. Rogner shrugs – not callously, but more like a man who's got to the end of his story and is wondering what to say next.

Silence fills the room. Silence, which is interrupted by a soft, disconcerting sound. All eyes turn to Hannah, who's started sobbing. It sounds like hiccoughs.

'She still thinks it's her fault,' Rogner says, getting up from his chair. 'Because she couldn't stand the baby. But she just hadn't got used to the new situation.'

I watch him walk around Hannah and plant a kiss on her forehead.

'It's not your fault that Sara got ill. None of it is your fault, my darling.'

Matthias Beck is straining to breathe. It's hard to watch this, but maybe that's how it is. Love. It's love. No matter how sick, distorted and misunderstood, it's still love. Love that spurs us on. That turns us into monsters, each in our own way.

'Lars,' I say, stifling a spontaneous retch. That's what he's called, Lars. That's his name, and it's the first time I've uttered it.

Kirsten tries restraining me. She grabs my arm, whispers, 'No, Jassy, don't.'

I shake her off. Get to my feet. Lars Rogner is here because of love. Love for his family. I'm standing now and my knees are shaking. But I'm standing. He didn't stop me from getting up. He didn't even make a move to. He watches me. I take a first tentative step towards him. He allows me to. I take a second.

'I want to go home,' I say.

'Don't bother, Jasmin,' he scoffs. 'You know it's over.'

I shake my head.

'If it really were over, you wouldn't have bothered coming here. And you certainly wouldn't have brought Hannah. You said you wanted Lena to finally take responsibility. But you bear some responsibility too, Lars. For your children, for me. Hannah wants us to be a family again, don't you, Hannah?'

He looks at his daughter, who gives a hesitant nod.

My hip brushes the work surface. Two or three more steps and I'll be standing right in front of him.

'I want us to be a family too.'

He narrows his eyes. 'That's a really pathetic attempt, Jasmin,' he says. But he doesn't try to attack me. Now I know I'm right. It's love.

Just one more step.

And a grab with the hand.

'In hospital they found out that I'm pregnant.'

Lars Rogner cocks his head. Sizes me up and down. He's the best journalist in the country; he knows if you're lying to him. And he can see it. But when he opens his mouth to hurl his verdict at me, all that comes out is a stifled gasp.

My hip brushes the work surface.

The knife block is right there.

And the hope, which is fixing his gaze on mine. Which has made him blind, at that moment or perhaps always.

His lips get narrower. His pupils flicker. His eyes say he doesn't believe me. The sharp, burning pain in his stomach. Lars Rogner isn't divine anymore, he's no god. Just a human being like the rest of us, with the spark of hope that allows us to be taken in by even the most pathetic attempts.

Chaos in the background. Kirsten screaming. Matthias Beck yelling.

We block it out.

Just him and me and the moment in which I ram the knife into his stomach. It cuts everything, including meat.

MATTHIAS

'No! Don't!'

I crawl over to Rogner, who's now lying on the floor. He's still breathing, albeit slowly.

'Tell me where Lena is!'

I press my hands on the spot where the red stain has seeped through the white material of his shirt and is getting visibly bigger.

'Please!' I beg.

There's a rattling in Rogner's throat.

'Call an ambulance,' I bellow at Jasmin Grass, who's standing beside the body, staring at it as if paralysed, the knife still in her hand. 'I promised her mother I'd bring her home,' I keep imploring him.

The hint of a smile darts across Rogner's face.

'From one father to another. Please!'

Rogner's breathing is getting shallower. His eyelids begin to flicker.

I take my hands away from his stomach.

Somebody touches my shoulder. Jasmin Grass's friend.

'Leave me alone!' I shout.

'The wood,' Rogner whispers hoarsely. 'Behind your garden. She loved the garden.'

'Garden? Do you mean the plot of land outside of Germering? Grandma Hannah's garden, yes?'

Rogner makes a sluggish movement with his head, which I take to be a nod.

I nod too, hastily.

'Behind our garden is Germering Forest. There, yes?'

'On the edge of the wood,' Rogner wheezes in confirmation. 'So she can always look at the hydrangeas.'

'That's where you buried them, is it? Will I find Lena and Sara there?'

'She loved the hydrangeas,' Rogner says, his eyelids twitching.

For some reason, I mumble, 'I know.'

Then the smile darts across Rogner's face again, quite clearly this time. His head falls to the side, his eyes stare vacantly. I sit beside him, his blood on my hands, his blood on my shirt.

After 5,013 days.

Ciao, Paps! See you soon!

I'm hit by a wave, which surges through my body. I jerk and sob and cry for my child. As if through a veil, I see Hannah, who's got up from her seat at the kitchen table, and now moves to Rogner's other side. She stretches out his limp left arm and sits on the floor, his arm around her. Puts her hand on his chest and her head on his shoulder. Whispers, 'Goodnight, Papa.' And closes her eyes.

Gruesome discovery of corpses in Germering

Germering (MK) – Yesterday afternoon the bodies of three adult women and an infant were recovered from a communal grave in a wooded area near Germering. According to Chief Inspector Gerd Brühling, two of the bodies were those of Lena Beck, the Munich student missing since January 2004, and of her new-born daughter.

So far nothing is known about the identities of the other two women. According to Brühling, an initial forensic inspection at the site suggests that the two unknown women were bludgeoned to death. The cause of death of Lena Beck and her daughter has not yet been determined. All the bodies were taken yesterday to the Institute of Forensic Medicine in Munich, where further examinations are now due to take place.

'Our intention is to identify the two unknown women as quickly as possible,' Brühling said. 'We have to assume that they were reported missing by their families, who now deserve clarity.'

JASMIN

'Really quite dry, isn't it?'

Kirsten puts down today's edition of *Bayerisches Tagblatt* and reaches for the bread basket. The swelling on the left-hand side of her face has gone down, leaving just a bruise that sometimes shimmers through the skin. The cut she sustained from Rogner is healing well. Ignaz strokes my legs, purring loudly as if he's being powered by a small motor. My apartment, the 'crime scene', is still sealed off. I'm living with Kirsten at the moment – 'for the time being', as we're calling it.

'What else do you expect them to write? That their very own star journalist was a murderer?' The thought that there were two other women sends shivers down my spine. Even though the police are bound to find out their identities soon, the question of why they had to die will perhaps never be solved. Perhaps they put up greater resistance, fought for their lives more doggedly than I did. Showed the angry god such defiance that all he could do was resort to extreme measures to prove his absolute power to himself and his children. Or they had to die because in his eyes their performances as Lena simply weren't convincing enough. Thinking about it now, I remember my first day in the cabin, when I awoke on the sofa, having blacked out in the storeroom.

Do you know what it sounds like when you bash someone's head in, Lena? It's like dropping a watermelon on to the floor. Bam!

Those words terrified me and I didn't think for one second that they were empty threats. I didn't doubt that he really had heard this horrific sound before. Several times, as it turned out. My thoughts are with the families of the two women, who will have to learn to live with the holes in their lives. And with the fact that they'll never get to the bottom of it all. I know how difficult, how cruel that is. Unless, of course, Hannah and Jonathan bring themselves to talk about it one day. But first they'd have to be capable of understanding all that happened from a different perspective. Dr Hamstedt thinks there's a chance. She compares the view the children had of the world in the cabin with a view through a keyhole. The door is open now, just a crack for the moment so as not to overwhelm them. But the more the door is opened over time, the broader their view of things will become. One day, she thinks, they'll manage to get things in the right perspective, even though that could take a long time and would also mean coming to terms with the fact that their father was a murderer.

I don't have to ask myself if he enjoyed what he did. Of course he enjoyed it. He loved playing the great God, with power over life and people. He loved torture. Perhaps he wasn't always like that. Perhaps the loss of his wife and son devastated him so much it drove him mad. Then all he had was you, Lena, who he loved,

331

but at the same time hated for your part in what had happened. Things got out of hand, isn't that the phrase? Things got really terribly out of hand.

'Yes,' Kirsten says, tearing me from my thoughts. 'Because that's exactly what happened. Don't they owe it to their readers to tell the truth? I mean, he was their star journalist, who even filed reports about the case. It's so perverted. But none of his oh-so-meticulous colleagues ever noticed anything.'

'I don't imagine writing that would be particularly good for business.'

'The other newspapers are printing it,' Kirsten says with a shrug and takes a bite of her croissant.

She's right, Lena. The media can't get enough of our story. And I'm assuming it's going to continue like this for quite a while. Until the next 'most spectacular crime of the decade'. You see, that's what they're calling it. There are requests for interviews and even a proposal for a TV movie. Our parts would be played by leading actors, and of course we'd be on prime time. Maybe it's something that they're leaving your children alone and switching the focus back to you instead. I mean, it can't hurt you anymore. All apart from the *Bayerisches Tagblatt*, which is quietly referring to you as a 'student' again, the media is depicting you as the notorious lover who was partly responsible for her own fate. It's about morality, of course. You mustn't get involved with married men.

Everybody is saying that Lena Beck wasn't the woman people thought she was, and most say it with raised eyebrows. But they've no idea, Lena. You were a mother who did everything for her children. Strong, that's what you were. Strong and brave out of love for your children, right up until your death. And I admire you for that. I promise to keep an eye on your children. Not yet, though; we all need a little more time. But I know they'll be fine. They've got the best therapists. Your parents are there. And I'll be there soon too.

'Jassy? Are you crying?'

Kirsten puts the croissant down on her plate.

'It's fine,' I say, sniffling.

'It's over,' Kirsten says, smiling. 'For good this time.' She takes my hand; we interlink fingers.

'Yes,' I say, smiling back. 'It's over.'

Lars Rogner is dead.

Less than two minutes after I'd rammed the knife into his stomach the police stormed my apartment. Frau Bar-Lev had called them. Because of the creepy, strange man she'd bumped into when she came back home from her trip that evening.

Your father, Lena.

Whatever one says or writes about Lars Rogner, at least he had the decency to tell him your story, rather than take it to the grave with him and let your father go on suffering.

He did, however, take a second story to the grave. As strange as it might sound, this was decent of him too.

It's the story of another fickle young woman. She'd had a bust-up with her best friend and was now planning her dramatic disappearance. She was going to go to the station and take the next train, no matter where it was heading, in the middle of the night without telling a soul. She just wanted to get away, switch off her mobile, give her friend a fright, put one over on her. That was her plan when, one late evening in May, she ended up in a bar on the way to the station, to give herself the last bit of Dutch courage. And he happened to be in this bar too. And it was she who offered to buy him a drink. And it was she who not only had a drink with him, but sat on his lap too. And it was she who whispered in his ear, 'Shall we go back to your place?'

'Anything else you want to tell me?' Kirsten asks, narrowing her eyes searchingly.

'No,' I reply. 'Nothing else.'

Nothing that matters anymore.

Lars Rogner is dead and I'm having breakfast with the woman I love.

'Do you think we could go past the shops later?'

'Sure,' Kirsten says. 'What do you need?'

I smile.

'Hair dye. It's time to get rid of the blonde.'

There's one thing all the papers agree on, Lena: Jasmin G survived. And I'm slowly beginning to believe that this is the truth. A good truth.

MATTHIAS

It's a late October day straight out of a picture book. The air is balmy. The trees are making a final show of their potency before winter, putting on their loveliest display of colour. The light has a golden quality. Says Karin. The perfect afternoon for a walk, she adds, reluctant to give up.

And yet both of us know that once again I won't be leaving the house today. I'm sitting opposite her at the dining table, on my plate a piece of cake I don't want. I'm in my pyjamas, my thick, brown towelling dressing gown and my slippers. I'm unshaven and my hair hasn't been combed. Like yesterday. Like the day before yesterday. Like all the days over the past week when I've done nothing but shuffle around the house. Having the odd rest, a few insipid mouthfuls at the dining table. A doze on the sofa. Or brooding in Lena's old room, which is now empty again. Just like me. Hannah's gone. Back to the trauma centre. Dr Hamstedt says her therapy is going better now that the story has come out; they can make a proper start now. Jonathan's making progress too. Karin said that on her last visit he was in high spirits. He's already calling her 'Grandma'.

'More tea?' Karin says, giving me a smile of encouragement across the table. I shake my head. Push the plate away. Leave the table, say I'm going upstairs, to Lena's room. Karin lets me go without passing further comment.

Gerd called yesterday. They've analysed the fingerprints from the two letters that Jasmin Grass handed over to the police. Of course they're mine. Gerd says he'll see what he can do. This is, after all, the second accusation against me. Even if Jasmin Grass were to refrain from pressing charges – and she will – the fact remains that I hindered the investigation, Gerd tells me. Anything beyond a fine of ninety days' wages and you're considered to have a criminal record, Gerd adds with a sigh. 'Why on earth did you do it, Matthias?'

I sighed too, just sighed, nothing else. Words fail me. I thought Jasmin Grass had something to hide. I thought the letters might help make her talk. Give her a bit of a fright. Remind her of Lena, who deserved the truth. But perhaps I wasn't thinking anything. I was just in another of my blind rages, being the useless, silly ass I'd always been. I put the letters in Frau Grass's mailbox on my way to the trauma centre. Gerd asked where I got her address. I sniggered down the phone. Oh, Gerd, good old naïve Gerd.

335

Anyone can find an address with a few clicks on the internet.

'You didn't make it particularly easy for anyone, Matthias.'

No, I'm a hopeless case, I know that myself.

'Ah well, it's all over now,' Gerd said at the end of our conversation. 'Maybe we should go fishing again sometime. Remember? Like in the old days?'

'Yes, maybe,' I said, and, 'Bye, Gerd.'

All over.

I go into Lena's old room. The bed is made, the swivel chair is pushed neatly up against the desk. The two orchids that Karin lovingly nurtures rise up from the windowsill.

All over and now I should be at peace.

I sit on Lena's bed, the stars above me.

Five thousand and thirteen days.

That's how long I spent looking for my daughter, looking for answers, certain that I would find peace if I got any.

Five thousand and thirteen days, which in the end fitted into a story lasting ten minutes. Rogner didn't take any longer than that.

Was that supposed to be it?

Yes, that was it, and it feels wrong. Unsatisfying. Who am I now? What remains of me? What remains when Lena's dead and Hannah's gone?

Dr Hamstedt has said we're very welcome to visit the children, twice a week, Tuesdays and Fridays, between three and four in the afternoon. Gradually, of course, the visiting hours can be extended, but right now, and especially in view of recent events, the children should focus on their therapy. Karin says that's 'sensible'.

I'm lying beneath a starry sky.

Thinking of Hannah.

My little Hannah . . .

I imagine how it would be if I were suddenly filled with life again. If there were hope, prospects. I would get up, because at once I would know what I had to do. It would feel like an epiphany. I'd go into the bedroom, take some clean clothes from the wardrobe. Then into the bathroom for my first shower in days. A shave. Comb my hair into a neat parting. Go downstairs where Karin's washing up and she looks pleased to see me, dressed and groomed like a normal human being. The sight of me gives her hope. Hope for a walk in the glowing autumn afternoon. I'd kiss her on the cheek and say, 'I'm just popping into the office to pick up the messages,' and Karin feels even more hope. We will cope. A few more good years together. It will be different, that's for sure. But we've still got each other and finally we've got closure. I'd smile at her again before I leave the kitchen, cross the hallway to the garage and get into my car. The garage door opens, I reverse. Drive off. Not to the office.

To Regensburg, to the trauma centre. To Hannah.

I imagine myself holding her hand and taking her out of the building to the car park. Putting on her seat belt in the back. Me sitting in the driver's seat. Starting the car.

'Let's go somewhere really far away, Grandad,' a squeak comes from the back seat.

I smile into the rear-view mirror and say, 'Yes, my darling, let's do that.'

I'm lying beneath a starry sky.

I could . . .

We're not that dissimilar, Herr Beck.

337

EPILOGUE

LENA, SEPTEMBER 2013

Our world has solid walls. No windows, no doors. Our world is small. If you measure by putting your heel to your toes, it's twenty-four paces from the bookshelves to the galley kitchen. Our world has its rules and punishments and its own time.

It's about power.

You think you've locked us in. We are your prisoners. Isolated from everything, from outside, from people. We belong to you alone.

Yes, it's about power.

Your power consists of four solid walls and twenty-four paces.

I know you'd love me to say your name. You practically beg me to say it, like in the past when it would fall lovingly, excitedly, admiringly or at least politely from my lips. But I don't do you this favour, no matter how often you try to remind me of the lovely times we had. No matter whether you beat me or kick me, insult me or hurt me in every conceivable way. As far as I'm concerned, you've become a stranger, and I'm going to make you feel this until the end. That's power. My power and it's inexhaustible.

338

You think you've locked us in?

If you can only see all of this as a prison, then you're a poor, sick man, a stranger. Every time you turn your back to me, I let a flower grow behind it, an entire field of shining yellow sunflowers. I can create bundles of cabbage-sized hydrangea flowers if I want to.

And I do. Every moment you leave us on our own here, I bring the world into our four solid walls. I create secrets and a private life. I take trips with our daughter, while our son sleeps sweetly and soundly after a cup of milk and honey, dreaming of flying. I take Hannah to our garden, to the hydrangeas. I introduce her to her grandparents and let ladybirds crawl over the back of her hand. You think we're stuck here, locked in. Whereas we're in Paris or by the sea or in all those places you think you're locking us away from if you just shut the door and board up the windows.

Power. Stranger.

I can bring the toy cat to life. I can flood the room with sunlight. I can fetch the stars from the sky. And one day I know my children won't just see all of this through my eyes and my stories. One day they will step through these doors and out into the world.

That is hope and it's in my power to ensure it never dies.

You haven't got us, not really.

It's your prison, not ours.

ACKNOWLEDGEMENTS

My untold thanks go to my agent, Caterina Kirsten, without whom this book simply wouldn't exist. Dear Caterina, I'll never forget how you've fought me and fought for me. May our journey together last for many, many more years and just as many more books.

I'd also like to offer my heartfelt thanks to Georg Simader, Vanessa Gutenkunst, Lisa Volpp and Felix Rudloff, for your support, the unforgettable experience of reading to an audience for the first time, and for schnapps at the right moment.

Once upon a time there was a little author and she cried torrents of tears when her agent called; tears of joy, happiness and disbelief . . . this is also down to you, Claudia Baumhöver and Bianca Dombrowa. Here I'd like to tell you again, as well as all the fantastically dedicated and enthusiastic staff at dtv, just how much I appreciate your efforts and your work, and how grateful I am for this very special time in my life.

Finally my family. I hope I tell you often enough what would fill a ridiculous number of pages – I hope you know every day. You are the point of, and reason for, everything in my life.

CV

I was born in the GDR, the child of very young and poor parents who were not especially loyal to the regime; their Stasi files were as thick as Tolstoy's *War and Peace*. My cot was a washing basket with a frame made of curtain rods and a home-made canopy. We didn't have a fridge, so we used to hang our sausages out of the window. Isn't that how a good story begins, with a sausage hanging from a washing line out of the window of a prefabricated apartment in Halle-Neustadt?

The story gets even better, for my parents, being terrific idealists, fled with me via Hungary to the Golden West. They worked hard, carved out careers for themselves and bought me a regular bed. They taught me to believe that everything was possible; they encouraged me to be more open-minded and instilled in me what I consider my greatest strength: I have no fear of failure. I like to test myself and see how far I get. If there are any limits to what I can do then I'm the one who sets them.

This is my pet topic and I've been regularly writing about it since 2016 at www.mymonk.com. In my articles I talk about my time in television. How I, a girl from rural Swabia with glasses and a big bum, ended up in this business in the first place. The reason? Because nobody believed I could make it. But it was what I wanted. I wanted to be in a profession where I could meet people, listen to stories and retell them, and I wanted to make a success of my career.

I talk about how, uneducated and without any training, I became managing editor of a Munich television production company at the age of twenty-four. I talk about the programmes I made and the hundreds of people I worked with over many years. The battered wives, the Somalian war refugees who brought me to tears in the middle of an interview, the neglected children and the gay Austrian farmers.

I talk about how fantastic a time this was for me, but also how I became ever harder on myself and no longer recognised who I had become. Letting go of stories wasn't always easy. I talk about how I sometimes felt so impotent and inadequate. How I slowly lost myself.

And I talk about Karl, my young son, who changed everything. For whom I wanted to get better and reinvent the world. Television was no longer to be a sixteen-hours-per-day job, but merely an activity to keep the wolf from the door. I started working with other stories that didn't hurt anyone. The job isn't as exciting as it used to be, but it's probably healthier.

Now I work at my old kitchen table rather than in an office. My workplace is no longer in the city, but somewhere where it's not unusual to see a racoon on the terrace in the evenings, gorging on wine grapes. I do yoga, chop wood and grow vegetables in the greenhouse.

And of course I talk about writing. About the first book that came about when, six weeks after Karl was born, I needed to process my separation from his father. And the second book that had to be written because after the first one I couldn't imagine *not* writing.

I also talk about all those other manuscripts that were rejected, I talk about the doubts and tears and the resolution I made on New Year's Eve 2006: I'm giving up; I'm never going to get anywhere. I strictly kept to my resolution until the second week in January. And finally I talk about the conscious decision I took to just keep going. Maybe on occasion you just have to convince life how seriously you mean something.

So I wrote my articles, most of which ended with: 'If I can achieve all of this, so can you.' But that's not actually true. You also have to be slightly naïve in this world, which at times can be very cruel. And I am naïve, really naïve, in fact, something I consider to be most advantageous. If you can believe, you have a reason to get out of bed in the morning. If you can believe, you don't ask yourself why you keep going. You just do – and then you're taken completely by surprise when your agent calls and says, 'They want your manuscript.' How wonderful and exciting life is – a very grateful Romy.

Romy Hausmann